Praise for Jim Williams' books

The Hitler Diaries

"...steadily builds up an impressive atmosphere of menace."
Times Literary Supplement

"...well written and full of suspense." *Glasgow Herald*

"...the quality of the storytelling is exceptionally high."
Hampstead and Highgate Express

Last Judgement

"...the author journalists read for their next scoop." *Sunday Telegraph*

Scherzo

"Sparkling and utterly charming. Devilishly clever plot and
deceitful finale." *Frances Fyfield – Mail on Sunday*

Recherché

"A skilful exercise, bizarre and dangerous in a lineage that
includes Fowles' *The Magus.*" *Guardian*

The Strange Death of a Romantic

"This is an extraordinarily witty and assured novel." *T J Binyon
– Evening Standard*

"...seriously good...technically brilliant...constantly suggestive...
dreamy but sinister glamour." *Times Literary Supplement*

With matters like these to think about, there was little time for thoughts of Jim Williams.

John Berendt, *Midnight in the Garden of Good and Evil*

My mind prefers what it has lost and gives itself entirely over to bygone memories. To be able to enjoy your former life again is to live twice.

Martial, *Epigrammata*

ACKNOWLEDGEMENTS

My thanks go to: my wife, Shirley, who listened patiently while I read to her and gave more love and support than I could possibly deserve; Audrey Hamilton, who typed the manuscript and gave unfailing encouragement; Shahid Qamar, for his deep knowledge of Magyar gained by a lifetime of study; James Hale, my agent, who allowed me to take risks; Nick Webb, my publisher, who understood the book; Pamela and Ian Shelton, who generously let Shirley and me use their cottage in Puybrun; Michael Mills and Marie-Paule, who dismally failed to provide some information I asked for and are therefore affectionately caricatured for their sins; and Helen Simpson, my copy-editor, who with erudition and dedication tries to make great literature out of the old rubbish scribbled by authors.

CHAPTER ONE

If it weren't for Harry Haze, this would be a boring story. In April when the trees were full of blossom and the daffodils in bloom, I felt the sap rising, decided to leave my wife, and ran away with my secretary. Let me say at the outset that this isn't a lament for the male menopause – or not entirely. Rather, it's a murder mystery.

Lucy and I threw up everything and moved to France, where I took a cottage in a small village, Puybrun, in the Aude. The location was my suggestion. Lucy didn't know France well, and I'd rented a place there for holidays with Sally and my son Jack. The fact that I chose the security of such a familiar location shows my innocent insensitivity to how Lucy might feel about the situation. However, she said nothing. We were in love.

I had no plan, but I was under no pressure. In London I'd been a partner in a commercial law firm and made my pile during the take-over frenzy of the eighties. I could abandon Sally with the house in Virginia Water and live off my fat for a couple of years without serious consideration of what I was going to do with the rest of my life. As the saying goes, I could take time to find myself.

I should say something about Puybrun to save you the problem of finding it on the map. It's an hour and a half's drive from Toulouse, about ten kilometres from Chalabre, on the edge of the Pyrenees, in a basin surrounded on all sides by mountains with sheer limestone faces except for the gap that takes the *route nationale* to Lavelanet. A broad, shallow stream runs through the centre and the older houses have been constructed right to the edge, so that on that side they rise like cliffs out of the water. There is a single crossing, a medieval bridge. It possesses the peculiar charm of a pair of latrines, as antique as the rest of the structure, offering an attractive view, and on the occasion I used one the results of my efforts were consigned by a windy drop into the shallows below. For the rest, imagine an undistinguished church, a war memorial, a *mairie* with the tricolor blown into knots around the flagstaff, and the Bar des Sports, which is run by Mike and Marie-Paule. Also a lake, which I shall deal with when I speak about Harry.

A kilometre or so outside the village the ground rises and forms a rocky spur on which stands a largish ruined castle. Simon de Montfort stormed it during the Albigensian crusade. Since then it has been left to the encroachments of vines and whatever bushes can cling to the thin soil. Puybrun itself is insignificant, but, as one negotiates the curves of the road from Lavelanet and sweeps down into the basin, the ruin and the lake come as a shock no matter how often one makes that journey. I have seen them in all seasons, all weathers, all colours, as moody as the sky: sometimes sombre and sometimes gay, but always with a sense of joy. It was my feelings about these features, as well as my instinct for the familiar and the comfortable, that drew me back.

Our cottage, Lo Blanc, stood (and, strictly speaking, still stands) at the foot of the spur, with its back to the castle. Here the ground slopes gently and there is a large garden with cypresses at the four corners like a cemetery. When we took the property, the garden was sparse and full of rocks, but that was an advantage since it kept Lucy occupied. I rented the place for two years. Only now does that fact strike me as significant. I could have taken it by the month, but I negotiated two years, telling myself that it was good business because of the saving against a monthly rental. Yet the truth was that, having fled a predictable and routine life, instead of travelling to expand my horizons and test myself against new experiences, I didn't wait to strike new roots. Lucy supposed that the two-year lease demonstrated my commitment to her. She didn't see how it showed that, though I'd broken with the physical circumstances of my history (and even then not entirely), I hadn't broken with my character.

I had no mind to work. I told myself I was a free spirit. Puybrun was my Tahiti and I would paint like Gauguin and maybe write a little. I was a competent amateur painter and, though I'd never tried my hand at literary writing, I was a practised legal draftsman. It seemed to me that the clarity of my analytical powers and the precision of my prose could be adapted to produce a work of worthwhile character, spare, clear and exact. But don't mistake me. I wasn't aiming at the artistic life. If there was any dominant theme in my incoherent vision of the long-term future, it was a vague notion of settling in the Cotswolds and opening a cheese shop. However I may view my time at Puybrun in retrospect, I saw it then as an entry into a world of change and excitement, but one that would necessarily end in my finding the peace and tranquillity that my middle-aged soul longed for. And Puybrun proved to be in every way mysterious and exciting. For instance, I never wanted to be suspected of murder. Harry made sure that I was.

I was nearly twenty years older than Lucy, and her appearance made the gap seem greater. I've kept myself in reasonable trim, but I wear every one of my years. Lucy was a petite brunette, slender and small-breasted. During our journey through France eyebrows had been raised when I asked for a double room. 'But surely, Monsieur, your daughter would prefer her own room?' Lucy used to giggle and make jokes about my advancing decrepitude. I took them in good part. Age genuinely meant nothing to her – though, on reflection, I should amend that remark to say that, at bottom, she too must have been in search of security. Otherwise, unless I attribute to myself astonishing powers of attraction, her love for me becomes incomprehensible. At all events we were at ease with the disparity, though I admit to being puzzled, since she was truly beautiful. Her hair was bobbed and perfectly framed a heart-shaped face. Her eyes were large, soft and brown. Her nose was of the small, neat sort that lifts and wrinkles when amused. At rest, her face and well-formed lips were always slightly open, suggesting surprise or curiosity so that, whenever I glanced at her, I expected her to speak; and it was this lively sense of expectation, this absence of anything heavy or inert, that delightfully troubled my stolid emotions and quickened even those still passages that comprised much of our days together. I remember these details because I shall certainly never see Lucy again.

Before that day of fateful cherry blossom and daffodils, Lucy had been my secretary for two years. Now I must be careful. In describing her laughing lightness, her winsomeness (a word not much used in conversation or legal drafting but which bears consideration), her disingenuous charm, I risk the accusation that the tired sentimentality which goes with my years is a veil through which I describe an inconsequential girl. However, I haven't described her intelligence. She was quick and perceptive and, if not deeply cultured, she had at least a university degree. She worked as my underpaid secretary because that's the nature of things and I'm not a social reformer. She belonged to that class of well-educated young women who staff the telephones in publishers' offices and are hired for their lovely voices. It could be said that I abused her, and, if so, I accept the accusation. On the other hand I gave her a gift which, admittedly, I possessed unwittingly and accidentally. I introduced her to glamour. I introduced her to Harry.

We arrived at Lo Blanc as summer was beginning and spent six months there before we ever met him. We engaged in enthusiastic sex and betweentimes walked, ate in restaurants and passed the sultry afternoons in pursuit of our hobbies. We talked a great deal and, unless, as is possible, in her stricken innocence and womanly patience she listened to me from politeness, I must suppose I had something interesting to say. I'd travelled a great deal to India and Nigeria and other places, had a fund of stories, and was esteemed as a raconteur. If my mood in this memoir is more reflective, it's the effect of experience and the limits of the medium. You can't expect to see the whole character from the written word.

Throughout the summer I painted. I did many sketches of the cottage, the castle and the lake; I went to Carcassonne with my paint box and (daring fellow!) took myself off alone into the mountains to brood pleasurably among the rocks and pines. Lucy tended the garden, applied herself to French cookery and kept a diary. Ill-defined and snaking about the village and its surroundings was a Cathar trail; and in the evenings, as the swallows swept in caracoles through the limpid sky, we would walk in the cool air and, as now and again she was ahead of me, I'd see the backs of her shapely calves, now bronzed, and the exquisite hollows at the tendon of her ankle, and would count myself a fortunate man.

Thus the summer. As the days prolonged themselves, so the energy and novelty that had first excited our enjoyment became attenuated. Our activity slackened, and during the midday hours when the sky was white, a torpor descended which, though not unpleasant, hinted at difficulty to come. I recalled that, in my first years with Sally, we hadn't known how to handle silences but felt they must be filled with conversation. It was a phase that passed and we learned that silence is not necessarily an absence of contact but is itself an amiable exchange. Nevertheless, Lucy and I hadn't reached that stage, and though I (already thinking of the long term) believed we would, I sensed that Lucy fretted guiltily at times and suspected that our quiet moments showed a lack of something essential in her.

It was a relief when autumn came. The onset of cooler weather revived our energies and we would go out in the middle of the day and Lucy even tried her hand at painting, for which she had some talent. At first, too, we had the lake to amuse us. The water was still warm, the tourists had gone, and the villagers could not occupy themselves with leisure during the working day. We swam for hours and sometimes, because I was still intoxicated with the daring mode of life I was engaged upon, we stripped and ran naked on the sand.

November. An ordinance posted at the *mairie* closed the lake to bathers until the beginning of March. In any case, the waters had cooled and it rained a great deal. We had to occupy ourselves for much of the time within the confines of the cottage and this wasn't without difficulty. I enjoy reading but had brought few English books with me and they weren't to be obtained locally. Although I spoke French well enough, it strained my powers of concentration to follow the television programmes, and they were wholly beyond Lucy's capacities. The satellite stations bored us both. I don't, however, mean that we were unhappy; and we rarely quarrelled. I began painting indoors, nude studies of Lucy. She enjoyed the attention, amused both of us by reading poetry aloud in funny voices, and, if she wished for more, would strike a pose indecent enough to inflame the ardour of a eunuch. In addition we still took our walks, fair weather or foul, and on one or two evenings a week would call at the Bar des Sports. Mike and Marie-Paule, who ran it, were a cheerful couple and Mike (who had his private fantasies) was determined to maintain its traditional character. He had banned electronic games machines but allowed the old-fashioned sort, the ones based on football or hockey, which the French play with ferocity, banging and spinning the control rods and hooting with determined enjoyment. Lucy and I both took part.

So, as I say, we weren't unhappy. Nor was I disturbed unduly by any guilt at deserting Sally after more than twenty-five years of marriage. Still less did I regret leaving the stress and long hours of life in the City. If I must characterise my disquiet it is that I could see that Lucy and I were living on the emotional capital of our relationship. I suspect that, initially, it's always so. The early raptures are depleted and dissipated in the many lesser pleasures of life together; but, if love is soundly based it begins to generate new and different energies to replace those that have been lost. I knew this and Lucy didn't. And, as from day to day we consumed the force of our first passions, I wondered: when will the change happen, and how? More fearfully, I wondered if it would happen at all.

Though bathing was now prohibited, our walks often took us to the lake. A long lane flanked by small houses leads there, beyond the medieval bridge and the square which holds the church of St Hilaire, the *mairie* and the PTT. It is at the lake, from which the highway can't be seen, that one has the most perfect sense of Puybrun nestling in its basin among the mountains. The lake is man-made. It isn't fed by the stream, which passes at a distance. I suspect that, originally, a marsh was there which drained on one side where one can see fields at a lower level. Some civic improver had the idea of constructing an earthen dike on this side of a shallow depression which duly filled. The dike is now grassed over and a path runs along the top through an avenue of osiers, and on the opposite side a narrow stretch of sand has been created. From the beach it takes no effort to swim the short length to the dike, and even a moderate swimmer can manage the long axis. Other than a small parking space and a refreshment hut, no concession is made to tourism. During the summer Mike and Marie-Paule abandon the Bar des Sports for the lake, where they serve *frites*, *merguez*, ices and cold beer. In winter the *buvette* is closed, the parking space empty, and the lake deserted.

The first day of December was cold and brilliantly clear. Both Lucy and I were in a good mood. I'd laid a log fire and, when it had settled to a crackling blaze, Lucy commented that we'd better make love now, because with the cold weather my penis was liable to shrivel. I therefore proposed that we test this theory by going for a walk, after which we might undergo a bout to establish if it were true.

I remember every moment of that walk because it was to define me: what I was and what I became; and everything since has been an exploration of that day. And yet it began in the same way as any other, with our laughing and holding hands as we strolled, and ended with an incident which, on the day itself, seemed of no importance whatsoever. Lucy wore a reefer-cut jacket of heavy tartan wool, a knitted white and red cap, jeans, and boots of soft red leather, a sort of lumberjack chic. I had what I'd brought from Virginia Water, a good Harris tweed jacket worn over a pullover, a silk cravat with my shirt, twill trousers, and hand-made brogues. I won't bore you with the makers' names since this isn't that kind of story.

There was frost underfoot and in the gardens along our path stood the dead canes of summer flowers and the air smelled of wood smoke. It was lunchtime and from the houses we could hear voices and the chink of glass or crockery. The church bell struck. I think it was one o'clock.

8

As we approached the water, Lucy nudged me and asked, 'What's that?'

She pointed and I said, 'A dead branch, probably,' though it didn't resemble a branch. Rather, something large, smooth and pale was semi-submerged.

'It looks like a body,' said Lucy, struck only casually by the thought so that it came out as a mundane observation.

'I shouldn't think so,' I answered. as someone in whose world corpses do not figure. And in fact I was right; or, at least, half right, since, though there was someone in the water, he wasn't dead, merely floating on his back and paddling lazily.

'He must be freezing,' Lucy remarked.

I said, 'He can't be warm, but don't be fooled by the frost. The lake's at its coldest in February.'

'Brrr!' Lucy snuggled up to me and I kissed her forehead.

We walked a little further and the swimmer noticed us. He waved a hand, turned over on to his front and swam for the beach. By the time we reached it, he was out of the water, had slung a towel over his shoulders and, from a strange sense of decorum, placed a large straw hat on his head. I saw an old man of medium height, who like many old men was fleshy in the top part and skinny in the legs. He beamed at us – that's the word, 'beamed' – and opened his mouth to speak the first words I ever heard from Harry Haze.

'Gosh, golly, gee!' he said. 'You must be the kids who live in the place on the hill!'

Gosh, golly, gee! I swear those were his words. And he said them in that aw-shucks-I'm-just-plain-folks way that James Stewart had. He took his time to rub down his hairy torso, and when he'd finished extended a hand.

'Haze,' he said. 'Harry Haze. You may call me Harry. And you'll be?'

9

'John – and this is Lucy.'

'One of the Derbyshire John and Lucy's, I'm sure.' He smiled and kissed Lucy's hands. 'Charmed.'

James Stewart was gone, replaced by James Mason.

I'd better deal now with Harry's way of speaking, because if I simply recite the words I won't convey its elusive quality. It was, I suppose, primarily American, though Harry himself wasn't. However, you shouldn't think of New York or the South. Whatever the words – from whichever repertoire of old films they were drawn – Harry spoke suavely, sometimes caressingly: a Hollywood English with a slight Yankee creak and always deep and slow. Even so, this in no way exhausted Harry's range of voices, some of which, I believe, were conscious affectations and others the relics of an obscure history. In the first category was his small-town Midwesterner: *Mr Smith Goes to Washington* comes to mind. Also his gangster voice: 1940s *film noir* rather than Cagney. He frequently lapsed into these, with a vocabulary to match. Piecing together his story I fancy he'd spent a deal of time in the movie theatres and drive-ins of the Truman and Eisenhower years. The second category comprised a substratum from a European past: Slavic fluidity, German gutturals and French nasals, and still more: Magyar, Rumanian and God knows what. As the mood took him, these would be accompanied by words or phrases in half a dozen languages.

Gosh, golly, gee! I've never heard a more pregnant phrase.

After our first, friendly introduction, Harry dressed himself, unembarrassed by our presence. When it came to removing his bathing shorts he remarked, ''Scuse my butt', turned away and got on with the task. Finished, he looked at me, smiled amiably and asked, 'How do I look, old boy?' and to Lucy, 'Am I fit to take my gal to the hop?'

Lucy could hardly contain her amusement, a fact that seemed only to encourage Harry in his determination that we were to be, as he put it, *'amigos – comprende?'* He presented us with the finished effect: straw hat, cotton shirt, a check jacket, rumpled linen trousers too short in the leg, no socks, and a pair of two-tones that looked like golfing shoes. He proposed we walk a ways together.

Let me say that I wasn't, at first, especially taken by Harry. He amused me but his exoticism was beyond my ken and I suspected it. I've come across old people whose surface of cheerful acceptance masks deep griefs and disappointments, and I thought Harry might be such a one and that, if we gave him opportunity, he'd become a leech on our existence. You must remember that at this date Lucy and I were in that solipsistic phase of love when nothing much mattered outside ourselves. I would have made an excuse that we had lunch prepared, and left. Lucy, however, was smitten. She couldn't take her eyes off him and he responded by catching her glances and returning a merry twinkle. This, I thought sourly, was what she'd expected when, as a pair of eloping lovers, we'd fled England. Harry had done nothing remarkable beyond open his mouth to say a few words of eccentric English. But those words, in their polyglot formation, opened vistas of travel and mystery of things we'd never seen, and above all, as we were to discover, of a history that was inconceivably strange.

We took the walk along the dike through the rows of osiers and across the sluice that controlled the level in the lake. We – mostly Lucy and Harry – made banal chat of the how-do-you-like-it-here? variety. I was alert to the threat that Harry was going to intrude into my idyll. In fact, however, his manner tended to assuage my fears. Old people, of the kind I've mentioned, let their loneliness and obsessions appear in the way they seize on conversation, turn it and monopolise it. Harry, on the other hand, was happy to let Lucy make the running. His answers, though far from grudging, were concise and to the point, and he was content with the silences, feeling no need to break them. I was given the opportunity to judge him.

I never found out Harry's age, and I learned it was pointless to ask. I think of him as eighty, but a well-preserved eighty. He bore himself upright and his movements were fluid, though he was reluctant to hurry. As I've said, he carried a little weight, but his face was long and bony with the strong jaw and set of mouth that produces deep-throated sounds. To my chagrin he had more hair than I had. It was white and he wore it short. His complexion was fair; so his tan had a hint of redness. His eyes were blue. In all of this, I don't mean to describe an ancient gaffer who lives out his years sitting by the village pond. Nor, on the other hand, do I mean to ignore that aspect of Harry's appearance. When he was good-tempered and in his wits (about which I have more to say later), he could seem like a gossiping old body passing the time of day. But when he was asleep or his face was still, or in shadow, or when he thought you weren't looking, it became something beyond my powers of description. It became, as best I can say, filled with an impersonal thoughtfulness.

We finished our turn about the lake and returned to the village by the way we'd come. Harry's path lay with ours but not as far. A lane led from the highway towards the castle hill and the graveyard and a scattering of farms. I was familiar with the row of houses, four of them, that stood on the left. They were plain in appearance, and, like most French village houses, shuttered at all times of day and revealing nothing. On this side were two storeys, but the ground fell away sharply behind them and I fancied that there was a deep cellar beneath, which extended under the gardens to the road beyond. The first two were occupied but somewhat shabby. The third was in disrepair, securely locked, and, I imagined, empty. The fourth had been spruced up and was normally let to summer visitors.

'Halt!' said Harry. 'Regretfully, I must leave you children.' He opened a metal gate that gave on to a short gravel path, a pair of steps and a small veranda. 'This is my place. Pretty, *nicht wahr?*'

'Yes, lovely,' I murmured, being by now tired and wondering if Lucy might win her bet about the effects of cold weather on men of my age.

'Yes, it is,' enthused Lucy, who seemed taken by the house.

'Come on, darling,' I proposed. 'Goodbye, Harry. No doubt we'll see you around.'

'You surely will,' he answered and, to be fair, he seemed easy at letting us go. He was talking, however, to Lucy and, following her gaze, to a plaque of wrought iron fixed to the wall, he added for her benefit, 'La Maison des Moines. In the olden days there must have been a monastery in this village – what do you think? It's a pretty name, ain't it?'

'It is,' she acknowledged wistfully.

Harry sighed. 'It was the name that attracted me to this house rather than another. It seemed, somehow, so appropriate.'

CHAPTER TWO

We didn't see Harry over the next few days. To some degree this fact was the touchstone that made further contact possible. At the back of my mind was the thought that he would come shuffling up the hill to Lo Blanc to borrow a cup of sugar of whatever, and that would be that: we'd never be free of him. Not that this occurred to Lucy, and when I mentioned it she gave me a look that suggested I was mean-spirited.

'I don't understand your problem,' she said. 'I'd *like* to see Harry again. He ... oh, I don't know. Where does he get his queer English from? Wouldn't you like to know? Where do you go, what do you experience to wind up with a language like that?'

I admitted I didn't know.

It wasn't that Harry didn't interest me; but he introduced a conflict between my curiosity and my desire to reconstruct and take possession of my life. When Lucy and I next dropped in at the Bar des Sports, I asked about him.

Mike, like me, was a middle-aged Englishman striving to forget the past and be someone different. Unlike me, he'd taken his wife along for the ride. He'd been born in Rochdale, had studied at Swansea, and emigrated to Brittany immediately after graduation; and, to hear him describe it, fought in the trenches of the French education system until he was sick of it. Then, with a ripening fifty years in his sights, he'd decided to desert and to become what he'd never been: that quintessential Frenchman, the

14

owner of a café-bar. I can only state this. The psychology escapes me.

A couple of years before my arrival, Mike and Marie-Paule quit Brittany and bought the Bar des Sports in Puybrun. The previous owners, a self-respecting and business-minded pair, had modernised the place as far as circumstances allowed and in due course, if their confidence in tourism had grown, would have transformed it into a tasteful restaurant for a discerning but decidedly English clientele. Mike would have none of this. He had a vision of a bar that had not been seen this side of Sartre's death: possibly not since the Occupation. And it embodied, I suspected, an essentially foreign view of France's unique character: a combination of sophistication and pure squalor to which only the Gallic soul could aspire. If the law had allowed, he would have torn up the drains to make people piss in the street. If his male customers had consented, he would have made them wear sweaty vests. Well, perhaps this is an affectionate overstatement.

Lucy and I went to the bar, and, while she tried her hand against the farmers at the football machine, I leaned my elbow on the zinc-topped bar, ordered drinks, and enquired about Harry Haze. Mike pushed his big nose in my direction and shared a lungful of *tabac brun*.

'Old Harry? Yeah, I know old Harry,' he said. 'And?'

'Has he been here long?'

'No. He came last summer – I don't mean the one just gone, but last year. It's odd that he took that place for longer than a single season.'

'I did the same.'

A grin. 'No comment.'

Lucy was playing for drinks. I knew though she didn't, that the yokels let her win. It amused them to see her get drunk and, provided that she kept a modicum of sense, I had no objection.

I asked Mike, 'Does he have any connection with Puybrun?'

'Not that I've heard. He speaks perfect French, so far as I'm any judge, but Marie-Paule says not. She says he speaks some sort of loony lingo. Where did you come across him?'

'At the lake four or five days ago. He was swimming.'

'Crazy bugger.'

'It's illegal.'

'Sod that. It isn't the law that keeps people out of the water in December.'

I took a spritzer, more seltzer than wine, over to Lucy. She said, 'Harry comes in here on Wednesdays.'

'That's right,' confirmed her partner, Antoine. He answered the question I had forgotten to put to Mike, but it explained why, in six months, we hadn't noticed him. We never called at the Bar des Sports on Wednesdays. The day meant nothing and I hadn't thought of it as part of a pattern that Lucy and I were building, but apparently it was.

Antoine was a strapping great moron, who loved to play against Lucy since never, even in his dreams, could he seduce a beautiful young woman. When I asked what else he knew of Harry he answered slowly, 'Ricard.'

'Ricard?'

'He drinks Ricard.'

'That's it? He's been dropping in here for eighteen months, and all you know is that he drinks Ricard?'

Antoine rolled his eyes sluggishly. 'He's not a talker, that one.' He thought some more and volunteered, 'Pierre knows him.'

'Pierre is Édouard Moineau's lad,' contributed Mike. 'But he's only thirteen or fourteen. He probably runs errands for the old bloke. I can't imagine that they've ever talked, if you take my meaning.'

I, too, doubted that young Moineau knew anything of Harry; and, in the end, did I care? I told myself that I was just making small talk.

The effect of a full moon on a frosty December evening can lend the night a strange clarity that seems sharper than daylight. Lucy and I had been dreaming over the fire, she resting cupped between my legs, and I idly parting the strands of her hair. Without warning, she turned, kissed my fingers and proposed, 'Why don't we go for a drink?' I had no objection and so we put on our woollens and went forth.

I remember one particular incident. Without thinking, I did something I should never have done in Virginia Water. I halted at the garden gate and pissed against the wall. It was a glorious stream, spangled with starlight and steaming fruitily.

Lucy laughed in sheer astonishment. She said, 'What on earth made you do that? We're only fifty feet from the house.'

I paused, also bemused over this little piece of earth magic, before answering, 'I'm not sure. I think it's a territorial thing. It means I'm at ease with this place – and with us.'

Lucy returned a few paces to smile and kiss me. She asked, 'Shall I drop my knickers and have a squat?'

'No. I suspect it's strictly male juju. If there's a female equivalent, you probably have to pee in the cooking pots.'

'Shame,' she said and, taking my hand, slipped it into her coat and over a breast.

'Sex, and so early?' I said, but she had sensed the atmosphere of the night.

'Not sex, magic,' she replied.

It was as we were approaching Mike's place that Lucy remarked that it was a Wednesday. 'Didn't you notice?'

I hadn't – or thought I hadn't. Yet, in the rhythm of the week I should have known instinctively that this was not a night on which we went out.

'You knew, of course,' I said.

'Oh, yes.' She hugged my arm. 'But I don't want rituals. I don't want us to become hidebound and stuffy.'

'Habits help us to get through life. They prevent our having to be always conscious of every least action. They reduce anxiety at the unpredictable behaviour of others.'

'I want to be fully conscious at the moment. I want to be able to remember everything.'

There was a certain naive sense to this remark. but it reminded me of how I had felt thirty years before.

We entered the bar. I nodded to Mike and Lucy blew a flirtatious kiss at Antoine. I glanced around and saw Harry Haze sitting peaceably in a corner nursing a glass of anisette. He recognised me and gave me a nod but made no move to impose himself. It was Lucy who, noticing him, gave a little squeak, exclaimed, 'Harry!' and went over to his table. Harry rose and, incongruously in the light of the words that followed, snapped his heels together and grazed her hand with his lips.

'Hi there, honey,' he said. 'How are two of my favourite kids?'

'Hardly kids,' I remarked coolly. 'I'm almost fifty years old.'

Harry was unimpressed. 'Whatever, you're still a kid to me. And as for you, *Liebling*,' he addressed Lucy benevolently, 'I could cry just to see you. In fact, just to see you is enough to put some fuel into these ancient loins.'

It was then that I knew that Harry Haze had no sense of shame and Lucy didn't mind. Nor, oddly enough, did I.

We sat together. We ordered drinks. Harry asked for another Ricard.

'I used to drink absinthe.' he said.

'I thought that was illegal.'

'It didn't always used to be.'

'A hundred years ago.'

We spoke a little more, the same ordinary stuff as last time, about the village. Then Harry took a box from his pocket and helped himself to a pinch of snuff.

'I know you children will forgive me,' he apologised, wiping his nose with a scarlet kerchief. 'A lot of people don't like the habit and in the flesh it's less elegant than in the movies. I used to smoke but…'

'Your health?' asked Lucy solicitously.

'Good Lord, no,' replied Harry. 'But it got to be more unsociable than farting at a funeral. At least snuff has a bit of class.'

Lucy had an eye for antiques and it dwelled on Harry's snuffbox. I also noticed it: a gilt enamel item set with stones, to my mind flashy and tasteless.

'Is that Fabergé?' Lucy asked excitedly.

Harry spun it in his fingers and answered, 'I wouldn't care to say one way or the other.'

'You mean you don't *know*?'

'It was given to me as a present by Grigorii Efimovich. I guess he might have stolen it.' Harry pocketed the box. Evidently, like me, he didn't care much for it. Lucy was still sitting with her mouth open, and the fact that Harry hadn't offered her the box for a closer look inclined me to the opinion that it was a fake. The conclusion suited me. Having reconsidered my first impression that Harry was a pathetic old man in search of friends, I now suspected that he was a snake-oil salesman. I was convinced that the old phony was going to sell me insurance or religion. If I were right, the faux Fabergé snuffbox was of a piece with the rest of him. Exactly why the Poughkeepsie Mutual Assurance Company or the Four Square Gospel Church should be peddling their wares in Puybrun was a question I didn't ask myself. Nor why I was so anxious, for my own peace of mind, to have Harry boxed and labelled.

At ten or so, the three of us decided to quit the bar. Lucy left a disappointed Antoine, with whom she hadn't bothered to play the football game. Outside the moon was riding high in an ice halo and an owl made its ghostly passage over the village square. Puybrun was buried in silence the way I loved it.

We crossed the *route nationale*, which extended as a pale ribbon left and right. Ahead the Cathar fortress seemed to ride like a ship on a sea of billowing bushes. The houses to either side of 'our' lane cast it in blackness so that, as soon as we entered it, I could see neither Lucy nor Harry.

I heard Lucy say, 'Would you mind if we took a look around your house some time, Harry?'

Harry must have been tired, or he wouldn't have misunderstood. 'Do you mean now?'

'Right now? Well … okay, Harry, if it's not too inconvenient.'

'A couple of minutes, and then I've got to get some shuteye. But, sure, why not?'

I was sorry for Harry and embarrassed for Lucy, who hadn't expected our request to be taken so immediately. Harry had locked La Maison des Moines, which wasn't usual in these parts, and it took him a minute to find the key and turn on the light. We went inside.

I think I was better prepared than Lucy. We were both building up our portraits of Harry, but mine was less exotic than hers. After all, he had rented the place and what we saw went with that fact. My guess was that the owners were English and had bought the house as an investment or a second home. It was furnished with kit furniture. sales-room stuff and one or two nice pieces that had suffered damage and not been restored. I felt immediately at ease in a way that I don't in most French homes.

However, the point is that there was nothing of Harry here, except for a print that seemed out of place. It was *Chronos Eating his Children*, by Blake, I think.

'May I get you folks something?' said Harry. 'A nightcap?'

Lucy, disappointed, was looking around. 'Whatever you have.'

'Me too,' I said.

Astutely Harry said, 'There isn't much to show, Lucy my lambkin, *n'est-ce pas*? I travel light, always have done. That way I've stayed ahead of the Revenue and the police.' He laughed.

Abashed, Lucy turned her innocence on him. 'I'm sorry' she explained. 'It was the Fabergé box. I had a vision of' – she laughed – 'I don't know what.'

I was unconsciously sniffing the air, seeking out the smells of old age: urine, unwashed clothes and mouldering dog food. But everything with Harry was spick and span. The house had a pleasant scent of herbs and beeswax.

Lucy, easing herself into a chair while Harry popped the cork of a bottle of muscadet, asked, 'What brought you to Puybrun, Harry?'

He hesitated. 'Oh, I was just going to and fro in the earth and walking up and down in it. Or, to put it another way, I have to park my old hide somewhere. I should have asked: is muscadet acceptable?'

'Fine, thanks. You're not so old,' Lucy added consolingly.

'Older than you may think.' He tipped his glass. 'Cheers.'

At the quotation from Job, I stared at Harry. Perhaps I was looking for Satan. The only light was from a reading lamp with a printed cotton shade. The light and shadow made a devilish play of his features, but the same was probably true of all three of us.

Lucy asked, 'How do you spend your days?'

'I walk a little. I think a lot. I try to make sense of things but don't get very far. None of it is very interesting.'

'I can't believe that.'

'As you please. But, as you can see, I don't carry much of my physical past with me. Such as it is, *mes enfants*, it's in there.' He pointed to a bag that lay discarded under a gate legged table. It was a grip made of a faded but fancy moquette with a leather handle and various patches of grey parcel tape; an old carpet bag such as a drummer from Sears & Roebuck would have used to carry his samples round the cattle towns of the Old West a century ago. I imagined Harry picking it up in an antique store in Greenwich Village.

'Where did you get it?' I asked.

Harry shrugged. 'It has no sentimental value. I bought it in an antique store in Greenwich Village.' He took the snuffbox from his pocket and opened the carpet bag to put it away. As he did so, something fell out. In amused surprise, he said, 'Well, whaddya know?' He smiled at Lucy. 'I must root in this bag half a dozen times a day and I could have sworn I'd lost this thing.' He handed it to Lucy, who gave it a puzzled glance and showed it to me. It was a room key with a wooden plaque attached. Written on the plaque in pokerwork were *Lone Pine Motel, Galena* and the number 13. I passed it back to Harry who rubbed it thoughtfully between thumb and forefinger for a moment and returned it to its place. He said wistfully, 'It'll mean nothing to you, *mes enfants*, but it certainly does to me. Dolly was forever walking off with keys. I don't know if she stole them or was simply forgetful.'

'Dolly was your wife?' asked Lucy sympathetically.

'Something like that,' answered Harry.

The Fabergé snuffbox – real or fake – and the undoubtedly genuine motel-room key had an effect on Lucy which I hadn't expected. Perhaps it was the contrast between the exotic and the ordinary – though the ordinary was not so ordinary since the key implied travel to places Lucy had never been. At all events she imputed a history to Harry: nothing definite but something vaguely romantic that would explain the miscellaneous treasures she imagined inside the carpet bag and the mishmash of vocabulary and accent with which he spoke. In other times and places, this wouldn't have happened, but Lucy had time on her hands and Puybrun was a place in which she had no roots, nothing to distract her. Of course, the theory was that our love was a sufficient occupation in itself, but the reality is that love is a perspective not an activity; or, at least, not a full-time activity. I thought that her interest in Harry was harmless, and, to be fair, my own thoughts turned to him at odd moments and I wondered what tide of events had beached him in this quiet corner of France.

You should understand that Harry did nothing openly to draw us on. Our first meeting at the lake was accidental, and it was Lucy who'd proposed our visit to the Bar des Sports that Wednesday evening and afterwards invited us to his house. The movement was all on our side. But isn't that the way with any magnet? The magnet seems inert and the iron filings move towards it. I don't mean that Harry set out to attract us. I simply don't know. I can say only that my half-hearted attempts to divert Lucy's attention were a failure and that one way or another she was determined to have Harry's story out of him.

Insensibly, we got into the habit of dropping in at Mike's place on a Wednesday evening, which meant, naturally, that we would see Harry. During the course of that winter I became familiar with his inexpensive but raffish wardrobe, the loud jackets, the baggy trousers, the two-tone shoes and a range of hats from a gay felt fedora with a wide brim to a dapper little number with a snakeskin band. I'd join him for a drink but spent most of the time at the zinc chewing the fat with Mike and breathing Caporals at second hand. Lucy sat with Harry talking brightly or listening intently to his creaky voice, now suave and now homespun, which I would catch only when a phrase came out in the tones of an English lord or a Russian boyar.

The only person who wasn't comfortable with this arrangement was Antoine, Lucy's partner at the football game. He was a slow-witted, taciturn bear of a man, aged thirty or so. If I make him sound like a stereotype, I acknowledge the fact, but it's difficult to divine the character of someone who speaks infrequently and in a thick patois. I could imagine dark and incestuous happenings in the dingy house he shared with his widowed mother, but have no reason to. Evidently, he had his dreams. He wore his hair slicked back at the sides, with an overhanging quiff in the style of Elvis, and sported a pair of mirror shades and some Heavy Metal jewellery. In summer, during my rambles after scenes to paint, I often saw him going up and down the fields in his tractor, his head rocking to tunes I couldn't hear.

To be fair to Lucy, she was conscious that she had in a manner dropped Antoine. It was scarcely possible to ignore his lonely hulk as he stood forlorn at the football table like the awkward child at school, and Lucy would always give him a kind word and, sometimes, a game unless she was too absorbed in Harry and forgot. But I don't think these small attentions helped: rather the contrary. Antoine was a simple fellow who couldn't handle inconsistency. When he came into the bar, not knowing if Lucy were his friend or not, it only confused him, the poor devil.

At that time, which was in the New Year, I wasn't paying close attention to the things Harry was saying. Mostly he was telling a loose string of anecdotes about America in the fifties and sixties. He mentioned

Hemingway and Norman Mailer and Truman Capote. He wasn't name-dropping. In fact, I wasn't certain if he was saying he'd met them or was simply relating stories that had done the rounds in New York. Lucy was fascinated because she was a student of American literature. I had the curious impression that Harry had read a great deal but derived very little from his reading; or at least, nothing direct or that he cared to quote. His comments were blunt: so and so was 'a lush'; such and such a book was 'horseshit'. I don't mean that he was opinionated. Lucy would contradict him and rattle on about *Zeitgeist* and subtext, and he would listen tolerantly, smile, shrug and say, 'I guess you could be right.' He was, I think, taking her measure in all of this: deciding how much of himself to reveal.

As often as not, we used to drop in at La Maison des Moines as we ambled home in the crisp starlight. There was no sign that Harry was doing anything more to stamp his character on the place. We sat always in the same plain, clean room which had nothing of Harry except the Blake print and the carpet bag. Then, gradually, it came to me that this did in fact reflect his character in its transient, nomad quality, and for this reason the room began to acquire a strange glamour. It seemed to me that, in its simple furnishings, it represented the magician's sleeves – 'Look, see, there's nothing up them' – and the carpet bag was the place from which, by miracle of prestidigitation, wonders would appear However, you should bear in mind that some of this is hindsight and also that on most of these occasions I was tired and had a few drinks inside me. Maybe to outsiders we would have appeared merely three people sipping wine and chatting in the dim evening light. This is a point I keep forgetting: how the situation appeared to me and how it might appear to others.

If I sound mysterious, it isn't because I was left without clues to interpret: hints at the direction in which our odd friendship with the old man might be going. I simply missed them – perhaps because my character is more prosaic than I care to admit, and certainly because my legal training and way of thinking led me down paths which were linear and logical. But, even allowing for my own limitations as a contribution to my blindness, I doubt that anyone else would have seen more clearly. In fact, I'm certain of it.

The first true pointer came in the middle of January. It was Antoine's birthday. Lucy was at her most affectionate and charming, with all the artless callousness that can imply. I recall that despite the weather (a bitter frost) she wore a black cocktail dress, beautifully cut, spangled and low in the neckline, to the chic accompaniment of a pair of Doc Martens boots. She had applied kohl to her eyes and a deep crimson lipstick, and decorated her hands with delicate patterns of henna. I was conservatively dressed as if to walk the dog and take a weekend gin and tonic at my local pub. I commented that she looked lovely (for which I received a 'Thank you, kind sir,' and a kiss), and remarked that she would quite turn Antoine's head.' It's the lad's birthday,' she answered lightly. 'He deserves a treat.'

I recall, too, that Antoine had appeared, in his own dim way, he'd risen to the occasion. His Elvis haircut was oiled to perfection. He wore a leather biker's jacket and a pair of jeans that descended below a copious belly to fall concertina-fashion over a pair of cowboy boots stitched with elaborate medallions. His first words on seeing Lucy were 'Hi there, baby,' the only English he knew. The poor fellow was entranced, and Lucy, thinking to do him a kindness, and in any case a little drunk, responded in the way she thought these things were done in the movies and draped herself over him. Mike, in beret and striped T-shirt, pursued his dream of non-existent France and played the accordion while singing some old Charles Trenet numbers. And Lucy and Antoine danced.

Throughout I smiled the smile of a tolerant fifty-year-old, and if I felt a pang at witnessing the passionate embraces on the small floor which Mike had cleared for dancing, I didn't show it amid the general laughter and uproar. What would have happened when Antoine found that on the stroke of midnight his Cinderella disappeared with me I don't know, since at about that time he had the tact to pass out dead drunk and was hauled off to his mother's house by Mike and the others. I was left with the cheerful, giggling wreckage of Lucy, and with Harry who'd spent the evening silently but good-humouredly drinking Ricard. As we surveyed the debris of the bar, with Marie-Paule looking at her watch and clearing tables, he proposed, 'I'll help you home with our little girl.'

'Are you sure, Harry?'

He placed a hand on my shoulder and said, 'It's the least I can do. You children have brightened my life here.'

So we grabbed Lucy and the pair of us supported her. We went outside and got smacked in the face by the cold. Slowly we made our way up the hill. I could hear that Harry was tired. The few remarks he made were in those dark middle-European tones he only occasionally used.

'I'm pooped,' he said as we reached the gate of La Maison des Moines.

'Okay,' I answered. 'I'll leave you here.'

'You won't make it on your own. Come in and have some coffee.'

I would have refused, but Lucy cried, 'Coffee! I'd love some coffee!'

Harry grinned. 'That's it, honey. Let's get some good strong java into you.'

I had no choice but to play along.

We went inside. Harry poured shots of cognac for himself and for me and went into the kitchen to fix coffee. Lucy, beautiful, dishevelled and sleepy, sprawled in a chair and, looking at her, I realised that I loved her more than ever.

Harry returned with the coffees. He fumbled in a small oak cabinet and took something from a drawer before sitting down. I dozed over my coffee and brandy, struggling to keep awake. The room held a fireplace made of fieldstone, an old-fashioned open hearth where the logs rested on iron dogs. Once Harry had lit the fire he turned off the reading lamp and we sat by the light of the blazing logs, listening to the flames flare and pop as the resin burned. Harry took a clasp knife from his pocket and began to pare at what looked like a twist of black pipe tobacco. As he fumbled with papers and a thin roll of card I recognised the routine, but, absurdly, I said, 'I didn't think you smoked, Harry?'

He looked up. 'I don't – not cigarettes, just now and again a Moroccan Marlboro.' He winked and ran his tongue along the edge of the paper. Finished, he admired the result, lit up and inhaled a lungful of smoke. I remembered the pleasant smell I'd always attributed to the kitchen. I should have known it was dope, but I hadn't smoked for nearly thirty years, not since the night before my solicitor's final exams. I didn't even know what the *cognoscenti* called the stuff these days. Putting a respectable face on the thought of Harry pottering in his kitchen, boiling eggs and bug-eyed with quiet satisfaction, I said, 'I suppose it has medical benefits. Has your doctor recommended it?'

'What?' he drawled. 'Oh, sure. It beats the hell out of aspirin, don't it?' He passed me the joint (if that is the current word) and, after staring at it a moment, I thought why not? and took a leisurely drag.

Lucy hadn't gone to sleep, as I believed. I felt her fingers tip-tapping on my thigh, and when I looked her lips were pouting like a fish's. 'Gimme, gimme,' she whispered. I passed the joint to her and she took a puff with more attention than she'd applied for the last half-hour.

So there we were, the three of us, more drunk than sober, smoking dope by firelight with no sound except the crackling logs amid the silence of night. It gave me a comfortable feeling and time for thinking on my arid existence in London, reflections which seemed enlightened at the time and which I have since forgotten. When, after ten minutes or an hour, Harry began to recount one of his tales of New York, I grunted appreciatively and my attention drifted in and out of his narrative, which was about Andy Warhol and how it was a bad idea to lend him money.

I said, 'Come on, Harry you'll be telling me next that you knew Elvis.' I was probably making a loose connection with Antoine.

'Yes,' murmured Harry deeply and slowly, 'I knew him. I met him in Las Vegas in ... when was it? Seventy-four?' He closed his eyes. 'Something of a gentleman in his own way.'

'*Please*,' I groaned amiably.

'You don't believe me?'

'No, no. If you say so.'

'I can tell you don't believe me.'

'Harry–'

'You don't believe me,' he repeated, too tired to be truly bad-tempered. He rolled over in his chair and groped for the carpet bag. 'Proof,' he said. 'I got the goddamn proof. Where is it? Got the goddamn proof,' he repeated, lingering with relish over the profanities rather than blurting them out.

'I believe you.'

'The hell you do,' Harry (or was it John Wayne?) drawled.

'Harry–'

'Got it, the goddamn proof.' Somewhere in the depths of the bag he found what he was looking for. He handed it to me and I twirled in my fingers a book of matches from the Sands Hotel. 'Open it,' he urged. 'Go on. See for yourself.'

'Okay, Harry, if that's what you want.' I opened the book and saw inside the cover scrawled in ballpoint, the inscription *To Harry from Elvis*. I gave a short laugh – or maybe a long laugh; my head was spinning. 'Anybody could have written this,' I said.

'Anybody *didn't* write it: Elvis did,' answered Harry.

'All right. But Elvis probably wrote hundreds, *thousands*, like this. It doesn't mean you *knew* him.'

'I didn't say I knew him well. We didn't have a lot in common – I was kind of a Cole Porter fan.' Harry took the matches back and dropped them into the carpet bag. He closed his eyes, opened them slowly, smiled and went on, 'Yeah, well I admit it's maybe not all that impressive, but leastways you can see I'm not a goddamn liar.'

'No, you're not a liar,' I said, soothingly. And that was where I should have let the matter rest. But, no, that wouldn't do. I was a lawyer and knew about evidence and that sort of stuff. I murmured. 'Of course. it could be checked. We could find out if Elvis worked the Sands in seventy-four.'

Harry looked at me more alertly. 'And?'

'And maybe the books would tell us that he didn't. Then how would things stand?'

'The books would be wrong.'

'Harry … please … I'm a lawyer.'

'I tell you the books would be wrong,' he insisted.

'Oh, really?'

'Yes, *really*. Because this is how I remember it. Do you understand me? I *remember* it.'

CHAPTER THREE

A la recherche du corps perdu

For a long time I used to go to bed early. Sometimes, when I had put out my candle, my eyes would close so quickly that I had not even time to say to myself: 'I'm falling asleep.' And half an hour later the thought that it was time to sleep would awaken me; I would make as if to put away the book which I imagined was still in my hands, and to blow out the light: I had gone on thinking, while I was asleep, about what I was reading, and my hands, which only in my reverie held the book, would, as if turning the pages, peel back my foreskin, first delicately, as when settling to enjoy the book and reluctant to read too fast lest it be over, and then with increasing rapidity, as if the book were a childish adventure that must be completed at a rush until with a gasp its mystery and my own inner mystery would seem to achieve a solution in that ejaculation. At the same time my sight would return and I would be astonished to find myself in a state of darkness, pleasant and restful enough for my eyes, but even more, perhaps, for my member, which appeared incomprehensible, without cause, something dark indeed.

I would ask myself what time it was; I could hear the creaking of a bed, which, now loud as if nearer and now faint as if farther off, punctuating the distance like the invitation of a whore in an alleyway, showed me in perspective the deserted city through which a petty clerk is hurrying towards the nearby station; and the path he is taking will be engraved in his memory by the excitement induced by strange surroundings, by the conversation he has had and the price agreed beneath an unfamiliar lamp that still echoes in his ears amid the silence of the night, and by the guilty prospect of being home again.

I would lay my cheeks gently against the comfortable cheeks of my pillow, as plump and fresh as the cheeks of my mother's buttocks. I would strike a match to look at my watch: nearly midnight. The hour when Monsieur Swann, who visits us as if on a journey and obliged to sleep in a strange hotel, having gratified his desire in a sudden spasm, sees with horror a streak of daylight showing under my mother's door. Good God, it is morning! The servants will be about in a minute: someone will ring and a servant will discover him. The thought of being exposed gives him the strength to suppress his cry of joy. He is certain he heard footsteps: they come nearer, and then die away. The ray of light beneath the door is extinguished. It is midnight; someone has just turned on the gas; the last servant has gone to bed; and he knows that, below, my father sits all night in an agony of self-abuse with no one to bring him relief.

CHAPTER FOUR

As January came to an end, I had a new idea. I took Lucy to dinner at a restaurant in Chalabre and explained it to her.

'I want to make a painting expedition into the mountains.'

'It's the middle of winter,' she pointed out reasonably enough and she might have added, if she'd been more familiar with my past life, that I wasn't the outdoor type and should likely get myself killed. I don't claim that I was making sense.

Behind my suggestion were the same agonies about being fifty, deserting my wife and running off with a beautiful woman twenty years my junior. I can't say how painting the mountains in the depths of winter would have cured these problems, but I think I told her something about existential freedom, the need for space, and the clarification of my thoughts which would lead to a deeper commitment to her. When I wear my advocate's hat I can spout such stuff and half believe it's true.

Thinking about it now, I believe that one thing in particular troubled me: that little thing which, perhaps more than love, sustains a relationship. I wanted to know: what were Lucy and I going to *talk* about for the rest of our lives?

I've already mentioned the subject of silences. Now I was concerned about conversations. One or the other: we had to speak or be silent; and whatever we chose had to mean something. I had had twenty-five years of talking with Sally and it was only in retrospect and in contrast with Lucy that I saw how multi-layered our conversations had been. Don't mistake me; I'm not suggesting they were profound; I'm speaking of structure, not content. It didn't matter if we were discussing the children or the car or Sally's mother or whatever: the idiom, the imagery, the things left unsaid as well as said were the effect of shared context and memory, and both form and intelligibility flowed from a private language that we remembered and also continued to create. The point may become clearer when I say that I recall food rationing, the coronation of Queen Elizabeth, cobbled streets, gas lamps and the arrival of the first motorcar in the road where I lived. Lucy knew none of these and even my shameful little secrets were incomprehensible. What was it to her if I once admired Denis Wheatley or Gerry and the Pacemakers? Indeed, who were they?

However, I fancy I'm falling into my vice of confusing recollection with hindsight and analysis. The fond lover who sought to convince Lucy of the necessity of his hike in the snow could hardly have thought it was an answer to a problem of semiotics. For the purpose of this story, it's enough that Lucy raised no insurmountable objection to my proposal. The next day I drove to Pamiers and bought the necessary kit and the following day Lucy and Harry took me as far as Montségur. I kissed Lucy goodbye and consigned her to Harry's fatherly care.

I was away for a week in the mountains and high pastures and saw no one except an occasional shepherd. I suffered no mishaps and painted a few bad pictures; and at the end of that time returned to civilisation bearing the manly badges of sunburn and mild frostbite. Lucy welcomed me home tenderly and I felt I'd accomplished something, though I couldn't put a name to it.

How had Lucy managed in my absence? I asked her.

'Oh, Harry took care of me,' she answered coyly.

'Took care of you?'

'I stayed a couple of nights at his place.' She laughed. 'Don't worry darling! Nothing happened between us. He has a spare room.'

In fact it hadn't occurred to me that anything might have happened. Sally tells me I'm not a jealous person and I think that's true. And even though Lucy had in my case displayed amorous inclinations towards the geriatric, I couldn't seriously regard myself as in competition with a man of eighty who dressed like a racing tipster and had a dope habit. Harry was engaging and exotic, but my imagination didn't go beyond that.

'I was lonely while you were gone,' Lucy explained affectionately. 'We had snow, and this house can seem very isolated at night, and I had nothing to do.'

'You could have gone to Mike's place.'

'I did, but I can't talk to him. He goes on about the past. I don't want to discuss the nineteen sixties. I was scarcely born then. Did you know he was a fan of Gerry and the Pacemakers? Have you heard of anything more ridiculous?'

Yes, I had.

'Antoine would be there.'

Shamefacedly Lucy confessed, 'I think I made a mistake coming on so strong to him at his birthday party. He's started wearing aftershave and he calls me "baby" all the time. "On s'en jète un, baby?" That sort of thing. And...'

'What?'

She stifled a giggle. 'He wiggles his bottom!'

'Like Elvis?'

'I suppose so – I mean *not* like Elvis, more like Jean-Paul Gaultier.'

'Oh dear.'

'Precisely. Poor lovey. I think I've messed up his emotional life and I don't know what to do. I ran into his mother at the PTT and she gave me the evil eye. She knows that the English trollop has set her cap at Madame's darling boy.'

'He'll get over it,' I said, though I wasn't convinced. A simple man like Antoine has room for only one idea at a time and doesn't discern shades of meaning. Perhaps the only solution was to stay out of his way. I asked, 'How did you spend your time with Harry?'

'Oh,' answered Lucy noncommittally, 'the usual way. He told me stories.'

'About Norman Mailer and Truman Capote?'

'And Sinatra and that sort of thing. He was amusing but the stories aren't very coherent – frankly, we smoked rather a lot. It's my impression that there's something Harry wants to say, but he's still marshalling his thoughts.'

'Did he give you any idea why he's come to Puybrun?'

'No. I don't think Puybrun is in any way special for him. I think anywhere quiet and out of the way would do. He hasn't said, but I've a notion that his decision is connected with the stories.'

'In what way?'

'Oh, nothing strange. He's an old man, and I think he's taking this last opportunity to make sense of his life: understand who he is, what he's done, where he's been. And find some meaning it it.' She paused to look at me affectionately. 'Like you, darling.'

I didn't see Harry for a few days following my return. Snow had fallen again and I stayed at home by the fire with Lucy, making love as the mood took us. It seemed to me that sex was affirmative rather than reflective. I wanted to demonstrate that I was in Puybrun for reasons other than the contemplation of my middle-aged navel. Or am I over-analysing again? No philosophical reason was needed to make love to Lucy. Her body quickened my desire whenever I saw it. Her skin was smooth and slightly downy, her breasts small and pale. The aureoles around her nipples were large and brown. Her belly wasn't flat; rather, it fell in a raindrop curve. Her hips and buttocks were plump and womanly, her legs long and shapely. When she wore jeans, a space opened between her thighs; only a small space, offering the tiniest glimmer of light, but enough to illuminate the shape and swell of the crotch. Since coming to France she had given up shaving and, though the conventional man inside me shuddered, I rejoiced in her scent and hairiness.

But enough! Read another book if you want that sort of thing. Buy a magazine.

Harry had decided that he, too, would celebrate my return. 'To say thank you, Johnny.'

'What for?'

'Because you and Lucy have spurred me on.'

'I don't understand. Spurred you to do what?'

'Oh, all those things old fellows like me should do before we meet our Maker.' Harry said this quite cheerfully. I don't think the prospect of death troubled him.

What he proposed was a dinner party for the three of us. We would do it in style. I didn't have a dinner suit with me, so I took Harry's hint that I should simply 'flash'. Despite the cold weather, I wore a printed silk shirt and my tropical linen suit with white canvas shoes. 'You look like a gun-runner, very *Nostromo*,' said Lucy appreciatively. She wore a Faerie Queen dress, long and trailing fichus of grey gossamer, a silver toque, and silver slippers bedizened with rhinestones. As for Harry he surprised me by wearing a sort of mess dress: black trousers with black patent pumps, and a white ducktail jacket. Admittedly the medals on the jacket were tarnished and the ribbons dirty and he wore a Hawaiian beach shirt, but the ensemble was oddly effective. The three of us reminded me of passengers on a liner about to cross the equator. I had in mind those parties thrown for King

Neptune, when the ship sparkles with coloured lights and the sailors dress as mermaids. Maybe Harry, too, had this idea since he'd decorated his lounge with paper streamers and from somewhere laid on a supply of Big Band records, slow fox-trots and girl singers with lush yet limpid voices.

He fixed us some Martinis, two or three each, American style that made my head buzz. After the first, Lucy mused dreamily over the second, her face set with a smile of unearthly complacency. I studied her intently for her imperfections. The record playing was Glenn Miller, I think – at all events it was dance music; and I reflected that, for all her beauty, Lucy wasn't graceful. Her walk and gestures had a mannishness about them, that is to say, they were matter-of-fact, even clumsy. This wasn't a quality peculiar to her. Most young Englishwomen have it. Then, on consideration, I remembered that tonight, in her jewelled slippers, she'd been different, walking with the level glide of an Indian. I smiled inwardly at that delicately erotic image. I've already said that the Martinis were good.

Harry was a fair cook, but his cuisine was as eclectic as his speech and clothes. We ate a cold beetroot soup, sweet but served with a spiral of soured cream, followed by *spezzato di agnello coi fagioli* (Harry's description, spoken like a New York mobster) and finished with a honey pastry I fancy was Turkish. A couple of bottles of claret saw off the meat, and a half-bottle of sauternes accompanied the pudding. For a *digestif* we smoked some dope – Oh yes! Wasn't I the adventurous one?

The meal over, Lucy slumped at the table. She wasn't asleep. She was smiling and kept one glassy eye open like a dozing dog in a cartoon. Harry and I took seats in a couple of old but comfortable armchairs. I produced some Havana cigars I'd bought in Pamiers. We lit up and puffed a while in amiable silence, broken when I said idly, 'What are we going to talk about, Harry?'

'What do you want to talk about? You want to tell me about yourself?'

That was the last thing I had in mind. My history was too bound up with Sally, and how could I talk about myself and Lucy? Our emotional relationship had begun in the time-honoured way with furtive coupling after an office party and, whatever it might mean for us, would sound sordid to anyone else. In a sense the whole point of our flight to Puybrun was to lift us out of the dreariness of common-or-garden adultery: a goal to which Harry was now contributing. After all, when this episode was over (as it inevitably would be) and Lucy and I returned to England to raise her first and my second family, then the memory of a hotel in Paddington could be decently buried and we would say that everything between us began in France – in a village in winter – on a night when the moon was a cracked mirror in a white room – before a log fire – talking to an old man – smoking dope. Thanks, Harry, for giving me a new beginning.

What I said was, 'You first.'

'Me? You want to hear my story?'

'Yes,' drawled Lucy from her torpor.

'Oh, my dears, I wouldn't know where to begin!' Harry protested. 'I'd make a start and forget something and have to go back and begin earlier.'

'Begin where you like,' I said. 'There must be something in this room you can use as a cue to memory: an object, a taste, a smell.' I smiled smugly and suggested, 'Begin with a madeleine biscuit.'

Harry raised an eyebrow. He mumbled, 'Proust.'

I was surprised. I hadn't expected him to grasp the allusion. Maybe he realised this. At all events, he gave me a quizzical look and got out of his chair.

'Wait … wait,' he said. 'I'll tell you my story all in good time, but first I've got something to show you.' He was a little unsteady and I thought he was drunk, but he was only searching in semi-darkness for his carpet bag. 'Where is the beast? Where? ... Ah! ... No! ... Goddamn it!'

'In the corner, Harry.'

'Where? Ah! To be sure, I'm obliged, *dziekuje bardzo*.' The bag was heavy and he dragged it to his chair, refusing my offer of help. 'No, no, it's all right, leave me alone. I'll find it.'

'Okay, fine, if that's the way you want it.'

'It is, it is. No offence, huh, Johnny? Now, where is it? Goddamn.'

I glanced at Lucy, who grinned vaguely. I closed my eyes. The momentary feeling of annoyance vanished and I let myself slide into well-being while Harry muttered in the darkness.

Suddenly he yelled, 'Ha!' I jumped, and I fancy even Lucy opened both eyes. Harry was waving a book before my face as if it were something he'd pulled from the fire. He wiped a rheumy eye with his left hand and with the right proffered his discovery. 'Go on, take it, it won't bite.'

'If you insist.'

'Hoity-toity, old boy. Go on, *mon brave*, take, read, learn something.'

'Very well,' I said, and took the book.

The binding was plum-coloured cloth, somewhat faded with dampness, and I couldn't make out the title. The endpapers were marbled and the pages had been hand-cut. It was a cheaply produced book, pretending to be something better. A quick riffle showed frequent illustrations. The chapters began with elaborate rubrics. The spine was weak and the book fell open naturally at a full-page plate comprising a black-and-white woodcut in *Jugendstil*. I had difficulty discerning the subject but that was more because of the complexity of the draughtsmanship than the poor light. The background was both biological and astrological, a composition of flowers, stars and tendrils intertwined to tie it to the main image. The latter composed itself into two young male figures, classical in their features but moustached as befitted the turn of the century. They were naked, and at first I assumed they were wrestling. Inspection showed that they were rather beautifully engaged in the act of buggery.

I turned to the title page. I saw: *Erotika Verlag – Hamburg 1923*. The text was said to be translated from the original French, but the title was given in German. I flipped a page and read: *For a long time I used to go to bed early...*

I read only a few pages, but they must have taken me half an hour since the text was in German and some words, though not their general sense, were unfamiliar. Lucy had emerged from her semi-slumber and was now sitting at my feet and stroking my knee with her fingertips. Harry was solemn and still, but wide awake.

'Where did you get this?' I asked.

The answer was hesitant, painful. 'Berlin. Clarence Quimby gave it me in ... I think it would be in thirty-four – at all events, some time after Hitler came to power.'

'Clarence Quimby? Should I know him?'

Harry shook his head, and again I had the feeling of a painful recollection.

'I doubt it. He was working for Bill Shirer in those days. I believe the term is a "stringer". As slick as shit on an ice-rink, and that was in the days when he was good-looking. He didn't get any better with age.'

'Your story begins with Quimby?'

'No. See what I mean? I'm getting distracted already. Maybe I'll tell you about Clarence another time.'

'So you're beginning with Proust?'

'No. *You* began with Proust, by feeding me that dinky reference to the biscuit. I simply picked up on your little joke because we were talking about the past and memory and that sort of stuff.'

'This book isn't by Proust,' I pointed out, pedantically. 'It's just a piece of pornography.'

'The front says it is by Proust.'

'That doesn't prove anything.'

'It *sounds* like Proust.'

'*Please*,' I laughed. 'It sounds like nothing of the sort. Whatever it may say about being translated from the French, this was written by a German with a filthy imagination.'

'If you say so. I won't argue with you, Johnny.'

'Thanks.'

'Except to say that it sounds like the Proust I knew. Marcel had a filthy turn of phrase when he was in company he could relax with.'

'Harry!'

'Sorry, sorry.'

I handed the book back. Harry ran his hands over it affectionately before replacing it in the bag. I leaned over to pick up a log and add it to the fire. The action disturbed Lucy, who must have been thinking over Harry's words.

She said, 'You couldn't have known Marcel Proust, could you?' More doubtfully, 'Could you? I mean, he must have died in nineteen twenty or about then.' In fact Proust died in 1922, though I wasn't aware of the fact – I mean, not then. Lucy said, 'At best you would have been a child. You couldn't have known him in any meaningful sense...'

'If you say so.'

'It isn't a matter of whether I say so, is it?' Lucy looked to me for confirmation.

'Lucy's right,' I said.

'Maybe,' answered Harry with a shrug. 'Perhaps my memory plays tricks. I'm sure I remember meeting Marcel.'

I didn't know what to reply. Harry seemed serious by virtue of the fact that he was minded neither to laugh nor to insist on his point. His tone throughout the brief exchange had been more level than the absurdity of the subject warranted. I wondered if he were being ironic, trying to state a facile philosophical thesis about the problem of memory. However, Harry's humour had always struck me as being of the direct sort and hitherto he'd shown no interest in philosophy. In a vague way, I felt we'd insulted him. As a consolation I reverted to where we had begun: with my initial invitation to tell us something of his history. I proposed, 'Let's have another drink or smoke another joint, or even both. It will put us back in the mood.'

We elected to smoke another joint and, having done so at a leisurely pace, we were at last (in the difficult and datable vocabulary of the topic) 'mellow' and in a mood to begin again.

'Do tell us about yourself,' urged Lucy in her most winning way. Harry grinned and, in a fatherly fashion, kissed her on the forehead.

He said, 'Sure. Who could deny you, honey? My story, why not? But not from the beginning, not from my date of birth. And you'll have to forgive me if I do it wrong and mention things and people you don't know about.'

'Like Clarence Quimby?' I said. Harry nodded thoughtfully.

'Like that sonofabitch, for example. So, are we agreed?'

'Yes,' said Lucy.

'Yes.'

'Good. Then I'll begin.'

Harry began in the way he started most of his stories. He dived into the carpet bag again and produced a bundle of old letters tied with ribbon. He shuffled them and took one out, which he gave me. It was on good-quality paper and bore a stamp with Victoria's head.

'Go on,' he said. 'Read it. It'll help prove that what I'm about to tell you is true.'

'Very well,' I said, to please him. I took the enclosure out of the envelope and read it.

Boulanger, Blanqui & Ravachol   Renfield, Jeofail & Mortmain
147 Avenue Macmahon   Solicitors
Paris   6 Scriveners Inn
France   Woolsack Street
                                      London
                           15th April 1890

Dear Sirs

We acknowledge with thanks the receipt of your communication of 30th ult. As we understand your instructions, your client, Count Esterhazy, wishes to dispose of certain hereditaments and chattels situate in the territory of the Dual Monarchy. The proceeds of the sale are to be applied: firstly to the purchase of a gentleman's residence in London; and, secondly, to be invested in the Consolidated Funds of Her Britannic Majesty's Government. That being so, we are pleased to advise that we are willing to act in the matter. Our fees will be according to our usual scale plus an addition of fifty per centum for the inconvenience of foreign travel, plus disbursements at net cost. Upon your written confirmation that our charges are acceptable, arrangements will be made for your correspondent to attend upon the Count at Linz on 10th. prox.

May I take the opportunity to express our gratitude and sense of obligation at your favouring us with this matter, and assure you of our best attention at all times, while remaining

    Yours faithfully
    R. M. Renfield, Esq.
       Partner

Finished, I passed the letter back to Harry. I didn't know what response he expected, so I said simply, 'Very interesting.'

'Isn't it?'

'But...'

'Yes?'

'It doesn't mean a great deal to me.'

Harry grinned.

He said, 'It will, my boy. I can assure you of that,' and he began his tale, this time ignoring the rough vocabulary with which it amused him to pepper his ordinary speech, but speaking, carefully, even fussily: modulating and playing with the smoother, darker tones of his voice so that they matched the darkness of the room and his subject. Imagine, therefore, someone reading Henry James in a slow Anglicised drawl – though neither the style nor the subject has anything to do with Henry James.

CHAPTER FIVE

Harry's Tale

I believe my name is Count Rudolf Heinrich Valdemar Drakul-Esterhazy; though, if someone were to contradict me, I should not call him a liar – it is unreasonable to expect me to remember all the details at my age. Let it suffice that I am fairly convinced about the 'Esterhazy' part. Indeed I am even sentimental about it; and, although I have had occasion to change over the years, I have tried to keep to something with euphonious similarity. *Esterhazy – Haze*. What do you think?

As to nationality, again you catch me at a disadvantage. In the last century it was a hazy notion, and whole tribes wandered across frontiers or were shipped across oceans without passports or any other let or hindrance. Consider only the peoples of the Habsburg state: Austrians, Czechs, Slovaks, Ruthenians, Hungarians, Rumanians, Croats, Slovenians, Serbs and doubtless others I forget. Not to mention proto-nations who had never converted their spoken gibberish into literature. Was it d'Azeglio who said: 'We have created Italy. Now we must create Italians'?

Certainly, in the year 1890, I was a French citizen, and an officer in the French army. But I was scarcely a Frenchman. In my youth I had spoken Rumanian to peasants, Magyar within my family, German to the authorities, and French to my mistresses. English was beneath my notice. It was learned by office boys who wished to become embezzlers. The last time I spoke

Magyar was with Lugosi Béla in 1947 . We had different accents and I'm not sure either of us understood the other.

A Magyar's definition of nationhood is the right to kick Rumanians. At all events that was the opinion of those of us who lived to the east, a bastion of civilisation in a sea of bumpkins (to mix my metronomes) It is scarcely to be credited that, at the end of the Great War, this historic land of the Magyar people should have been lost and its inhabitants converted into Ruminants. However, the injustice done to my race is not my subject.

My family owned a number of properties, including an ancestral castle. This was located on a forested mountain in the Carpathians, many miles from a village, many miles from a town, many miles from any place you ever heard of. It was, in short, situated in that pleasant rustic land that, in my American days, I learned to call 'the boonies'.

It is an Anglo-American conceit that the Industrial Revolution and its accompanying Agricultural Revolution occurred only in those countries and in Germany. A movement towards capitalist farming was also current in the East, and it was that which, in part, enabled us to sell Castle Bunicetate to a consortium of Viennese Jews who believed they could make a profit out of the timber. I mention these facts because some people have given a gothic twist to matters best explained by macro-economics.

Certain financial difficulties in France made me wish to put my funds outside the reach of my creditors. Hence my employment of Renfield. We agreed to meet in Linz, which was a convenient midpoint in our journeys, with the added advantage that my family owned a town house there.

I think it was May? There or thereabouts. Renfield presented himself at Linz and booked into a modest *pension* near the New Cathedral, which at that date was still under construction. He sent a porter to my house in the Landstrasse to announce his arrival and followed this with a visit in person to pay his compliments to his client. I had never met an Englishman before and my opinions were based on the current prejudices. I forget exactly what those were in 1890, but something along the lines that Englishmen were arrogant, snobbish, bloody-minded, hypocritical pederasts, though I couldn't swear to 'bloody-minded'. Also they had a sense of humour.

Renfield was an unprepossessing little man in his late thirties with sparse fair hair, a nose that would have looked better on a girl of five, and a voice of distressingly variable pitch. We conversed in French, which he spoke comprehensibly if one did not attend too closely to his accent. Out of politeness, I complimented him on his mastery of the idiom and he said complacently, 'That is because I have been to Deauville several times with my mother,' which made me wonder whether the English had gained India in the same sublime way: because Clive had once been to Delhi with his sister and her friend, perhaps?

I can't say that we hit it off. I don't say that we quarrelled. Renfield sat primly in his Norfolk jacket and declined any refreshment, while I lounged in the semi-darkness of the shuttered room, nursing a considerable hangover and sipping from a glass which contained the pelt of the creature that had bitten me. This last condition was attributable to my having spent the previous evening carousing with an old friend, Alois. In the circumstances, I refused to spend much time on the subject of business and it was agreed that we'd discuss it as we travelled and that we should start the following day.

Our journey took us by train via Vienna and Budapest to Bistritz. Alois accompanied us, and tried to relieve me of some of the burden of conversing with Renfield, though with little success since the latter had a limited command of German. (Alois was a petty government official aged sixty or so and fond of drink. I had met him when drunk in some *Bierstube* or other and collected him rather in the way that one collects stray bits of other people's property or mysterious bruises.) At Vienna Renfield and I paused for a day while Alois pressed on to prepare our reception at the castle.

Renfield's manner was restrained but unremarkable until we had travelled beyond Budapest. Until then he kept up an occasional chat about Surrey and maiden aunts and his mother, and tried to interest me in an obscure dispute about Anglican liturgy. Looking out of the window every now and again, he drew comparisons between the Hungarian countryside and that of England. However, the closer we approached to Bistritz, the more silent he became and he adopted an uncomfortable wariness.

Andere Länder, andere Sitten. Wallachs, Slovaks, Szekelys, Szgany – to me they were all familiar neighbours. At Bistritz we changed from the train to a public *diligence* which would take us into the mountains by the road leading to Bukovina by the Borgo pass. To my mind, it was a pleasant ride in May, though rather slow and bumpy. To Renfield it was … well, something else.

At Bistritz, he began paying attention to the peasants in a way that one doesn't if one lives there.

'What does "Ordog" mean?' he asked.

'Satan,' I told him.

' "Pokol"?'

'Hell.'

'And "voolok"?'

'Vampire – I think. My Slovak isn't the best.'

'I noticed that they were making a sign,' he said. 'Something like this,' and he repeated the gesture.

I laughed. 'Oh, yes. They do that to ward off the evil eye.'

'Why should they be doing and saying these things?' he asked, giving me a look that was more pointed than polite.

'Because they're frightened of you,' I told him. 'You're the first Englishman they've ever seen.' I was surprised that this perfectly obvious answer had not occurred to him.

The road rose by degrees through the forest. I shan't elaborate the details since they may confuse those unfamiliar with the area. It should suffice that, for me at least, I was spending a delightful late-spring day in a countryside I loved. However, this was not so for Renfield.

'Those trees are…?'

'Firs,' I said. 'Surely you have them in England?'

'They seem very dark.'

'Do they? I suppose they do. There are rather a lot of them. But, then, there are – in forests, I mean.'

'We don't have forests in England.'

'Epping Forest?'

'It's not the same.'

'No? Is "Epping" a verb? Can one go epping? I am trying to learn English if I am to buy a property there.'

'One can't go epping.'

'I see. Is it illegal?'

He examined me with a very cunning expression in his eyes, but I assured him my question was entirely innocent. In my studies I was coming to grips with continuous tenses and present participles. I returned to my book and to gazing out of the window.

Some little while later Renfield jogged me with his elbow.

'At that last village,' he said, 'The people crossed themselves as we passed.'

'Quite possibly. They are very religious.'

'I thought that the sign was directed at you.'

I'd not been paying much attention, so now I stuck my head out of the window and asked the driver where we were and he told me.

'Ah, yes,' I said to Renfield. 'My family used to own this village. The peasants were probably showing their respect.' Again this rather commonplace explanation seemed lost on my companion.

The journey from Bistritz over the pass is rather long and night fell while we were still under way. Speaking for myself, I am rather fond of wolves. Their howling at night is the very essence of the countryside and I'd grown up with it in childhood. The poor beasts never attack humans, and most peasant families have raised a wolf cub in their time. I tried to mention this to Renfield as distraction, since there was little to see in the darkness.

'The wolves,' I said, sociably. 'Would you like to hear about the wolves I used to keep?'

'No, I would not,' he said sharply.

'Very well.'

After a spell during which we were silent except for the jolting of the *diligence* and the occasional howl, he enquired: 'You can command wolves?'

'I don't think I'd put it in those terms.'

'What terms would you use?'

'I would – oh, look!' I said, pointing out of the window to a will-o'-the-wisp which was flickering over a marshy spot somewhere out in the forest.

Renfield's train of thought was interrupted, and he asked me solemnly, 'Was that a ghost?'

He was beginning to tire me.

'Probably,' I said, and closed my eyes.

Our destination was not Bukovina. I had arranged that, at a point on our descent from the pass, we should be met by a *calèche* driven by one of the castle servants. As the *diligence* began its way down the winding route, I saw a pair of carriage lamps flickering among the trees and the driver swinging a lantern to attract our attention. I called to the coachman to halt our vehicle. Inexplicably, this prospect seemed to terrify Renfield.

'For God's sake, don't stop!' he cried.

'Why ever not?' I asked.

'You *know* why,' he answered meaningfully. But I didn't and I wasn't to be prevented by an Englishman with a fit of the vapours.

When the driver of the *calèche* approached, I recognised Alois. This was a surprise.

I exclaimed, 'Alois, old friend, I hadn't expected you to turn up in person. I thought you would send a servant. Where's the usual driver?'

The old fellow took me aside – which was probably unfortunate given Renfield's nervous condition as he peered from the window of the *diligence*. Alois whispered, 'I have some unfortunate news. The servants haven't been paid for months and they've decamped. There's no one at the castle except myself and Maria.' Maria was a village girl, buxom as I recalled from last seeing her.

'There's no need to whisper,' I said. 'He' – indicating Renfield – 'speaks only English and bad French.'

'Also,' said Alois, 'the Jews are kicking up some fuss about the boundaries of the estate and the amount of commercial timber. They won't pay until these problems are resolved.'

This was embarrassing news. I had no desire that Renfield should see the distressed state of my affairs. I returned to him, reassured him that everything was in order and invited him to join us in the *calèche*. He did, but only after telling the driver of the *diligence* to remember his face and pressing into the man's hand a note which, when it was shown to me, contained details of the Englishman's next of kin. I shrugged and gave the driver a tip.

I shan't trouble you with a detailed description of the castle. It was gloomy and gothic enough for any number of tales, but I was fond of the old pile and the habitable parts were homely enough, and in summer it was distinctly charming. The Turks and the Austrians had besieged it several times over the centuries, and various marauders had sacked it whenever no one was paying attention. In consequence, whole sections were barred off for safety's sake and we lived in an apartment furnished in what to my mind was a tasteful manner with items ordered from Liberty of London. If the electricity generator had been working and if there had been servants, I daresay Renfield would have been content after a good meal, a warm bath and a comfortable night's sleep. However, in my absence the place had been neglected and was dark, damp, dusty and full of cobwebs; and, as Alois and I banged about in our search for keys and kerosene, we hit our heads and stubbed our toes and muttered curses in Magyar and the impression we might make on Renfield's imagination was forgotten.

Maria provided us with a cold chicken and Renfield and I dined alone in the great dining room, lit only by a few candle stubs. It was a miserable occasion and I was distracted by money concerns.

Renfield said, 'I haven't seen any servants since I arrived here.'

'They're very discreet,' I lied.

After a pause, he went on, 'May I make a tour of the castle in the morning?'

'I may have to be away all day,' I answered. Alois had arranged a meeting with my Viennese investors.

'Ah,' murmured Renfield.

'Of course you may wander about if you like, but you'll find much of the castle is inaccessible.'

'Ah.'

For the rest our conversation was stilted. My guest's was mostly about his relatives, and when that failed he tried to engage me in an explanation of the rules of cricket.

I grunted through this tedium and amused myself with the speculation that foreigners often indulge in on first meeting an English gentleman. How do they reproduce?

I showed Renfield to his room and bade him goodnight. As I walked away from his door, I heard him moving the furniture.

The following morning I was up early and off with Alois as far as Bistritz, where the would-be purchasers were holed up in an inn. The distance meant that it was ten at night by the time I returned to find Renfield chewing on a cold dish that had been left for him and in an excitable and petulant mood.

'Where were you all day?' he enquired sharply.

I didn't deign to reply.

'Don't you eat like normal people?' he asked.

'I've eaten already.' In fact I had eaten on the road.

'Hah!'

'Hah?'

'Yes! Hah! Don't think you shall keep me imprisoned here!'

'I have no such intention.'

'Hah!'

I'd had enough of this 'Hah!' business, which seemed to be a form of retort learned at an inferior boys' school. I stalked off and left Renfield to go to bed, move the furniture, or do whatever he liked. That night the wolves were very active. I heard them howling, which brought back comforting memories of childhood, and I slept well.

I pass over the next few days, which were in substance a repeat of the first: a tiring journey in the *calèche*, an hour's wrangling with the Jews, and an even more wearisome return journey. The only change was that on the third night Renfield retired to his room and refused to come out, and I had to leave a plate of food outside his door.

The fourth day was a Saturday, when my pious Hebrews refused to conduct business. Feeling refreshed, I relented a little towards my guest and had it in mind to take him into my confidence as to how my financial affairs stood. However, when I went to hunt him out of his room he wasn't there. I began a search of the castle.

It became evident that Renfield had been making his own investigations. I found various objects had been moved in the dust, and somewhere, he had come across a set of keys: several of the locked rooms had been opened. I began to be concerned. As I say, the place was dangerous.

A ruined chapel stood in the courtyard. The crypt was a family vault, though the sarcophagi were empty, since we had moved the bodies to inter them in more decent surroundings once we had decided to sell the estate. I had meant to tidy the place up but never found the time.

Even as I was in the courtyard, I heard Renfield clattering in the crypt. This seemed to me most uncivil behaviour, and I decided to give the man a piece of my mind. I went down into the crypt, where I found him standing among the open sarcophagi in a litter of broken coffins and the odd wayward bone. He was holding a lantern and his face looked ghastly.

'Risen!' he said. 'All risen!'

'Now look here!' I began.

He turned like a reptile and seized a pair of batons, which he held in front of him in the form of a cross. I strode towards him, intending to shake some sense into him, but tripped over some damned skull or other and went flying into the dust.

'It works!' he cried. He came and stood over me, still holding his makeshift cross, while I lay dazed and spitting dust and other things I hate to think of. Clearly the man was off his head and I could do nothing except listen to his rantings.

'Monster! Undead! Nosferatu! Vampire!'

'Be practical and reasonable,' I said. 'Even if I were a vampire, I'd hardly eat my lawyer.'

'Monster!' he repeated, and more of the same; and then fled. Where he went to, I have no idea, for the castle was a rambling place and he was missing all day.

You may imagine that my situation was a somewhat depressing one. I was deeply in debt, I was in difficulty with my consortium of investors, and now I had a mad Englishman rattling in the attic. Maria, Alois and I spent the day mulling over these problems and refreshing our lucubrations with a couple of bottles of plum brandy.

Maria's appearance belied a placid good nature. In later years she became fat and thick-ankled, though with the compensation of being a good cook. At the age of twenty, however, she was a dark-haired, dark-eyed beauty of plump voluptuousness which I had reason to know well.

After we had drunk liberally, she proposed, 'I'll sort him out.'

She had a simple and mechanistic view of male psychology: '*Ghab tatey bhare hoon, to demagh khailee hota haa.*'[*]

'Trust me,' she added. And indeed we had to.

Maria stole softly to Renfield's room, but he wasn't there. To her surprise she found the place festooned with garlands of garlic flowers. The Englishman must have made an expedition from the castle to gather them in the forest, where ramsons grew abundantly in the damp clearings. Faced with the overpowering smell, she gathered them up and disposed of them. In addition she found a crucifix which Renfield had lugged from the chapel. It was the height of a man and hung precariously over the bed, threatening to brain the occupant. It was beyond her strength to take this down, and so she returned

[*] 'When the balls are full, the brain is empty.'

to the kitchen, where Alois and I had broached a third bottle of brandy.

So once more to Renfield's room, this time three of us, all rather the worse for wear.

'Good God!' said Alois, studying the crucifix. We were mightily impressed by the Englishman's fanaticism and energy in heaving it on to a nail protruding from the wall. 'Give me a hand.'

I stood on the bed with him and together we lifted the crucifix down and then considered what to do with it. It was extremely heavy and, frankly, we were in no state to struggle under it back to the chapel in darkness.

The room contained a small closet. Probably it had been an oratory, but at some date it had been filled with travelling chests, stuffed animal heads and general junk. While Alois and I endeavoured to prop the crucifix in the closet so that it shouldn't simply fall over and crash through the door, Maria helped herself to more of the brandy we'd brought and began to remove her clothes. I admit now that I was always an enthusiast for her body. Her breasts were slightly on the pendulous side of fullness, with nipples like saucers, and she had a luxuriant thatch. Regarded aesthetically she fell short of the ideal, but viewed practically, she was admirably equipped for the business in hand, which was to seduce Renfield back to sanity. I say nothing for the merits of this idea, except that it made sense at the time.

Thus engaged, we heard a noise outside the door. 'Quickly!' whispered Alois. And as fast as possible we squeezed everything into the closet: two drunks, one naked strumpet, a man-sized crucifix, and several stuffed animals. Renfield fiddled with the door handle and then entered the room, as we could tell by the sigh he emitted when he saw the result of our handiwork. Doubtless he thought that the Powers of Darkness had spirited away his instruments of protection.

Of course, Maria should have been disporting herself in the bed. Certainly that was the idea. But in drink and panic she had come into the closet with Alois and myself, and there was nothing to be done about it. She could scarcely emerge now, revealing her accomplices, without giving Renfield the fright of his life. We reached a silent consensus that we would wait until our guest had gone to sleep and then sneak away. In the meantime we listened to Renfield's furtive manoeuvres, the wind buffeting the shutters, and the evening chorus of my friends the wolves. And we polished off the rest of the brandy.

I don't know how long we stayed in the closet. From muttered prayers and various creakings, I surmised the Englishman had gone to bed. Unfortunately, however, he did not extinguish the candle. In his excited state, he had evidently felt the need for the comfort of a night-light. It followed that, if he woke as we were making our escape, he would inevitably see us.

To add to our troubles, Maria began to complain that she was cold. I was in no position to do anything about this, since I was in an uncomfortable embrace with Jesus, but I felt Alois stirring his ancient loins, and by whatever ministrations he was delivering, he succeeded in soothing Maria. So to the sound of the wind and the wolves was added the cooing of a woman who was no longer afflicted by the cold.

I have failed to mention the dust. The closet was full of it. The plastered walls had long ago crumbled. Spiders' webs hung everywhere. The various animal pelts were thick with dust.

My difficulty was the crucifix. It was by design top-heavy and it took both hands and all my strength to keep it upright. Alois was otherwise occupied and I couldn't ask him to relieve my burden. As I say, the problem was the dust. It was in my hair and my eyes and all over my clothes. If it had ended there, all might have been well.

However, once it attacked my nose my situation was frankly hopeless. I sneezed.

I sneezed not once but three times and dropped the crucifix. Though I grabbed it again, I couldn't stop it crashing into the door, and that was too much for our cramped circumstances. We came bursting out of the closet into the bedroom, where, as luck would have it, a sleepless Renfield was reading his Bible by candlelight. He was – how shall I say? – not a little affected at the sight of the spectral apparition of his host covered in plaster dust, a fat, elderly Austrian naked below the waist and clutching a stuffed wolf, a nude woman of voluptuous appearance, and a large crucifix that seemed to be advancing upon him under its own motive power.

'Excuse me,' I said, as one does, no matter how inappropriately.

'Forgive us if we–'

Renfield screamed.

In due course I tried to explain matters to him, but the English sense of humour is greatly overrated.

CHAPTER SIX

Common sense tells me that Lucy and I must have said something even as Harry was telling his tale; but for the life of me, if we did, I can't remember it. What I do recall is sitting by firelight over the remains of our ample dinner, listening intently to this crazy old man.

Perhaps the explanation lies in Harry himself. Despite the obviously comic structure of his story his manner made no concession to humour. Of his varied voices he had selected, as I have mentioned, his mannered, suave Hollywood European, which had all sorts of menacing undertones. Yet, there was a degree of archness and irony; and as he revealed his prejudices against Jews, Rumanians and Englishmen he granted us a wry smile: but of an outright invitation to laugh with him there wasn't a shred. It was this preposterous yet compelling pretence of seriousness that kept us silent. I can't say otherwise than that he was trying to convince us his nonsense was true.

He finished and poured himself another glass of sauternes. I believe I threw another log on the fire, stared at the sparks rising in the open hearth and murmured, 'Very interesting, Harry,' without knowing what I meant.

Lucy was sitting at the table, leaning on one elbow and smiling dreamily and sweetly at Harry. Her silver toque rested cock-eyed on her head. She said, 'So you're telling us that you were the original model for Count Dracula?'

'After a fashion,' said Harry.

'And poor Mr Renfield?'

'He had a breakdown and we packed him off to England. I never saw him again.

I asked, 'Did you ever meet Bram Stoker?'

Harry glanced away from Lucy. 'Yes – but that was after he had written his book. I was in London. I believe it was nineteen hundred and eight. We chatted about the theatre.'

'But not his book?'

'No. I didn't find it interesting.'

Lucy giggled rather prettily. 'You are a darling, Harry,' she said and kissed him on the forehead. 'I need to wee. I've drunk too much.' She collected her little evening bag and wove her way towards the bathroom.

I said to Harry, 'So the whole story about Dracula and vampires was based on a misunderstanding.'

'Not entirely.'

'Not entirely? What does that mean?'

Harry didn't answer.

I asked, 'Why did you tell us the story?'

He shrugged. 'You asked me to, don't you remember?'

'I think we asked about your life. You don't suggest that what you told us is true?'

'It's true.'

'In what sense?'

'In what sense is it true?' Harry reverted to one of his folksy grins. 'Aw shucks, Johnny, I'm just a simple guy. I don't know that "truth" has got all that many meanings. I just told you things the way that I remember them happening.'

'You can't have,' I objected.

'As you please,' said Harry. His attention was diverted by Lucy's return. She'd tidied her hair and repaired her make-up. I was so used to her as a pleasant companion that I hadn't considered before how dark and dramatic her beauty could be. Examining her now, an uncomfortable image came to me. Black-haired, black-eyed and clad in a gossamer dress made insubstantial by the dim light, she reminded me of the three brides who inhabited the fictional Dracula's castle. There was something lascivious in the smile with which she greeted Harry's stare. She sat down again, leaned on her elbow again, and gazed at him, large-eyed and intent.

She asked, 'Are you a vampire, Harry?'

The question chilled me. But only for a moment. Harry flipped through his repertoire and simpered in the voice of a Californian hairdresser, 'Just because you're a vampire, it does *not* mean that you're a bad person.'

Lucy laughed. I laughed. Harry lounged back in his chair, grinning. He drawled, 'I've got to tell you, *mes enfants*, that there's a lot of horseshit talked about vampirism. It isn't a change of being, more a fashion statement. In fact, in the Old Country where I came from, it didn't even carry a social stigma – at least, not much of one. It's like spouse beating: some people disapprove, and others say it shows how much you care for your wife.'

'That's a dreadful analogy!' said Lucy, stifling another laugh.

'I guess so. But it's the truth.'

That word again: truth.

We walked home. Alcohol, dope, frost and starlight. We didn't speak, but no particular meaning should be attached to our silence. Although we'd already drunk too much, I poured us each a nightcap as Lucy stripped for bed. We made love somewhat ineptly, chuckling over our breathless endeavours to achieve an anaesthetised climax; and afterwards, through the open bathroom door, I watched Lucy at the bidet, and then squatting to dry her crotch. The simple carnality of this vision pleased me, and, despite Harry and his vampires, I felt myself in the land of the living and thought that on this night there was no one in the world so happy as me.

My winter expedition into the *garrigue* had exhausted my passion for painting. I didn't give it up entirely, but my restless quest for novelty looked for another outlet and I turned again to writing, for which I'd the notion that, as a lawyer, I would necessarily have some talent. In my heart, I knew that the saga of my abandoning Sally for Lucy would appear banal to others, whatever it might mean to me. I was never so far gone in my delusions that I was unaware of the essential ridiculousness of my situation.

There's an obvious connection to be made between listening to Harry's fantastic autobiography and my deciding to write a fictionalised account of my affaire. However, I have to caution you, just as I caution myself, against reading such a connection into my story. For one thing, the apparent sequence of the two events is specious. From adolescence, I'd always wanted to write and, although I'd never produced anything much except the usual juvenilia, the desire had never gone away. Quite the opposite. During the five years or so preceding my elopement with Lucy – as my dissatisfaction was growing on me – I'd sketched out a few ideas and written one or two introductory chapters. I recognise that my career as a writer is as ordinary as the rest of me. The point is that the notion of fictionalising aspects of my life came earlier than my encounter with Harry. The connection is snapped. Or, at least, I think so.

While I was brooding over the start of this new enterprise, I broke off any regular contact with Harry. Naturally I'd run into him at the grocery store and the PTT and we'd have a friendly chat; and, as spring came in and the osiers by the lake broke into leaf, I took a stroll there more often and sometimes saw Harry in a straw hat, cutting at the long grass with a walking cane, an elderly *flaneur*. If we were in hailing distance we'd call to each other, and if not he'd give me an old fashioned tip of his hat and I'd smile and respond in kind with a bow. But I no longer went to the Bar des Sports on Wednesday evenings and there was, for the moment, no repeat of that first exotic dinner party.

Lucy didn't understand the change and I had difficulty explaining it since I didn't want to say anything against Harry. And what was there to say? Harry's conversation was stimulating and I enjoyed his zaniness. Lucy and I often laughed over our recollection of the dinner and made light-hearted references to our neighbour the vampire. Above all, Harry never intruded, never imposed himself on us. I repeat: what was there to say against him? It was a puzzle even to me and I worked it out only slowly, and the solution was this. No matter how affable and entertaining Harry was, at bottom I didn't like him. It was quite otherwise with Lucy.

My novel will never be published; so I'd better say now what it was about.

In April when the trees were full of blossom and the daffodils in bloom, the narrator, a fifty-year-old lawyer, abandoned his wife for a woman twenty years younger ...

In fact, the detail was rather different from my actual situation. I had to recast it in order to achieve the necessary detachment, and wanted to make the whole business colourful. However – so I told myself – though the detail might differ, I would use my own insights to arrive at an essential *truth*: the 'T' word again.

For seven years I'd been involved as advocate in an arbitration in India: six or more trips per year of seven or fourteen days each, say forty visits in all. Long enough for an affair of the heart to develop. In this version of my life I was called Rex, my wife was called Allison, and the part of Lucy was given to a beautiful Indian lady-lawyer called Susheela.

The actual arbitration was a curious business. It went on so long as to take on a life of its own and the participants, bored of the affair, decided to take it on tour. And so with a cast of lawyers, judges, wives and children we moved from resort to resort, Goa, Ooty, Kodai, mixing law with sunbathing, and meantime wondering if it would ever end. I hesitated long over turning these implausible facts into fiction.

In the fictional arbitration, I set the opening scene in a temple-cave complex. Here, during a visit made by our unlikely caravanserai, Susheela was to disappear. Here were my Marabar Caves, my Bibighar Gardens, where East and West were to confront each other in an atmosphere of ambiguity and sexual violation.

I had the idea of structuring the novel around the seven days of the week to track the seven years of the arbitration. The narrator would be examined each day by the detective investigating the disappearance. Each day the narrator would describe the events of the corresponding year to build up a picture of his reaction to India, and in particular to women. On the third day the tone of the story would darken as a body, apparently that of Susheela, was discovered in one of the caves. The narrator would deny murdering her, but the lies and evasions with which he had sought to deny his adultery would trap him in the semblance of guilt.

As for Susheela, she was the key. I was conscious that Indians had an ambivalent attitude towards the West – admiring it because of its achievements; hating it because they were ashamed of their own failures. There would be two Susheelas, whose differing reactions would keep the narrator in a state of sexual excitement and uncertainty. The resolution of the mystery would come when it was revealed that Susheela was in fact a twin and that one version of her identity had murdered the other.

In brief that was my book. Admittedly, in summary it seems to wander from the starting point of a fifty-year-old man's tribulations. But you should bear in mind that I intended a multi-layered novel in which the full meaning would hide within the subtexts.

I got the idea of the twins from reading John Fowles's *The Magus*, or possibly Agatha Christie.

With the above as my plan, I began to write. As with everything I did during that year in France, I flung myself into the task with an immoderate passion. If I woke early, I began writing before breakfast. I normally worked late until I heard Lucy calling from the bedroom. As the weather improved I wrote at the table in the garden. I was reluctant to take trips to Mirepoix for the market or to go anywhere else, since this would take me away from my mission.

Lucy bore with me patiently. We didn't talk much about the book, but I wasn't worried about this. I thought that our silences were beginning to acquire the character of quiet communication which I've already mentioned. Also, my book contained two prominent female characters, and I was complacent enough to suppose that they were well realised. In my confusion, I saw this creation as a vicarious dialogue with Lucy.

She bore with me, but I bored her – at least a little. She was, as always, honest enough to mention it. And I was a liberal fellow and suggested she go to Mike and Marie-Paule's place and play the football game with Antoine and even have a chat with Harry. When the lake opened for the season, she used to take herself off there during the afternoons when Harry would be taking his walk; and so she met him on these occasions too. She told me of their encounters. I had no reason to be jealous, and I wasn't. In case you should misunderstand me, I should explain. This story is not about jealousy. Possibly it is about vampires.

I attacked my novel. Lucy pottered in the garden, painted a little, walked, swam, spent evenings at the Bar des Sports, came home drunk occasionally. Her affection for me never diminished.

From hints, I learned that Harry was telling her more of his life story.

'More of the vampire stuff?' I asked.

'Not exactly.'

'Then what?'

'I'd rather not say. It would spoil it for when Harry tells you.'

'Do you think he will?'

'Only if you ask him. Why do you never see him nowadays? Are you avoiding him?'

'Why should I do that? I'm just busy, that's all.'

'Do you mind if I have dinner with Harry?'

'No, not if that's what you want.'

She did, and afterwards she had dinner with him once a week. Whatever my feelings about Harry they were personal and I didn't want, still less expect, Lucy to share them. And dinner with Harry seemed to be good for her. She would come home stimulated, stoned and amorous, and in this way Harry seemed to be making a positive contribution to my love life.

Not that it was always so. Sometimes she came back thoughtful.

'Have you ever heard of Clarence Quimby?' she asked once.

'The journalist?'

'You've heard of him?'

'He worked with William Shirer in Berlin. But that's only what Harry told me. Otherwise I've never heard of him.'

'What about Volodya Botkin? From what Harry said, I gather he's a famous Russian author.'

'The name means nothing to me – but then, I'm no expert on Russian literature. Is he important?'

'I think so, but I'm not sure. The name has been mentioned a couple of times, but so far Harry hasn't actually said where he figures in the scheme of things.'

I couldn't comment on that.

On another occasion: 'Harry was in Berlin. Do you think he may have been a Nazi?'

'He doesn't seem overfond of Jews.'

'No,' said Lucy. 'It isn't as simple as that. Harry admits he used to be anti-Semitic. He says he isn't now that he understands better. Whatever he may be, he isn't a hypocrite, John. His explanation is that he has never thought much about morality but has simply gone along with current ideas.'

'What makes you think he may have been a Nazi?' I asked.

'He was rummaging in that bag of his. A small enamelled badge fell out. It had a swastika on it.'

'Harry's bag means nothing. And swastika badges can be bought in junk shops.'

'Where is Hotzeplotz?'

'*Please*, Lucy, I can't keep up with these changes of subject.'

I should have asked more about Hotzeplotz.

The subject of the carpet bag puzzled me. It was clearly the source of whatever 'evidence' Harry used to support his stories. It was from the bag that he'd produced the Elvis matchbook, the pornographic Proust, and the letter from Renfield which he used for the Dracula episode. Obviously the letter couldn't be genuine: Harry had faked it. Or, alternatively, he'd come across it as a page-marker in an old book or in a shop that sold these things. There had, perhaps, been a solicitor fortuitously called Renfield. He had a client called Count Esterhazy – *not* Drakul-Esterhazy. The lawyer in me saw that there was no evidence that Harry Haze was Esterhazy; and, even if he were (which was impossible because of the date), the contents of the letter said nothing in detail to connect it with the tale of Dracula. No, it wasn't the letter *as evidence* that troubled me. It was the fact that Harry had it available and tailored to fit what he chose to reveal of himself. To a lesser degree the same was true of the Elvis matchbook and the pseudo-Proust: the 'proof' was there.

What it showed was that Harry's stories weren't improvised. Either they were true in the most superficial sense ('the way I remember them happening'), or they'd been prepared to some purpose and before Lucy and I ever came to Puybrun. Since the former proposition was fantastic, the latter must fit the facts of the case. That was an extraordinary conclusion, because it implied that the farcical parody of Dracula actually meant something.

I'd never thought much about it, but for a dark-haired, dark-eyed woman Lucy was quite pale-skinned. I'm not much attracted to the fashionable bronze look, and Lucy's fair complexion was one among her many attractions. She merely commented à propos that she'd always suffered from heavy periods, and indeed for several days a month she struggled with lethargy and cramps which I affected to ignore.

She grew paler. I noticed that her skin was smooth, white and marbled. The effect was gradual and I didn't remark on my own necrophile pleasure in the pattern of blue veins that showed faintly on her breasts, and the contrasting brown of the aureoles. In case this sounds perverse, you should remember that for twenty-five years I'd been acquainted only with the pleasant familiarity of one woman's body. I had no conception of the range of the possible; and so Lucy's pallid beauty was, to me, both exotic and normal at the same time.

I don't wish to suggest that I ignored Lucy entirely during my preoccupation with writing. Whatever my weaknesses, I do consider myself a kind person, and even in my distracted mood I was concerned that Lucy's health seemed to be deteriorating. One afternoon, when I'd agreed to take a walk with her among the ruins of the Cathar fortress, I raised the subject.

'Ah, so you've noticed,' she said. She raised a hand whose ivory nails were tinged with blue, and stroked my face reflectively.

'Is it anything serious? Have you been to a doctor?' I asked.

She shrugged. 'It's a family thing. All our women are prone to anaemia. I've been taking iron tablets, but they don't seem to work.'

'And the doctor?'

'I haven't seen one yet. I've been looking for a specialist. There's a Doctor Moreau in Pamiers who deals with women's illnesses. I'm thinking of contacting him to make an appointment.'

'You should.'

She looked at me thoughtfully and stroked my face again.

'You are sweet,' she said. 'Even if you are mad.'

I've never cared for being 'sweet'. Sally used to call me that. Still, there are worse things.

My writing was in a temporary lull. I was waiting for some books to arrive from England. I'd asked my son Jack to get them for me the next time he went home. I could have approached Sally directly, and I don't doubt she would have obliged, but I was ashamed to do anything that reminded me of my conduct towards her, which was inexcusable except on the grounds of personal necessity. I took up my paint-box again and sketched the hills as viewed from the lake and, on my walk home, dropped in the Bar des Sports.

'Long time no see,' said Mike.

I apologised and explained something about writing.

'I thought maybe you'd killed yourself,' he said cheerfully. 'I wondered if Lucy had driven you to it.'

'That's an odd thing to say.'

'Pardon *me*.'

'All right – but what made you say it?'

'Just a joke. We see Lucy here quite often.'

'I know. I don't find that a problem.'

'I wasn't suggesting you did. But Antoine is finding it a problem. The poor bugger is going nuts at the sight of Lucy. Mind, I'm not saying there's anything deliberate on her part. It's just an effect she has. It was him I was thinking of when I mentioned suicide.'

'He won't kill himself,' I said, indifferent to the exaggerations of bar gossip. However, I did mention the matter to Lucy.

'It's that bad, is it?' she said sympathetically.

'Oh, I doubt it's as bad as all that.'

'The problem is that Antoine misinterprets everything. I do try not to give him a come-on, but just my being there sends him a signal and I can't control that.'

'You could stop going to the bar.'

She bridled. 'That isn't fair. You can't impose the solution on women when the problem lies with men. Also, I see Harry there.'

'You see Harry often enough.'

'I like to see Harry, especially now that you're spending so much time writing. Oh, darling! I'm not criticising you, but you have to have some understanding of my position.'

I did. But I couldn't give up my writing.

That night, I noticed a mark on Lucy's neck. It had bled.

'Did I cause that?' I asked.

She put her pale fingers to the spot.

'No,' she said. 'I snagged myself on the chain of a cheap necklace.'

I used a kiss to disguise my closer investigation of the mark. It was a puncture wound, or possibly two: shallow and not very serious.

'Can I see the necklace? I may be able to fix it.'

'I've thrown it away. It was only a cheap piece of costume jewellery.'

'What was it?'

'It had an ankh pendant.'

From the description it sounded like an ethnic item. Lucy wore such things when she was minded to float around in her guise of Earth Child, though I couldn't specifically recall it.

Her fingers caressed the place again and suddenly she laughed and said perceptively, 'You're thinking of Harry!'

I admitted I was.

'Don't worry it's not the Kiss of the Vampire.'

'I didn't say it was.'

'Did you think that was why I am so anaemic?'

'Of course not.'

'Liar!' she said, snuggling against me and laughing as she buried her head in my breast.

I was lying – or half lying. Of course my rational mind refused any credence to Harry's absurd vampire story, but in the dim world of the unconscious it had an effect, if only as symbol rather than literal truth. I was always acutely aware of the stark fact of my age. Recalling my youth, I remember my attitude towards people of my present age. Insofar as I thought of them at all, I didn't credit them with lively and authentic emotions. The notion of middle-aged passion was, to my adolescent eyes, even more ridiculous than I now find it. The appearance of emotion in older people was a mere simulacrum. They were faking it. The ranks of my parents' generation were filled by the Undead.

To give you a further idea of the effect of Harry's story on the meandering pathways of my memory, I'll tell you something else it brought to mind. It concerns the curious habits of the English. We were in Bergerac on holiday. The day was hot. The shops had closed for the long afternoon break. We were taking lunch in a restaurant overlooking the small leafy square where a statue of the famous Cyrano stands. Beyond the window, the square formed a stage of sunlight and shade, torpid and dusty and empty. Until there hove into view the shimmering apparition of a family of three. I see them now: father in shorts and sandals with white socks; mother in a dress of printed cotton; son, fair-haired, wearing a T-shirt and trainers. The child is hungry and fractious; the parents haunted and uncomprehending. Why is everywhere closed? It couldn't happen in England. They make a lonely tour of the square and disappear to eat their sandwiches. And I turn to Sally and comment, 'There they go – the midday vampires.'

The problem with this story is that it makes me sound like a snob. An Englishman looking down on other Englishmen. So typical.

Lucy told me it was Harry's birthday. I asked, 'How old is he?'

She answered,' He didn't say. But he wants to give us dinner, in order to celebrate.'

'You go,' I said.

Exasperated, she retorted, 'Look, John, it hasn't escaped me that you don't particularly like Harry. But I do. And it isn't kind to say no. He's just a poor old man…'

'And?'

'I think he's dying, John. That's why he's come to Puybrun. It's just a quiet place to die.'

I don't know why I was surprised. Harry was, after all, very old. I asked, 'Why do you think he's dying? Is he ill?'

'I suspect he has cancer. He takes something for it – morphine, I think. It may be the drugs that are affecting his mind and causing him to tell his stories.'

'Has he been telling you more stories?'

'Some,' she said evasively.

'Such as?'

73

'I can't explain. They'd sound silly. You have to hear Harry tell them in that way that he has.'

Lucy's voice was drawing on a well of tenderness that was quite different from whatever love was between us, and I was moved by her concern for Harry.

I agreed that we'd both take part in Harry's birthday dinner, and I'd listen to whatever he had to say.

CHAPTER SEVEN

Hôtel d'Alsace
2nd February 1898

My dear Esterhazy,

It was so delightful to meet you over dinner, that I had to write. For, having spoken with you, I feel so ignorant as to your true character that I am sure we have the basis of a lasting friendship.

I have given much consideration to the difference between our trials and it seems to me plain. You were guilty and were therefore acquitted. I was morally innocent and was therefore convicted. Lawyers insist on a challenge, and there was nothing I could do for them.

Your problems are all attributable to having written down your treasons in the infamous bordereau. *Since you endeavoured to keep it secret, naturally all the world knew. If you had published the thing, you may be assured the public would have ignored it.*

I should not advise you to confess your crimes at this late date. The time for that coup de théâtre *was immediately before poor D's wrongful conviction. The éclat would have been splendid. I speak as a dramatist. Confession for the state of your soul is another matter; but even in that case I should recommend that you keep repentance for your deathbed, when it will help to pass the time on an otherwise dull evening.*

I was enchanted, dear Esterhazy, to learn that you are a Vampire. I had, of course, heard of the stories, but I thought they were creatures of fiction, like Christadelphians or Belgians. My disappointment is only that you have made the condition sound bourgeois and respectable. Please reply promptly to assure me that it is truly wicked. I should hate to join a club of which Prince Albert was a suitable member.

Even so, you sorely tempt me. To enlist in your Society would solve much of my present predicament. On death a man's debts die with him. Certainly it would be convenient to rise from the grave with one's credit restored!

Your disclosure that Vampires are more numerous than I supposed goes far to explain my downfall. Despite my genius, I had entirely misunderstood my situation. I went to my trials blithely prepared to defend myself against the Philistines. I had not thought to arm myself against the Transylvanians. And this notwithstanding that it was evident my enemies were after my blood. It was remiss of my lawyers not to advise me of this possibility: though doubtless they will excuse themselves on the ground that I did not put the question and pay the fee.

I am these days often sad and should welcome Death. Until now, however, I had always worried that, like so many guests, he would stay too long and monopolise the conversation. The matter is quite otherwise once one understands that Death calls, dines, and goes away leaving one a little wiser for the experience. He is a friend whom I could accept: provided that he does not want to borrow money, of which I have none.

The price of eternal life is a kiss. A Vampire's kisses can be no worse than the rest. I have suffered those of women – which were like ready-made clothes, wearable but tailored to the figure of other men. And I have revelled in the voluptuousness of rosebud kisses as fragrant as Turkish tobacco and coloured the deepest purple. All alike have been fatal. Do I not sigh, then, at the thought of baring my throat to a kiss of another sort? One which is frankly cruel, sensual, sharp-toothed and unutterably selfish and which brings immortality! I can almost believe in a paradox whereby beauty leads to death, and horror to eternal life.

Alas, however, everything I see of Death tells me that it is indiscriminately democratic. I imagine an eternal wait with the other third-class passengers for a cheap excursion to Weston-super-Mare and no entertainment except a Methodist travelling salesman from Barking, who will tell me his life story.

Pray extend my felicitations to your good lady. Forgive my lack of tact in proposing you make an honest woman of her. I have since learned that she is a demimondaine whom you met at the Moulin Rouge and therefore an honest woman already. Furthermore, I find her sobriquet of 'Four-fingered Margaret' most charming.

So farewell. I doubt I shall see you again unless perchance you appear on bat wings outside my window, enter my sanctum and take me naked and sleeping into Eternity.

Until then I remain weary and oppressed and ever your
Sebastian Melmoth

Postscript
Are there any boy Vampires? I have in mind a youth with doe eyes and a bee sting mouth. He must wear black and be gentle in appearance but very severe in manner. And honest – I am tired of being robbed by waiters and tourist guides; I imagine it was they who were the downfall of Socrates. It is so easy for youth to corrupt the corrupters of youth. Degenerates should be protected from the innocent. We are deprived of free will by the urgency of our vices, but the innocent are the more criminal for having no excuse. There is nothing so culpable as innocence. When I believed myself innocent, I was cruelly punished.

CHAPTER EIGHT

Harry's Tale

A man who agrees with both sides of a case is deficient in logic. If he agrees with only one, he is lacking in sympathy. I might add that if, in addition, he lays claim to only one identity, he is incapable of self-awareness.

So far as the Dreyfus Affair is concerned, I believe I resolved these conundrums quite prettily. As Esterhazy I stood for the honour of the Army and the perfidy of the Hebrew race. But as Charles Haas I proclaimed the paramouncy of Justice and the liberal values of a secular state. Admittedly Esterhazy had precipitated the entire Affair by certain petty treasons, namely the sale of French military secrets to the Germans, the crime of which the innocent Dreyfus was convicted. But to suppose that on that account I felt guilty is to misunderstand the depth of sincerity within every successful hypocrite. Charles Haas, of course, considered Esterhazy a bounder and a cad, an opinion I felt entirely justified in holding since I knew Esterhazy thoroughly.

A bee had flown into the studio as if seeking refuge from the rich odour of roses, the heavy scent of lilacs and the more delicate perfume of the pink-flowering thorn which were stirred by the light summer wind. I was lying at the corner of a divan of Persian saddlebags, unwisely smoking one of Marcel's asthma cigarettes instead of my usual fine Turkish blend with its hint of opium. From here, though it stirred only a languid interest, I could just catch the gleam of laburnum blossom, honey-sweet, honey-coloured and posed against the sky with artistic eccentricity like the sprigs painted on a kakiemon vase; blossom which would fade to dry, brittle pods from which one could make a poisonous tisane, an emblematic display that age poisons the joys of youth.

'My dear Haas,' said Elstir as he poised his brush over a pot of noble carmine, 'you speak in paradoxes which you seem to feel under no obligation to explain.'

'The paradox is the explanation. You expect me to be wiser than my words. Believe me, if I had another explanation I would have given it. Why should I trouble your mind with one notion, if I intended to disturb you with another? I am not a shopkeeper who desires to go on holiday to Venice but decides to come to Balbec because it is cheaper; and therefore pretends that Venice and Balbec are one and the same place.'

'I should like to go to Venice,' intervened Marcel. 'But I should need good health and the permission of my mother.'

'Or more accurately a good mother and the permission of your health. In such case only the latter would pose an obstacle and your problem would be halved.'

The object of our study smiled. He was a young man of saturnine appearance, not uncomely, but neither of any singular beauty. Dark hair, well-groomed but limp, fell either side of a parting. Dark eyes seemed at one moment to stare exophthalmically and at another to shelter like anchorites in dark caves. Dark lips budded from the pale skin of a sallow, angular face.

I said, 'For your portrait, Marcel, you should have dressed in black in the Spanish fashion. I swear I have seen your twin in a picture by Velázquez. Do you not think, Elstir, that our boy is a Renaissance figure? I speak of the hero in a revenge tragedy.'

'I think,' replied the painter thoughtfully, 'that he is the perfect type of our age. We live in the dying years of the century and face the future uncertainly. Marcel possesses youth but looks as if he has seen death and been frightened yet not daunted. He has none of the physical qualities of the hero, but when I look at him I see a fevered shine of heroism.'

'Is that what you are trying to capture in my picture?' asked Marcel, allowing his lids to uncover slowly the jewelled eyes of a lizard. 'May I look at it?'

'If you wish,' said Elstir. 'It is almost finished. I wish to apply another glaze over the cheeks. They must be bloodless but hint of blood. I want the effect of a bowl of *pai ting* porcelain in which a single rose petal has been allowed to float.'

'That's all very well, but may I see it? Come, Haas, you must look, too! I want to remember this moment. And if I see how you feel, then that will become a part of how I feel. Come now.'

I allowed Marcel to take my hand. My glance fell on a Turkey rug and then upon some splashes of paint, which, as though the design had broken free of the weave, seemed to continue the pattern towards the easel where the portrait was placed. There a patch of mauve and white bismuth had spread among a pool of viridian so that the easel appeared to stand on a bed of dead irises.

'Here it is,' said Elstir, reluctantly. 'Whatever you do, dear boy, you mustn't mock. You have inspired me to the best work I have ever done. I feel ruined, as though I have expended the treasure of my talent on this one painting.'

'I shouldn't dream of mocking,' said Marcel.

'And you. Haas?'

'If I like it, I shall certainly mock. Mockery is the highest form of flattery. No talent is worth having unless it is envied by others. Sober praise is reserved for those subjects where we are sure of ourselves. It is a medal awarded for long service and good conduct – not for bravery.'

'Where do you get your aphorisms from?' asked Marcel.

'I never acknowledge my sources. That is how I persuade myself I am wise. A truly learned man must think himself irredeemably stupid. The only knowledge he can claim as his own is the whereabouts of his ties.'

Marcel turned from me. In his eagerness it seemed as if he would flee, but the boy was only avid to view his immortality. I followed with my own tired immortality in his train and we stood before the picture to view it.

I looked at the portrait first in its pictorial aspect. Elstir had painted the lad in three-quarter face, bringing his eyes to bear as if he would challenge the viewer. In contrast to the rest, where the painter had suggested a certain flatness of tone and a delicate outline of form in the Japanese manner, the facial mask floated off the canvas in a succession of glazes as if it were painted in air and tied only by the finest of gossamer anchors. In his left hand the sitter held a carnation. His right hand rested weightlessly on a table on which stood a *famille rose* bowl of the Ch'ien Lung period whose delicate pinks, playing counterpoint to the green of the flower, whispered that the rosy tints of flesh had escaped and here made their home. Thus the figure. My eye then continued to the background, which was divided. To the left was a screen of silk that appeared dipped in ancient gold and decorated with bamboo in smoky greens and browns with touches of cinnabar. To the right one saw beyond the window into the garden, where the laburnum was weighed with blossom and a twist of woodbine grew in the long grass. And finally, in undying emblem of that summer's day, a dragonfly was imprisoned on the window, printing the transparent pattern of its wings like a fragment of cathedral glass.

This was the picture considered only as paint. The portrait, however, insisted that it should not be dismissed with such facility. In lifting itself from its physical bounds, the face of the sitter compelled one to consider it in itself, as if it had being and soul independent of both canvas and its origin in the purely human world. Of course it was a likeness of Marcel. But, if that were the only aspect from which it might be viewed, then it was rather a bad one. I do not mean that one would doubt the representation. The lineaments were unquestionably Marcel's. Yet in contrast with the boy, who was a changeable creature of vagrant moods, the face in the picture displayed a uniform intensity. I returned to the challenge contained in the darkly painted eyes. Glancing at the original, I saw that these eyes had fixed on his and were engaging in a dialogue to which any other person must be deaf. Then, on reconsideration, I saw that the likeness was in fact perfect in its truthfulness. What had confused me was the lack of correspondence to any particular one of a dozen familiar expressions. Elstir had avoided such a partial solution to the mystery of the boy's soul. No, he had created not Marcel as he was in a passing humour, but the very Platonic type which underlay all manifestation. So, if I had not seen Marcel in fifty years, I would look at that picture and say: 'That is how I remember him.'

'Well?' enquired Elstir, addressing me but with a loving eye on the lad, who had picked up the carnation and crushed it between his fingers. 'Does it meet with your approval?'

'I am dumb with amazement.'

'What? Do you not intend to mock me? Was your epigram false, then, and mockery not the sincerest flattery?'

'As to that, you must not expect me both to amuse you and to tell the truth. Next you will criticise a beautiful woman because she does not ride a bicycle.'

'I should be in the right, if she had promised that she would.'

'Only moneylenders insist that promises be kept. But do not let us quarrel. I shall mock you as viciously as you like if it will cause you to believe how greatly I admire the painting. What does the boy say?'

Thus far Marcel had not spoken. His face had become pale and I thought for a moment that he was unwell. Then he said, 'What a beautiful object.'

'You are admiring your own beauty?' asked Elstir.

'No ... no. I am not beautiful. The face in the painting is not beautiful. I was referring to the work of art, that is all. What shall you do with it? Do you intend to exhibit it at the Salon?'

'Perhaps. If I can bring myself to do so.'

'You must!' I stated flatly.

'No,' said Marcel. He looked at both of us and smiled gently. 'I should be frightened if it were moved from this room. It might be damaged.'

'One runs that risk with any work of art,' I reminded him.

'It is a condition of its existence. Even *La Gioconda* will turn to dust and ashes, if only when the stars themselves burn in their last glory.'

The boy bit his lip and then exclaimed passionately, 'I could not bear that!'

'You should be more concerned about your own youth. That will pass.'

'Oh,' sighed Marcel, 'that doesn't trouble me in the slightest. I am condemned to die for my sins. But the picture is innocent.'

'It would be more truthful to say that we live for our sins, but die for the sake of our relatives. If that were not so, neither music halls nor lawyers would be in a prosperous way of business. As for the picture, would it not be preferable if you could borrow its innocence?'

'I do not understand you.'

'I mean only that, if one had a choice, it would seem desirable that our age and our sins should be borne by a picture and that we should live on in unblemished immortality.'

'I should not like that at all.' said Marcel.

'Why not?'

'Because such an existence would be that of a vampire. It would be impossible to experience love, since our friends and loved ones would change and finally die, and it would be both dangerous and cruel to watch while that happened. Have you considered that one would be journeying through an emotional desert? Who would be our companions except similar unclean spirits?' He put his hand to his mouth and cried, 'No, the thought is too frightful! If I thought it were possible' – he picked up a curved knife of curious oriental workmanship which Elstir kept for no other purpose than its beauty – 'I should take this knife and tear the picture to shreds, even though it tore out my own heart!'

Elstir said nothing, but he caught the vehemence in the lad's eye and he interrupted gently to remove the jewel-bedizened blade from between the other's trembling fingers and replace it. Outside, in the torpor of the sun-drenched day, a cricket chirruped in the long grass. Turning again to Marcel, he asked, 'Then what would you desire?'

'Only that the picture should never change but always be preserved exactly as it is today.'

'Not change? Surely that would scarcely matter after your death?'

'Even then,' said Marcel. 'While I am alive, whenever I look at the picture I shall recall being here today with my dear friends. And when I am dead, others will look on it and remember me and, in imagination, this day and I shall exist immortal in a million memories.'

'A million?' asked Elstir.

'Well, perhaps not a million,' conceded Marcel modestly. 'But as many as see the painting.' Addressing me, he continued, 'In comparison, what is your vampire existence but a furtive and specious thing? There would be no true immortality but merely a succession of shifting identities as one was forced to abandon each in order to avoid one's shame and the world's horror. God willing, I shall be Marcel for seventy or more years, but you, dear Monsieur Haas, why, you couldn't continue in your present condition above five or ten years – or let us say twenty at most – without your unholy state becoming evident. In comparison, which of us is closer to immortality?'

As he spoke, I noticed a furrow in his brow that was not present in the painting, and this poignant reminder made the latter seem more beautiful and precious. At the same time a blossom petal that had lain in the grass was lifted by the breeze and blown through the window, where it settled on the painting at that spot of carmine placed by Elstir only a half-hour before. The effect was quite pretty, as if a portion of the wing of the painted dragonfly had become detached, but it was the beauty of decay and an agony for the dear boy to watch.

'Do you see?' he cried.

I said, 'You seem reconciled that everything else should be consigned to the ravages of Time. Why not this painting?'

'You mistake me. I am not reconciled to Time. I look to overcome it by the action of memory and art. But whereas a book has a hope of immortality, being an abstract thing free of the loss of any particular copy, a painting is unique and concrete. When Time destroys this painting, it will be entirely destroyed.' The boy turned away listlessly and threw himself upon some cushions, causing a small array of peacock feathers in a vase nearby to tremble. 'I wish I'd never seen it!' he sobbed.

Elstir was greatly moved. He was immoderately fond of the lad and in bitter pain at so distressing him. He begged, 'Marcel, tell me what I must do?'

Marcel raised his head and the ashen rosebuds in his cheeks quivered. He said,' Do nothing except preserve it.' He raised his eyes to Heaven and prayed fervently, 'Let no harm come to this picture: not dust or dirt, nor damage nor decay. Let fire not burn it nor sunlight bleach it. Let woodworm and mite stay far from it. Let nothing fade the sharpness of its line or the brightness of its colour.' He gazed at me and I saw in the original the same challenging eyes as in the copy, and in a final heart-rending intonation he chanted, 'I pray that whatsoever force shall bring change to this picture shall be deflected and that, rather, age and dissolution shall fall upon my body.'

With that terrible plea to the Almighty still ringing in our ears, the boy and I left the distraught Elstir. It was difficult to believe it was the same day and that the sun still shone and the bees hummed among the flowers. Yet Marcel, though not physically robust, was mentally strong, and as we strolled from the study back towards the hotel he regained his spirits and we talked. He was curious concerning my thoughts on the Affair of Captain Dreyfus. Naturally he was ignorant of the hellish pact by which I, Charles Haas, was also the villainous Esterhazy, or how nearly his conversation of vampires and immortality had touched me. Unlike Marcel, I was aware of the world's strange alchemies, and it was with dreadful foreboding that I reflected upon that accursed portrait.

Briefly, the position regarding Dreyfus was that, needing money, I had, in my character of Esterhazy, sold some trivial secrets to the Germans. In their stunning inefficiency, the counter-espionage section of the French General Staff had wrongly identified the culprit as Alfred Dreyfus and procured his sentence to a term on Devil's

Island, where he was now rotting. As Esterhazy I considered it a very desirable outcome. As Haas I thought it monstrous.

'How do you suppose Esterhazy lives with himself,' asked Marcel, 'knowing of his own guilt?'

'Very comfortably, I imagine. Guilt is a sentiment experienced by a weak personality, rather than the moral consequence of sin. A true sinner blames other people, never himself. The hallmark of his conscience is anger rather than guilt.'

'But surely he is shunned by Society?'

'On the contrary. Before the Affair, Esterhazy was a mere nobody, but I hear that these days he dines very well. The more his guilt appears, the more vociferous Society is in his support. One judges a man not by the company he keeps but by the company that keeps him. The former reflects his amusements: the latter his obligations.'

Marcel continued to express his dismal commiseration with the poor captain of artillery. In doing so the dear boy displayed the melancholy intensity captured so perfectly by the picture, which I had only today realised was the quintessence of him. I offered him one of my cigarettes with its soothing admixture of opium but he declined.

'I am sorry but I may only smoke my own blend. You know I'm an invalid.'

'I know no such thing!' I protested. 'An invalid is someone from whose illness we all suffer. You are merely occasionally unwell. Wait, here comes a tramcar.'

The vehicle in question travelled along the rue de la Plage more or less to the doors of the Grand Hotel. This convenience was the only excuse for Elstir's having taken a lease on a new house of exceptional ugliness.

'Oh,' said the boy when I commented that Elstir's edifice of art was constructed on the very material foundations of good plumbing, 'I had understood you to think that the gardens were charming. In fact you said expressly that they reminded you of those described in *The Dream of Red Chambers*, of which you had seen a scroll painting.'

'We seem to have paintings on the mind today. They are somehow more convincing than the originals. Elstir's garden was charming when I found it in Peking; but, like a button detached from its shirt, it has no value when found in Balbec.'

We dressed for dinner and I joined Marcel and his grandmother. Madame enquired of the picture and I allowed her to express her opinion of this object, which she had never seen, and then agreed with it. I was still concerned that the boy's prayers might have invoked sinister consequences and I had no desire to pursue the matter. Instead I drew attention to some of our fellow-diners.

'Who do you think that chap is?' I asked, indicating a corpulent fellow wearing a suit of clothes more lavender than grey. He sat in conversation with an epicene young man.

'I don't know him,' said Marcel, 'except that he is excessively ugly and Irish. I don't say that the two qualities are connected. In fact, I believe the Irish can be excessively other things. Now my turn. Who is that?'

An elderly lady with her own servant was sitting to my left. She was wearing a dress that might have been elegant in the Empress Eugénie's day.

'I am acquainted with her,' I answered. 'Her title is Princesse de Vittoria. No, do nothing. One is not obliged to recognise her. She is merely in the Corsican nobility. Her grandfather was Marshal Boucher, but she has come into property and risen in the world; so that she is now Madame de la Charcuterie. This is not a very interesting game, dear boy. I am feeling sad. Amuse me.'

The mistake was mine, for the lad would return to the painting. Addressing his grandmother, he said, 'Monsieur Haas has suggested that, in order to preserve my youth, I should pray that all the ills which would ordinarily attend me should instead fall on the picture. I have said that that would be to create a vampire of myself.' He looked at me. 'But I have also read a book, recently written, in which a doctor devises a potion which causes personality to divide between its angelic and daemonic parts. Are you familiar with the work, Haas?'

I nodded. It had been prompted by meditations on the connection between my Esterhazy and Haas identities. I regretted talking to the Scotsman, who had not disclosed that he was a writer.

Marcel continued, 'It occurs to me that the division of the personality into good and bad halves and a similar division between the individual and a painting are essentially the same idea.'

I reassured Madame that her grandson did not desire to be a vampire. He was content to achieve immortality in Art.

'And, if necessary, to sacrifice myself so that Art may survive,' the boy reminded me.

I could not bring myself to drink the hotel wine with the pudding. I commanded my man to bring me my own Tokaji, a souvenir of my life in Hungary. Madame had already retired, and soon afterwards Marcel claimed a slight indisposition and followed. I thought he looked horribly pale.

I took my cigarettes and decided to contemplate the brief perfection of this pleasure by walking along the shoreline from where I could see the lights at Rivebelle. Still it seemed to me that the boy's fervent prayer had not been hollow words; nor was it a prayer to which the angels give ear. Rather, I felt that his speech had resonances in the text of some infernal *grimoire* to conjure up a spirit to inhabit the portrait. Full of foreboding, I returned to the hotel.

I had no sooner entered than I was accosted by Françoise, the family servant. She told me that the boy's condition had deteriorated suddenly and he was now experiencing a burning fever. I left her to search out a doctor, and, ignoring the lift, bounded upstairs to his room.

My first impression on entering was that it was remarkably hot. I ascribed this to the elevated position of the room – it received heat directly through the roof – and to the effect of my own exercise. Marcel was lying in bed and Madame was applying vinegar to his temples. I remarked on the heat and also on a faint scent of smoke. The source of the latter was unaccountable, for when I opened the window the night air was sweet.

Neither the vinegar nor the ice Françoise brought had any effect. The poor boy moaned, 'I'm burning.' And I swear that his face was so inflamed that it seemed it would break into blisters purely from an interior cause. His voice faded to faint mouthings, and to hear better I approached closer. Only then did I receive the force of his breath. Though no smoke was visible, the stench of it came in a gust as though from an inferno within him. At once I suspected the hellish source.

I descended the stairs even more quickly than I had ascended. Outside I discovered the brougham belonging to the Irishman and his companion, who were not guests at the hotel but merely dined there. I threw a gold louis to the driver and told him to ignore his masters and drive me directly to the villa of Monsieur Elstir.

To my horror the coachman replied, 'So, Monsieur wishes to see the fire?'

At my urging, the coachman whipped the brougham along the rue de la Plage. He was forced to compete with the wagons of the *pompiers* and the carriages of vulgar spectators hastening to the show. God forgive me but I could not but rejoice in the beauty of destruction as in the distance I saw the fire exploding like bursts of chrysanthemums on a black backdrop of Japanese silk.

We arrived at the villa. It was aflame, and Elstir, with the solemnity of a hierophant presiding at a sacrifice, was studying the pyre.

I asked him, 'Have you managed to save anything?'

He shook his head. He said, 'It seems I have reached too high and the Divinity is inclined to remind me of His existence. Magnificent, is it not?'

I grabbed his arms and forced him to look at me. I demanded, 'What of the portrait of the lad?'

'Gone – everything is gone,' he replied with a sad yet whimsical smile.

'No!' I cried. 'Don't you understand? The painting *cannot* be destroyed! Rather, the fire will kill the boy! Think on the prayer he made. He has drawn upon his own head any ill that might befall his portrait. Curse you, but he would give his own life to preserve your Art!'

These words seemed to stir Elstir. He said. 'Come. The picture is still in the studio. The fire began in the kitchen. It is still barely possible that the flames have not yet reached so far.'

I did not wait on any further speculation. Pushing Elstir roughly, I opened the street gate and, ignoring the objections of the *pompiers*, bundled the painter before me towards the rear of the house, where the studio, adapted from a conservatory abutted the main part of the building. Already I could hear blasts as the tortured window-glass shattered.

'This is madness!' cried Elstir. 'You will kill us both!'

'Remember your love for the boy!' I answered, who should have known better that the selfishness of an artist is limitless. Then I reflected that I did not need him. I could risk my own damned immortality to save the picture. I released Elstir and went on without him.

The garden, which by day had been so beautiful, was now fitfully lit by the flames of the house and the exquisite composition of form and colour was broken. The studio did not appear to be burning: rather it was as if a cauldron of smoke were boiling against the remaining panes of glass, issuing from them in tortuous coils as if Hell were venting daemons. I tried the door and, though the handle was scalding to the touch, it opened.

I entered and through the further door could see into the morning room, which was ablaze; the fine Turkey carpet, the Chinese porcelain and the curiously chased silverware from the Maghreb were all fallen into the general ruin. Even as I watched, an Indian cabinet inlaid with ivory and rare woods burst into flame and was reclaimed by its Hindoo gods.

The danger was acute. Only the fact that Elstir had put away his pots of oils and varnishes in cupboards the fire had not reached saved the studio from the conflagration. Still, there was the heat. It had touched the canvases – the seascapes off Balbec, the studies of rocks around the bay, the landscapes around Rivebelle. They yielded their paint as if it were being conjured from them. The frames buckled, the varnishes crackled and blistered, pigments bubbled and burst in small inflorescences. The outer layers, like a blackened calyx, opened and from within bloomed petals of bright colour only to assume the same dark form and in turn reveal the underlayers of paint so that what once had been images of sky and sea became brief glories of *millefiori* before decaying in a second to waste.

All except the portrait of the boy.

That picture, though all those canvases around it had turned to wreck and mockery was still there in its pristine perfection: wholly unblemished, seeming, indeed, to be even brighter, as though it were the true day and source of light. I paused momentarily, the aesthete within me marvelling at its beauties, accepting almost that an object so ideal had no place in the concrete world and must of necessity be excepted from the ruin of Time. The wonderment flickered and passed. I seized the diabolic object and rushed with it into the garden, where the *pompiers* had gathered like mourners around the forlorn figure of Elstir. I thrust the painting into his hands.

The artist looked at the miracle of his handiwork. Astonished, he cried, 'It is not possible! There is not a mark on it! It is – no it can't be – *fresher, better* than when I made it!'

'It is cursed,' I told him soberly.

'How so?'

'It owns the immortality that belongs properly to the boy's soul.'

'No … no!' cried the painter.

'Take it! Keep it! Do not show it – ever. It must be kept safe and inviolate in the most secure of caskets in whatever fastness your imagination can devise. Do you understand me? Whatever happens to it will happen to Marcel!'

I extracted a solemn oath from Elstir that he would do as I commanded. And upon that I returned to the hotel, my heart heavy that I should be too late.

Listlessly I bore with the joltings of the brougham until we were returned. Almost I wished not to do so. I was afraid that my action was too late and that, instead of that fine lad, I should find only a cadaver smouldering under the ensorcelled gaze of his dumbstruck relative.

However, as I mounted the stairs I came across Françoise bearing a bowl of water and a clean white towel, and she informed me that the crisis was past. She was amazed to hear me chortle like a child – or a madman –

and seemed to doubt that I should see her young master. I brooked no obstacle but hurried past her.

I found Marcel lying on the bed and indeed his fever had diminished. He smiled feebly and said, 'I feel as if I've been inhaling smoke. I fear that my asthma has taken a permanent turn for the worse.'

'Hush now,' said his affectionate servant as she proceeded to bathe his face.

I saw that it was flushed and had erupted in blisters. I saw, too, that it was covered in fire-blackened smuts though the window had been closed.

CHAPTER NINE

The night of Harry's birthday party was the night Lucy disappeared.

The evening itself followed the earlier pattern. The food was good but curiously varied and I remember only the blinis with caviar and soured cream, which I'd never tasted before, and it was for this reason that we drank vodka rather than wine. Harry produced half-litre bottles covered in rime, and, in the Russian fashion, threw away the cap of each one since, once open, it must be finished. Afterwards we smoked several of his interesting cigarettes.

My wardrobe was limited and I dressed as before in my hot-country wear. Lucy wore a long, straight sheath of black taffeta with a silver necklace holding a single white stone, and a silver anklet to grace her bare feet. To me she looked pale and ill in a slightly feverish way. Her eyes were unnaturally bright, and the spots of colour applied to her cheeks were clumsily done and served only to emphasise her bloodless *morbidezza*.

The door to La Maison des Moines was open, and Harry called to us from the kitchen. When he emerged, he was dressed in white tie and tails. Lucy gave a little gasp. On examination the tails were an ancient set of black gabardine, shiny with use and inexpertly repaired. The stiff shirt-front and waistcoat had begun to turn a parchment colour. Round his neck he wore an order. An elaborate star of tarnished silver and some dull stones hung by a blue ribbon bleached by sunlight. His feet were tucked into heavy woollen socks and carpet slippers.

I picked up an allusion to Harry's story. We were intended to see Harry the Vampire – but with a crucial difference from the conventional image. This was Dracula in his dotage. Or perhaps we were seeing a frozen section of the final transformation scene in which the Prince of Darkness, fixed by a stake in the heart, begins his corporeal dissolution. Move the film on a few frames and Harry would crumble to a pile of hideous dust smouldering in a pair of tartan slippers. Or perhaps, too, the socks would survive. Devoid of support they would rumple, fold, tilt, and spill his ashes in two trickles on to the floor.

'Welcome, my children,' he said in a mellifluous Slavic accent. Following my glance at his feet, his voice saddened and he said something about age, coldness and poor circulation.

'But let us eat, darlings,' he resumed. 'Whaddaya say, kids?'

So we ate a little, drank a lot, smoked a few; and Harry told us the next episode of his life story. I didn't know what to expect, but I was determined not to be shocked. I'd decided to convey the appearance of urbane amusement so that he'd realise I was up to all his games. If his story had some purpose or subtext, he should know that I thoroughly understood it. I was determined to be master of the situation. I was faking.

The preliminaries were simpler than on the previous occasion, since we were tacitly agreed on the agenda of the evening. Harry began as before by delving into the magic bag to produce the 'evidence' that would prove the truth of his statements. This time it was a letter written in French, in purple ink, on handmade paper, both very faded. It was signed 'Sebastian Melmoth', which meant nothing to me. The date on the letter was 1898 and it gave every physical appearance of age and authenticity. But I expected no less. I read the letter and passed it to Lucy.

'You told him you were a vampire?'

Harry shrugged. 'I was in my cups. You must also remember the date. *Dracula* had been published the previous year and the subject was very topical.'

'Who was Melmoth?'

'Just a guy. You're missing the point, which isn't Melmoth. Read the reference to the Dreyfus Affair.'

I remembered it. 'You were *that* Esterhazy?'

'The very same,' said Harry. And he began his tale.

The story of Dreyfus – I mean the true story – is one of betrayal. Esterhazy betrayed France. The Army betrayed Dreyfus. It's also a story of fraud and imposture. The real Esterhazy (assuming he were not Harry) was very like him in his fantasies and pretensions; and the whole sad train of events was extended by the lies and forgeries perpetrated by the counter-espionage section of the French General Staff. The Melmoth letter was appropriately of a piece with the fabrications produced in those years. Indeed it occurred to me that, if the letter were, as it appeared to be, contemporaneous with the Affair, it might have been forged by one of Dreyfus's supporters in order to implicate Esterhazy and then somehow have come into Harry's possession. It's a measure of the confusion wrought by Harry that I found it necessary to formulate such an elaborate explanation to deal with what was plainly nonsense.

Lucy and I ambled home a little unsteadily. I'd noticed earlier in the evening, that the first bats of the season had emerged. They brought back a memory. At the age of seventeen I passed a summer vacation as a labourer at a small château in the Dordogne. In the evenings, after a day in the vineyard, we ate under a magnolia on a small gravelled terrace. One evening during dinner, as the bats circled overhead, my host took a small stone and threw it into the air. A bat followed the stone, mistaking it for an insect, and landed on the terrace, from where we picked it up, passing it from hand to hand, stroking its fur and astonished by its warmth. Yet another memory. Sally and I were living in our first home. Jack was a baby. It was a summer evening and Sally came to me to say that a sparrow had found its way into the house. I caught a brief glimpse of the creature and followed it upstairs into Jack's room, where I found a bat describing perfect circles around the central light. It was so unlike a bird. Whereas a sparrow would have panicked and flown into walls and window, the bat circled calmly until, tired, it lit upon the curtains and hung upside down. I scooped it up gently, feeling its warmth and all the while telling Sally the story of my first encounter with a bat. And then I released it in the garden. Tonight the bats were small pipistrelles; I'd seen them sweeping in circles as the sun went down. They caused me to reflect on the subject of vampires but not too seriously. I was troubled, but not insane.

'What do you make of Harry?' asked Lucy as if she were an indulgent parent speaking of a naughty child. She squeezed my arm affectionately.

'I think you know my opinion.'

'You still don't like him?'

'I enjoy his company – in moderation.'

'And his stories?'

'Those, too.'

'I *love* them!' she said brightly. 'They remind me of horoscopes: how one reads them as if they apply to oneself, as if the astrologer is speaking to one personally – though they're all rubbish, of course.'

'Which part of tonight's tale struck you as important?'

'Four-fingered Margaret.'

I was surprised. She was a detail I had forgotten: merely a passing reference in the Melmoth letter and, to my mind, quite insignificant.

'Why her?'

'Because she was a prostitute and a vampire's moll. Can't you imagine how curious her situation must have been? Living with a vampire can't have been easy. I imagine her sitting in of an evening while her lover popped out for some blood, or staying at home in the daytime, frightened to go out shopping in case a visitor called and stumbled across the coffin. She must have passed the time reading novels. She would have read *Dracula*, since it was very popular, and said to herself, "No, it isn't like that at all. Life with a vampire is very quiet and domestic." '

I let myself think of the practicalities of vampire existence, taking it for a fact. 'She would have to go shopping in order to eat,' I said. 'It wouldn't be difficult to disguise the coffin, especially in Victorian times. She could cover it with a piece of velvet plush and put photographs on top. In any case, Harry goes about in daylight, so there doesn't seem to have been a problem.'

'Yes, he does. Still,' Lucy said thoughtfully, 'I can't help being impressed with how devoted Four-fingered Margaret must have been. She would know in her heart that she was living with the wrong person – that it was all a terrible mistake. And yet she was in love and there was nothing she could do. Like falling in love with an alcoholic or a drug addict. Waiting every day for the disaster that will inevitably happen. Placing her trust, but knowing it will eventually be betrayed.'

'My poor darling,' I said. I held her close, and kissed her white neck on the place where the broken necklace had drawn blood.

'Not me, *her*,' retorted Lucy, returning a peck on the lips and gently pushing me away.

I smiled at this last exchange and it was a minute later before I asked, 'Didn't the story of Proust and his portrait interest you, then?'

'No, no – you're wrong if you think I didn't enjoy it.'

'But?'

'Well, we've heard it before, haven't we? Even I recognised that it was a retelling of *The Picture of Dorian Gray*.'

'With an important difference.'

'Oh?'

'In Wilde's version Dorian Gray wishes for all the signs of age and sin to fall on the picture. In Harry's version the situation is reversed. Marcel wishes that all the accidents and decay that might affect the portrait should, instead, fall on the original. Or, to put it another way, Dorian Gray sacrifices Art to himself and creates nothing. But Marcel sacrifices himself to Art and – possibly in return – creates his book.'

'I see.' Lucy grinned and whispered, 'And do you suppose that's *the message*?'

'I've no idea. If it is, it doesn't amount to very much.'

'Perhaps you've only scratched the surface.'

'Maybe. I admit I'm a sucker for hints of Profound Subtexts and Ineffable Wisdom. But mostly they're phony – just an old storyteller's trick to grab the attention of the punters.'

'And the critics.'

'Them, too,' I agreed as we passed through the garden gate.

Over Lucy's shoulder I thought I saw the shadow of a man in the bushes.

'Is there someone there?' I asked.

Lucy spared an idle glance. 'It's probably Antoine,' she said. 'He's taken to following me home. I don't mind. There's no harm in him.'

Whoever it was was having a pee. I could hear the splash, and that mundane fact made the incident seem natural. 'Shall we go in?' I asked, and we did, leaving the night and its vampires behind us.

That night I dreamed of betrayal and imposture, and wondered if all men kill the thing they love. I knew I'd betrayed Sally. I feared I would betray Lucy. I was a phony. I was a middle-aged man pretending to be twenty years younger, a painter and a writer. These were the plain facts of my case, evident not only to any observer but also to me, and it hadn't taken Harry's story to bring me to this realisation. I was convinced there was nothing to be learned from stories beyond their lending an accidental focus to what one knew already. Nor were they a spur to action. I knew I'd betrayed Sally and would betray Lucy. And, in the morning, in that knowledge, I would continue with my betrayals: as cruel, sensual, sharp-toothed and unutterably selfish as Melmoth had said.

In the morning Lucy wasn't beside me. She wasn't in the house. She hadn't had breakfast.

I supposed she'd gone to the baker's. When she didn't return after an hour, I made myself a cup of chocolate, dunked some stale bread in it, and then attended to my writing.

By lunchtime Lucy still hadn't appeared and I experienced a small knot of anxiety. Putting away my manuscript, having written very little, I searched for a note but found none. I looked for Lucy's purse and it was gone – and this, at least, was encouraging since it suggested she had an intelligible purpose even if I didn't understand it; or couldn't remember it. In all likelihood Lucy had told me of her plan for the day and I'd forgotten, or, more likely, had paid no attention. Thinking over recent events, the only thing I could recall that might have taken her any distance was a visit to the doctor to be examined about her heavy periods and anaemia. She'd mentioned a Doctor Somebody-or-other in Pamiers. That must be the explanation.

Except that our only car was in the driveway and there was no taxi in Puybrun.

Unable to concentrate, I strolled down to the Bar des Sports for an aperitif and a snack. I knew that I was vexing myself over nothing. Lucy's disappearance was like that of a keyring, which causes one to tip out the wardrobe and the sock drawer until reduced to looking in absurd places like the sugar bowl, when the solution is obvious and one has left the keys in the car. Lucy would come back from shopping in Chalabre where she had got a lift from a friend and would bring me a present of a tiepin, and I would be stupid and resentful and blame her.

The bar was closed. I remembered that the season had begun and Mike and Marie-Paule had opened the booth by the lake. I decided to go there and have a beer and some *frites*, comfort food.

'Have you seen Lucy this morning?' I asked.

'No,' said Mike. 'Has she gone somewhere?'

'She said something, but I can't remember what. I wanted a word with her.'

Harry was also there. I could see him in the distance, walking at a leisurely pace on the path at the far side of the lake. He was rooting with his stick among the detritus of winter and the dead chicks of spring. I sat over my beer and *frites* as with insufferable slowness he completed the circuit and came towards me.

'Ahoy, matey!' he boomed in the unbearable manner of a bar-room bore at a sailing club. 'How are my children this morning?'

'We're not your children,' I snapped. 'Have you seen Lucy?'

'Since last night?'

'Of course since last night.'

'I … no, I don't think I have. Mind if I sit with you? I'm pooped.' He ordered a Ricard and mixed water to the colour of a stomach medicine. 'Has she gone out? Did she say where she was going?'

I mentioned the doctor in Pamiers. Then I remembered a vague conversation about a shopping expedition to Carcassonne and another to Lavelanet and talk of a friend who would be on holiday in Béziers. The car was a problem in every case.

'The doctor sounds the most likely,' said Harry. 'I said to my little girl that she was looking pale. Of course, I didn't think there was anything wrong with her.'

'The car…' I said.

Harry brushed my observation aside. 'I don't have a car but it's not a problem. My doctor is in Chalabre and I've no difficulty getting a lift. Lucy probably met someone at the baker's.'

'That sounds unlikely.'

'Things do sound unlikely when you're not in possession of all the facts.'

Harry then did something I didn't expect and wasn't sure I liked: he placed his hand on mine and patted it. He checked his watch and said benignly, 'Have another drink and things will seem better. Lucy is a grown-up lady, even if I do call her my little girl.' So I did, and we passed a couple of hours with my thoughts like waves lapping on a beach, advancing to engage in small talk with Harry; retreating to wonder as to Lucy's whereabouts. On our return through the village I enquired of the baker, but he hadn't seen Lucy.

She wasn't at home. I searched for a note again and, in a drawer, found an old wallet and a credit card I'd reported lost. Now I remembered: I'd taken the wallet on one of my hikes precisely because it was old, and the credit card in case of emergency. There was no reason to suppose that Lucy would leave a note in an old wallet in a drawer, but I looked anyway.

I went to Harry's house, thinking that if Lucy had returned to the village she might have dropped in on him and even now be taking tea. I didn't believe this for a second.

The door was open; I went in. Harry was sitting in an armchair shooting drugs.

'Jesus Christ, Harry!'

He could say nothing. His teeth were gripped round one end of a tourniquet and I caught a glimpse of a needle. Beyond that I didn't need to look, and couldn't. I'm squeamish about these things. Turning my eyes away, I waited until I heard the needle drop, and then, still not looking, I asked: 'Is there anything I can do? Make tea or something?'

Harry sighed. 'Yes, make some tea,' he answered. 'I'm sure you could do with a cup.'

In the kitchen I found a kettle and some Twinings teabags. I made tea like an idiot, chatting through the doorway about Lucy and how she hadn't come home yet, and had Harry seen her, in the most inconsequential fashion. When I took two cups into the lounge, Harry waved his away. He was half dozing. The tourniquet was loose about his arm. The needle was on the floor.

'I heard you were ill,' I said, trying to apologise for my shocked reaction. 'Lucy told me. Is it … cancer?'

'Not cancer,' he murmured.

'I see … what are you taking?'

'Heroin … horse … smack.'

'Your doctor…?' I wasn't certain of my own question.

'No doctor.'

'No doctor?'

Harry smiled and moved sluggishly in his chair. 'Isn't it plain to you? I'm what used to be called a dope fiend, dear boy. A smack-head. A junkie.'

'In Puybrun?' I said disbelievingly, thinking of the village lost in its dream among the hills.

'I buy my supplies in Mirepoix. I get there only once a month, but my habit is very moderate.'

This was scarcely more credible. Mirepoix is a charming little country town.

'Ah, the world is a wicked place,' answered Harry.

He drifted off and I couldn't leave him, though he must often have found himself in this state and come to no harm. I helped myself to a brandy and sat and mused a while, hoping the old man would sleep peacefully. If he'd overdosed or there were any other form of emergency, I'd no notion what to do.

Half an hour of this and Harry still quiet. I looked at him with what I suspect were my first feelings of true affection. Then I thought, 'What on earth have I got myself into? I've deserted my wife, my mistress has vanished, and I'm sitting with an ancient junkie who says he's a vampire.'

I returned the glass to the kitchen and, in my methodical way, washed it and the tea cups. I was about to go back to Harry when I noticed the old fellow's bedroom, and I thought, 'Shall I go in there? Will I find something to tell me about him?' I pushed open the door and entered a darkened room with the shutters closed. I tested my emotions and to my surprise found I was afraid, not with a gothic dread that the denizens of Hell were about to spring at me, but more in the way that we are afraid of ourselves: of forgotten incidents, dark corners of memory and unadmitted longings. The room, which showed no more than a bar of sunlight and some motes of dust, was an invitation into my past: the nights when I had gone to bed and my mother had come to visit me bearing a digestive biscuit and a mug of Ovaltine, and I read a Biggles book by torchlight, and my parents, downstairs, talked quietly and reasonably about divorce. The room was full of whispered voices: *Brains Trust* on the wireless; my mother asking my father where she had put her knitting pattern; or silent as my parents listened to Sir Anthony Eden broadcast on the Suez Crisis. Things I could never discuss with Lucy, who had not been born.

I turned on the light and was in a pleasant bedroom, simply furnished in that comfortably shabby way that second homes often are: a repository of the not-quite-best; the duplicates of things already possessed: presents from elderly relatives; quaint objects that are almost but not quite useless, such as cut-glass dressing-table sets. The used and the second-hand bring an old-fashioned air to a room; and it was at this flickering transition point between time present and time past, this double image of things remembered and things there before me, that I tried to find Harry.

I found a photograph.

It hung on the wall, faded and fly-spotted. At first I passed over it, thinking it belonged to the house. Instead I hesitated over whether to violate Harry's confidence entirely, and go through his wardrobe and tip out his drawers (where, doubtless, I should find some lost car keys); or whether I should open the carpet bag, which lay on a peg rug by the bedside, and lay bare its content of foul totems and talismans of a fabulous past, all in a cloud of unhallowed dust. I shuddered. No, I decided, not that.

I returned to the photograph. I took it from the wall, turned it over, and read the framer's label. *Jesse Shuttleworth, portrait photographer, 27 Union Street, Oldham.* But it wasn't a portrait: rather a shaky snapshot of an Edwardian bedroom, briefly caught in the flare of flash powder, and, on the bed, two naked figures.

Though the subject was sexual (the man was going at it doggy fashion against a well-filled rump), it wasn't pornographic. Lacking the artificial lubricity of true pornography, it was more sordid, more appalling. The lighting was poor; the composition eccentric; the positions, gestures and expressions of the actors impromptu. The setting was the last word in seediness. Closed curtains had partly broken from their rings. A fly paper hung from the ceiling. A chamber pot stood on a shabby dressing table. Clothes and bedding were strewn in a heap. I sensed rather than saw the mattress stained with bodily fluids; sensed rather than smelled the sour coal ashes in the cast-iron grate, the sweat and cheap scent that infected the clothes, the musky fishiness of body heated sperm and vaginal secretions. I thought 'hotel room' and remembered the hotel in Paddington where Lucy and I had first coupled. I stank of red wine and cigars: Lucy of the beer an office drunk had spilled on her dress. I was noisy with booze, jokes and guilt. Lucy was doped from a furtive drag in the ladies' loo. She stared into my eyes, which were heavy-lidded and wistful. I stared at her uncertain smile: at her teeth, which were stained with beaujolais and lipstick. I shudder now at these recollections.

To return to the photograph. The man and woman had been surprised in their coupling. She was a big woman, her thighs and shoulders puckered with fat, her left breast (the only one visible) drooping and full. Her face was masked by the coils of a hair piece that had come loose. He was a heavy man, still young; but I could imagine him become old, fat and pig-faced. Indeed I thought I knew him. Indeed, if this were one of Harry's fabrications, I was *meant* to know him. But, for now, his identity escaped me. I saw only the sordid spectacle these two had created, which, unwittingly, they had filled with meaning for me. And for someone else. I wondered: who was the eye behind the camera?

Meanwhile Harry came to. I found him, open-eyed and motionless. His expression was tender and affecting.

'Hullo, John,' he said, slowly.

'Harry.'

'I nodded off.'

'You did.'

'Yes. I'm sorry about that. You have enough, worrying about Lucy without concerning yourself with old Harry. My excuse is that you weren't supposed to be here.'

'I forgive you,' I said, and then, 'But why, Harry? Why do you take that stuff?'

'For the vampirism, *mon ami.*'

Here we go again, I thought, but I wasn't inclined to argue. The heroin explained his fantasies. I needed no other explanation.

However, Harry went on, 'I get withdrawal symptoms.'

'From heroin?'

Harry shook his head, slowly, ponderously. 'The other thing,' he said.

'Being a vampire? You're no longer a vampire?'

'What made you think I still was?'

'I didn't know you could give it up.'

'You can give up anything if you try hard enough.'

'I'll make you some more tea,' I said.

'Yes, do that,' he answered. And then he did something which I hadn't expected – not from Harry, zany, fantastic Harry. He began to sob, first a little, and then uncontrollably.

'There's no need for that,' I said gently. 'It's just an effect of the drug.'

He nodded, but the explanation didn't comfort him. He looked at me with his ancient eyes and wiped a dribble of spit from his mouth, and cried, 'You can't imagine the agony of it, John! To become old! To lose my immortality! To seek something other than people's blood to fill the hole where my soul used to be!'

'We all grow old and die,' I answered.

'Not vampires!'

No, not vampires.

'I'll make the tea,' I told him.

CHAPTER TEN

Harry was subdued when I called on him that evening. I prepared an omelette *aux fines herbes* with a green salad and we cheered ourselves with a bottle of cheap Blanquette de Limoux. I'd left a note for Lucy, if she chanced to come home.

We chatted by lamplight. The season was too advanced for a fire to be necessary. Harry was tired and I was conscious of his burden of years, but he was sympathetic. He asked me about Sally and my family, and I understood that he'd had Lucy's version of my situation on the evenings they spent together while I attacked my great Indian novel. It was a fairly general conversation, and I won't bore you with too many details since I have few insights into the human condition, and such insights as I had into my own position and character seemed to be of little use. I was like an alcoholic aware of his own addiction. I possessed a purely intellectual comprehension, insufficient to control the practical direction of my life. However, you shouldn't read this as self-pity nor conclude that I was oppressed by a great weight of guilt. That would be to misunderstand the generally even tenor of my emotional life and the degree of rational detachment and amusement I experienced in observing my own behaviour: qualities which, though not admirable, had contributed to my success as a lawyer. Though I wasn't free of self-doubt and passed moments and even days of agony at the thought of the hurt I'd caused Sally, my reaction in the main was to say to myself, 'So that's what I'm like. Well, well! How odd! I hadn't expected it.'

For the sake of the record, I told Harry, 'I still love Sally, but I couldn't continue my life as it was. I'm not immortal and I can't bear the thought that whatever years are left to me will comprise the same sameness, and that all my unused talents, including any further capacity for love, will go still unused into my grave with me.'

My actual words sounded less phony than those I've written, but what I said was in essence the plea of every dissatisfied adulterer, and I'm reminded of the habitual thief who, with complete predictability, excuses himself on the grounds that he was unemployed and drunk at the time of the offence. The difference is that I've never known a convicted burglar who doesn't have a job to start next Monday, if only he's allowed to go free. I had no such mitigation.

Harry didn't comment and didn't criticise. Perhaps he murmured a few agreeable truisms about the difficulty of life, love and marriage. I wasn't looking for a shoulder to cry on, and, having disposed of my tedious affaire, I opened another bottle of wine and proposed that Harry go on with his life story. If this seems strange, given my troubled thoughts after the earlier tales, it was because I'd changed my attitude. I knew that his stories were fiction, but I was prepared to treat them as truth. I would suspend disbelief and give the limited engagement of a reader, knowing that, in the last analysis, I was secure in the world beyond the book covers.

I remembered Lucy's curious concern. 'What happened to Four-fingered Margaret?' I asked.

'I didn't call her that.'

'No? What, then?'

'Margaret – what else?'

'Lucy thought she must have been very devoted to you.'

Harry smiled sadly. 'Did she? Lucy has a kind nature and likes to see the best in people. But the answer is that

Margaret was less devoted than you might think. In the end, whatever their feelings may be, women know that vampires are losers. The only ones who stick with you to the finish are those with scarcely a drop of blood left in them, who are halfway to being vampires themselves.'

'She left you?'

'As it happens, I left her. It was in the August of the same year I met Melmoth. An eventful time. In January I was tried and acquitted. Zola – who, by the way, was what the Americans call "an asshole" – printed an article in *L'Aurore* accusing me and then fled after his trial. Then, at the beginning of August, Major Henry confessed to forging some of the documents in the case and killed himself. That was enough for me. I could see that everything was *foutu*. I took the train to Maubeuge, shaved off my moustache and strolled over the Belgian frontier.'

'And then?'

'I went to England.'

Harry's Tale

My plight was miserable (said Harry in a creaking American bass which I thought of as his John Huston impersonation). I had a severely limited education, my reputation for honesty was in shreds, I had a poor command of English, and I was plagued by my unfortunate taste for human blood. The only work I could find was as a journalist.

This was a time when popular journalism was taking off.

Great Britain was engaged in the Boer War and, as I've discovered, anyone can pass himself off as a military expert. For a year or so I wrote despatches for the London papers from Pretoria, and Bloemfontein; and it was only after it was discovered that my base was Hammersmith, not Ladysmith, that I lost this source of income. I left London to try my luck with the provincial newspapers. And so I arrived in Oldham as the new century dawned.

Let me tell you, Johnny, that the advantage of a taste for low company and shameful pleasures is that it can be satisfied as well in Oldham as in Paris. I lived in cheap lodgings in Greenacres and entertained myself in the public houses of George Street. During the day I worked as a reporter for the *Oldham Evening Chronicle*. At night it was … otherwise.

One of my colleagues was a man named Shuttleworth. He was a short, fat, beery fellow in a rusty frock coat and a bowler hat, who had a taste for women, liquor and gambling. He was a photographer. One day he came to me with a proposition.

'Now, listen, lad,' he said. 'Tha seems a feller as can take care of issell. In fact tha's reat up my street.'

Shuttleworth spoke no more English than I did.

The substance of his offer was this. In his spare time he worked as a private investigator for several local lawyers. The cases he handled were separations and divorces for which his skill as a photographer was useful in gathering evidence. He'd done this work for several years.

One of the hazards of his occupation was facing the anger of lovers and husbands. 'Th' problem, lad,' he explained,' is that I'm getting too owd. I'm short of breath and slow on me pins, and I can't run away from th' buggers like I used to.' To prove his point, he indicated his nose, which was spread across his face like a red cabbage. He suggested that we go into partnership and divide the profits.

We worked together successfully for several months, until one day – it was in October 1900, I remember, since the country was in the throes of an election – we were given the case of a Mr Albert Henshaw. The facts of the matter were straightforward. His wife, Mrs Bella Henshaw, had been an *artiste* before her marriage and of an enthusiastic and amorous temperament. Mr Henshaw a respectable man, had believed that the attractions of religion would be greater than those of the music hall and been proved wrong. He had reason to suspect that the love of his life was sharing her favours with a travelling corset salesman named Spencer. According to Henshaw, he'd only that day seen the fellow in town.

The night was rainy. Shuttleworth and I were at our 'office', drinking brandy and water at the Prince William of Gloucester, when a boy came, sent by Mr Henshaw. He brought a message that *la belle* Bella had had a quarrel with her husband and stormed from the matrimonial home saying she was going to have some fun 'and not drinking tea, either'. Summoned by the clarion call of duty, Shuttleworth collected his Kodak camera, a hefty apparatus with a tripod, and we set out to make a tour of the public houses, in the hope of finding one where Spencer had rented a room.

Oldham had a lot of public houses, and we visited a good number of them. As I say, it was election time, and the streets were hung with bunting. On every rainy corner a speaker was haranguing his audience about the South African War. Bands played, tramcars rattled, the cobbles sparked under the iron-shod clogs of the workers, the rain brought down tears of soot from coal fires and mill chimneys. Oh, yes, it was a fine night to be staggering drunk and wet under the weight of a camera.

We arrived at last at an establishment called Doctor Syntax, a red-brick gin palace at the head of the High Street, bursting with boozy colliers, mill workers, refuse men, night-soil collectors, clerks, cotton-brokers, loafers, riffraff, and a splendid collection of tarts. In fact it was just my sort of place. We ordered brandy and joined in the singing and ordered more brandy, and, at last,

Shuttleworth remembered why we were there. He stuck his florid nose over the bar and collared the barman.

'Thee, lad,' he said, 'I'm talking to thee! 'Ast tha seen a feller name of Spencer an' a big bonny lass 'oo looks no better than she should be?'

'What business o' thine is it?' replied the barman.

'This,' said my friend, flashing a half-crown and then covering it with his hand.

The barman indicated that Mr Spencer had in fact taken a room.

'Champion!' said Shuttleworth and gave the honest tapster his money.

We drank another brandy. Shuttleworth complained he was feeling 'poorly'. He explained, 'It must be summat I ate.' I confessed that I was also feeling unwell, and we drank another brandy to settle our stomachs. 'Champion!' repeated Shuttleworth, smacking his lips. And again we recalled our purpose.

We found the staircase and began our ascent. Shuttleworth fell on his face. He rose and looked at me sternly. He asked, "Ow many of us are there?'

'Two,' I said, with reasonable confidence.

'Which bugger tripped me, then?'

'I think it was the camera.'

He examined the instrument. He said, 'Between me and Mr Kodak 'ere, *one* of us is drunk.' He stared at me belligerently. "Oo the 'ell are you?'

'Harry.'

'Which Harry?'

'Your partner, Harry.'

'Champion!' said Shuttleworth.

In this fashion we arrived at last on a gas-lit landing smelling of chamber pots. On one side it looked down on the High Street. Two or three bedrooms gave on to it from the other. Harry was wrestling with the camera and trying to fill a contraption with flash powder. He halted.

'Remind me,' he said. 'Why are we 'ere?'

'Mr Spencer,' I said.

'Oh, aye.' A pause. 'Which room?'

'I don't know,' I answered. 'I thought you knew.'

He reflected and then said, 'I don't suppose it matters. They all look the same when they're shagging. Eeny, meeny, miney, mo! Let's try this one.'

The room we entered was in darkness except for a night-light burning on the bedside stand. Two people were vigorously occupied on the bed. Behind me I heard a clatter of equipment and Shuttleworth muttering, 'Which one's the bride's mother?' and then there was a flash and, by a miracle, we had our photograph. Which was as well, since, within a couple of seconds, the man in question had covered his loins with a towel and the lady had buried her face in the pillow so that only a pair of quivering buttocks was visible.

The gentleman rose from the bed. He was in his middle twenties, with reddish-brown hair, porcine features and a bold stare which he turned on us.

'Who the devil are you?' he demanded icily.

'Thee tell 'im,' said Shuttleworth to me. 'I'm buggered if I can remember.'

'Well?' enquired the gentleman. 'Am I to be given an explanation?' He was a cool customer and no mistake.

Now, you must remember that I was drunk and at this date had a very uncertain command of the language. On the other hand, I was an aristocrat and a soldier and as calm under fire as the next man. I treated my interlocutor to a look of withering contempt.

'We, sir, are private defectives,' I said.

'Indeed, indeed … may I smoke?' Moving from the bed, he took a case from his jacket pocket and, puffing the while as he lit a fine Havana, murmured, 'Do go on, please. Who am I?'

'You?'

'Yes, I'

I was nonplussed. I collected my thoughts and declaimed, 'You, sir, are a brazen philanthropist!'

'Ah. How so?'

'You have alienated the afflictions of this lady from her lawful spouse, Mr Henshaw.'

'The devil I have.'

'Indeed you have. My colleague and I have just now caught you in an act of flagellant adulthood.'

'Thee tell 'im, lad!' contributed Shuttleworth.

However, my supply of English was running dry and, from the amused curl on the gentleman's lip, I was conscious that I might have committed some solecisms. Nor did I feel that I had the entire support of my companion, who now announced that, if the bride and groom didn't choose to buy him a drink, he was tired and wanted some shut-eye.

Meanwhile the gentleman, acting as if he were master of the situation, continued smoking thoughtfully. He asked me, 'What do you propose to do with the photograph?'

'We shall give it to Mr Henshaw.'

'Henshaw? I don't think I know this Henshaw.'

'A likely story when here you are formulating with his wife.'

'This lady is not Mrs Henshaw. I believe her name is Bertha Hardcastle.'

'I see. And I am to take it that your name is not Spencer?'

'Spencer?' The gentleman burst out laughing. He said, 'My dear fellow, you must have a cigar, you really must!'

'I'm obliged,' I said stiffly. And so we sat a while longer, smoking in silence except for the voluptuous Bertha, whimpering on the bed, and the inebriated Shuttleworth who was snoring in the embrace of his camera. Finally my fellow smoker said, 'This is a pretty pickle and clearly a case of mistaken identity. Still, you catch me in an embarrassing situation, but one which can be cured by a little mutual accommodation.'

My English was not so poor that I did not understand the sense of his offer. But I was still at a loss as to his true identity and this ignorance was a defect in any negotiation. I stirred the recumbent Shuttleworth with the tip of my boot. He woke.

'Do you know this gentleman?' I asked.

Shuttleworth opened an eye that looked like an out-of season oyster. He mumbled, 'Mr Churchill, sir. I'm pleased to meet thee, sir. Tha can count on my vote.'

'Mr Churchill?' I repeated. 'You are Mr Winston Churchill, the candidate in the election?'

'I am,' said the gentleman.

'*Bon Dieu!*' I exclaimed.

'Ah,' murmured Churchill, 'I see that you are French. That explains a great deal.' He cleared his throat. '*Monsieur, je vooz propose que nooz arrivonz ah oon petite accommodation. Je vooz donneray bow-coop d'arjunt si vooz me rendray la photographie. Que ditezz-vooz?*'

'I see,' I replied. 'And exactly how much money would that be?'

'*Sink-aunt levers.*'

'Fifty pounds!'

'*Oui. J'ay l'arjunt ici dance ma red-ink-goat.*'

'Hey up! Take it, lad,' urged Shuttleworth who had somehow got the drift of the conversation and was now alert. 'Tha'll not get a better offer or I'm a Dutchman.'

'You're a Dutchman?' I asked, confused.

'*Il estt Hollandezz?*' enquired Churchill. '*C'est l'explication pork-war je ne le comprend paz?*'

'Dutch or double-Dutch, it's all the same. Take th' money, lad!' said Shuttleworth.

Churchill: '*Prenay l'arjunt!* '

Shuttleworth: 'Ay, lad, take th' brass!'

Harry: 'Brass?'

Churchill: '*Quiver joan – prenay le quiver joan!*'

Harry: '*L'argent est le cuivre jaune?* The silver is brass?'

Shuttleworth: 'Nay, brass is gold.'

Harry: 'Brass is gold? What is silver?'

Shuttleworth: 'Silver is only coppers by comparison with what yon Mr Churchill is offering thee!'

I paused.

'Shall we all speak English?' I asked.

Shuttleworth accepted a cigar from Mr Churchill and we settled to negotiate. With our permission he was allowed to dress, as was the lady, who was promptly despatched home. We sent down to the bar for brandy and soda.

Mr Churchill stood. He tucked his thumbs into the pockets of his waistcoat. He fixed both Shuttleworth and me with a pugnacious glare. He spoke. 'Gentlemen,' he began. 'You see me before you, a war hero and a candidate in the present election. I pray you: shall you let it be said by generations yet unborn, in a country whose future we are here shaping, though we see it but dimly – shall you let it be said, in that far land beyond the bourn of our knowing, whose ripe harvests are the fruit of the seed we sow: that land which shall be Hell or Eden according as we are wise or foolish – shall you let it be said that all its fair hopes were blighted by present, selfish greed? No! I repeat *no*! – I trust not. For are we not all Englishmen – or Frenchmen, or Dutchmen, as the case may be – at all events stalwart men and true? Assuredly we are! Let us therefore put our shoulders to the wheel and drive the chariot of History not down the strait and winding paths of Selfishness, but towards the broad and sunlit uplands of the Future so that, at our resting, we may smile at the contemplation of our Past and comfort our Old Age with the knowledge that we have done our Duty! In brief: take the money.'

Insofar as I understood this, I considered Mr Churchill's offer. The attractions of cash were, of course, obvious. However, I knew that he was an up-and-coming politician, and I foresaw that at some date in the future I might have need of his services to extricate me from the difficulties posed by my irregular life.

So, instead of accepting, I said: 'I am grateful for your offer, Mr Churchill. And for my friend Mr Shuttleworth I am happy to accept twenty-five pounds. For myself, however, I am a poor foreigner and would sooner prefer a powerful friend to cash in hand. At some time in the future I may have reason to ask a favour of you – one favour only, and I do not know what it is. If you promise to grant me that favour, and it lies within your power, then I will exchange your promise for my silence about the events of tonight. What do you say, sir?'

What could he say? I had him.

'*Dieu vooz blesse!*' sighed Mr Churchill.

And that was Harry's tale. I listened through it, nodded, asked a couple of questions, fixed myself a drink, for all the world as if it made sense and this was the sort of stuff that happened in Reality. Did I believe him? I should know and yet I don't. That night the world did not exist outside the walls of La Maison des Moines, and, within the little world of Harry's dining-room, he was the Demiurge, spinning universes out of his own fantasy: giving colour and substance to them; consistency and interior logic. And was the 'proof' not there? Recalling the photograph hung in Harry's bedroom, I realised now that it *was* Churchill as he'd been in his youthful days; or, at all events, someone who resembled Churchill enough for Harry's purposes.

It was only necessary to listen to Harry long enough to become a little crazy.

I asked, 'Did you ever collect on Churchill's favour?'

'Sure,' said Harry. He yawned and stretched his old bones. 'I'll tell you about it some time.'

'Not now?'

'Another time. I'm pooped. You don't want to listen to an old guy rattling on. Not when there's Lucy to consider.'

'Then I'll say goodnight.'

'Yes, do that, Johnny.' He hesitated '.I'll tell you one thing now. I sometimes wonder if I didn't ask for the wrong favour. I should have asked Winston to kill that bastard Clarence Quimby.'

'Quimby? Why?'

Harry looked pained, as he had before when first Quimby was mentioned.

'That's another story.'

CHAPTER ELEVEN

The next morning I drove to Chalabre. I drank coffee and a cognac to clear my head, read the newspaper, and bought some groceries. I debated whether to go to the police about Lucy's disappearance. From a call box I phoned Dr Moreau to check again whether she'd fixed an appointment concerning her anaemia. She hadn't. I went to the police.

Chalabre was home to a small post of *gendarmerie*. The station chief was a *brigadier* by the name of Gérard, a calm, slim, dapper man of forty, with the inexpressive face of someone who habitually listened to lies. He ordered coffee as I explained briefly that I'd come to report a missing person, and, while we waited, asked me a few questions about my own circumstances. He was interested that I was English and that, though I was only fifty years old, I no longer worked. 'You are very fortunate, Monsieur Harper. You have, perhaps, a pension.' I explained, a little impatiently, that I was able to live on my investments. He put down his pen, looked at me, raised his eyebrows, and picked up his pen again. I waited for the Gallic shrug but it didn't come. Instead he took a *carnet* from his drawer and flipped through several pages of photographs. I speculated that he thought I was a drug-dealer.

'We must complete a report,' he began as coffee arrived. I gave my particulars and produced my passport.

'And the name of your wife?'

'Sarah Elizabeth Harper.'

He wrote it down.

'And her age?'

'Is that necessary?'

'But of course. How else shall we find her, if we do not have her details? A photograph would assist.'

I corrected his error. 'It isn't my wife who is missing. It's another lady. Her name is Lucy Victoria Western.'

The pen went down again. 'I see. And she is…?'

My mistress? My paramour? In English the words sound old-fashioned. 'Girlfriends' belong to pop stars, 'partners' to feminists, gays and lesbians. 'Common-law wives' cohabit with unemployed men who have convictions for assault. 'Bits on the side' sleep with the elderly captains of golf clubs.

'I live with her,' I explained.

'I see,' said Brigadier Gérard, and noted the point.

As we completed the form, I realised how little I knew of Lucy: her birthday, her last employment (my secretary), her address in London. She'd told me about her parents (I believe they were dead) and the place where she was brought up (Nottingham – Rugby – some damned town in the Midlands, but I couldn't remember which). She'd told me and I hadn't thought it worthwhile to remember. I understood she had a brother called Willie, but I couldn't put an age, address or other particulars to him. 'His name is William,' I said, and spelled it. 'I don't know if they were close.'

Gérard's assessment was as I knew it would be. He completed the report with impeccable method, passed it to me to sign, signed it himself, and placed it in his tray. He examined me studiously and said, 'You will understand, Monsieur Harper, that these matters – especially when they involve people of mature years – usually resolve themselves. Mademoiselle Western has been gone only a little over twenty-four hours. Has she really disappeared?'

'She left no message. She had no cause to go,' I answered feebly.

'I cannot say.' He didn't believe I was telling the truth.

'She hasn't taken any clothes.'

A smile. 'Are you sure? Speaking personally, I shouldn't know if my wife had taken clothes or not.'

'She has no transport.'

'Taxis, hire cars, friends – there are many possibilities. You say she took her purse?'

'Yes.'

'Containing cash and credit cards?'

'Yes.'

'It does not sound like abduction, Monsieur.'

No, it didn't sound like abduction. It sounded like … nothing I could imagine.

'The case is noted,' said Gérard formally. 'But it is not our practice to investigate after such a short period and when all other explanations for the disappearance have not been exhausted. I suggest you telephone Mademoiselle's friends in London and her brother' – flicking a page – 'William. I suggest you wait and come to me again in several days. In other words, be tranquil, Monsieur Harper, and the matter may solve itself.'

I knew it wouldn't.

I retired to a café for another cognac and to call myself a fool for raising my problems with the police. Gérard, of course, was right. How could I say Lucy had taken no clothes? I knew so little of her wardrobe that I couldn't even tell him what she was wearing when she left me. My mistake in trying to understand what had happened was to look for a seamless explanation of the facts when all my experience as a lawyer told me that nothing was ever totally explicable. Some facts are simply unknowable. Others have nothing to do with the matter in hand but are mistakenly included within the compass of things to be explained, like the fingerprints of persons who are not involved in the crime but have by chance touched an object or been present in a room. Yet others are relevant but incapable of interpretation: facts that are of meaning only for a single person: such as Proust's memory of a madeleine he ate as a child.

I turned from this last thought, seeking distraction and making a connection with the events of the previous evening (a connection having a meaning only for a single person). Two points came to me out of Harry's Churchill story. The first was that the reputation of every great man is vulnerable to the slander of the future; for the future controls the evidence: interpreting it, selecting it and, if necessary fabricating it for its own purposes. I saw no relationship between this conclusion and my own situation. The second point concerned the ambiguity of language. Harry's example of himself, Shuttleworth and Churchill debating in a mishmash of tongues was farcical, but it was easy to think of more meaningful examples. To take one: myself and Lucy. According to my recollection, nothing had been said between us to indicate that Lucy no longer loved me or that she was discontented enough to leave me. Of course we'd had differences over small things but, in my estimation, they'd amounted to nothing. Yet, had I misunderstood her? Had I construed the surface of language and ignored the metamessages of gesture and context, the languages of silence?

'*Darling, can you come home on time and pick up the children after school?*'

'*Darling, why don't you love me any more?*'

Perhaps these two sentences do mean the same thing.

The 'true' facts and the 'true' meaning of language. Both are debatable. However, neither subject was new to me. If these were the point of Harry's story they were commonplaces. So what? Why consider them?

As I brooded over confused thoughts of Lucy and Harry I drank another couple of cognacs and my unfocused attention wandered across the landscape of the café, noting indifferently how sunlight, shining through the window, fell upon coffee stains on a table top, a wine glass with lipstick on the rim, an ant crawling on a bread roll, a paper napkin on which the waiter had scrawled the bill, writing in blue ballpen and using continental sevens. I followed the sunlight to its source, broken by the leaves of a young plane tree planted in the pavement. Early summer leaves, still fresh and green and not the leaves of August which (the cognac prompted me) drooped dull and stained like the folds of a flasher's raincoat. At home in England I had no plane trees. Instead, at the bottom of my garden, two hawthorn bushes stood, ranked one behind the other, spilling cream and pink blossom in May. Sally and I called this event 'the blossom fall'. At breakfast I would look through the kitchen window and see sunlight strike it with bright glory. And in the evening the sun set behind it and I would think of a waterfall in the shadows of a deep combe.

Here it was daylight and I followed the track of sunlight back into the café where it fell on my table, on which lay the crumbs of a roll I had eaten. I stared at the crumbs and mentally ordered them into patterns. I thought of old ladies reading tea leaves. I thought of my Latin lessons at school and of Roman priests divining the future from the entrails of beasts. I thought of university.

Once, in my final year, stressed at the prospect of exams, I smoked too much dope. I was at a party and, while the charivari went on around me, I sat peaceably meditating on an empty wine bottle. Such was my single-minded concentration, it seemed to me that, simply by the force of contemplation, I could extract all colour and form from the bottle, leaving merely an illusion that was empty of substance; or that by the same effort I could annihilate the bottle in itself and reduce it to a mere shape or pattern and paste it into a pattern of other shapes like a painted object on a theatrical backdrop.

The breadcrumbs lay on the table, hard and bright like diamonds poured from a jeweller's velvet bag, and an ant moved over and between them, assaying each one.

I couldn't see the wine glass clearly, but I imagined the pink pattern of a lower lip, one half of a Cupid's bow impressed upon it, and saw in my mind's eye (as I had seen when Sally and Lucy had left the same tokens on a glass) fine clear lines rising vertically through the film of lipstick: tea leaves and auguries, foretellings of the future when the lines would turn to wrinkles and an old lady, wearing too much make-up, would sip wine and slander her daughter-in-law in a voice made hoarse by cigarettes.

I returned to Puybrun and went to Mike's bar. I ordered cognac and asked for some *jetons* for the telephone.

'Watch yourself,' said Mike, 'You're nine parts drunk already. Christ, you haven't driven from Chalabre in that condition, have you?'

'I'm all right.'

'As you please, but I don't recommend making telephone calls when you're drunk. It's always a mistake.'

I had the number of Lucy's flat, the one in Earl's Court where we'd once or twice fumbled on the couch settee. She'd shared it with a children's nurse called Trish and an Australian who was something lowly in films and went by the name of Birdie. It was evening and I calculated that one or other would be at home. I got Birdie.

'Hullo? Birdie? This is John Harper.'

'John who?'

'I'm calling from France. John Harper.'

John…? Oh, yeah, Lucy's bloke.' She sounded tired.

'I'm sorry to disturb you…'

'S'all right, I was only eating a Chinese.'

'…but I was wondering if Lucy was there.''

A pause. A rustle.

''Scuse me, I had a mouthful of beansprouts. Lucy? Why would Lucy be here?'

'Has she phoned?'

'What, Lucy? No – I mean, not for months, in fact not since last year. Last I heard was a card for Christmas. Hullo? John?'

I composed myself, forced myself into pseudo-sobriety. I said, 'You wouldn't lie to me, would you, Birdie? I could understand if Lucy had told you to say ... look, it's very important that I speak to her.'

She wasn't fooled. Like all women she could smell drink down the telephone line.

'You've been tying one on, haven't you?' she said matter-of-factly. 'Still, I suppose it's none of my business. Have you two had a falling-out?'

'No – at least, I don't think so.'

'You don't think so? What the hell does that mean?'

'I don't know.'

'I see. Well, I swear to God she isn't here and I haven't heard from her.'

She put the phone down abruptly. I fumbled for more *jetons* and called back.

'Birdie?'

'Listen, John, piss off! I don't want to get involved.'

'Don't hang up!'

Wearily: 'What do you want?'

'A phone number or an address. Lucy's brother.'

'Lucy hasn't got a brother.'

'William!' I was shouting. 'She has a brother called William!'

'She doesn't have a ... no, wait a sec, I tell a lie. Willie!' Birdie laughed. 'You mean Willie! She has a *sister* called Willie. Oh, Christ, didn't you even know that?'

'Willie?'

'Willie – short for Wilhemina. Okay? Satisfied?'

'The number?'

'I don't have it.'

Birdie rang off again. This time I didn't call back.

My drink was standing on the zinc. Mike gave it to me and advised me to ease up a little. I couldn't remember if I'd told him that Lucy had left me, or been kidnapped, or died, or been abducted by aliens. Mike confirmed he hadn't seen her. He gave an ear while I told him a rambling tale of love in a Paddington hotel and the problems of language. I noticed Antoine playing gloomily and alone at the football machine. I asked him, 'Have you seen Lucy?' He looked back guiltily, stopped his game and quit the bar. I recalled that two nights ago Lucy and I had seen a figure lurking in the lane by Lo Blanc and had supposed it was Antoine. I followed him. I saw him dodging in the shadows and I knew that he was guilty of something unspeakable. I cried, 'Where is she, you bastard? What have you done with her?'

I set off up the narrow street, bellowing his name, but stumbled, and his lumbering form disappeared. Instead of Antoine, I saw Harry coming towards me, ambling with his walking stick. He sized up the situation, smiled and said gently, 'Hullo there, John. I see you've had a tiring day.'

I gasped, 'Antoine ... Antoine...' but nothing more. I felt my eyes sliding like fried eggs in a pan.

Harry guided me back to the bar. When Mike looked doubtful, Harry waved him away. He ordered a Ricard for himself and a cognac for me and posted me at a table. I looked at him blankly. 'It isn't Wednesday,' I said.

He grinned and shook his head. 'No, it isn't Wednesday. I wanted to speak to you. I wondered how you were getting on – whether Lucy had come back. When you weren't at your house, I thought you might be here. Did you go to Chalabre?'

'Yes.'

'And saw the police?'

I nodded.

'And they told you it was too early to raise the alarm and you should speak to Lucy's friends and family? I tried to give you the same advice.'

I wasn't interested.

I said, 'You saw me and Lucy together. Did you ever think she would leave me?'

'The Lucy I saw may not be your Lucy, just a nice girl being kind to an old man.'

'I'm not a bad person,' I affirmed.

'No. In fact you're quite a good man, though occasionally selfish and foolish. That's fairly normal. If women left men for that reason, there'd be a lot of lonely men.'

'Some do.' I said.

'Indeed they do,' agreed Harry.

Oddly enough I'd become moderately sober. Perhaps it was the effect of Harry's calming presence. Tonight he seemed just a decent old fellow, tired and feeling his years. The dangerousness which I'd always sensed in him was replaced by sympathy. Regaining a sense of proportion at the end of a disastrous day, I raised a subject which had vaguely troubled me.

'I want to tell you a story, Harry,' I said.

He looked mildly surprised.

'This isn't one of your stories. It's about a novel I was writing.'

'Lucy said you wrote.'

'She did?'

'Uh – huh.'

I was disappointed, as though my toy had been stolen. 'Did she tell you what it was about?'

'She told me what she *thought* it was about. Your version may be different. Go on.'

'I will,' I said, and began.

It was April and the trees were full of blossom ...

Harry listened good-naturedly as I told him my tale of the lawyer, the lawyer's wife, the lawyer's mistress, the cave temple, the disappearance and the suspicions. I fumbled only over the arbitration, which had really taken place, and where fact and fiction became mixed up in my disordered brain. When I'd finished, Harry said, 'I think I understand.'

'You do?'

'After a fashion. But you tell me. I take it there's a point to all this.'

'A point? Of course there's a point! What's the point if there's no point?'

'Hush now. Calm yourself, Johnny. Of course there's a point. You tell me what it is.'

'Can't you see it?'

'I can see all sorts of things. It reminds me...' He chuckled. 'No, no, this is your story Johnny, not mine. Go on.'

'The similarities to what's happening!' I cried.

'You have something particular in mind?'

'Susheela,' I said, and I found that I was sobbing. 'In my novel she has a twin sister. It's the sister who murders her.'

'And?'

'Lucy has a sister! Her name is Willie. And now Lucy's disappeared!'

I was still sobbing, but I didn't know if it was for Lucy or Susheela. I loved Lucy, but she was real and what I felt for her was the qualified love that we have for the real: the love that is mixed with guilt and fear of rejection; the love in which the lover shields himself from his beloved by a veil of deceit, for he can never allow her to see him as he is. Susheela was different. I had her caged within the page: blind to my existence, while I could know her thoroughly. And, though I might describe her in my inept prose, I could attribute to her all those qualities of intelligence, mystery and beauty I desired. I could feast on her and kill her at will and, indeed, had done both; and afterwards, secure in my immortality, had cried sweet, poignant tears.

'*Is* Lucy a twin?' asked Harry matter-of-factly.

'I don't know.'

'Have you any real reason to suppose Lucy's dead, or that this sister – Willie or whatever – is in France?'

'No.'

'Mike,' called Harry, 'another Ricard!' To me: 'You've had enough, Johnny.'

Marie-Paule came over with the drink.

Harry turned to me and resumed. 'Your similarities are starting to fall apart. D'you hear what I'm saying? You're making patterns, where they don't exist. Have you finished writing this novel of yours?'

'No.'

'Then give it up – especially now. In any case it sounds like it was written by a sad bastard. Okay? Are you listening?'

'Yes.'

'Get a grip on yourself. Get some sleep. Tomorrow make a few more calls. Lucy's probably left some numbers lying around. Phone them. Act rational.'

'You're right.'

'Darn tootin', *mon cher ami!*'

I wasn't finished. It had been a bad day. I knew I couldn't sleep. My mind was a jumble of images: fact and fiction, present events and past recollections; and I was struggling to find the connections. I asked, 'Have you ever been in love, Harry?'

He hesitated before answering, 'Once upon a time, as the old story goes.'

'Four-fingered Margaret?'

'I was fond of Margaret, but I can't say I exactly loved her. We had a comfortable understanding.'

'Maria?'

'She was a good lay. She thought the same of me. We liked each other. She married a guy called ManziaIy.'

'Dolly?' I remembered the keyring from an hotel in Galena, Illinois. 'You were married to her, weren't you?'

Harry paused. For a moment I thought he was angry. Then he spoke. 'I never said that,' he answered. His glance drifted and he raised a finger to order another drink. He let his eyes fall to the glass before him and I thought he wasn't going to continue. But, at last, he said, 'No, I wasn't married to Dolly. I didn't even realise I loved her – not until afterwards. I thought it was a sex thing.'

'Tell me about her.'

'In time maybe.'

'Tell me something – anything.'

'Go to bed.'

I shook my head. 'I'll never sleep.' I looked at his face, which had become calm and thoughtful. I urged him, 'Help me, Harry! Tell me a story that'll help me to sleep.'

'What kind of story, *mon enfant?*'

'Something about yourself. I want something' – I couldn't find the word – '*wonderful*. Astonish me, Harry. *Astonish* me!'

He smiled, shrugged, and the mood lifted. The thoughtfulness was gone and his old eyes brightened with puckish wrinkles.

He said, 'Did I ever tell you how I murdered Rasputin?'

CHAPTER TWELVE

I woke with a hangover: not a splitting headache, but an insatiable thirst and a feeling of floating muddily inside my skin. I reached out a hand for Lucy, but she hadn't returned. And so I got up, drank a litre of Évian, took some tablets and had a shower. Afterwards I ate a good breakfast, a habit from which even a hangover doesn't break me.

I could recall very little of the previous evening. Some time during my conversation with Harry I'd switched to automatic pilot. I vaguely remembered asking him to continue with his life story, but I'd forgotten what, if anything, he'd told me. My last memory was of his suggestion that Lucy might have left some phone numbers lying around. I decided to search for them.

Like others who have to be organised at work, Lucy was disorganised at home, a trait I shared with her and which explained my perennial hunt for car keys. It was a vice that wasn't without its compensations. At home I would search in my desk, and among my papers often find a photograph or a birthday card or a scrap album compiled on holiday when Jack was young. The album contained sketches I'd done and an ephemera of tickets for boating lakes and funfairs, a castoff snakeskin Jack found in Crete, and a Napoleon III coin that lay in the dust of a yard outside a house near Laval we took for a summer. And Malabar wrappers. These were made of waxy paper with cartoons printed on them. Ten years later they still smelled of bubble-gum. Searching for a pleading in my Indian arbitration, I would come across the old album made of thick beige paper that waited for the drawing of a treasure map, and I would open the cover, which had a picture of Worzel Gummidge on the front, and find a page containing a sketch, a ticket or postcard, and a Malabar wrapper. And I would forget the pleading and, instead, subside contentedly into a chair with the album open in front of me. I would lift the frail album with both hands, like a priest elevating the Host, and bring the Malabar wrapper to my nostrils and sniff that faint scent of past summers, letting my mind wander down trails of memory.

So I recalled the holiday at La Rochelle when Jack had ridden the double-tiered carousel to the music of a calliope; or gliding with Sally along the weed-covered canals of La Venise Verte while the sun shone through her cotton dress; building a sandcastle on the beach at Woolacombe in September among the debris of the season, shards of polystyrene cups and lollipop sticks. Once that elusive scent of Malabar had me in its thrall, my memory could not be held within confines bur would fasten, seemingly at random (though not really so), on the new objects in the way that (as I recall) Sally and Jack and I had collected sloes in autumn, not methodically but moving from this bush to that as a fat bloom-covered berry caught our attention.

So we had holidayed in La Rochelle, and years later I bought Jack a copy of *The Three Musketeers*, which described the siege of La Rochelle in the French wars and brought the holiday back to memory. La Rochelle, where I bought an Agatha Christie novel in a yellow-covered French translation, and discovered that the solution to the murder turned on a pair of twins. La Rochelle, where, so the album informed me, I had once bought some Malabar.

At this point my memory which had wandered down one path, our holidays, would take a turning down another. As a child in England I could not buy Malabar, but I remembered other bubble-gums. Some were sold for a penny from a vending machine which stood outside a newsagents that advertised Condor Tobacco and the *Daily Sketch*. Others were sold inside. These came with transfers that could be licked and stuck on the arm like a tattoo. They were the sort I would buy, and I would not wash that arm, but carry my trophy for a week. In my early childhood, sweets were still rationed. In Lucy's they weren't.

I opened a drawer, and Lucy's lingerie smelled of Poême. It was a perfume she shared with Sally. I used to buy it as I returned from India. Smelling it now, I thought not of Lucy but of Sally and Jack and holidays and Malabar and all the other things I have mentioned until, dizzy and distracted, I broke off to fix myself some coffee. Even then, I couldn't free myself from the spell of memory. I sat at the kitchen table with the coffee in front of me and at once my thoughts began to follow a new coffee-flavoured direction. My mother used to buy her groceries at a shop that kept its wares on open display: loose biscuits sold by the pound; butter in great pats that had to be carved and weighed. The shop smelled of ham, cheese and coffee.

I wondered if I were going crazy. My life seemed to have broken free of the ordered sequence of years. Instead of a story composed of events in series, it seemed that I had lived another life – or rather *lives*. I had visited my Malabar-life and set foot over the threshold of my coffee-life. I've always liked to buy second-hand books and, as I buy them, I sniff the pages and relish the mustiness of the paper. I own over a thousand books. If I were now, in my present state, to pick up a book, what would happen to me? Would my memory ever release me? It was tempting to try the experiment. By my bed lay a copy of *Miscellany at Law*. I'd read it thirty years before at university. Already I knew the contents of the first room within my book-life. It was filled with students and old girlfriends. I should meet

Sally in a mini-skirt, descending with long legs the steps of the law department. I would stop her and ask her to a college dance. She would agree, we would go to the dance, and, in two days' time, fall in love. As for Lucy, she wouldn't be there at all.

I finished the cup of coffee and resumed my rummage through Lucy's possessions. Except for the scent of Poême, which still caused flashes of recall like the last fireworks in a display, they meant nothing. Finally, in a discarded handbag in a shoe box in a wardrobe, I found what seemed to be an old address book. I flipped through it and came across an entry simply for 'W' and an address in Peckham. I guessed it might refer to Willie/Wilhemina. Although it was eleven in the morning and most likely that she wouldn't be at home, I decided to phone her.

A man answered. At first I thought there was a mistake. Birdie had said that Willie was a girl, but she could have been wrong.

I said. 'Willie?'

The man said, 'Naw, Stuart.'

'Have I got the right number? Does Willie live there?'

'Sure.'

'May I speak to her?'

'Naw.'

'Can I leave a message?'

'Naw.'

'Will she be back later?'

'Naw.'

My prejudices threw up the image of an unshaven Neanderthal in a vest. I was about to lose my temper when Stuart said, 'Sorry mate. You caught me at a bad moment. The dollar's been going fucking ape and I've been sitting at a screen all night watching Tokyo burn. I was just grabbing some kip when you called. What can I do for you?'

'Willie.'

'Yeah?'

'I need to get in touch with her urgently.'

'Tough. Like I said, she isn't here. Fucked off on holiday some place.'

'France – *is she in France?*'

Voices offstage. 'Nigel! Where did Willie fuck off to? … Where? … Sorry can't hear you. Where?' Then to me, 'Nigel doesn't know either. Probably France, but maybe not. She was shagging some Greek, so it could be Athens. At least I think he was Greek.'

I asked when he expected her return, but all I received in reply was a laugh. I took another couple of tablets and made another cup of coffee. This time, no memories visited me.

I wandered down to the lake and Mike's hut where I ordered a Fernet Branca to clear my head and an Evian to slake my thirst. Mike made a few grumbling remarks to the effect that I hadn't been his favourite customer last night. I scanned the beach. It was still too early in summer for the French to be out in force, but the Germans had begun to arrive and were doing much the same as everyone does. There was no sign of Harry.

I took a stroll for the sake of the fresh air and returned to the *buvette*, where I parked myself at one of the tables. I'd brought a pen and paper with me, thinking to occupy myself with my novel. But when it came down to it, it didn't interest me.

I began to sketch, not the scene before me but doodles in free association. I wrote inscriptions under them so that they were linked by a sort of jabberwocky. The result formed a recognisable composition and this suggested that it should have some meaning, but when I examined it I found only drawings and words juxtaposed in a pattern that lacked significance. I tore up the sheet.

The sun continued to shine on the righteous and the unrighteous. The crowd on the beach, which at first had been an incoherent whole, began to break into a series of tableaux and I identified lovers, families and knots of friends. This little group was domestic and self-contained. The next was expansive and noisy. The third was tense and dramatic, watching a toddler hesitating at the water's edge, prompt to seize her if she fell. The overall sense of unity was maintained by the children, who ran like couriers between the groups, asking for the return of a ball or help to find a pair of mislaid parents. At this last event, an embassy was despatched and two groups would make contact as the emissary of one met the emissary of another and a child was exchanged for an invitation to a beer.

I began to write. My subject was Dracula. As accurately as I could, I set out Harry's story of his encounter with Renfield. My problem was how to include the significant detail, when I didn't know Harry's intentions behind the tale. In addition there was the question of language. Harry's use of words was idiosyncratic and, again, I didn't know the intent behind it. Was it accidental, the product of an uncertain command of English? Or ironic? Or an attempt at a peculiar exactness? Forget for the moment the difficulty of recollection, the weakness of my own skills in reproducing another's speech, and the intangible qualities of accent and emphasis that couldn't be reduced to writing: had Harry even succeeded in his own purpose? Or had the message become lost in the medium? Had words facilitated or resisted expression? At all events, I wrote down what I could and, with a few later corrections, that's what you have before you. I don't suggest it means anything. Or rather, I do – but I don't know what.

The afternoon wore on and I tired of sunshine and writing. I ambled back to the house, sparing a glance for the shuttered windows of La Maison des Moines. I had in mind to phone my son Jack as soon as he returned home from work. I would take a snooze, freshen up and do it.

Jack was twenty-four years old and very bright, if not exactly a genius. Unlike mine, his inclinations had always been towards science and technology and he had a first-class degree from Cambridge, plus various other diplomas, and now fooled around in a software house based in London. He'd moved away a year ago and taken a room some place in Hammersmith. His character was orderly, tending towards obsessive, clear-thinking, unemotional, a little waspish in speech, good-humoured and generous. His cerebral mind-set meant that his relationships tended, on the surface at least, to be instrumental rather than deeply involved: exchanges of information rather than feelings. But he had an amused and intelligent insight into his own character, and I suspected and hoped that all would turn our well for him. He found me to be, like most parents, an embarrassment.

We got on well together. My own intellectual rigour was tempered by a degree of imagination, and Jack borrowed my imagination to supplement his own. He didn't understand that it is a quality that comes with risk and cost: that imagination is a product of childishness and that it clouds reason and judgment. In my professional life I continually had to struggle to synthesise the creative and the rational. And in my personal life I reaped the rewards of kindness and sympathy that come from a free and open imagination; and paid and caused others to pay the penalties of my foolishness.

Jack's puritan streak, when combined with generosity, made him see my faults and tolerate them. However, I hurt him deeply when I abandoned his mother to flee with Lucy. We had a meeting at which he cursed me bitterly for the pain I'd caused Sally and the disruption I'd brought to his ordered life. But he wasn't one to hold grudges. When he discovered that Sally, whatever her inner feelings, accepted the situation calmly, he relented and mediated between us over the practical matters of our separation. He even met Lucy. We flew to London one weekend to collect some of her stuff from the flat, and Jack had dinner with us at an Italian restaurant in the West End. He pronounced that he liked her – but thought I was an idiot all the same.

I don't know why I phoned him. I didn't have an agenda or any requests to make. Perhaps I was following the old adage that a problem shared is a problem halved. We began with the usual subjects: weather, work, the state of his social life (dismal evenings in the pub with other fans of *Star Trek*). Finally I got round to the matter of Lucy.

I said, as if unconcerned, 'My news is that Lucy has disappeared.'

'Uh-huh. When did this happen?'

'Two nights ago.'

'You mean she left you.' Statement, not question.

'No, not really. I don't understand what's happened.'

'Come off it, Dad.' Calm, knowing and impatient.

'I'm telling the truth.'

'Suit yourself.'

'I *am*. She simply vanished during the night. She didn't leave a note and didn't take any of her things.'

'Oh yeah?'

'Honestly.'

Someone else might have enquired as to my state of mind or my relations with Lucy. Had we quarrelled? Jack confined himself to the reported facts.

'Have you been to the police?'

'Yes.'

'What did they say?'

'It's too early to become alarmed.'

'It probably is.'

'They suggested I speak to her friends and family.'

'Good advice.'

'I've phoned a couple of people, but they haven't heard from her.'

'Then go back to the police.'

'I shall.'

We both meditated a while, then Jack asked: 'Do you want me to mention this to Mum?'

I suppose I did.

'You might do that,' I said. 'By the way, how is she?'

'All right. Much as usual. Working too hard. I'll tell her you called, once she gets back from holiday.'

'She's on holiday?'

'It's that time of year.'

'Where has she gone?'

'Spain, I think. I wasn't paying attention. Pauline and Ivor suggested she go away with them.'

'Their cottage is in France.'

'Whatever. Maybe they haven't gone to the cottage. I thought Mum said Spain. Does it matter?'

I didn't know if it mattered. I remembered that Willie might be in France; and now, apparently, so might Sally. But, as Jack had remarked, it was that time of year. There was nothing else to say on that subject, nor any other unless I intended to open my heart to my son's unreceptive scrutiny. I decided to end the conversation with my usual call-off sign, which on this occasion was heartfelt.

'I love you, Jack,' I said.

'I love you, too, you silly bugger.'

I strolled down to Harry's place, intending to invite him to share Marie-Paule's cooking at the Bar des Sports. I found him sitting in an armchair reading, with his gear for injecting heroin on open view on the table.

'Shouldn't you put that kit away?' I asked.

'Do you think anyone gives a hoot if I shoot myself full of shit?'

He closed the book and laid it down. It was Freud's *The Interpretation of Dreams*.

'I thought we might grab a bite of dinner together.'

'Fine by me. How are you feeling?'

'Okay.'

'Any news?'

I told him of my inconclusive conversations with Birdie and Willie's flatmate.

'I doubt it means anything. She may have gone back to folks and friends in Nottingham.'

'You know she's from Nottingham?'

'That's what she told me.'

I remembered the evenings Lucy had spent with Harry during that spell when, obsessed with my writing, I had avoided him. Suddenly I felt a spasm, not of jealousy, but a sharp injection of mystery. I envisaged them, sitting by firelight, replete with food and wine, with the contents of the carpet bag laid out on the floor. Harry, I knew, would have told her *everything*. His bony hand with its shaky fingers had picked over each talisman and the old magician had taught his beautiful apprentice the meaning and function of every one. I could hear his voice. For this he had selected the velvet cadences of James Mason (flash! – a scene from *The Wicked Lady*), whispering explanations and conjurations as Lucy, pixie-like, crouched in fascination over his treasures. These I could see in my mind's eye, but without focus. I stared harder, hoping by force of will or application of reason, to make them resolve themselves. But – God help me – they glowed! The whole pile of baubles was suffused with a vaporous white light. What was it? Suddenly I knew. The objects from within the carpet bag were radiating memories, and as I tried to penetrate the white glow I saw that it was not static but compounded of ghostly images that shimmered as they drifted to and fro, in and out of the depths of the nimbus. I was dazzled. I turned away. Where was Harry? He had vanished in my concentration on Lucy and the contents of the bag. Now he was back. I could see him, frail, trembling, standing behind Lucy like a spectre, smiling a benevolent smile. See how he stoops. See him kiss Lucy like a lover on the neck.

I remembered that I'd never asked Harry about the two puncture wounds on her pale throat, which Lucy said came from the chain of a cheap necklace.

'Are we ready?' asked Harry. He had changed and was prepared to go for dinner. He wore a battered panama and had draped a white foulard round the neck of his T-shirt to guard against the cool of evening. I answered that I was ready, and together we walked to the Bar des Sports where we ate a meal and cheered ourselves with a couple of drinks.

I hadn't realised that we'd eaten early. The disturbance of Lucy's disappearance had broken the even flow of the hours, and now, as we finished our *digestifs*, I looked out of the window and saw it was still light. I felt stale from the excesses of the previous night, which I recalled only dimly, and proposed that we walk off the food by taking a turn round the lake.

The beach was empty of children, who had been taken away for supper and bed. Some teenagers had set up a radio and were dancing on the sand. Mike's boy, Andy, was manning the hut and half a dozen middle-aged Germans were sitting at the tables drinking beer and unconsciously massaging their ample bellies. Harry and I took the path on the opposite side from the beach, the one leading through the avenue of osiers. The swallows were out in force; the bats just stirring. The low sun was by now gilding only the tops of the distant limestone crags, the rest was in soft tones of indigo and dark honey, and the trees were grey and olive.

'What happened last night?' I asked as we walked.

'When last night?'

'I was smashed. I remember telling you about my visit to Chalabre.'

'That you did.'

'And then?'

'You don't recall?'

'I think I asked you to go on with your story.'

'And?'

'It's a blank.'

'Well,' said Harry 'we went back to my place. I don't like telling my business in public, even if it is all ancient history. I gave you a small nightcap and we smoked a joint and I told you what happened next.'

'Next after the Churchill episode?'

'Kind of. I mean, you only get the edited highlights of my life. There's a lot of other stuff which would take too long.'

'I see. So you did tell me a story? What was it?'

'You truly don't remember?'

'No.'

'Gosh, golly, gee!' sighed Harry and grinned.

I looked away to the lake, which lay still in the shadows of the trees. A bar of sunlight fell on the beach and the kids were working themselves up to the music until they could slip away to make love. I didn't know whether to press Harry or give up and go home. But my mind and body were jumpy from their broken rhythms.

I said, 'Tell me again, Harry.'

CHAPTER THIRTEEN

This is the story of how Harry Haze came to write *Mein Kampf*. He told me about it as we sat under the osiers on the dyke. But, before I go into that, I want to return to the murder of Rasputin.

Harry never did repeat that bit of 'history' to me. He pretended he'd never spoken of it. I don't know the tale and so you don't either. Sometimes, in my dreams, or sometimes when I walk by a lake of a summer evening, I have this feeling that it's there at memory's fingertips and I have only to reach out and grasp it. But I never can. The feeling fades and I walk away from my dreams and the lake, always with the hope that it will all come back to me. It should be unimportant, but isn't. Without it, I have a hole in my memory and, in a sense, my life.

My problem with the lost history of Rasputin concerns its place in the overall structure of Harry's stories. If – and it's a big 'if' – there is some purpose to them, *if* they form an architecture or have a pattern, a missing piece may be crucial to the intelligibility of the whole. Without it, I may be piling up bricks without a plan or applying paint to the canvas without seeing the scene before me.

Nor are my concerns limited to the overall scheme. I've already explained my problems in transcribing Harry's account of events: the difficulties of recollection and language. As I set each story down, I have always before me the thought that, in the process of remembering and selecting the details, I may be missing some significant point. And I ask myself: is there a clue within the Rasputin story which would affect the way I have written the others? In other words, even in respect of the stories that I have related, is there, so to speak, a second version, a lost version, the version I would have written if only I could remember the tale of how Harry killed Rasputin? I *know* this is unlikely. I *know* that the speculation is hopeless. But that's the situation I find myself in.

In the meantime I suppose I should press on and tell you what I know and can remember. I would also mention that tonight, for reasons best known to him, I am dealing with Harry the Horse.

I am never having a country (said Harry) to which I owe my undying loyalty. Or my undead loyalty, for that matter. Rumania, Hungary Austria, Germany, Russia, France, Britain, America – I am seeing them all, and, though I have my preferences, when the chips are down they are nuts to me. Stalin knows a trick worth two when he calls vampires 'rootless cosmopolitans' and spends sweat to clear them out of the Party. Are you ever wondering why they are driving an icepick into Trotsky's skull instead of shooting him in the way normally approved for unpopular citizens? The whole point about vampires is that we are bloodsuckers and not exactly the selfless types which are the pastrami in the sandwich of Socialism.

The Great War and the Russian Revolution are over and I find myself in Berlin. This, you understand, is nineteen twenty and the citizens are still sad more than somewhat and the streets are full of beggars and doughboys and you are asking yourself what I am doing there. This is a good question since it is not a town for regular guys. However, I am not a genuine regular guy but a citizen of the bloodsucking persuasion, and Berlin is a fast track on a sunny day and I am a horse used to hard going.

Like the guys in those stories by Raymond Chandler and the other citizen whose name I do not remember but he writes *The Martian Falcon*, which is also a movie, I get myself an alias. I am born in Egypt with German parents; my father is a wholesale importer; I serve as an officer in the war – da di da di da. This is pure hokum like some of the race tips I get.

At this time I have a pal and he is called Ernie Röhm, which is also an ex-officer. Ernie is a fag, which does not necessarily make him a bad person, but in fact he is a bad person. He is one of those macho types and his idea of a good time is loading himself with beer in the company of his soldier buddies and then breaking a few Red skulls. To look at him, he is packing his beef into tight pants and jackboots, shaving his scalp and carrying a whip, and his face looks as if he eats a pound of chillies for breakfast.

One day – I think it is April and the daffodils are in bloom and the sap is rising – Ernie tells me there is a citizen which he wants me to meet. He takes me to a place in Dahlem, an old drill hall, I think, that is now a vets' club. Leastwise it is full of soldiers putting away beer and complaining that the Jews and the politicians are stabbing the Army in the back, which is also my opinion when one of my hay-eaters is losing my rent money and I ask who is giving him his nosebag.

(By the way, I have to tell you, Johnny, that in those days I am kind of anti-Semitic. Everybody is – except the Jews, I guess – and it is no big deal. I do not become a liberal until I vote for Truman in '48.)

Well, I am sitting at a table, nursing a glass of Weissbier, when Ernie comes over with this other guy. He is a skinny type: dark hair, blue eyes, moustache, felt hat and trenchcoat. When I put his appearance together with the anger that is coming off him, I conclude that he is a guy going through an alimony suit.

We set to talking. He tells me he comes from Linz. He tells me he is a great painter. He tells me he is a war hero. He tells me he has a plan for the salvation of Germany. He is full of the brown stuff we do not mention in the presence of dolls.

However, he is also Alois's kid – Alois, my old drinking pal from the days when I am Dracula, Prince of Darkness. I am figuring this from the details that Adolf lets slip, though I do not tell him this, since today I am Rudi Hess (Esterhazy – Hess – Haze – you are getting me?) and since on first acquaintance I do not want him to remember the vampire stuff about which ordinary citizens are saying bad things. Later I find it is not a problem because, apart from the racial thing, Adolf is an easy-going guy. Also he is from that part of the world where everyone has an Uncle Béla in the family who works the night shift and likes to sleep during the day.

So we talk and we drink (it is a lie that Adolf does not drink, but some citizens say anything to destroy another citizen's reputation) and he tells me of this political party. And before I know where I am, I am joining the party as member number sixteen and they give me a badge which is still in my bag if you want to see it, Johnny.

In these early days I get to meet Joe Goebbels, Manny Goering and Hank Himmler, who are also very patriotic citizens. Also I am made chief of this and that and get to wear the neat brown shirt and the jackboots, which is this year's fashion in our social circle and does not show blood so much when we discuss baseball with those citizens who play for the Bolshevik team.

It is a busy and fulfilling life, chewing over politics during the day and pursuing my private hobbies at night, and sometimes I become very tired and do not know if I am Rudolf Hess or Rudolf Valentino. So one day when I am carrying a headache which I buy the night before, I find myself in the Nollendorfplatz outside a coffee shop which is run by a Joe, name of Minsky. Now, normally Minsky's is not a joint I visit, since the citizen who owns it is a Russian and it is not on the social calendar of patriotic persons. However, I am wearing a nice number in grey wool and not my brown shirt and I am not too concerned that Minsky will ask me to leave by the window. So I go inside.

Minsky's is very popular with people of the Russian persuasion and is very crowded because there are a lot of Russians in Berlin who are not anxious to attend an early funeral in the old home country. I find myself a space and am sitting at a table with another citizen who is reading a book about butterflies. Bats or butterflies, I am not one to throw stones.

'Botkin, Vladimir Vladimirovich,' says the citizen and he sticks out his hand.

'Hess, Rudolf,' I answer and take it.

'You can call me Volodya,' says Volodya.

'And you can call me Rudi,' I tell him.

'Vodka!' cries Volodya.

'Fine,' say I.

Now this is not the first time I drink vodka. In fact I many times drink it with Grigorii Efimovich, who is an expert in this matter, up until the night when Yusupov and I dump his body into the water, and even then I am not certain if he is drowning or drinking the river. However, today at Minsky's I am not in training and, if I am a horse, I am definitely scratched from the card.

This Volodya is not the ordinary citizen beloved of bookies. He is a writer and poet, as well as knowing everything about butterflies, which I do not hold against him. In fact, where literature is concerned, he is almost as smart as Joe Goebbels, who is the world's best in that department.

So we talk, and I am thinking that Minsky sells pretty good vodka except the bottles are too small and I order another. Volodya tells me that I am 'a character', which I do not understand since I am trying to be a regular citizen. But, clearly, he is a nice person, and soon I tell him that I am a vampire and stuff like that. In fact I am thinking that maybe being a vampire is not such a bad thing though a little unsociable. I remember my Shakespeare and tell him, 'If you prick us, do we not bleed?' – though, as it happens, we do not bleed unless you stick a stake through our hearts, or an icepick in the head, as in the case of Leon.

'Vampires!' says Volodya. 'You are evidently a Symbolist.'

In fact I am a Fascist not a Symbolist, but Minsky's is not the place to point this out. We leave it that Volodya tells me he is certain I have a great contribution to make to world literature. And, strange to say, he is right. Because when we meet again, thirty years later in America, I am teaching literature, though my students are football players at a college in Hotzeplotz, Ohio.

For me 1923 is a busy year. First I have some loose ends to tie up from my life as a journalist; namely, I must go to England in order to be buried. Next I have to overthrow the German government and establish a dictatorship.

The dictatorship thing is Adolf's idea. I am easy about it, since, as I see things, we are already breaking all the heads we can break, so who needs more heads? However, Ernie, Joe, Manny and Hank think the whole notion is just peachy, and that's what we decide to do.

We begin the National Revolution in Munich. Why Munich? I have not a clue. However, Adolf has one good idea which is that we kick off the revolution by filling ourselves with juice at the Biirgerbräukeller. In my experience most revolutions are fuelled by beer – or vodka in the case of Russia, which is the same principle.

Von Kahr, who is head of the Bavarian government, is in the beer cellar holding a public meeting. He is protesting about inflation and martial law and similar stuff, when I march in with Adolf, Manny and a bunch of other patriotic citizens who are waving their roscoes and setting up a machine-gun to persuade the other citizens that they are not as brave as they may be thinking they are. We shuffle von Kahr and the other ministers into a side room, where Ludendorff, the old general who is to be our figurehead, is joining us. Ludendorff is not happy. He thinks we should make an appointment for the revolution so that it fits his diary.

I leave the hall. I have ministers to arrest and more heads to break and I drive around Munich in a car. I am still taking hostages and driving around the following day when I learn that the Bavarian government is putting down the uprising and Adolf and Ludendorff are arrested. And that is the end of the Beer Hall Putsch.

In my opinion the mistake is to begin in Munich. It is like overthrowing Washington by starting in Minneapolis.

At the time they put the arm on Adolf, I am in exile, and so I do not go to the Landsberg prison when he gets eight months – which, by the way, is a very good stretch for high treason, and if I get the same price on a horse then my life is very different from what it is being. However, exile is not suiting me and, treason being very cheap with a lot of it about this season, I decide to go back to Germany. And that is how I also find myself in Landsberg.

Life in Landsberg is not so bad. The judges who sentence us are very patriotic, and the prison governor and the guards are also patriotic. In fact, everyone is so patriotic that I wonder why the revolution is not succeeding. However, I am just your regular working vampire and I leave explanations to the real politicians.

The problem is boredom. We play cards and we get the occasional beer and some of the guys do the things guys do when they do not find any dolls. Then I remember what Volodya tells me, which is that I am going to make a contribution to world literature. And so I propose to my fellow citizens that we write a book.

First we have to agree the subject and the title. Adolf wants to write his life story. He calls it 'Four and a Half Years of Struggle against Lies, Stupidity and Cowardice'. I tell him that the title sounds like the grounds in a divorce case and finally we call it simply *My Struggle*. It is to be a cowboy story.

Now *Mein Kampf* is one of the best-selling books ever written, and I suppose that is making Adolf a better writer than Volodya Botkin. I mean: who would you rather publish? Even so, I do not think it is a very good book. It has too many ideas and not enough action. Later, when the patriotic citizens are running the show, Joe looks it over and decides that even he cannot make a film of it, though maybe a musical, in which case plot and characters do not count. I do not wish to be a dog on a racetrack about this (if that is how the expression goes), but I think that if Adolf leaves me alone to write the way I am wanting to write – which is like Zane Grey, who in my opinion is a writer who knows his business – *Mein Kampf* is an even better book than it is being, and we sell even more copies and Joe makes his film or even Hollywood, and Gary Cooper gets to play Adolf. In this case maybe I am a better writer than either Adolf or Volodya. However, that is all water under the whatever the thing is that water goes under when it is going under someplace. It is not to be.

Adolf is still beating the drum about the National Revolution, which, from where I am sitting in Landsberg prison, is a horse that is not going to run. He takes over the writing and we have to do it his way. This means that he is using my plot – exchanging Russia for the Wild West and Jews for Indians, but it is still the same story in which the good guys steal the land and shoot the natives. But then he has to put in all the political stuff, which to my mind is not necessary.

Also Adolf takes out the jokes.

I think this is a mistake. Life is full of light and shadow. My version of *Mein Kampf* has a lot of jokes.

CHAPTER FOURTEEN

We sat while Harry spoke, and, when he'd finished, one of us suggested we walk on. The sun had slipped behind the mountains and we were into the long twilight. We skipped the rest of the lake path and, instead, went down the other side of the embankment to pick up the Cathar trail as it wandered through fields dotted with poppies. We decided on the short circuit, which goes towards the *route nationale* at the point where the shallow slope of the spur begins that ultimately leads to the castle. This is the edge of the village an only a few farmhouses stand among the fields, so we walked alone.

I didn't interrupt Harry's story as he was telling it, but I knew it wasn't the truth. I'm referring not to the details, which were the usual incredible nonsense, but to the basic narrative line. Whatever Harry had promised, this wasn't the same tale he'd told me the night before. The latter had come back to me while he was talking: not the whole thing by any means but, so to speak, the title. The little piece of history that Harry had imparted on the previous night was how he, Harry Haze, together with Prince Yusupov and others, had murdered Rasputin. It had nothing to do with tonight's story.

When I realised that Harry had gone off on a new track, I said nothing. It wasn't a mistake on his part. He knew I was trying to fill in a gap in my memory and had decided he wouldn't help me. It was to be as if the Rasputin incident had never happened. I don't know why. Perhaps Harry

feared I'd catch him in a contradiction between the first and second versions – though that would scarcely make the incredible less credible. Perhaps I'd failed him by forgetting, and his unwillingness to go back was a form of censure. Perhaps – and this makes a senseless sense to me – Harry's stories were only for telling once. Thereafter they exhausted their magical quality. Like the wishes granted by a genie, once used or misused,
they were gone.

We dragged our footsteps in amiable silence in that last half-hour when the sky is a slice of light over an earth that is already dark and the half-moon, pressing urgently to become full, waits on the horizon for the sun to be finally done. The path now turned sharply as if bored with wandering and wanting to make a dash for the road, home and fireside. At this corner was a blackthorn speckled with brown rags of blossom. Torn and hanging from it was a lady's linen jacket.

The jacket belonged to Lucy.

'Dear God!'

The sound of my voice is locked away in my head. I don't know how it appeared to Harry: whether I cried out aloud, sobbed, murmured or what. At that moment I felt only shock. Horror, sadness, puzzlement: these all came afterwards and then so mixed up and overlaid one on another that I can't put a name to my feelings as if they were a single thing.

'Are you sure it's Lucy's?' asked Harry and he was about to reach out to take the jacket from the branch when I grabbed his hand.

'Don't touch anything!' I'd already seen that there was more: a blouse, a pair of briefs, a shoe. The night was now closing so fast that they were disappearing into blackness even as I saw them.

Harry repeated, 'Are you sure it's Lucy's?'

I nodded. Of course I couldn't be sure. I'd already established, to my shame, that I knew so little of Lucy's wardrobe that I couldn't swear to what was missing or what she was wearing. But I remembered that she had a linen jacket; and, whether I remembered or not, I had that moral certainty which determines our judgments.

'We mustn't disturb anything,' I said to Harry. 'We must' – I put my hand to my forehead as if to stop my head falling off – 'call the police.'

'Johnny?'

'That's what we've got to do. Yes. We mustn't touch anything. We must call the police.'

'That's right, Johnny,' said Harry affectionately, and he put his arm round my shoulders.

It is at the heart of any story that the Reader should be induced to suspend his disbelief. Before that night, however – before, that is, I found myself staring at the rags of Lucy's clothing – I hadn't thought how it is necessary at times to suspend our disbelief in 'real' life.

When I was a child, I had a friend named Alan. We played together with colouring books and soapbox carts and the old gas masks that were found on bomb sites after the war. He was killed in the street by, of all things, a horse-drawn rag-and-bone cart; and I remember him whenever I smell wax crayons.

I think of his parents, who expected, as we all expect, that they would die before their child. At least, that was what they expected until life presented them with the unconvincing fiction that their child was dead, and invited their belief. Did they believe? I mean: did they believe in their hearts? It seems to me that the sudden death of a child is such an outrage against the moral order of creation – against any conception that it may have form and meaning – that I cannot imagine how any parent can truly credit it. Surely, at that moment, the flow of reality would stop, and life, which seemed to be at one with reality, become something other? At such a moment true life ceases and we are compelled to take part in a horrible fiction, and only by suspending our disbelief in this pretence at life can we continue. Yes, I suspect that is how it is. Yet is that all? Or is it that reality, the structure that sustains our faith, does not retreat entirely but waits at the edge of our consciousness? For in our tragedy we live a fictive life as if it were a book that forces itself on our attention. Yet, because it is fiction, it can never fully engage us. So we read the book, not giving ourselves wholly to it, but waiting for faint sounds from outside: the whistle of a kettle which will make the nightcap we drink before we put down the book and seek the bliss of sleep; or the soft crying of a baby alarm which reassures us that our child is alive and well.

'We must call the police,' I said to Harry. I was outwardly calm. The discovery of Lucy's clothes did not mean that she was dead.

We took the path leading directly to the highway on the other side of which soared the spur of rock and the Cathar fortress. There was silence except for the birds settling in their roosts, and stillness except for the circling bats. When I heard the sound of a twig breaking underfoot somewhere in the bushes or the nearby field, I called out, 'Antoine?', remembering the incident of two nights ago, but no one answered. We pressed on.

Harry's house was nearest and we decided to phone from there. I called the *gendarmerie* post at Chalabre, but it was closed. There may be a system for obtaining emergency service in rural areas at night, but I have never figured out what it is. We decided to go down to the bar to get Mike's advice.

Antoine was there when we arrived. He was standing at the football machine, staring at it morosely. I looked at him searchingly. He returned my gaze and seemed to flinch. Then he put down his drink and left abruptly.

'What's wrong with him?' I asked.

Mike tapped his right temple. 'He's crazy. Now, what can I do for you gents? Ricard for you, Harry? You look out of breath, John. Been running? – ha ha – Any news of Lucy?'

This was the question I didn't want to answer. Whether to Mike or to the police, I didn't know what to say. A sentence was trying to form itself on my lips, inviting me to suspend disbelief. 'I think that Lucy's been murdered.' But I could not say it. I *would* not say it. I had no other explanation than murder to account for Lucy's discarded clothes but I could not concede this version of reality. There *had* to be another explanation.

I said, 'We've found something that concerns Lucy. I need to speak to Gérard, the *brigadier* at Chalabre. He's the only person who'll understand me without a long explanation, but I can't get in touch with him. The place is closed for the night.'

Mike accepted my seriousness. He didn't interrogate me. He asked Marie-Paule to tend the counter and invited Harry and me into the back room. He said. 'I don't know Gérard except by sight, but I've got friends in Chalabre who may have his home number. I hope to God this really is urgent.'

'It is.'

'Okay. Then give me a moment.'

Mike began to rummage for his book of private numbers and then riffle through the pages. He made three calls, using a voice that was sociable yet urgent; chewing the fat over kids and weather while trying to get the other party to give him Gérard's number. Harry and I were left to wait anxiously, like persons accused of a nameless crime, who expect to be asked unanswerable questions and in the meantime are left to study the wanted posters and the police regulations as if they mean something. Of a piece with Mike's fantasy, the room was lit by a dull bulb behind a parchment shade; a radiogram in a walnut case with a fretwork front like a sunburst played low music from bakelite records; the window was shuttered and curtained as if in anticipation of an air raid.

'This is it,' Mike said, passing me the number.

I called and a woman answered. I asked to speak to Monsieur Gérard. She covered the mouthpiece and I heard a murmur. 'Hugo, it's for you. An Englishman.'

'Allo?' came a man's voice. 'Gérard here.'

I began. I spoke as if words were stones and I was throwing them by the spadeful into a hole. I mumbled. I apologised. I tried to reach a coherent formulation in the teeth of my desire to disbelieve. I recollected what I was doing and tried to speak carefully like a lawyer obscuring clarity of meaning by precision of expression: choosing my words so that I should not concede that I was convinced by the new turn of events. I merely told a story. I did not subscribe to its truth.

'You are certain that this clothing belongs to Mademoiselle Western?' asked Gérard.

'As certain as I can be.'

'And you have not disturbed it?'

'Of course not!' I snapped, exasperated.

Voices off. Gérard speaking to his wife. He returned to me wearily. 'Very well, Monsieur, I shall come now to Puybrun. I shall be … what shall I say … an hour? Where are you speaking from?'

'The Bar des Sports.'

'I know it. Bien, wait there for me.'

'Well?' enquired Mike.

'He's coming here.'

'I couldn't help hearing. Where did you find Lucy's clothes?'

'On the Cathar trail, a couple of hundred yards from the road.'

'Christ,' he murmured. That was all he said: all the commiseration offered man to man, though it was heartfelt enough. He showed his concern through practical steps. 'It'll be dark there. I've got a torch somewhere. Why don't you and Harry help yourselves to another drink while I find it.'

'I don't want to trouble you, Mike.'

'What are mates for?'

He disappeared to find the torch. I turned to Harry who had said nothing. He was sitting hunched in a chair. His old face seemed desolate and doubtful. At this point someone was supposed to say,' Cheer up: look on the bright side! Lucy may have…' whatever. The problem lay with that 'whatever', that alternative explanation. I couldn't see what it might be and Harry made no suggestion. In the absence of a body, the evidence still pointed unequivocally towards Lucy's murder. And wasn't evidence the touchstone of my approach to the truth? God knows, I had demolished enough arguments because they were not in accordance with the evidence. I'd humiliated less rational minds by that implacable appeal to the facts. In my occasional bouts of domestic warfare with Sally, it had been the principal weapon in my armoury and, if I was intent on getting my own way, I didn't spare to use it. Not that she was impressed. 'All you're really doing is bullying me with your brain instead of your fists,' she said. And on another occasion, 'There's never enough evidence to satisfy someone who doesn't want to be satisfied.' She might have added that, conversely, a believer is satisfied on no evidence at all.

I looked at Harry. That brief reflection on my own mindset made me think of Harry's magic carpet bag, which was crammed full of 'evidence' if one chose to believe it. Faced with a choice between Harry's vampiric existence and Lucy's murder, I would have chosen to believe the former. Almost, I thought, I was free to make that choice, in the way that a fundamentalist chooses to believe the biblical account in preference to the material evidence of evolution.

My mind, unoccupied by action, was rattling down avenues of memory and speculation. I suppose I was experiencing grief and bewilderment. I say 'suppose' because, before this night, I'd seen only the outward effects of grief: Alan's parents weeping at his funeral; Sally at the death of her mother.

The image of a tabloid newspaper headline sprang before my eyes: SALLY HARPER SAYS: 'I CAN'T BELIEVE THAT MOTHER IS DEAD.' Did I really know more than that about how she'd felt?

Another headline: ELVIS ALIVE AND WELL IN BURGER KING! Suddenly it didn't seem so absurd. Rather it was a heroic refusal to suspend disbelief in the face of life's ridiculous fictions.

Rattle-rattle. Thoughts like marbles in a tin. Alan and I used to play marbles. We cleared a space on the bomb site, scooped out a hole and placed in it the rusty ARP warden's helmet we had found. We pitched marbles into the helmet. At the time he died, Alan's parents were planning to emigrate to Australia with an assisted passage. (Flash! Another memory. A certificate given to my Uncle Joe when his ship to Australia crossed the equator. It was this old memory that caused me to think of a shipboard party on the night Lucy and I first had dinner with Harry.) Alan and I promised to meet again when we were eighteen years old. When he died I was too young to grieve. Death and Australia were much the same place. We would meet when we were eighteen. Possibly in a Burger King. Rattle-rattle.

Gérard arrived as promised. He'd come from home and hadn't changed into uniform. He was wearing slacks, loafers, a chambray shirt and a tartan cap. He carried a serious-looking torch. His manner was sombre but as if concerned with his own affairs (an argument with his wife, perhaps?) not mine. We shook hands.

I said, 'This is Monsieur Haze, who was with me when we found the clothes.'

'Monsieur.'

'And this is Mike.'

'I know Monsieur Miller.'

'I'll come with you if you don't mind,' said Mike.

Gérard raised no objection.

We went by the road, which was quicker than the route by the lake. Mike was familiar with the ground and was able to point out where the Cathar trail made its exit on the right-hand side. It was pitch dark, the moon behind a cloud and nothing to guide us but stars and constellations of farmhouse lights in the distance. Gérard switched on his torch; it conjured images out of the blackness, but they seemed flat and unreal like a slide show.

As the path made a turn to the right, I said, 'Here. Somewhere around here.' Mike switched on his torch, which punched a small hole in the gloom. Gérard made a sweep with his. I said, 'There is a' – I couldn't recall the French for blackthorn – 'bush. We saw Lucy's jacket hanging.'

'Hanging?'

'In the bush. It was in the bush.'

My brain fired off another recollection. A film. *The Draughtsman's Contract*. In one of the artist's sketches, the murdered husband's shirt appears laid out on a bush like laundry put to dry. As the beam of Gérard's torch caught the bush, it formed a round vignette of greys and sepias, and in the middle was Lucy's linen jacket, looking improbably flat and creamy as if pasted on to a background.

'There was more,' I said. 'I found a shoe and…'

'Briefs,' said Harry.

'And other things.'

Gérard grunted. He reached for the jacket. I didn't stop him, though my lawyer's mind told me that this wasn't the thing to do: the scene should be photographed before being disturbed, otherwise evidence might be destroyed.

Gérard took down the jacket. He held it out to me and asked, 'Can you confirm this belongs to Mademoiselle Western?'

I said I thought so.

He tucked his torch under his arm so that he could examine the jacket with both hands. It seemed undamaged except where snagged by the spines of the blackthorn. But there were copious stains. Blood, said one part of my mind. Dirt, said another.

Gérard slung the jacket over his forearm. He stooped and began searching the ground beneath. He found the shoe, a flat-heeled, practical pump such as Lucy wore normally. He found the pair of briefs. My throat caught as he sniffed them, seeking traces of urine or semen: traces of fear or violation. He found a skirt. I knew it because I'd been there when Lucy bought it at a shop in Kensington High Street that sold fashions with a certain oriental style. It was of russet cotton vaguely printed with figures as if in batik. A green blouse accompanied it which Gérard produced.

'There is no brassiêre,' he said.

'Lucy didn't wear a bra.'

'Stockings?'

'No.'

And not always knickers, though I didn't say that.

'May I borrow your stick?' Gérard asked of Harry.

'Sure.' Harry gave it to him.

I asked, 'What are you looking for now?' but received no answer. Gérard placed his discoveries on the ground and told us to stand guard over them. Then he disappeared into the undergrowth behind the blackthorn and we could no longer see him but only the fugitive light of his torch; and we heard nothing except his thrashing among the brambles and the alarm call of a disturbed bird.

I looked at Harry, who still had an expression of profound sadness, and at Mike, who shrugged. I said, 'What kind of a bloody fool is Gérard, trampling over the evidence?'

'Strictly speaking there is no evidence since there's no crime,' said Mike. 'Anyway, he seems to know what he's looking for.' He lit a cigarette, one of his Caporals.

'What do you mean, "there's no crime"?'

'Where's the body?'

'The body?' I halted and turned away. And, from somewhere deep inside, the distress and confusion welled up and I began to sob. Then I felt Harry's hand on my shoulder and his kindly voice said, 'Keep your chin up, old man. Stiff upper lip and all that.' Through my tears I smiled at his mock-Englishness. He went on, 'Did I ever tell you – No, no! Not the time. I'm forgetting myself.'

'That's all right,' I answered. I may even have been laughing. Then I said, 'I have something to tell you.'

Surprise.

'You do?'

'I do,' I said, and then and there I told him about Alan and the death of children: everything, including my Uncle Joe's fabulous sea voyage to Australia.

I don't know if this is relevant. It's another story about my Uncle Joe, and I mention it only because I told it to Harry.

My Uncle Joe was a figure of myth. I met him only once as a small child when he and my Aunt Blodwyn returned to England on a visit. Later, when Blodwyn died, I inherited her papers which, in the main, were photographs and a few letters and certificates relating to her career as a nurse. Joe was a publican. The photos of him dating from the forties, show a dapper little man in a double-breasted suit. His hair is slicked back with Brylcreem, his eyes are bright and waggish. His mouth is broad and sickle-shaped and gives the impression of a ventriloquist's dummy. Blodwyn spoke affectionately of him and said he was 'a card', which is what his photographs bear out, for he looks like a music-hall comedian, Uncle Joe the Cheeky Chappy, who refers to women as 'girls' and tells jokes about underwear and Blackpool landladies.

Blodwyn died and her box of memorabilia arrived in the mail. Among the rest was Joe's ancient passport. It showed that for some reason my uncle had travelled to Germany in nineteen thirty-eight. One of the pages was stamped with a visa and the Nazi eagle and swastika, and others contained entry and exit chops.

Now in my fancy I saw that Joe Wilson bore a more than a passing resemblance to another dapper little fellow, Joe Goebbels. The shape of his face, the hair, the suits. And, if these points of fact were true, didn't the rest follow? My uncle was Reichsminister for Propaganda and fled Germany at the end of the war to run a pub in Blackburn and thence, not to Argentina, but to Australia in the company of a plump Welsh nurse. It was possible. Truly – in Harry's fantastic world it *was* possible. All that was required was that I free my imagination and then my existence would depart from its pedestrian course and become a thing of glamour.

When Gérard returned from his ferreting, he found me and Harry laughing. He shone the flashlight in our faces and asked, 'Is there a joke I should understand?'

'No, no,' I answered lamely. 'I'm sorry. I'm very tense. I find it hard to control my feelings.'

'The poor chap is close to a breakdown,' contributed Harry. I remember the word 'chap' – very English – Harry as David Niven.

Gérard waited in case we had more to say and then continued, 'I have found nothing else. We shall have to wait for daylight and then search further.'

'What were you expecting to find?' I asked.

'A body naturally, Monsieur. Mademoiselle Western's clothes are all here. She did not walk away naked from the scene. No attempt has been made to hide the clothes and therefore there is no reason to suspect an attempt to hide any body.' He directed his torch at the ground and said to Mike, 'This path is well used.'

'Yes. It's a trail used by tourists who're interested in the Cathars.'

'So I supposed. A day cannot go by without many people walking here.'

'I shouldn't think so.'

'Monsieur Harper, when did Mademoiselle Western disappear?'

'Let me think. Today is Wednesday. Lucy disappeared on Sunday night or, more likely, early on Monday. I can't be exact as to the time, since I was asleep.'

'You went to bed together on Sunday night?–'

'It may have been after midnight. In fact it probably was.'

'And you woke on Monday morning to find her vanished?'

'Yes.' Stated so flatly, it seemed impossible that Lucy could have gone without my knowing.

Gérard said, 'That is how I understood the position from our conversation at the *gendarmerie*.'

'Yes?'

'And it is most strange.'

'I don't follow.'

'Really? You astonish me, Monsieur. I understood you are a lawyer and used to things such as evidence.' I had nothing to say. He went on, 'The facts are plain. If Mademoiselle Western had been assaulted or murdered here on Sunday, then her clothes would have been found on Monday. A similar point can be made of Tuesday, or indeed of today at any time before evening. So now you understand? Whatever has happened to Mademoiselle Western, herself, her clothes were deliberately placed here this evening.'

He added, 'I think there is an element of a joke in this, don't you think so?'

'It's possible,' I conceded, and I imagine Gérard detected in my sudden levity a confession that I was wasting his time on some strange trick that only the incomprehensible English could play. He couldn't feel, as I did, the sudden rush of joy and hope that Lucy was alive. Indeed it was beyond hope: it was certainty. It couldn't be otherwise. I'd refused to believe in the fiction that had been imposed on me and now, as if in reward for my disbelief, life had relented and reverted to its mundane, credible course.

This euphoria lasted until the following morning, when Harry came to tell me that a body had been found in the lake.

CHAPTER FIFTEEN

Quimby – my Fate, my Fortune, my Kismet, Kiss me Hardy, Kiss my Ass.

In the learned opinion of Dr H. Haze, Emeritus Professor of Comparative Literature (Ted Gottlos Baptist College, Hotzeplotz, Ohio) and distinguished, not to say cultivated, European gentleman, 'quim' signifies in Olde Englysshe the female organ or *cunnus*. Therefore, officer, in the interest of forensic enquiry (if you will forgive my excursion into polysynonymoglossalalia) you may identify the villain under one or more of his many aliases such as: pussy, cunt, vige, snatch, twat, beaver, crack, joy hole, pit, quiff, purse, snapper, trim, ginch, box, furburger, furrow, hairy prawn, lotus, cabbage, couchie, love muscle, chinchilla, kitty, monkey, pink eye, slice, slit, fireplace, oven, cock inn, Cape Horn, snack bar, sardine can, ace of spaces, coffee shop, mink, cuzzy, chacha, twelge, futy, futz, gigi, giggy, jazz, jelly roll, jing jang, nautch, piece, cunny, honey pot, fruit cup, shaf, fern, muff, Garden of Eden, mount, receiving set, goldmine, moneymaker, puka, dark meat, the Y, middle eye, Venus fly-trap, beauty spot, crack of heaven, cavern, vertical smile, baby factory.

I first met Mr Clarence Furburger at the Adlon Hovel in 1933, shortly after Riotous Rudolf (yours truly) – or, more accurately, his Jolly Japers – had burned down the Reichstag.

(Speaking of arson, was it Manny and his boys who actually torched the old place, or did the mad Dutchman, Marinus van der Lubbe, *really* do it? So much in history is unclear, even to its participants. Ah me, the debt to truth is so hard to pay.)

Mr Beaver accosted me and said, 'Please forgive me, Herr Deputy Führer. My card' – forcing a pasteboard on me. 'May I introduce myself? The name is Clarence Quimby. I'm a correspondent for CBS. CBS? You may have heard of us, or met my colleague Bill Shirer? I wondered if I might have a word with you.'

The Adlon was drastically landscaped during the war. So, to continue this conversation, my memory must invent two chairs in red plush, a lobby with marbled columns and potted palms, and an entourage of Hank's charming young men in black, who are eyeing Mr Snatch with a desire to give him a sincere talking-to. Reasonable Rudolf, on the other hand, is comfortable in the glow of a good fire.

'Very well, Herr Quimby. What may I do for you?'

I digress – but all that is of interest in history is digression. There was about Mr Poontang a certain something, a certain *zher ner say quoits* as delicate as the flavour of a small cake (whose shape, by the way, is owed to the pilgrims of St James of Compostella) taken with tea. I savoured it. What could it be? Not Sterno or Thunderbird. I sniffed again. A certain earthiness, as of newly turned clay, leaf mould and those little packets of doodoo that poochikins so obligingly leaves behind. I sniffed yet again. There was no doubt! It was that subtle fragrance Terre de Cimetière ($50 an ounce in all good graveyards), my own favourite perfume.

Gentlemen of the jury! You will learn little concerning Mr Cuzzy from the case of *The State of Ohio versus Haze*, since on the advice of learned counsel and three psychiatrists (Larry, Curly and Mo) the defendant did not give evidence. However, the *Hotzeplotz Picayune* for 1 December 1950 contains a photograph of Mr Quiff (and I swear that in this case I am not making the name up) which shows him to be about forty years of age, bespectacled, with the plump, flawless features of Caspar Milquetoast , and a spotted bow tie. If we allow that fashions in bow ties change, there you have him also as he appeared seventeen years earlier in 1933, which is no surprise since, as with our heroic dead, the Grateful Dead, and the not-so-grateful undead, age did not wither him nor the years condemn.

In addition, the *Hotzeplotz Picayune* ('the Voice of Middle America') had its fact-checkers work overtime to produce the following gem of biographical information, psychological insight and judicious neutrality:

> Mr Clarence Quiff was a news reporter in Berlin during the period of Hitler's rise to power and a fearless critic of Nazi tyranny. After the War, he became a valiant crusader against the virus of Un-American Activities and responsible for uncovering those corrupters of youth and decency who hide behind the mask of our liberties. The alleged offender [I particularly like that fair and disinterested 'alleged'], Harold Hoess, is a stateless alien, also under investigation for degeneracy and perversion – though your correspondent would not wish to prejudice the outcome of his trial by implying that these accusations are true.

There was no doubt from Mr Pussy's silky smile, as we sat in the Adlon at this first encounter, that he had also detected the sepulchral whiff of my aftershave. He insinuated himself into a chair with the insulting familiarity of a cat.

'Well, Herr Hess,' he began, grinning to disclose a set of perfect American teeth (though a little long in the canines), 'it has taken me quite some time to secure this interview. But, now that we *have* met, I feel that we're going to become great pals – in fact, I just know it.'

'That's very kind of you, Herr Quimby,' answered Hesitant Harry. 'But you will understand that my position as a Minister precludes any intimacy with members of the foreign press corps.'

'Of course. You've been a minister from the beginning of the Thousand-Year Reich, and' – he winked – 'who knows, we may both be around for its ending.' I don't believe he had 1945 in mind, the subtle cad.

He had a reporter's pad and a pencil. 'By the way,' he continued with a little moue, 'let me say, *à propos* of nothing, that I admire the Führer's dress sense. Those SS uniforms have a definite funereal chic. Together with Coco Chanel's little black cocktail dresses, they may become the fashion statement of the century.'

'Clothes interest you?'

He fluttered his eyelashes. 'If one is forced to deny oneself the normal pleasures of food and wine, is there anything left? Of course,' he added with slight distaste, 'there is sex. But given our ... um, ah ... medical condition, our amorous transports may result in inconvenient outcomes. And there is, after all, only so much space available to house our loved ones in the backyard, *n'est-ce pas?*'

'Please,' quoth Reluctant Rudi, 'I have other appointments. May we confine ourselves to business?'

'Business? What a wag you are! As if you and I didn't have all the time in the world. And, speaking of time, may I ask: have you read any Proust?'

'No.'

'Really?

'*Ça m'étonne!* Well, I'll send you something, a *recherché* folio that I came across in a dear little shop in Hamburg. But to work, to work! I must put my questions for the benefit of our listeners in the US of A. Tell me, then, Herr Minister, did the Nazis burn down the Reichstag?'

'No.'

'No? So that's your official answer? How disappointing! I'd hoped that, now that we have established our little rapport, now that our two souls are, as it were, as one, you might admit to the teeniest weeniest little flame. No?'

'No.'

'Very well. Next question. Is it true that there is a tunnel from the Reichstag President's Office to the Reichstag? I speak of a little passage that carries the central heating.'

'I have no knowledge.'

'*Trés bien*. Next question. Whaddaya say? Did Herr Goering order his SA leader, Karl Ernst, to lead a detachment of storm troopers through said passage on the night of 27 February carrying gasoline and chemicals for incendiary purposes?'

'I deny it.'

'Excellent! We're getting on famously.' He flipped another sheet on his pad. He murmured, 'Names, names ... Esterhazy, Hess – so confusing. Here it is. Marinus van der Lubbe.' He leaned forward confidingly. 'Can you tell me, Herr Hess: according to my information, in the days when Marinus van der Lubbe still had a head on his shoulders (he having become recently shorter than he was of yore), it was none too good a head: he was, shall we say, a little touched? A little crazy? Far too crazy to burn down the Reichstag on his own. Any comments, pal?'

'He was a Communist terrorist.'

'Succinctly put. You have a way with words, really you have! So there we have it: *"Reichsminister Hess denies that the National Socialist Party had anything to do with burning down the Reichstag".*'

'Exactly.'

'Then that's what will go in my official report.'

'Just so.'

'In my *official* report.'

'I don't follow you.'

'I think you do,' said Mr Futz pleasantly. He leaned back in the armchair I have invented for the purpose, and the shadow of a rubber plant fell across his face, revealing only his eyes glittering like spikes of mica. Cunning eyes – *cunnus* eyes – cuzzy wuzzy little eyes – eyes which, Your Honour and members of the jury, esteemed citizens of Hotzeplotz, would have explained (had you seen them) my implacable hatred for Mr Quim. 'I think that *sub rosa*' – (or did he say '*sub rosebud*'?) – 'you may be able to help me by giving me, strictly *entre nous*, a fuller and more frank account of current events in the Third Reich.'

And thus, as I explained in my many submissions to the Parole Board, I began my career as an American spy.

Before I leave off this section of my history I should like to draw the attention of any surviving Freudians to the use of the *Rosebud* motif in the film *Citizen Kane* (for a fuller explanation, you may refer to my monograph on the subject, which is in the archive of the Hotzeplotz County Sanatorium for the Morally Insane). Learned doctors, knowing what you now know about the symbology of roses, maybe your time would be better spent investigating the subconscious of Mr Orson Welles instead of turning over the grave of my memories. I appreciate that Mr Welles is dead and buried, but who knows what fame awaits him who approaches the subject with a fresh mind, a spade, a crucifix and a consulting couch?

Speaking of films, I should like to apostrophise movie buffs everywhere, and say that you are not alone in your solitary vice. No sirree! From the word go, Adolf and the boys were fans of the silver screen. From the day when, to our surprise, Hitler became Chancellor and asked, 'What the fuck do we do now?' the movies provided the direction of our policy and the solace of our leisure hours. Indeed on the night that Manny burned down the Reichstag, we were watching a movie and shooting the breeze (or do I mean 'sowing the wind'?) *chez* Joe Goebbels.

The Boss's favourite movie was *Lives of a Bengal Lancer*, starring Gary Cooper. Mine was *Queen Christina* because I detected in Garbo that touch of immortality, if you catch my drift. On reflection, I think we'd all have liked *Mr Smith Goes to Washington*, because its tale of how an innocent small-town guy takes on the political system describes what Adolf did.

Not that Adolf spoke like James Stewart, though his voice had something of the other's homespun quality. For further study I refer philologists to the dialect of Linz and the *argot* of the Viennese gutters *circa* the year of Our Lord 1900. It was news to Larry Curly and Mo that Adolf had spent time in Vienna at much the same dates as their revered Sigmund and they wanted to know if the Master and the Monster had sounded the same. For their benefit and yours, I improvise the way that Hitler spoke.

'So,' he said at a *tête-à-tête* a few days after my interview with Quimby, 'Hindenburg, the *alter kocker*, wants I should get rid of Ernie and the SA already. Me! I should tell my oldest *chaver* he's no longer wanted? My father, *alav ha – sholom*, would turn in his grave!'

(I am loath to disrupt the fluency of my narrative by yet another diversion into history but needs must if my case is to be understood: Hitler was Reich Chancellor but not yet Head of State. Hindenburg, giving a convincing show of immortality, was still hanging on. In addition, the Army was keeping a beady eye on the activities of Ernie Röhm and his storm troopers. The latter had it in mind to displace and absorb the Army. A showdown was inevitable, yes indeedie!)

I disclaim responsibility for what followed. As I told His Honour Judge Bullwinkle, at my trial: 'Herr *Justizführer*, I deny all guilt in the case of the Night of the Long Knives.' Perhaps he understood, perhaps he didn't.

He said: 'Professor Haze, I should be grateful if you would confine your defence to your relations with Mr Quarmby. If not, and if you continue to be so excitable, you may be excluded from the rest of these proceedings.'

Very well. But had I not a duty to the integrity of my own memories – to history to forensic science, to alienists and students of aliens? It cannot have been often that a self-confessed thanatophile appeared in His Honour's court with bootleggers and mere child-molesters. Had he no sense of compassion – no sense of showmanship? Apparently not. Larry Curly and Mo took furious notes, and at my side Perry Mason pared his nails, smiled and said, 'Keep going, pal. Either the judge will lose his cool and we'll move for a mistrial, or you'll earn your ticket to the funny farm. Whichever way, you'll avoid a date with Old Sparky.'

As if that were my object! I was expounding philosophy, and these clowns were making a circus out of my agony. These vampires were drinking the blood of my madness and waxing fat on their fees. And when I explained to them that I was the incubus who had fastened on their dreams and feasted for generations on the flesh of their ancestors, what did they do? They laughed!

Meanwhile, back in Berlin we had to sort out the business of Ernie Röhm. Slowly Hank and Manny gathered enough evidence to persuade Adolf that Ernie was planning a coup.

'All right already!' he said. 'So I'm convinced! So the *tsedoodleteh faygeleh* thinks he can take over the show. So what are we going to do?'

Well, as to that, Your Honour, there is no secret. We are going to resort to that universal panacea for the problems of *la condition humaine*. We are going to send Ernie on a trip beyond that bourn from which no traveller returns. We are going to – let's not be mealy-mouthed about this: we are going to kill the son of a bitch before he kills us. Adolf, Rudi, Manny, Joe and Hank are going to whack their old pal Ernie. And while we are about it, and in the interests of economy, we will add to the list of whackees the names of anyone else who has got in the way and one or two who haven't but whose names resemble those of our preferred candidates and, what the hell, they probably would have turned traitor some time or other. It's to be a whacky affair.

Let us return to the movie theatre where we came in. Let us hunker down in the back of our old Packard with a root beer and a sack of popcorn and watch the fun. Let us fumble with a co-ed's brassiere strap while, beyond the drive-in, the night settles over the Ohio cornfields. Are we comfortable in the darkness and the haze of sweat and hormones. the *Nacht und Nebel* of desire? Speaking of haze, old Prof Haze who teaches Comp. Lit. has written a book (or perhaps – more truthfully – has just *read* one) about subtext and intertextuality and Texaco and Tex Ritter and *il n'y a pas de hors-texte* and, well, kind of literary stuff, you know. He says there's kind of a connection between life and art, and art provides a means of looking at life and at other forms of art and yet *nothing* is to be learned from art – at least nothing you can grasp and write down, which is kind of a bummer when it comes to those end-of-semester papers. Prof Haze is kind of inconsistent, kind of nuts, kind of spooky.

Okay, *mes enfants*, here comes the picture, flickering into black-and-white life. It's one of those silent movies of Hollywood's Golden Age of Yesteryear when Comedy was King and we all laughed at the antics of Chaplin, Keaton and Hitler. Here we see Fatty Goering in his famous role in *The Murder of Ernie Röhm*, one of the hits of 1934. Fatty starred with Hitler in such great movies as *The Beer Hall Putsch* (1923), *The Invasion of Poland* (1939) and *The Battle of Britain* (1940). His popularity was at one time almost as great as the Führer's. Ha ha!

And here, too, we have that master of slapstick, Hank Himmler and his Keystone Kops. Sadly Hank's career was brought to an end in his forties by a scandal when he was accused of murdering six million Jews. A studio enquiry found that he was acting under superior orders, but the public never forgave him. He took poison in 1945 and so ended the career of one of the Giants of the Silver Screen.

For your end-of-semester paper, boys and girls, I wish you to write a thousand words on the theme: *'Was the Career of Hitler a Satire against Charlie Chaplin?'* Consider the following points: First, Hitler was a tramp in real life at a time when Chaplin was a tramp in fiction. Second, Chaplin's career was already at its peak when Hitler began his own. Third, Chaplin had obtained the copyright on his famous toothbrush moustache before Hitler adopted it, and Hitler must have known of its comic associations. In your paper, please reflect on the absurd importance attached to comedy as an interpreter of life, and therefore how desirable it may be that life should prick the pomposity of comedy using its own tool of satire. Marks will be given for entirely conventional thinking, or your parents will complain. And by the way, Dolly, I should be grateful if you would not make eyes at Adolf, Manny, Joe and Hank. It distracts them from their classwork and Professor Haze will have to tell your mother.

On my oath, Your Honour, I do not recall if Dolly bought training bras for my darling girl at K-Mart. Indeed I cannot recall if there was a K-Mart in 1948, though I swear by God and *E pluribus unum* that the Patriotic Prof was in America trying to get citizenship at the time. I appeal to your sense of fairness. Given such a failing memory of important matters, how can I be expected to recall in verifiable detail a trivial massacre in 1934, simply on the grounds that I happened to be there? It is this kind of slapdash epistemology and heuristics that has given philosophy a bad name. However, I am now upon my oath, so help me. I promise to speak epistrophe, the whole epistrophe, and nothing but epistrophe. What follows is the lowdown on the Night of the Long Knives.

In reel one of our little movie we have seen Manny and Hank pouring poison into Adolf's ear, so that he can bring himself to whack good old Ernie. The storm troopers have been stood down and sent on holiday. Okeydokey, let's cut to the chase.

Reel two, scene one: the Hanslbauer Hotel at Wiessee (which, by the by, is a nice joint but does not call up the same sentimental associations as the Lone Pine Motel where Dolly and I exercised our philoprogenitive proclivities). Big buck Ernie Röhm is in bed with a young male companion, who is definitely not his wife, no sir. Sadly, movie fans, the career of Loveable Ernie was also cut short in its prime by scandal. He violated the Haze Code and his contract was terminated by the studio. And so into the twilight of that Golden Age passes another King of Comedy.

But I am in advance of my tale. Scene two: a country road between Munich and Wiessee. A convoy of black Mercedes motor cars. Adolf and Hank are in the front. The Keystone Kops bring up the rear, together with the paraphernalia of steel helmets and machine-guns which make these scenes of slapstick so memorable.

Scene three: the Surprise! Adolf enters the bedroom like the unsuspecting husband. Ernie, the Popular Pederast, extracts the old pork sword and pulls the bedclothes up to his chin. Adolf faints into Hank's arms.

FLASH CARD:

ADOLF
My word, these are queer goings on!

ERNIE
Dearest, I can explain all!

ADOLF
Liar! I see from the state of your
shlong that you have betrayed me! You
love another!

Reel three: the Dénouement, or Justice Triumphant. This
contains only one scene: the Stadelheim prison in Munich,
and I'm reminded of Cagney going to the chair in *Angels
with Dirty Faces* (a fate which was spared Hateful Harry
the Hotzeplotz Horror, thanks to the efforts of Larry, Curly
and Mo). Damp-eyed Pat O'Brien begs his boyhood friend
to repent.

FATHER ADOLF
Well, boyo, it looks like this is the end,
begorrah!

TWO-GUN ERNIE
It sure looks that way, father.

ADOLF
Yes. But you know, my son, there's
still something you can do – something
for all those young, idealistic Nazis out
there who still look up to you.

ERNIE

I've told you already, Father. I won't play yellow for nobody!

Enter HANK. He is solemn and carries a gun.

HANK

I'm sorry father, but his time is up.

ADOLF

Do you hear that, Ernie? Once more, I'm begging you – for the boys! God will know that in your heart you weren't yellow.

ERNIE

Tell me, Butch, is there a guy with a white hat out there? (*In tears*) Where am I?

ADOLF

I guess it ain't Kansas.

ERNIE

(Shaking *his head sadly)* Of all the prisons in all the world, you had to come into mine.

HANK points the gun. *Blam! Blam!* Ernie falls dead, but – this being 1934 – we aren't allowed to show the blood.

FADE TO CAPTION:

THE END

CHAPTER SIXTEEN

When Harry told me how he came to write *Mein Kampf* he said that a story, like life, should have light and shade. I could think of other pairs of opposites: sophistication and vulgarity, action and reflection, interest and boredom, clarity and obscurity. The list of antitheses stretches as far as language. It came to mind because the existence of these contradictions marked, so it seemed to me, a boundary between life as it's lived and as it's narrated. No story, if it's to be successful, can wholly accept life's ragged plotting, its failed outcomes, its unexplained events like unsolved murders; or depict life using its true palette, with shocking contrasts in one place and muddied colours in another. Narrative imposes form and coherence. Life resists both.

For example: Hitler was a farter.

Sally used to comment that my memory and education were like an old lumber room where I staggered in darkness, stumbling over relics of things past. My occasional fanfares of erudition were a toot on a broken trumpet found in an old toy box. I dimly recall a historian who said that bad guts and a vegetarian diet made Hitler fart. During his rise to power he flew around Germany in a light aircraft with Ernie, Manny, Joe, Hank (and Harry Haze, if you believe him), and the boys gagged as the Führer tooted his anal trumpet. The Reich was conquered in a whiff of rotten eggs.

If that tale is true, it's pure Harry and enough to make me wonder about everything else he said. But my interest is, for the moment, not in validating Harry's histories, but more in the way that a small detail can change the impact of a painting or a story. The Nazi episode has been translated into stark and terrible theatre: dramatic in its narrative line; uniform in its tone of unrelieved blackness. But how would it be if suddenly the stage were occupied by Hitler the Farter – Hitler the Clown? Though the fact of horror would remain, would not the mystic images dissolve; and, in the world of symbols, would the Third Reich evoke any more resonance than the tinpot regimes of a thousand other shoddy dictators?

Returning to the Bar des Sports with Harry and *Brigadier* Gérard after our discoveries on the Cathar trail, I found my mind turning over these points. Granted, it was strange that I should think of Harry rather than Lucy, but I can't answer for the workings of my brain under stress. Although I was clinging to a hope that Lucy was alive, any effort at calm reflection was battered by anxieties. In the end, all that Gérard had done was indicate the oddities surrounding the finding of Lucy's clothes: the anomalies of timing; and in these facts alone lay my grounds for hope, when every other circumstance cried out that Lucy was dead. So, as we walked back in darkness and silence, my thoughts turned to other matters, and I don't find that so surprising.

My notions about the relationship between art and life are commonplace enough, and if they rested there they wouldn't be worth mentioning except as a trivial detail. But, that night, they came to me with a peculiar force that seemed beyond their merits. Bewildered by Harry's stories, Lucy's disappearance and the ridiculousness of my own position as the errant husband, I felt my existence teetering between reality and fiction. And in this situation the most banal ideas, which on the surface lacked any novelty even for me, suddenly seemed fresh and powerful, and, God help me, it was as if I had received a revelation.

We entered the bar and Mike called to Marie-Paule to fix a drink for me and Harry. Gérard declined to join us and left for the comforts of home. Antoine hadn't returned. Harry downed his Ricard and I my brandy, and we left together, ambling up the lane, across the highway and on as far as La Maison des Moines, where we paused and he proposed a nightcap as I knew he would. I took a seat while Harry busied himself with the glasses. I rested my head on my hands, feeling it spin with half-formed thoughts and emotions.

When Harry had handed me a cognac and taken a seat for himself, I said quite abruptly, 'I don't want to talk about Lucy.'

'I understand.'

'Do you?'

'Sure, Johnny.'

'Good. Then tell me a story.'

He did: the one about how he first met Clarence Quimby, and some other stuff about the Nazis in the nineteen thirties. As he did so, a false memory came to me.

I am ten years old. It is night and I am wearing striped pyjamas and a dressing gown of maroon wool and sitting at the dining table playing with my Meccano set. Outside it is dark and raining. Inside it is warm. My mother is studying the *Radio Times*; my father is watching television and his face shimmers with black-and-white reflections. The only other light is from a standard lamp covered with a shade printed with a hunting scene, which is by my mother's armchair. My mother says, 'Arnold, they're showing Quatermass at nine.'

She nods sideways in my direction and my father says, 'That's enough for tonight, John. A story and then bedtime.' So the television is switched off and my father takes down a copy of *Jennings* in a red cloth cover from a shelf where a row of books is supported by a wooden elephant and a brass model of a Spitfire. My father reads a chapter to me, as he does every night.

As I've said, this is a false memory. I didn't have a Meccano set, being too ham-fisted to manipulate the tiny nuts and bolts. My father never read to me that I can recall. He was a more physical man and used to spar with me or play rough-and-tumble games on the floor. The memory which came to me quite vividly as I listened to Harry was no more than a pastiche of images of forty years ago. It was false, but its vividness was as sharp as if it were true. Make of that what you will.

I was still putting in the odd hour on the Great Indian Novel. (GIN – gin? As it happens, the arbitration in India involved a fair quantity of gin, an association as firm as rum and the Royal Navy. One of my colleagues was a Scot named Fergus who each evening, when we returned to our hotel, would drink a glass of gin mixed with a feeble local tonic water. He would sigh over the result and then reminisce about his ideal recipe of Bombay Sapphire and Schweppes, for which he claimed to be famous in the golf clubs of the Wirral. And, as he told this story with such sparkle and relish we would be lifted from our mundane surroundings – armchairs in the executive lounge of the Delhi Sheraton, surrounded by attentive Indian waiters, and listening to the clamour of the roseate-necked parakeets which nested in the trailing plants that overhung the window – and be translated to a fabulous country near Liverpool.)

Harry came rapping at my door at about eleven as I was writing. I called out, 'Come on in, it's open,' and, putting down my pen, asked, 'Would you like a coffee?'

He seemed busy and excited, like the little guy in the Western, who breaks into the barber's shop to announce, 'Marshal, the Clancy boys are in town!'

'What's wrong?' I asked as I took steps to fix the coffee.

'They've found a body by the lake.'

I put the percolator down. 'Is it Lucy?'

'I can't say. French policemen don't tell you very much. The village is full of them.'

I felt an odd calmness, perhaps an effect of shock. I said, 'I think I'll have some coffee anyway.' I set about the task, feeling very conscious of my own physical movements, at once slow and precise. 'How do you know?' I asked.

'I was taking a walk. I didn't get as far as the lake before I found the lane full of cars and people.'

'And they couldn't tell you? Who found the body?'

'I don't know.'

'I see. Sugar? You take sugar, don't you, Harry?'

'Yes. You don't seem very concerned.'

'Milk? Yes, I am concerned. I just feel … strange. Last night, I was certain that Lucy was alive.'

'Maybe she still is.'

'Maybe.'

We drank the coffee. Harry picked up his stick, and I took a hat to guard my eyes against the dazzling sunlight. We set off together down the lane by Lo Blanc and across the highway into the village, which was peculiarly alive with doors and windows open, quite unlike most days, and caught in that moment of brightness when the sun is almost overhead and for the space of an hour the street isn't closed in shadow. I was conscious of the gaudy boxes of geraniums, and these, the sunlight and the stir of people gave almost a festive air.

I noticed that the door of the Bar des Sports was ajar. Evidently Mike hadn't been able to open his place by the lake. I stuck my nose through the door and called, 'Mike?'

'Hullo?' Mike emerged from the back of the bar. Seeing me he said, 'Christ, it's you. Hi, Harry. I take it you've heard the news?'

'Harry told me. Is it Lucy?'

'I can't say for certain, but I don't think so. Someone – who was it? – said it was a man's body. Probably one of the Germans went swimming last night and got into trouble.'

'Let's hope so. I mean...'

'Have a drink. It's bedlam down there at the moment. I don't...'

'I'll take a cognac.'

Mike poured the drinks, brandy and Ricard as usual. He took a seat on our side of the zinc and said, seriously, 'I still think there's hope for Lucy. There's something odd about what we saw last night. Everything seems to have been placed deliberately and Gérard is right about the timing. Lucy disappears on Sunday night and her clothes are found on Wednesday lying where anyone can see them. It makes no sense.'

'That's true. But the whole incident makes no sense. Why did Lucy vanish?'

'Only you can answer that.'

'Me?'

'Who else?'

Indeed, who else?

We finished the drinks and Mike called to Marie-Paule to say we were going down to the lake. As we walked through the village square I was conscious of being the object of scrutiny. It was known that Lucy had gone and now, *mon Dieu*! it was possible that this tawdry affair of the English was altogether a different matter, *qu'est-ce que vous pensez, Madam?* Madame thought it was a very fishy business; and, in all honesty, I agreed with her.

The path by the cottages with their flower borders was surprisingly clear of vehicles. The police hadn't cordoned off the whole lake. Whatever had happened had happened at the furthest end, away from Mike's refreshment hut. It was an area which to my eye had always been a little mysterious. Though in no sense remote, it was some distance from the car park, the strip of sand and Mike's place. The osiers were denser there and a stretch of rushes grew in the shallows. Sally had often scanned it for reed buntings and I'd painted its secretive corners, though they'd proved less mysterious on closer examination. The discovery of an occasional pair of tights or used condom had exhausted their nefarious possibilities.

Here by the hut a crowd had gathered, mostly of summer visitors so far as I could judge. The girls had the air of flirtatiousness that seems more acute the further away they are from home, and the boys that additional hint of swagger. Some adults were there and one of them called out, 'Herr Mike, you open for some beer, hein?' and Mike, a little embarrassed, said he thought he would. I was reminded of those accounts of the eighteenth-century theatre, where the audience went to be seen, gorged itself on food and made discreet love in the boxes while ignoring the actors. The patch of trees and shadows formed a stage and I could imagine someone remarking casually, 'This is the part where Macbeth murders the King. I've seen it before.'

Mike was soon in business and jabbering to his customers. Harry and I decided to get closer to the scene by taking the path through the osier avenue but didn't get far before we were turned back by a gendarme. We returned to the hut and I ordered a beer since the sun was still beating down.

Mike said, 'I hear they've identified the body. It's Edouard Moineau's lad. Do you know him? You do, don't you, Harry?'

'He's run the occasional errand for me.'

'What's he like?'

Harry shrugged. Mike said. 'He's ... what ... thirteen or fourteen, wouldn't you say?'

'About that.'

'A cocky little type, the sort you can imagine getting into trouble.'

'Did he drown?' I asked.

'Franz, the fat guy over there, found him at about eight o'clock when he was walking his dog. He was in the water, bollock naked, so he may have been swimming. But Franz doesn't think so.'

'No?'

'His head was bashed in. He could have fallen, I suppose; or dived and hit his head; something like that.'

'His family...?' My first notion came from my prejudices. I saw a black-clad widow in the last stages of distress, making furious and frantic appeals to the Virgin, while her other sons stood around her: dour unshaven men in caps and waistcoats who carried shotguns. On reflection it was more likely that the Moineau boy's mother was in her thirties. I saw a woman with bleached hair and pale legs who had married a husband with a fondness for beer and Alsatian dogs. By one of life's dispensations, the children of such women seem to die in their cots or in house fires.

'He lives with his dad,' said Mike. 'His mum died of breast cancer. Do you know Edouard Moineau?'

'No,' said Harry. 'Only the kid.'

'You're not missing anything. He's a piss-artist. I've had to bar him from my place. He sits at home and drinks. I don't think he does anything else much.'

'Is that Antoine?' I asked. I pointed to a figure at the farthest point along the sand, where one of the gendarmes was holding him back from the scene-of-crime tape. I debated whether to go over and speak to him. It was still in my mind that Lucy thought she'd seen him haunting her on the night of her disappearance – and then, last night, I'd been conscious of someone in the darkness near the blackthorn bush. Of course, neither person might have been Antoine: indeed, I couldn't be certain anyone was there on either occasion. Mike proposed another beer and, in my lassitude, I accepted; the next time I looked up, Antoine was gone.

'I'm going home,' I said.

'I'll stay,' said Harry. I thought the old man looked distraught and puzzled. Since calling at Lo Blanc he'd exchanged nothing but a few clipped sentences. Perhaps I should have pressed him as to the cause of his troubles – with hindsight, I think I should – but I was inexplicably tired. Although it was barely eleven o'clock I wanted to go to bed.

I strolled back through the village. I paused at the grocery to buy some dried spaghetti and a bottle of wine. The heat was more than I could bear, but no more than I was used to in India, and I wondered if I'd caught a bug of some kind which might account for my general malaise. The death of the Moineau boy also disturbed me; not because I saw any connection with Lucy but for quite the opposite reason. Perhaps because I refused to accept that anything untoward could have happened, my concern for Lucy seemed factitious, even shameful. The boy's death on the other hand was real and wholly credible: one of the shabby tragedies that afflict the poor everywhere. He would be buried not with the pomp of kings but to a chorus of reproaches and family quarrels: and instead of sermons there would be whispered lectures from ignorant relatives about child-rearing, and an uncle from Tourcoing or some other god-forsaken hole would get drunk and tell jokes.

A police car was parked outside Lo Blanc and the door was open. I caught a glimpse of Gérard, who, today, was in uniform. He noticed me, came out and offered a handshake.

'I am sorry to have entered without your permission, Monsieur Harper. But you were not at home and we thought you would not mind if we came in and searched for anything that would tell us the whereabouts of Mademoiselle Western. Something you may have missed, for example.'

'We? You said, "we".'

'I have a colleague with me. He came because of the other matter – I see you know of it – and thought he would take the opportunity…'

'You think there's a link?'

'Who can say?'

'I thought the Moineau boy had an accident?'

Gérard said nothing. He merely gave me a look of sadness mixed with curiosity.

I couldn't be bothered to argue the proprieties of this intrusion. I followed Gérard into the house and saw that he and his companion had been turning over my possessions. The other man was in one of the bedrooms. I offered to make coffee – tea, or coffee? sugar and milk? – and made a few remarks about being anxious to help. Perhaps I added sarcastically that I was glad they'd finally decided to take Lucy's case seriously.

The other man emerged. He was in civilian clothes: loafers, slacks and a well-made tweed jacket, an ensemble that in France can pass for business wear. I estimated he was forty years old, a neatly made man with small, neat features, light brown hair and round spectacles of the kind worn by intellectuals and torturers. He smoked Marlboro cigarettes and I would have bet that his tipple was malt whisky.

'Monsieur Barrès,' said Gérard.

'John Harper.'

We shook hands. He was a Freemason and I wasn't.

'Please be seated,' he said politely. 'Gérard has apologised, I think, for entering your house when you were not present.'

'Yes.'

'You are not angry?'

'No.'

'Excellent!'

I waited, preparing myself to discuss Lucy. Forgetting present circumstances, it was always difficult for me to speak of her. Some older men take pride in having a young mistress, but I wasn't one of them. I always felt like a fool who'd got into this situation because I'd misunderstood something.

Perhaps that's one of my better qualities. Barrès, however, didn't appear to have Lucy in mind.

'Pierre Moineau…'

'Yes?'

'You knew him?'

'No – at least, I don't think so. I may have seen him about the village.'

Barrès tendered a photograph. I recognised a travelling fair that had been set up on the open ground by the lake. A boy and girl stood laughing. He wore jeans and a T-shirt. She wore a blouse tied to expose her midriff and a short denim skirt. They looked the sort of kids who maintain their self respect by laughing at older, richer people without knowing why. I pass them by in their thousand and pay them less attention than I do beggars.

I shook my head.

'Can you explain your movements last night?' asked Barrès.

'From what time?'

No answer.

'I was with Monsieur Haze.'

'Haze? He is also English?'

'No. He is – I think he holds an American passport.'

'Go on.'

'We spent the early part of the evening at the refreshment hut by the lake.'

'Doing what?'

'Drinking, talking. This must have been before the boy died.'

'What makes you think that?'

I was a little impatient with Barrès's even tone. 'It's fairly obvious, isn't it? It wasn't dark before nine, and the boy couldn't have been dead so early or he would have been seen. The lake was crowded with tourists.' I looked to Gérard for support.

'Continue,' said Barrès.

'We went for a walk, along the Cathar trail. Monsieur Gérard knows about this. We found Lucy's clothes and then went back to the bar and telephoned. What time did you arrive?'

'About eleven o'clock,' said Gérard neutrally.

'Eleven, that sounds likely. We kicked around in the bushes until midnight or so, and when we'd finished I went home.'

'Directly?'

'What?' I paused to recollect. 'No. I went to Monsieur Haze's house and we talked for an hour. I got home at one thirty or two this morning.'

'I see.'

Barrès took notes. Gérard simply stared first at me, then at his hands, then at me again.

'Who proposed the walk?' asked Barrès.

This was a question I hadn't expected. I couldn't see any immediate relevance to the case of either young Moineau or Lucy.

'I can't remember,' I said.

'Please consider harder.'

I did, but for the life of me I *couldn't* remember. It was too ordinary an event, too unimportant a detail.

'Why do you want to know?' I asked.

Barrès tapped his pen against his notepad for a moment and then said mildly, 'I was reflecting that Mademoiselle Western's clothes seemed to have been arranged so as to be discovered. So I ask myself: did you ask Monsieur Haze to take a walk so that *he* would find them or did he ask you to take a walk so that *you* would find them?'

Now I understood. But I still couldn't answer. Certainly I hadn't contrived to discover Lucy's things, but I couldn't exclude the possibility that I'd suggested to Harry that we go for a walk. I wondered what Harry would say.

CHAPTER SEVENTEEN

From the interview with Barrès and Gérard I wasn't certain whether they were asking me about Lucy's disappearance or the death of the Moineau boy or both; or if they saw a connection between the two events. The conversation ended inconclusively and they went to pursue their enquiries in the village. I made myself a light snack. Too disturbed to work on the Great Indian Novel or my notes of Harry's stories, I decided to go for a walk.

Apart from the path round the lake and the excursions along the Cathar trail, my favourite walk was in an anticlockwise circuit that took me round the castle rock and back to Lo Blanc via the cemetery. It meant a short stretch alongside the *route nationale* in the direction of Quillan, then a turn by a steep path through bushes past a votary chapel that celebrated a small nineteenth-century miracle. This path led to a shallow saddle that linked the fortress on its spur of rock to the higher reaches of the hills, from which there was a descent on the further side through thickets of hawthorn and broom to the graveyard. The saddle was high enough to offer a panorama of Puybrun and the lake as far as the distant cliffs and crags that enclosed the basin. The Cathar trail could be seen as a narrow line snaking among the fields.

It was too close to high summer to take this walk at noon, but I hadn't considered the weather. I heard singing from the chapel, where I paused for breath. I remembered that it was tended by a group of ladies who had the bright copper hair that afflicts French women in middle age. Lucy and I had once gone inside and listened to the choir practising. They were trying to raise money for repairs and explained politely how the chapel had come to be built. The Blessed Virgin had saved the patron from a shipwreck somewhere in the Indies and he'd dedicated it as a testimony of faith. Unfortunately, no endowment had been provided, and wind and rain had damaged the faux marble columns painted on the walls. I rather liked the place for its faded, gimcrack prettiness.

By the time I reached the high point I was in a sweat. The sky was a glassy whiteness. A lark was singing, but when I looked for it my searching eyes were dazzled as if I were trying to penetrate a vision: a painting, perhaps that of the Holy Spirit descending as a dove. When I looked away, I found that the earth itself dazzled me: that sunlight lay on the land like a hoar frost at the point where the air itself freezes and everything dissolves in a liquid of mist and light.

I heard the clock of the church of St Hilaire chiming the hour. From here the steeple dominates the view of the village, defining it as a village rather than town, and acting as a point around which the cottages compose themselves so that they form a picturesque whole rather than a straggle of buildings. The same overall impression of Puybrun may be gained if it is seen from the lake or as one descends into the basin by the highway from Lavelanet, though there are crucial differences: in particular from the viewpoint of the saddle the Cathar fortress is invisible, while from the others it stands in different degrees of counterpoise to the church, and those views are therefore more dramatic. In itself the church is unremarkable, even dreary.

I thought of another landscape, not so dissimilar in general concept, though very different in other respects. It had been our habit, when Jack was a child, to holiday in the west of France, Brittany or the Dordogne, and to take the ferry between Plymouth and Roscoff. Near the latter is the pretty town of St-Pol-de-Léon which boasts a cathedral and a fine church, the Kreisker. There are three steeples, but they are quite different from the steeple of St Hilaire. Whereas the church of Puybrun has in itself no beauty but borrows it from its situation, the steeples of St-Pol-de-Léon are pierced in the Breton fashion so that they form a lattice of granite and sky, a juxtaposition that prevents them from being static; for, as one approaches the town by roads bordered with fields of artichokes, so the three spires change, each in relation to the other two like parties to a stately dance, and also each in itself as the sky-lit apertures in the stonework open and close, slowly like a lizard's eye or glittering like a diamond, depending on the speed of the car.

Within Puybrun, like a prophet in his own country, the church of St Hilaire is not significant. From the narrow streets, overhung by the houses, it is invisible and a stranger visiting the village may not realize it has a church. But then – and always with a degree of surprise – one emerges from a lane that is bound in shadow like a prisoner in chains into the sudden sunlight of the square, and the church is there in its brilliant dullness, its exciting tedium. It is a shock that may cause a visitor to enter the building, thinking there may be more; and, indeed, he or she will, at first glance, find more.

In the chancel is a window dedicated to Albert the Good, Comte de Puybrun at the time of the Albigensian crusade; and in the opposite space one to his ancestress Geneviève, Châtelaine d'Échalote, descendant of the Merovingian kings. However, examination shows that the windows date from the year 1920 and are dedicated to somebody's son who died in the Great War. Other bits and pieces of decoration possibly refer to Masonic or Rosicrucian symbolism. There is an unspoken hope in the village that an American student with a doctoral scholarship will take the geography of the basin, the iconography of the church and the unrecorded history of the castle, and by geomancy, necromancy and any-othermancy construct a cosmology out of Gnosticism, the Templars and the Maya, which will solve the Mystery of the Universe – or how to make money and sleep with attractive people without working or being good-looking.

It should be clear that there was no consistency to my thoughts, which seemed to rise and fall without purpose like a kite on the thermal currents of midday. The highs were my recollections, glimpses of the past with Sally and Jack that were at best poignant and at worst painful. The lows were a mélange of loosely connected thoughts and vagrant humour. Or possibly I've invented the highs and lows, since no description is perfect. Such coherence as existed was external. It lay in the heat of the sun, which agitated a flow of thought and emotion outside their usual congealed boundaries. Turning from these events of the mind, I saw the sun-bleached, sun-misted landscape again and, as the sweat dripped from me, melted into it – not like water but like syrup.

I lay back exhausted and shut my eyes, though that scarcely diminished the glare, and felt my body flowing away. This was accompanied by a mental detachment – I am careful not to say clarity. In a flash of insight I realised that I was experiencing a revelatory moment of the same kind as I'd had in the café at Chalabre when the objects around me had for an instant lost their quality as objects and become reified metaphors for obscure memories. Again, I could feel the stirrings of recollection. This time of a villa we'd rented in the mountains overlooking the coastal plain at Mojácar. In the mornings Sally and I would take breakfast on the terrace and watch the blue-greys of dawn illuminate two hills which stood alone and abrupt in the middle of the plain, so sudden in fact and so well-formed by the elements into the shapes of pyramids that they seemed to be not natural features of the landscape

197

but rather the tombs of mighty kings, sealed and bound with spells, and standing sentinel against invasion from the sea. Nor was this air of solemn magic fleeting or a mere effect of dawn and distance. As we pottered about in our hired SEAT, sightseeing and supermarketing, so we would see the various facets of these grave monuments at midday and in the evening: lit now on this side and now on the other according to the sun's path until they finally dissolved in dusk and shadow. And always I had the same feeling that, in their grandeur, they were simply enclosures for some further secrets that were deep, dangerous and magnificent.

However, today I was tired of revelations that revealed nothing, like the burning bush without the voice of God. I told myself, no doubt accurately, that I was under stress and putting myself in the way of a dose of sunstroke; and that, just as the incident at Chalabre was brought on by alcohol, so this one was only another effect of my disturbed physical equilibrium. In short, there was no wisdom to be obtained from these visions.

I opened my eyes and at once saw that the lark had dropped from the glassy reaches of the sky to the softer blues where it met the ground. I got to my feet and now, having shaken off the heat-induced trance, felt businesslike. I looked down to the road and saw a police car parked at the end of the Cathar trail. Further examination gave a glimpse of a couple of men beating the blackthorn bushes at the turning of the path where Harry and I had found Lucy's clothes. In my detachment I felt vaguely pleased that the police were treating the matter seriously: pleased in the way that, I suspect, distraught parents are when they appear on television to make appeals to a murderer to give himself up; which is to say that, however futile the gesture, it relieves suffering to be the centre of attention.

When I returned to Lo Blanc I noticed a postcard on the floor behind the door. Lucy and I received little mail and I wasn't in the habit of checking. We'd given few people our address, though my credit-card company had found me and was spreading the good news to sellers of things I didn't want. The card was addressed to Lucy and bore a Greek stamp and a scene somewhere in the islands. The date was three weeks ago. The message read:

Dear Lu

  Theo and I have finally tipped up on Mnemonikos after the horrors of Athens. Sun, donkeys, ouzo and all the usual stuff one remembers about Greece. The VW was impounded in Piraeus, but the fine will probably be cheaper than the cost of parking. We leave here tomorrow, and, if we can get the van back, intend to return to England toot sweet since we've run out of money. Now for the bad news. We may drop in on you and the Bozo for a few days before the last leg of the drive home. No need to make a fuss: the fatted calf will do for your prodigal sister, and the Bozo can show Theo the fleshpots of Puybrun (ho! ho!). Until then …

  Love
  W

Presumably 'W' was Willie and I was 'the Bozo'. The insult was gratuitous since I'd never met Willie and I couldn't imagine Lucy had called me 'the Bozo': more likely it came from Willie's feelings about the old guy with the limp dick who'd seduced her sister (by miraculous means, one supposes). That, however, didn't concern me since I enjoy my own prejudices and don't begrudge them to others this side of violence. More curious were Willie's message and the date of the card. Giving in to my prejudices – i.e., assuming Willie to be a disorganised tart and Theo a dubious Greek – it was reasonable to allow an extension to the indicated itinerary. Add a couple of days to leave Mnemonikos and another couple to clear the van from the bureaucrats in Athens. Allow a further week for a journey from Athens to Puybrun that could be done in two or three days. In theory – quite a reasonable theory – Willie should have arrived at Puybrun before Lucy's disappearance, had she kept to her intentions.

Clearly Lucy hadn't seen the card. She would have told me about it and wouldn't have left it on the floor by the door. It would seem almost equally obvious that Willie hadn't turned up; she'd been delayed or changed her plans. (I imagined her lifestyle as chaotic and impulsive.) If she had reached Puybrun, then again I would have expected Lucy to mention the fact. At least that would have been the natural course of events.

But the natural course of events was precisely what had *not* happened. Lucy had vanished, and that stark fact had to be explained. I speculated. Had Willie arrived in Puybrun on Sunday evening? Had she come to the house unannounced that night while I was asleep and had a conversation that had caused Lucy to leave urgently? I could make obscure sense of this scenario, but if it were true why had Lucy left no note for me and why had her clothes been found on the Cathar trail?

I considered a more sinister variant of this scheme. Willie had arrived on Sunday and come to the house at night. She and Lucy had talked and either Lucy had left the house, thinking that she was stepping out only briefly (say, to look at something in Willie's van), or there had been a quarrel and in either case Lucy had been abducted (Theo acting the part of a Greek cut-throat for this purpose). Hence, Lucy's departure would be sudden and there would be no note.

Whether or not this supposed encounter between the sisters had occurred as I imagined it, it was possible that Willie had come to Puybrun – even that she was still in Puybrun or nearby. How should I know, when I'd never met her? She could pass unrecognised among the tourists. The only risk of identification would be if she and Lucy bore a striking resemblance – if they were twins, for example. This nagging possibility, for which I had no evidence, came back to me; and although in common sense I should have dismissed it, I couldn't. The mystery of Lucy's fate had such a factitious quality that I was searching for the element of contrivance: the convenient symmetries that my dear Agatha Christie would have invented to unravel the plot. Willie's involvement (with its hint of sibling rivalry dark passions and family inheritances) provided that missing element which seemed to me so necessary to complete the story.

I was making myself a cup of tea when I heard a car pull up outside. I glanced through the window and saw Gérard and Barrès. I anticipated them by opening the door before they knocked. Gérard made an apology for calling on me again and seemed to mean it. Barrès, on the other hand, was impatient with such politeness and eager to be at me with whatever questions he had to ask or information to impart. I decided that, while I rather liked the *brigadier* for his air of grave decency, I didn't care for Barrès. He had a foxy intelligence – genuine, but too overt and self-assured.

They came inside. I offered seats, which they occupied, and drinks, which they declined. I took a seat, too, and composed myself to convey the impression of someone who wished frankly to co-operate; but in fact I felt like a habitual liar whose dishonesty must be patent on his face, though I'd no idea why I should feel like this when I didn't even know the reason for the second visit.

'We have some further questions,' Gérard began.

'About? Are we talking about Lucy's disappearance or the accident to the Moineau boy?'

'You think it was an accident?'

'Excuse me? Isn't it? I'd assumed…'

'Possibly.'

'I … I've no opinion one way or the other.'

'Between accident and what?'

'Do you suspect that Pierre Moineau was murdered?' intervened Barrès.

'No!' I said emphatically. 'I don't have an opinion. I don't know anything about that case.'

Gérard and Barrès exchanged glances and I had a vague sense that our conversation had gone in an unintended direction, in the way that sometimes Sally and I had argued about some trifling matter only to stop suddenly and wonder how a perfectly normal exchange had diverted itself and whether we had the courage and wisdom to abandon the argument, even though that meant that one of us would 'lose'.

Gérard resumed. 'We should like to go over the events of the last few days again.'

'Very well. What do you want to know?'

'On Sunday night you had dinner with your American friend, Monsieur Haze?'

'It was his birthday.'

'And you returned home…?'

'Probably some time after midnight. I can't be certain. We were drinking and not paying attention to time.' In fact we were doped and didn't know our own names.

'You woke up on Monday, and Mademoiselle Western had disappeared?'

'Yes.'

'And…'

'Yes?'

Gérard sighed. 'You did nothing in particular during the rest of that day?'

'I made some enquiries in the village. I think I phoned Lucy's doctor in Pamiers. I assumed that I'd forgotten something – that Lucy had told me where she was going and that, if I waited, she would come home.'

'Then on Tuesday you came to the *gendarmerie* at Chalabre and you made your report to me.'

'Yes.'

'And afterwards?'

'Pardon?'

'Afterwards,' said Gérard patiently. 'What did you do afterwards?'

'Does it matter?'

'Please answer,' said Barrès with a smile.

'I returned here to Puybrun.'

'At what time?'

'At...' I searched my memory for a guide to that day, but certainty was lost in the fitful amnesia of alcohol. 'I think it was about seven in the evening. I went to the Bar des Sports. Mike may be able to give you a better idea. I was...'

'Yes?'

'Drunk.'

At that I heard a mental Aha! from Barrès.

'You left the *gendarmerie* at one. You should have been in Puybrun by two or two thirty at the latest.'

'I...' What *had* I done after I left the *gendarmerie*? 'I went to a café. I can't remember the name but could point it out to you if necessary. I had a drink there – several drinks, I suppose.' Yes indeed: several *large* dinks. I remembered passing the time having visions of the past and the present and, though I hadn't thought about it, must have spent three or four hours there if my timing for my arrival at Mike's place was even halfway accurate. I said, 'I don't see how anything to do with Tuesday is relevant.' Gérard appeared not to hear me. He made rapid scribbling motions with his pen, as if the flow of ink had stopped.

Barrès took up the thread. 'So you returned to Puybrun – *drove* to Puybrun in an intoxicated state?'

'I suppose so.'

'And were in the Bar des Sports for seven o'clock.'

'Thereabouts.'

'And then?'

'And then … I phoned England, to try to contact Lucy's sister in case she had news, but couldn't reach her. Then … Harry – Monsieur Haze – came into the bar and we talked.'

'Until?'

'Until…' I tried to concentrate, but my memory wouldn't yield anything more of that evening. Harry and I had talked, and he'd told me another of his stories, and then … 'I can't remember,' I said, and explained with every appearance of guilt, 'I was under a lot of stress. I drank myself stupid. One moment I was in the bar talking to Harry and the next I was in my bed with a hangover and it was Wednesday. Why does this matter?' I repeated. 'Who cares about Tuesday?'

Barrès had a bag with him. I was reminded of Harry's Magic Bag, though this one was plastic. It seemed I was going to be presented with evidence, and I wondered, as I did with Harry what it would 'prove'. Barrès was clearly pleased with himself, even smug. He produced a ladies' leather purse.

'Do you recognise this?'

He meant was it Lucy's purse and I felt a flush of shame. I did not recognise it. I had paid no attention. I shrugged. Barrès smiled and opened it.

He dealt a series of plastic cards, snapping each one down: Barclaycard, a Debenhams charge card, the swipe card that gained access to my London office (evidently Lucy had forgotten to turn it in when she left). He produced a few hundred francs in cash and a miscellany of receipts. I wasn't surprised that these objects were Lucy's, but I couldn't escape the ominous implications. Without cash or credit, Lucy hadn't hired a car or taken a plane. In fact she hadn't gone anywhere.

I sighed. It is curious how in life the display of emotion is more restrained than in art. Sally and I used to laugh at the exaggerated enthusiasm of sexual scenes in films and the sweats and screams of childbirth. Thinking of my friend Alan, I can imagine circumstances in which death is greeted with cries of grief. But even in that case, since I knew his parents, I find it more plausible that the news of his death was answered with a discreet sigh. *'I'm afraid your son is dead.'* Sigh. *'You must appreciate, Monsieur Harper, that Mademoiselle Lucy is dead.'* Sigh. Barrès didn't in fact say that, but he implied it, and I replied with my polite English sigh.

'Do you have anything to say?' he asked.

'No. Have you found anything else?' I meant a body.

Barrès smiled and produced a watch. For once I recognised it: Cartier, very elegant and simple, with a plain black leather strap. 'It's Lucy's. I bought it for her.' I saw that it was broken and felt a fugitive and inappropriate flash of annoyance that such a lovely and valuable object should be ruined.

'Have you found Lucy?' I asked slowly.

'No,' said Barrès. 'You think she is dead, then?'

'I don't know. It seems so.'

'You are taking that prospect very well.'

I tried to suit my posture to that of an innocent man, and failed. 'I've had four days to get used to the idea. Is there a body?'

'I just said not.'

'So you did. I forgot.' I held out my hand, thinking to take the watch; thinking to hold something that had touched Lucy's skin. But Barrès withdrew it.

'There are some strange circumstances surrounding the watch,' he said more briskly. 'I am speaking of the time and date.'

'Oh?'

He leaned over. I don't know if he expected me to bleat out a confession or what. He said, 'It seems, from the time and date, that the watch was broken at eleven thirty on Tuesday evening. Where were you at eleven thirty on Tuesday evening?'

'I don't know. I've already told you, I was drunk. Mike – Monsieur Miller – or Monsieur Haze may know.'

'We shall ask them,' said Barrès and leaned back. He put away his bag of tricks and then simply looked at me, inviting me to go on. I glanced at Gérard, who was silent, solemn and sympathetic.

Finally Barrès said, 'Perhaps you now understand some of my difficulties concerning time. According to you, Mademoiselle Western disappeared on Sunday night or, more probably, in the small hours of Monday morning. But according to her watch, she was alive and active until late on Tuesday night, *after* you had reported her absence. Still more curious, it seems impossible that her clothes and possessions could have been placed where they were found until Wednesday afternoon or evening.'

'I see your problem.' I added, lamely, 'I don't know what answer to give you.'

Suddenly I realised, with a sense of relief, that Barrès was as tired of me as I was of him, and that his shrewd and knowing air was, as much as anything, a pose to impress Gérard. In one of my rare moments of insight I saw that he was a simple provincial detective who, if he'd ever handled a murder enquiry before, knew only those cases which involved the disorganised poor: the miserable, murderable women and children who are killed by husbands, boyfriends and stepfathers. At night the cities are lit by their burning apartments. In daytime the murderers blink before cameras and appeal to the public to help solve their crime.

'We are going now,' said Barrès, 'but I do not doubt we shall return. In the meantime you should think about the events between Sunday and Wednesday. We must investigate this lost time.'

CHAPTER EIGHTEEN

Perhaps I should have been thrown into confused speculation about the anomalies Barrès had disclosed concerning the events between Sunday and Wednesday evenings. Instead, once he and Gérard had left, I went to bed and slept for a couple of hours. In retrospect I sometimes amaze myself.

Barrès, of course, was right. There were holes – lost time, if you like – in accounting for Lucy's movements. If I were to be believed, Lucy had vanished on Sunday night. Yet her watch suggested she was alive as late as eleven thirty on Tuesday evening. Yet again, her belongings had been disposed of in the blackthorn bush some time late on Wednesday. There were plenty of grounds for speculation if I thought of Lucy – if I could bring myself to think about Lucy. Instead, I slept.

When I reflect on the year that we spent together, I realise that I wasn't in search of a lost time. It is sometimes thought that a middle-aged man who finds himself in my situation with a younger wife or mistress is trying to relive his past, but this isn't so. On the contrary he is trying not to relive but to eliminate it, as if the years between thirty and fifty have never happened. And the past resists: it recurs in habits of thought, speech and action, in flashes of recollection and longer spells of brooding in quiet moments when one's guard is down. For me, memories which would have been irrelevant or merely the subject of sentimental reflection had acquired a new and sinister potency, changing their character in the way that one's attitude to a familiar friend might change when, coming home from work, one finds him taking tea unexpectedly with one's wife. Then, though the circumstances are outwardly innocent, and though his conversation is amiable and much as always, one looks at him with different eyes: eyes filled with distrust and dislike; and, even when he makes his excuses and goes, he leaves the essence of himself behind to poison a quiet evening, always with a promise of his return. Between Lucy and me, the past intruded like an adulterer.

In my struggle to eliminate the past, I eliminated the present. Our months spent in Puybrun were not spent in true time, in a true present. They were an escape from the commitments and difficulties that engage us and ground us in the flow of true time. Of course, our days were filled with events which gave the impression that life continued in the normal way, a sequence of real events as tangible as objects. But this was not so. The happenings at Puybrun were like those in a story, carrying conviction for so long as we believed in Puybrun like the text of a book, only to become unreal and implausible when, for whatever reason, the covers were closed.

As I say, once Barrès and Gérard had left, I didn't think about the present, I simply went to sleep.

At six I got up and ambled to the lake, thinking to get a snack at Mike's refreshment hut. My mood was too torpid to cook. The mad glitter of midday had gone, and the sun, which had almost deranged me, had settled into gentleness and the air was soft with blues and golds, as if I were seeing the world through cataracts.

The police had disappeared from the far end of the lake except for a small roped-off area guarded by one gendarme. Mike gave me the time of day and I ordered a beer and some *frites*.

'What's new?' I asked. 'Have you seen Harry?'

Mike flipped a finger. I followed it and saw the old man cruising on his back in the middle of the water.

'The story,' said Mike, 'is that young Pierre had his head bashed in.'

'Who told you that? I thought the French police never gave out information.'

'His dad.'

Mike pointed to one of the further tables, where a man was sitting over a glass of wine and staring over the lake. He wore a broad-brimmed straw hat. His face was middle-aged, weather-beaten and unshaven, but strangely gentle and intense. His clothes were old-fashioned and comprised a blouson and baggy trousers in faded blue cotton or linen, and he wore clogs.

Aware of my own gaze and Mike's upon Édouard Moineau, I was reminded of a picture, *The Boyhood of Raleigh*, in which two children listen enraptured to an old seadog who tells a story while at the same time appearing not to address them.

'Likely as not, it was his dad who killed him,' Mike went on, speaking remotely as we watched Moineau. 'Assuming that he was killed. I can't see any connection with Lucy,' he added, meaning to cheer me up.

I nodded. Of course that was the explanation. The mute, disorganised poor, doing the decent thing by keeping their misery to themselves and murdering each other. Édouard Moineau and the boy lived alone in a cottage like a pigsty full of empty Valstar bottles and mouldering food. The boy would have gone to the bad, so what was more natural than that his father should do us all a favour by slaughtering the brat?

He glanced round and I saw that he had melancholy, alcoholic eyes, large, wet and seeming to nestle in folds of damp brown tissue paper.

'I want to talk about Tuesday night,' I said to Mike.

'What's to talk about? You were drunk and a fucking nuisance, though that's forgivable under the circumstances.'

'I don't remember. Tell me, what time did I leave?'

'Search me. Ten o'clock or thereabouts? Harry helped you home.'

'I went home?'

'I'm guessing. Ask Harry if you need to know. I was just glad to see the back of you.'

'I'm sorry about that.'

Mike shrugged and, as if to confirm my forgiveness, pulled the tab on another beer.

Harry came out of the water, rubbing himself down. He paused as he passed Moineau, exchanged a few words and patted him on the shoulder. It was in small things, especially timing, that I noticed Harry's moods. I mean, for example, a fraction of delay in smiling an otherwise conventional smile; a second pat on the shoulder rather than just one. It's conventional, if accurate, to say that comedy is a matter of fine timing, yet no one says the same of sadness, even though the smiles on the masks are but a flicker apart. Admittedly the timing is what makes comedy – what's the word? – funny. But doesn't it also make sadness sad? At all events, according to my two-beer philosophy, Harry seemed sad. And yet the low sun sparkled in his white, water-beaded hair as if he were an angel.

He said: 'Hi there, amigo.'

'Hullo, Harry. I hadn't realised you knew…'

'Moineau? Sure, to talk to. I used to pay his kid to … aw, fuck it, Johnny. The poor son of a bitch…' He paused. *'Quel dommage.'*

He ordered a beer from Mike, stared at it and fooled around as if it was a TV recorder and he wanted to record some time next week, and then looked at me.

'Any news of Lucy?' he asked.

'Why do you care?' I asked. I surprised myself by my cruelty. But I'd seen him sympathise with Édouard Moineau, and when you sympathise with everyone you sympathise with no one – or, from another viewpoint, the miserable are selfish. I added while Mike's back was turned, 'After all, you're a Nazi vampire, *n'est-ce pas?*'

Harry smiled an accidental kind of smile, like a fold in melting wax. 'A palpable hit!' he drawled softly (*pace* Sir John Gielgud). 'But feeling is not morality, dear boy, and even a monster may experience pain. Himmler – and I speak as one who knows – absolutely *hated* killing Jews.'

'That's tasteless,' I said, annoyed.

'So was the Crucifixion. Are you having a bad day, dear?' He coughed.' Hey, *hombre*! What say we take a walk?'

I paid the bill and we walked.

Or, rather, Harry shuffled.

'You don't seem well,' I said, concerned.

'Lucy, the Moineau kid, heroin – three things I love and miss. I need a fix.'

'I'll take you home.' He was shaky and I put my arm under his. 'How old are you?' I asked.

He seemed to consider the answer. 'Six hundred.'

'Liar!'

'So I rounded the number. So sue me.'

'I love you, Harry!' I joshed. I don't know if I was drunk or becoming American.

'I know. It's a vampire-thing.'

We reached La Maison des Moines and the door was open. I led Harry inside and dumped him in a chair. All his stuff for injecting, including a dinky spirit burner, was on a table beside him. I murmured 'Christ!' and went to make some tea.

I returned. I don't know much about heroin. In fact, I told myself as I looked at the old guy, I know several people who don't take it. After an hour or so he came back to life and felt like talking, but in the meantime, as he dozed and murmured in his obscure dreams, I gazed on him tenderly – as tenderly as Himmler, a simile which few but Harry would understand.

I asked, 'Do you know anything about Lucy's sister? Was she ever mentioned?'

'Willie? Lucy said something, not a lot.'

'Go on.'

'Willie was the wild one.'

'That's it? How old is she?'

'Their ages are fairly close.'

'Are they twins?'

Harry looked at me wearily. 'So you're going back to that theme? I don't know if they're twins. There's no reason to suppose they are. And what does it matter?'

'Did Lucy tell you that Willie was planning to visit us?'

'No.'

'A postcard arrived. I don't think Lucy saw it. If Willie did what she suggested, then she would have got here a week or so ago – before Lucy disappeared.'

'It doesn't ring any bells.'

'Have you seen anyone about the village who might be Willie?'

'No.'

This was futile, and I changed the subject. 'Do you remember Tuesday night?'

'Sure – though you don't seem to recall much.'

'I don't. I came back from Chalabre drunk and went to Mike's bar. What time did we leave?'

'Ten thirty.'

'Mike said ten o'clock.'

'Maybe ten. No one was paying attention to the time. Mike asked me to take you home.'

'Did you?'

'You were restless, upset. You wanted to hear more about my life.'

I waited, wondering if Harry would admit to telling me the Rasputin story or if he would persist in the fiction that he had told me of his life as Rudolf Hess.

'We came back here,' he continued. 'You had another drink and smoked some dope. I shot up some shit and we dozed for an hour or so. Then I told you the tale.'

'And when we were finished?'

'I walked you home.'

So far so good. But I wanted to be clear on one point.

'What time did I go home?' I asked slowly.

Harry gave me a cautious look. 'One o'clock.'

'Are you certain about that?'

'Of course I'm not certain,' he answered testily. 'I was out of my head on smack. It could have been later.'

'Could it have been earlier?'

'A little, maybe.'

'Before eleven thirty?'

'Not a chance. Definitely not this side of midnight.'

'You would swear to that?'

'If you like. Now what's all this about?'

I told him about the finding of Lucy's watch. That it had been broken at eleven thirty on Tuesday night.

'You see where the police are coming from, don't you?' I said. 'They think I was lying when I reported her disappearance. They think Lucy was alive as late as eleven thirty on Tuesday, and suspect that I killed her.' I paused. 'But I couldn't have, could I, Harry? Because I was here – with you.'

'That's right, *mon brave*. You were with little old Harry Haze.'

I was with Harry Haze. He was my alibi. 'It's all right, officer. At the time of the crime I was smoking dope with a Nazi vampire who was shooting heroin and telling me how he murdered Rasputin or wrote *Mein Kampf*. I'm not certain about this last point, but maybe it doesn't matter. The thing is: Harry will swear it's all true.'

On reflection I realised that, even with these limitations, Harry's testimony wouldn't get me off the hook. If he was right, we'd returned to La Maison des Moines at ten thirty, and almost immediately Harry had injected himself with drugs and passed out for an hour or more. Who was to say what I did during that time? I *could* have gone out. I *could* have killed Lucy at eleven thirty and then gone back to wake Harry. It wasn't true and it made no sense of Lucy's disappearance almost two days before. But it didn't necessarily have to make complete sense, since I was clearly a madman; and, in any case, the police didn't believe my disappearance story.

Another point occurred to me. One I didn't like. If Harry was my alibi, so was I his. But the truth was that I couldn't swear to where he was at eleven thirty on that night. Maybe I'd inverted events. Maybe it was I who had lain in a stupor at La Maison des Moines, and it was Harry who'd gone out and killed Lucy. That made no more sense than the first version but, again, did it matter? I was reminded from my legal training, and not for the first time, that explanations were rarely complete: that, in the complexity of real events, exiguous details intruded, unconnected facts that were only coincidentally contemporaneous with the issues in question, and which would always remain as unexplained anomalies spoiling the perfection of any solution.

I looked around the room. It was littered with Harry's drug-taking kit and his carpet bag stood in the middle of the floor. And I remembered that the rest of the furnishings had nothing to do with Harry. I recognised the deep sadness of his existence. He was an old man with nothing but a few pathetic possessions and equally pathetic stories. I wondered if there were a real Harry Haze, with real memories and a real history or whether he had killed his past even more comprehensively than I had killed mine.

I said, 'You need to tidy this place up, Harry. The police are going to pay you a visit and we don't want them to drag your old hide off to prison.'

'It wouldn't be the first time.'

'Tell them that we left Mike's bar at ten or ten thirty and you took me directly home. Forget about the rest of the stuff.'

Harry seemed deflated. He answered: 'If you say so, Johnny. But I don't mind telling the truth.'

The truth: the good old 'T' word.

'Oh, I really don't think we can do that, do you, Harry?'

I needed a drink and so I went to Mike's bar. He'd returned from the lake.

He asked, 'How's Harry?'

'He seems depressed.'

'It's this business with Pierre Moineau. He really liked that kid. I liked him myself, the poor little bugger. He was always up to tricks. He was the sort who was always at the hospital with a cut or a broken bone. I'm not surprised that he had an accident.'

'Was it an accident?'

'Who can say?'

Marie-Paule poured a beer from the tap, slapped it on the zinc and disappeared into the back room.

'Was it something I said? Is she cross about Tuesday?'

'No. She likes you. She liked Lucy too. She's annoyed because she had some washing out to dry and it's been stolen.'

'You're joking!'

'Scout's honour. It's the third time.'

'That often?'

'It happens all over the village. I had an idea that Pierre was doing it and I tried to catch him out. But apparently I was wrong.'

I asked, 'Have the police been to see you?'

'They came down to the hut. They asked if I'd seen Lucy on Monday or Tuesday, and I said I hadn't.'

'Anything else?'

'Stuff about whether you and Lucy seemed happy together. Whether you quarrelled. Things like that.' He smiled. 'I told them you were a pair of lovebirds.'

'How did they react?'

'Gérard played the sphinx, but the other one seemed disappointed. He asked about Tuesday. I told him you came in drunk and left with Harry at about ten. What else could I say?'

'You did right.'

Mike said, 'They think Lucy's dead, don't they?'

I nodded.

'What about you?'

'I don't know. None of it makes sense. All I want to do is sleep. I think I may be grieving for her, but I can't tell. I've no experience to compare it with.'

'Don't start drinking.'

I glanced at the beer, which was still untouched, and realised that I didn't want it. I'd spoken the truth when I said I wanted to sleep. Leaving the glass, I made my farewell and took the path home to Lo Blanc.

Sally was there.

CHAPTER NINETEEN

An unfamiliar compact blue Renault saloon was parked in the lane. The door to the house was open and I detected movement. I felt a surge of anger, thinking that Barrès had returned and was turning the place over again. Then I caught sight of Sally and, in my surprise, all I could say was, 'Christ, you're the last person I was expecting!'

She came out to meet me and, with only a flicker of hesitation, gave me a kiss on the cheek. I hadn't expected that, nor its peculiar quality. It was more than a dry peck, and although it did not linger as long as it once would have done, it seemed filled with unfeigned affection, so that I felt a frisson of physical shock mingled with guilt.

'I've only just arrived,' she said. 'I've made a pot of tea. I hope you don't mind.'

'No, not at all. You're looking well.'

She was slightly tanned, which was unusual for her fair skin. She had re-styled her hair. It was auburn with streaks of white at the temples, which she didn't bother to colour. We'd joked that I had enough money to give her a face and boob job if that was what she wanted. As I say, it was a joke. Sally preferred to look her age, and she wore her fifty years gently, keeping her elegant figure and her bright eyes. Because of those eyes and her high cheekbones, I thought she would always look beautiful and, even though I'd run away with Lucy, I found her sexually desirable: a desire to which she had responded with soft and mature enthusiasm. Today she was wearing a sleeveless cotton dress, very simple but attractively printed in scarlet and yellow. She had very little desire for jewellery and only for

218

silver, never gold. I'd offered to bring emeralds or rubies from India, where they could be picked up cheap, but she'd always refused in favour of a plain necklace or ring, decorated perhaps with a single semi-precious stone. Nothing had changed except that, wearing sandals for the summer, she'd taken to painting her toenails, something she'd never done before.

We went inside. Sally poured tea with a little milk. 'I couldn't find any biscuits,' she said. She took her cup to a chair and sat with her back to the window: behind her the evening sky was banded in turquoise and cinnamon.

'I thought you were in Spain,' I said. 'Jack said something...'

She smiled. 'Jack never pays attention. I've been with the Mortimers. They've taken a summer's lease on a place near Montaillou, so I've not been far away. But it's awkward being single, and there's a problem with the swimming pool. So generally it's not been much fun.'

'What made you come here?'

'I phoned Jack yesterday and gathered from him that you were having some difficulty.'

'Lucy's disappeared.'

Sally's cup rattled briefly. 'Left you?'

'I don't know. I don't think so. The circumstances are ... peculiar.'

'How?'

I looked at my watch. 'Are you intending to drive back to Montaillou tonight?'

'I haven't thought. No, I suppose not. Are Mike and Marie-Paule still running the bar? They have a spare room, haven't they?'

'Yes.' And so had I. But I didn't suggest that Sally take it. I wasn't certain of the exact terms on which our relationship stood, and a sudden cold thought had come to me: the construction that Barrès would place on the situation, with Lucy gone and Sally moving in with me.

'You sound worried for her – for Lucy,' she said. The note of sympathy was quite genuine. She'd known Lucy and met her several times in that year or so before we'd run away. I even caught them discussing me – wife and secretary – at some dinner or other. It was odd to think that, before the fateful Christmas party and the shabby hotel in Paddington, there was a period in which Lucy and I had worked together and I had thought, wrongly as it turned out, that I had no more than a fatherly feeling towards her. I lay claim to a natural kindness and this hid the trap into which I was falling. I simply couldn't imagine abandoning Sally, and it followed that my feelings for Lucy were not such as could lead to that conclusion. This same kindness condemned me to go the whole hog once I'd been overwhelmed by Lucy's attractions. I was unable to sustain a cynical duality of wife and mistress. Though I ruined my marriage, I would, in an imitation of decency, be true and faithful to Lucy.

I went to the telephone and put through a call to the Bar des Sports. I told Mike that Sally was here and enquired about the spare room. I sensed Mike's curiosity and it sparked my own. I wanted to know: exactly *why* had Sally come? Was the explanation really as simple as the one she'd given? It's a feature of my character that I'm given to contemplating hard, cruel thoughts. I don't mean that I hold to unreasonable jealousies and suspicions: simply that I can face up to the questions, if only to analyse and dismiss the answers. And the matter which troubled me now was this. When my mistress had disappeared, my deserted wife had been only a short drive away.

When the call was finished, Sally asked, 'Well? Are you going to tell me what's been happening?'

It was unreasonable to refuse an explanation, but I felt reluctant. It seemed indecent to discuss Lucy with the woman I'd betrayed, and, moreover, impossible to think of a way of telling the story in language that did not reveal that I loved Lucy: that I was grieved and confused by what had happened. I had to assume, from the trouble she'd taken, that Sally wasn't indifferent to me. Was I now to trample on her sadness and memories?

However, it had to be done and I did it as best I could, keeping the story brief. I stayed away from the detail of our life over the last year at Puybrun, and confined myself to the events following Sunday. I didn't mention Harry except to say that we had a friend. The facts were absurd enough without piling the old man's craziness on top of them.

'I've never heard anything so strange,' Sally said thoughtfully.

No? I asked myself. You should listen to Harry.

'Neither have I. It makes no sense.'

'Presumably it will in time.'

If I had difficulty in describing Lucy to Sally, so I have difficulty in describing Sally to anyone who cares to listen. A true image is overlaid by the distortions caused by my own sense of guilt. There was no rancour between us, but to say that we treated our situation 'in a civilised manner' or 'like adults' is to convey an impression of coolness and detachment that was never there. Yet I'm conscious that in setting down the words of our conversations, our tactful, reasonable language, that is exactly the impression I may give. The problem is that one has to be present in order to understand. One has to place the words in a context of gesture, facial expression, the exchange of glances. Sally was a strong person but strong through her gentleness and sympathy – a description which is accurate but misleading if it suggests a nice, homely little wife. In fact she had a career of her own as the director of a children's charity and was used to tough decisions and unfazed by them. But none of this seemed to affect her inner core or shake her quiet integrity.

You may suspect that we had a good marriage and wonder why I gave it up. It *was* good. It was always good. The years didn't make our affections stale or convert life into a routine so emotionally flat that one doesn't realise one is unhappy. I stepped out of my marriage like a man stepping out of his house, expecting to return home that night to its warm comforts, only to meet with an accident. It may be said that a failed marriage must have had an inner flaw, but I don't see it; I can't accept it. There was no flaw in the relationship, only in one of the parties to it. As I say, I am clear-minded in normal times and able to think hard, cruel thoughts. And it isn't a sense of guilt particular to my break-up with Sally, but the cool contemplation of a lifetime that explains my predicament. At heart I'm a fool.

So I told my tale and Sally listened with genuine concern. And when I'd finished, we had to talk about something else. I didn't want to go over the history of the last year under the pretence that we were making nothing but small talk. Instead I commented that I was being troubled by flashes of memory.

'What do you mean?' asked Sally curiously.

I was uncertain how to explain. 'I find that, if I don't keep control of my thoughts, they wander off into the past. I don't mean that I keep mulling over events as if I regret them and dream of putting things right. Rather my memories are sense impressions: images, scents, tastes; and the stories that go with them. It's more like day-dreaming, I suppose. Some of the things I think of are genuine memories. Others aren't. I don't know where they come from – books or films? Whatever, they seem to explain whatever impression it is that I have in mind.'

Since she was clearly interested I told her of some recent occasions: at the café in Chalabre; the business of the Malabar wrappers; the heat-exhausted vision I'd had only that day while walking near the castle.

'Were you drunk?' she asked with not very serious malice, which made me grin.

'I admit to being drunk at Chalabre. I had an excuse,' I added hurriedly without going into it.

I recounted the various things that had passed through my mind at the café and paused when I came to the image of the old woman imprinting her wrinkled lips on the rim of a wine glass. That wasn't a recollection of anyone I'd seen. The sight of the wine glass hadn't stimulated a memory; it was more like a premonition. The old lady was an archetype, an emblem of the end to which all women would come. She, or someone like her, was a version of what Sally or Lucy might change into when worn down by years. My cold reason had forced her before my eyes so that I could contemplate her and say to myself: this is the end of everything – this is the woman you must love if you are to know what it is to be faithful.

The story of the Malabar wrappers passed off more light-heartedly since it was a shared memory, and we spent a happy half-hour rehearsing the incidents of our holidays in France when Jack was a child. This was the conversation that I couldn't have with Lucy and – God forgive me – it felt so good that I could almost forget her. At the end Sally said, 'From what you tell me, your flashbacks seem to be a sort of Proustian recollection.'

'No,' I said, shaking my head, which was still filled with thoughts of Malabar wrappers. 'Well, perhaps in the vulgar sense: in the same way that we say "Freudian slip" or "Machiavellian" when we've never read either Freud or Machiavelli.'

As a matter of fact, it wasn't strictly true to say I'd read no Proust. There was a time – when I was nineteen or so and a student, which is an heroic age for reading – when I felt that I could manage anything. So, after limbering up on *War and Peace* and *Ulysses*, I felt ready to tackle *A la recherché du temps perdu*. It would be right to say that I do not remember the book in any detail, only the experience of my attempt on it. It had no aesthetic or literary component, only a sheer physicality that had to be attacked by blocking out all sense impressions, like a boxer with deadened nerves who persists by act of will despite the bludgeoning he has received. So I would become engaged, as if in the thraldom that must affect a man caught in a whirlpool, in Proust's seemingly interminable sentences with their cascades of dependent clauses (and the parentheses which would lead one into them as if they were just a short aside, but which would come to dominate the sentence as if the words before and after them were a skin sloughed by a snake revealing the essential snake within) the similes which, in a similar fashion, would begin as illustrations of the matter under comparison, only to go off and become small stories of their own, stories of a strange and inappropriate character, not true similes at all, like a remark made by a man whom we have met on a train and whom it would be impolite to interrupt, who under the pretext of making some point chooses to elaborate it from his own experience at such length that the illustration becomes the history of his life and we are at once fascinated and repelled; yet sentences that never wholly forget their thread, but, like a mountebank on a high wire, teeter either side of meaning without ever wholly losing their balance, so that after every diversion (no matter how long and parenthetical) they resume their course and purpose and, spun with other sentences of the same character, form eye-defying paragraphs that one reads at a rush in the hope that one can reach the end before dying for want of breath.

At the end of *Swann's Way* I put the book down and said to myself, 'That's that!' and turned to reading murder mysteries. I considered this pause after the first volume a sort of base camp at which I would recuperate and gather strength before scaling the central massif of Proust (before reading *Lucille disparue* perhaps). However, I have remained for ever in this temporary refuge, only occasionally venturing out of my tent to test the weather before retiring to warmth, a cup of tea and a paperback. Not that I have entirely forgotten the experience. Occasionally, other readers with their teams of sherpas come to my camp, glance up, dazzled, at the heights and ask, 'Have you done Proust?' to which I reply, 'I've been up by Swann's Way,' as if it is an old and familiar path.

It is impossible to predict the effect of a book. For the most part it goes into the general stock of knowledge and when it emerges later, processed and distorted by our own experience and understanding into forms the author would not recognise, we are unable to attribute the idea or attitude to its source, or even know that it had a source outside our own wisdom. This element of the subjective was apparent to me as, fascinated and baffled, I tried to quarry some meaning out of Harry's stories. And my debt to Proust? Who can say? I doubt he would recognise it. I doubt he would have predicted it. The fact is, it was my encounter with Marcel Proust that gave me a life-long love of Agatha Christie.

Sally and I didn't pursue the subject beyond that brief exchange concerning 'Proustian recollection'. I waited for her further reaction to my tale of memories and visions, but she was too tactful to give it. I've said that I don't think they were fuelled by regrets for the past, even though many of the memories were of times with Sally and Jack. But that was an obvious interpretation and I suspect Sally made it and then decided wisely that it was a conclusion I should come to by my own efforts. My own opinion is that I was struggling towards a point more obscure but more truthful. In my blind and foolish way, I believe I was trying to understand the significance of memory and shared experience as a foundation for love. I hold to the view that, despite my selfishness and folly, I have a loving nature. And though I still felt the symptoms of love within me, both for Sally and for Lucy, I had (I now realise) somewhere lost its essence. My memories were not an attempt to recover Time. They were an attempt to recover Love.

Tonight, however, we were just chatting as old friends who have known each other a long time.

Sally said,' I see that someone has been working on the garden here. But it needs watering.'

'That was Lucy's handiwork. I've forgotten to water it since she … I'll do it tomorrow.'

'If you remember.'

'If I remember.' I laughed. The failings of my memory, so far as the chores and details of everyday life are concerned, were a regular subject of good-natured criticism from Sally. I warmed at this familiar joke. I asked: 'How is the garden at home?'

Sally smiled with pleasure. 'Thriving! At long last I've done what you never got round to doing. I hired a contractor to deepen the fish pond, so that instead of a foot of water, we have six feet in the deepest place. I've bought some Koi carp – absolute monsters, but they should do fine.'

'And the heron?' There was a grey heron that cruised the area, dining off garden ponds.

'I asked Barbara' – a sculptress friend – 'to make me a dummy. She has, and it's a beauty – you'd love it.'

'I probably would.'

'And it seems to have done the trick.'

'Are the flowers good this year?'

'The drought hasn't helped. Spring was lovely, with a fine show of bluebells under the trees.'

I nodded in agreement with her satisfaction. The garden was her especial delight. We'd bought a house with a wilderness. Sally had designed the garden and did as much planting and maintenance herself as she could. We hired a service to do some of the regular work and I provided unskilled labour. The result was the fruit of ten years' effort and itself had a history. Sally would look at it and tell when and where she had acquired the plants and describe the campaigns she'd fought to landscape each portion. We could, of course, have hired a designer and contractor to do the lot in a season, but that would have gone against the grain of her character. It was a matter not just of prudent economy (which she hadn't forgotten from the early days when we struggled), but of creativity. Sally had no talent for craftsmanship. Even my tatty paintings and inept attempts to write were beyond her. But she needed an energetic and creative outlet to relieve the stresses of her work, and the garden was it.

Sally recounted with relish her gardening year, and I sat placidly with a smile on my face and drifted off into one of my trances of memory while outside the night closed in.

She took an overnight bag from her hire car, leaving the latter parked in the lane, and I walked her down to Mike's place. She proposed a nightcap, which I declined, and we parted with another exchange of kisses on the cheek. I walked back past La Maison des Moines; I noticed a light burning and considered paying Harry a visit. On reflection I decided not to. Since he wasn't expecting me it was quite likely that the old fellow had given himself a treat – a good fix of heroin and sweet dreams. A bleak image formed in my mind of Harry in his drooling decay. That was the reality and it was only the spells he conjured which prevented me from seeing behind the robes of the magus to the seedy fraudster within. I'd no desire to detract from the feeling of inner calm I was experiencing, and so I passed on. I remembered that I'd failed to ask Sally how long she proposed to stay.

Sally came for breakfast at ten the following morning. I'd already watered the garden. We sat outside and ate melon and some croissants she had bought warm from the baker.

She remarked, 'I've seen a very odd man in the village. He looks like a bumpkin version of Elvis Presley.'

'That'll be Antoine.'

'Has he always been here? I don't remember him from our previous visits.'

'I think so. But he's a farmer, so normally he's out working in the fields. Did he do anything? Was he behaving strangely?'

'Not exactly, but he looked not altogether there.'

I felt confident enough of Sally to say, 'He was in love with Lucy, the poor devil. She was kind to him – used to play on the machine at Mike's, dance with him, that sort of thing.'

'Well, you never were jealous.'

'No. Even so, I didn't particularly approve. Antoine isn't very bright and I fancy his life has been spent pretty much around Puybrun. He doesn't have the ability or experience to judge situations. I thought Lucy risked giving him a false impression.' I remembered the mysterious figure in the lane and told Sally the story.

'You mean he's a stalker?'

'No. Things never got as far as that, and I may be mistaken, but Lucy and I both thought it was possible that he'd taken to following her.'

'Do you think he could have hurt her?'

'I doubt it. You know as well as I do that educationally backward people are no more inclined to violence than the rest of us. Antoine's never struck me in that way. But he may be confused and love-sick.'

'I fancy sunbathing. I'm getting a good tan this year. Shall we go to the lake?'

'If you like.'

We gathered up some towels. I picked up a Sue Grafton paperback. Sally noticed the manuscript of the Great Indian Novel and asked, 'Is that what you're working on? May I read it?'

'I suppose so,' I said reluctantly.

We chose a spot on the sand. I noticed that the police had dismantled the cordon near the spot where Pierre Moineau had been found. But they were still around the village. I'd spotted Barrès talking to the owner of the grocery and I had an idea that he was interviewing everyone – not an impossible task in Puybrun – but whether about the boy or Lucy, I didn't know.

Sally stripped to a stylish green one-piece costume. She hadn't favoured bikinis since Jack was born. As with Lucy's imperfections, which I'd so coolly studied, so with hers. I was conscious of and liked her womanly reality. It was that convincingly frail and mutable flesh that had sustained my sexual desire and – until Lucy – I'd wanted to get old with Sally and the prospect of an amorous tangle when we were both seventy didn't perturb me in the least.

I went to the *buvette* to get a beer for myself and a spritzer for Sally. Mike said, 'Have I gone stupid, or is there something between you two?'

'I didn't ask her to come. She showed up unannounced yesterday.'

'I hope for your sake that's true. I'm not trying to be offensive – God knows I like the pair of you – but it doesn't look good if the mistress vanishes under mysterious circumstances and then the wife turns up. Sunbathing together – it doesn't exactly appear as if you're grieving for Lucy.'

'I know,' I admitted. 'But what can I do?'

Mike shrugged. 'Hint that she ought to go?'

Jesus, Mike! I've been a big enough bastard towards Sally as things stand. Am I supposed to throw her sympathy back in her face?'

'That's your business. All I'm saying is watch your step.'

I returned to Sally. She was applying lotion. I thought she might ask me to oil her back, but she didn't. She'd placed our pair of mats a discreet distance apart, and this gave me some confidence that I could rely on her delicate tact. Though, of course, it might simply be that she didn't want me to touch her.

Sally is a strong swimmer and on our previous visits to Puybrun she had plunged into the lake and spent a good part of the time in the water. But today, to my surprise, she declined this suggestion. She seemed absorbed in my manuscript. I was flattered that she cared.

Around us the lakeside scene went through its slow, hot summer rhythm like the patterns of a ballet one has seen often but in which each performance is subtly different. Puybrun is a place for families. The older teenagers seem old-fashioned and out of the general run: shy kids who are content to be with their parents. I watched them diving from the raft while their mothers took care of the infants and the fathers sat at Mike's tables and talked of cars. In contrast with yesterday, the light was iridescent and soupy and the sun seemed to be nowhere in particular.

When I saw Harry he seemed to have resumed his old, chipper form. I was about to take a plunge from the raft and saw him in the no-man's-land between the end of the lane where the cars park and the lakeside proper. He was striding out with his malacca cane and, though his face was shaded by the brim of his panama, I had the impression he was whistling. He wore a beach shirt, 1960s style, with a pattern of cocktail glasses and Tabasco bottles, the trousers from an old grey pinstripe cut off below the knee and supported by suspenders, and emerald-green plastic sandals. He looked, as they say, 'the business'.

He called out, 'Hi, Johnny!' and I dived and swam the few yards to the shore. I asked him how he was feeling and he said, 'You're looking at a happy camper.' His eyes were glittering and I suspected he was stoked up on something.

Sally had glanced up as I dived, and she was looking at me now. I realised that, if she were to stay in Puybrun, she had to meet Harry. I regretted that I hadn't prepared the ground by discussing him last night. She was going to get a dose of Harry cold and I had no idea what he was going to say, particularly if he was hopped on pills.

'You've got company.'

'My wife,' I said.

'Your wife,' he said with a pause and then an old dog look in his eye. 'I guess you'd better introduce me to the pretty lady.'

'I've not told her much about you.'

'What's to tell, old sport? I'm a perfect English gentleman, don't you know?'

Sally got up and gave Harry one of her engaging smiles. Harry removed his hat, took her hand and gave it a kiss.

'*Encantado!*'

'This is Harry Haze,' I said.

'*Count* Esterhazy.'

'Stop that, Harry,' I said, restraining a grin. 'Harry – Sally. Sally – Harry. Harry's a friend.'

He squatted on the sand. His flies were held with a safety pin and a curl of pubic hair peeked out.

'What brings you to our fair domain, dear lady?' he enquired.

'I often used to come here on holiday.'

'Ah, an *habitueé – quelles délices!* Puybrun is such a heavenly place, the climate so equable and the soil so gentle to rest on – or do I mean "in", Johnny?'

'Probably both.'

'Probably.' He looked at me and added, 'Why don't you shake your tail, Johnny, and get me a beer. And while you're at it, ask Mike if he has any chow. Whaddaya say, doll? Something for you? Go on, Johnny. It's just old Harry not some jigaboo with a big pecker. You can trust me with this broad.' He turned to Sally and drawled, 'My apologies, dear lady, one has to address the staff in a tongue they comprehend.'

I went to get the beer and had to stand in line, and when I returned Sally was laughing and her face glowing with a fine sweat. I handed the beer to Harry.

Sally said: 'I think I'll stay another day, if you don't mind, John. Harry's invited us both to dinner.'

As I have already suggested, there was nothing impromptu in Harry's stories. That possibility was excluded by the elaborate props contained in the magic bag. Even so – and as if Harry had had foresight of Sally's arrival and decided to knock her dead with a bravura performance – nothing prepared me for his next tale.

It was in the form of a play, recited by Harry with his full panoply of tricks. And for it he produced the text, vellum-bound, on hand-made paper, in seventeenth century typeface.

This is it.

HASLET

or

*The Flight of the Führer's Deputy to England,
with a True History of his Imprisonment and
Miraculous Escape to America
with the aid of Master Churchill*

An original play in Verse
by
FRANCIS BACON

performed to popular acclaim by
Harry Haze Esquire
and Company

Act I

The Palace of King Adolf. The KING, LORD
BLITZKRIEG, *the* DUKE OF AUSCHWHITZ *and*
PRINCE HASLET *ponder a map of conquered Europe.*

ADOLF: (*pointing at a photograph of Churchill*)
        Now is the summer of our great content
        Made odious winter by this piece of pork;
        And all the force we aim against his house
        Must 'cross the English Channel first be ferri'd.
        Now bow the French to our victorious wreaths;
        Our legions march beneath their monuments;
        Our curfew puts end to their merry meetings;
        Our dreadful S.S. takes its dreadful measures.
        Grim-visag'd war still keeps his wrinkled front,
        But must now against England be directed
        To fright the souls of fearful adversaries,
        The capon Chamberlain's fat successor,
        And all the scum who would deny my loot.
        (*To Blitzkrieg*)
        Whadd'ya say, my Lord? How goes it, kid?
BLITZKRIEG: (*Placing his finger with relief at the place
        on the map where London is marked*)
        If they go down Lambeth way
        In the evening of the day,
        I'll put them all
        Under a funeral pall
ADOLF: My Lord of Auschwitz breaks out in a sweat?
AUSCHWITZ: Rather I'll sweat pain out of England's
        blood. (*He explains cheerfully*)
        When the shades of night are falling
        Come the men whom everyone knows:
        It's the old Gestapo
        Spreading fear where'er it goes.

RECHERCHE

We often give free beatings
Because we know full well,
That there's no such thing as innocence:
Just tomorrow's clientèle.

Exeunt ADOLF, BLITZKRIEG and AUSCHWITZ *to*
                    invade Illyria, Arcadia etc.

HASLET: Though loth to grieve
        True evil time's sole patriot,
        I cannot leave
        My horrid thought
        For the priest's cant
        Or statesman's rant.
        If I refuse
        My study for their politique,
        Which at best is trick,
        The angry Muse
        Puts confusion in my brain.
        Fate aids them – so a desperate game I play:
        For Russia, too, they'll fight one day they say.
        Ah! Our armies vanquished! Heroes fled!
        Our people murmuring and our commerce dead,
        Our shattered panzers pelted, bruis'd and clubb'd
        By Britons bulli'd, and by Russians drubb'd,
        Our name abhorr'd, our nation in disgrace,
        How should I act in such a mournful case?
        What shall I do – confess my labours vain?
        Or whet my tusks, and to the charge again?
        Can we at once with both our foes contend,
        And fight the villains on the world's green end?
        The pangs of parting I can ne'er endure,
        Yet part we must, and part to meet no more!

Exit HASLET *to make sandwiches, put on warm*
    underwear and commandeer an aeroplane.

Act II

A blasted heath – more particularly an airfield near
Augsburg. HASLET *and the* FOOL *are examining an*
aeroplane.

FOOL: I can see, sir, that you're a gentleman. There's
        no use denying it. Wait till I tell Mrs Fool!

HASLET: The fuel capacity will meet the case?
        I'd hate for want of it to lose the race.
        The flight to England takes a lot of gas,
        Remember – if I fail – then it's your ass.

FOOL (*pausing*): Verse, sir – you're speaking verse?
        Whoa! Wait till I tell my wife, I was with a
        gentleman who spoke verse – well, I guess I
        don't know what she'll say! Now me, sir – can I
        speak confidentially? – I use prose. You may
        have notic'd. It ain't got a lot of class, but it's
        very hard-wearing. You should try it, sir.

HASLET: The radio? We'll test the radio next.
        Should it not work, I warn, I shall be vexed.

FOOL: Doggerel, sir – if I was to try verse, it'd come
        out as doggerel. You, sir – well, like I say, you
        got class. But me, if I was to try verse … (*He*
        turns a switch). The radio is tun'd to the
        Luftwaffe stations in Norway. Speaking
        personally, I like Ted Gottlos's *Hellfire and*
        Happiness Hour on SX4U Las Vegas. Mrs Fool
        listens to it all the time. You shouldn't have no
        problems with this radio, no sir.

HASLET: The weapons now. To put you at your ease,
        They need not work, for what I seek is peace.

FOOL: Those are very fine sentiments, sir. Mrs Haslet
must be proud of you. The guns are still covered
in the manufacturer's grease. By the way, sir, did
I hear rightly that the Führer intends to kill six
million Jews and one Australian?

HASLET: (*examining the sky leerily*)
Love not such nights as these; the wrathful skies
Gallow the very wanderers of the dark
And make them keep their caves.

FOOL: Six million Jews and one Australian. There's a
point that's been puzzling me, sir. I wondered if
you could help?

HASLET: Through the sharp hawthorn blow the winds.
Hum! go to thy cold bed and warm thee.

FOOL: I don't doubt you're right, sir. When Mrs Fool
and I take a vacation, it's the weather gets us
every time. You remember my question about
six million Jews and one Australian?

HASLET: Marry come up! Thy prattling tires me out.
Australians! Australians!
What talkest thou about?
(*He climbs into the cockpit and waves to the*
FOOL)
Good-night, sweet Fool,
And flights of pigeons sing thee to thy rest.
(*He pauses*)
Australian? Why the Australian?

FOOL: That's my point, sir. *Nobody* asks about the
Jews!

Act III

Scene I

Another blasted heath – this time in Scotland (suited to low budget productions in the Globe Theatre, London, England, and to the John Wilkes Booth Junior High in Hotzeplotz where the senior class puts on an annual play. Students and critics in search of artistic sources will note that Professor Haze, the Transylvanian Terror, took the lovely Dolly there in the summer of 1948 to watch *Timon of Athens*. The play was favourably reviewed and the Hotzeplotz *Picayune* stated, 'The weather did full justice to the production').

And, by the by, there are three shepherds tending their flocks by night when they see a light in the sky, which could be a star, a plane, or the moon, an arrant thief who snatches her pale fire from the sun.

LARRY: Lo! There is a star in the East!
CURLY: (*Adjusting his head-dress which has flipp'd over his eyes*) Yes! Lo! and again Lo! Perhaps it is He who of … whom of … of whom it is written that … (*forgets lines*).
MO: Yes! Lo! and thrice Lo! We must not loll. It is Surely He … Him! Come, let us adore He!

LARRY *nudges* CURLY, *who drops his crook and bursts into tears.*

Exeunt shepherds.

Scene 2

Another part of the heath. HASLET stands by the burning wreckage of his aircraft. The shepherds, on seeing him, are startled.

LARRY: Ae dreary, windy, winter night,
        The stars shot down with skelantan light,
        Wi' you, mysel', I got a fright.
HASLET: Poor Rudi's a'cold.
CURLY: Rudi!

The shepherds confer and, in a manifestation of low comedy characteristic of the genre, conclude that they are dealing with Rudolf Valentino, or, possibly, Rudolf the rhodorhinophoric reindeer.

MO: Great is thy pow'r an' great thy fame,
          Far ken'd an' noted is thy name;
          An' tho' yon lowan heugh's thy hame
          Thou travels far;
          An' faith! thou's neither lag nor lame
          Nor blate nor scaur.

        Exit MO to return shortly with a policeman.

HASLET: Poor Rudi's a'cold.

POLICEMAN : (*offering food*)
          Wee, sleekit, cowran, tim'rous Nazi
          Will ye tak' a bite o' pasty?
          Thou need na start awa sae hasty
          Wi bickering brattle:
          I wad be laith to gin an' chase thee,
          Wi' murdering Prattle!
          (*He examines the wreckage*)

HASLET: I am the shadow of the Führer ta'en
    By the false allure of an aeroplane;
    I am the schmuck in feldgrau stuff and I
    Came here, flew here, through the defended sky.
POLICEMAN: Aye weel, sir. But before you go on: do
    you remember the case? Miranda? Do you
    remember the case? You have the right to remain
    silent. You have the right to an attorney …
HASLET: First let us kill all the lawyers!

The POLICEMAN *arrests* HASLET.

Exeant omnes.

Act IV

*A prison cell at Maryhill Barracks, Glasgow, HASLET sits
alone. His body, deprived of its vampire food by reason of
wartime rationing and the delicate habits of the British,
writhes in agony.*

HASLET: Is this then a touch? Quivering me to new
    identity,
    Flames and ether making a rush for my veins,
    Treacherous tip of me reaching and crowding to
        help them,
    My flesh and blood playing out lightening to
        strike
    What is hardly different from myself,
    On all sides prurient provokers stiffening my
        limbs,
    Straining the udder of my heart for its withheld
        drip,

Behaving licentious towards me, taking no
    denial,
Depriving me of my best as for a purpose,
Unbuttoning my clothes, holding me by the bare
    waist,
Deluding my confusion with the calm of the
    Sunlight and pasture – fields,
Immodestly sliding the fellow senses away
They bribed to swap off with touch and go and
    gaze at the edges of me,
No consideration, no regard for my draining
    strength or my anger,
Fetching the rest of the herd around to enjoy
    them a while,
Then all uniting to stand on a headline and worry
    me.

Enter the DUKE OF HAMILTON.

(By way of digression: during the Interval, which is
normally placed between Acts III and IV for the usual
reason that the audience is getting bored – though an
artistic case can be made for placing it at the end of Act II
to denote the passage of time and distance – Professor
Haze, in anticipation of the last soliloquy, is in a
lachrymose condition at his recollection of the first time he
experienced Haslet's loss of his vampire condition. He
tries to lighten the atmosphere with a feeble riddle. He
asks his students, 'Why does the text demand that the
Duke of Hamilton be played by the worst actor in the
company?'

'Search me,' answers Largizione, a pretty co-ed, a gift
of a girl with magnificent mammaries, who will go far on
answers like that (and indeed is a reputed mistress of JFK).

'Is this another of your dumb jokes?' asked tousle-
headed Ricciuto, with a curl of his lip.

'Because,' persists the Prof, 'the part requires a Ham!' Ho! Ho!

'In which case, he'd better not be Jewish,' says Morris jewdiciously.

Exchanges like this – though scarcely qualifying as literary criticism – do give rise to insights. The pedantic Professor wonders if the perspective of student humour would yield a reading of the text more plausible than any imputation of wit or wisdom. He makes a note to ask Volodya Botkin when next he sees him – which turns out not to be a smart move since *unbeknownst* (as the complete Comp. Lit. *aficionado* of English has licence to say), the Resourceful Russian is raising a rap sheet on the Prof – namely his hateful best selling biography of H.H. And, in the foolishness of time, poor Harry's hopes of attaining his own immortality will be firmly nailed with a wordy, worthy, woody stake through the heart. *Tant pis* for American literature! Who steals my name steals nothing. Who steals my royalties had better pack a shooting iron.)

HAMILTON *rouses* HASLET *from his painful slumbers, in which, perchance, he dreams.*

HAMILTON: I'm truly sorry your dominion
           Has broken Europe's social union,
           An' justifies my ill opinion
           Which makes thee startle
           At me thy poor, earth-born companion
           An' fellow mortal.
HASLET: How mutable is everything that here
           Below we do enjoy? with how much fear
           And trouble are those gilded Vanities
           Attended, that so captivate our eyes?
           Oh, who would trust this World, or prize what's
              in it,
           That gives, and takes, and changes in a minute?

RECHERCHE

There comes a knock at the door HAMILTON *opens it.*
CHURCHILL *enters and stares at the bloodless form of*
HASLET.

CHURCHILL: So fallen! so lost! the light withdrawn
    Which once he wore!
    The glory from his grey hairs gone.
    Forevermore!

He signals HAMILTON to leave so that he and HASLET
may enjoy a private conversation.
          Exit HAMILTON.
HASLET: You have heard, I suppose (and I know
    you'll confess)
    Of the mermaids that live in the sea,
    Of Baron Munchausen and poor Rudolf Hess
    (Esterhazy to you and to me).
    He still has a snap of a guy – maybe you? –
    With a *shlong* that hangs down to his knee
    And a doll with no clothes, and there's more he
    can do.
    Rudolf Hess, Baron M – namely me!
    Oldham, God damn!
    Pork sword ain't spam.
    Wham bam, thanks M'am.
    Take me to Uncle Sam.
CHURCHILL: (*After considering this proposal*)
    My Mother's land, her Puritanic stock
    Still has some loot bound up in Plymouth Rock.
    And now her son is squarely in a mess
    I'll use the cash to help you, Rudolf Hess.
    Yes, Rudolf Hess, I Churchill, stern and true,
    Will tell the English what they need to do.
    When in a scrape that's definitely tight,
    Who gives a shit for 'loyalty' or 'right'?

('Considered dramatically,' says Prof Haze during a short interlude caused by the luscious Miss Largizione who has gone to the ladies' room complaining of a headache, as she does once a month, and where she is presumably changing her head – 'considered dramatically, this moment represents the resolution of the problem posed by the play, the point at which the tragic tone at the hero's loss changes to a note of gaiety at his escape from danger. This mixing of moods is not without its artistic risks and is made no easier by the flatness of words on a page and the tiresome twang of somnolent students as they twist their tongues around them. But, gosh, golly gee! Are we going to try, boys and girls!')

HASLET: (gaily) My bote is icummen in
    Lhude sing Whoopee!
    War endeth, cash spendeth
    Joyous 'tis for me.
    Sing: Whoopee!
    Blude to suck and brodes to fuck
    Alle of thys comes free.
    For this sap no more crap
    So I sing: Whoopee!
    Whoopee! Whoopee! For free! For me!
     Whoopee!
    And Rudolf Hess – who he?
    Sing Whoopee! Who he? Not me!
    Sing Whoopee! Sing Whoopee! Whoopee!

Enter all players. They form a chorus to symbolise symbolism. The chorus reprises the final verse in song – excepting FOOL, *who only does prose.*

        Exeunt omnes, pursued by critics.

CHAPTER TWENTY-ONE

Since we were committed to dinner with Harry I had to explain to Sally what I knew about the old guy. I had to assume that during the course of the evening he would tell one of his stories, and it would have been unfair to leave her unprepared. Even so I couldn't be certain what direction Harry would take. His caginess in the matter of acknowledging and repeating what he had told me about Rasputin had made me wonder if his tales had some unique and unrepeatable character tailored to his listener – in which case God alone knew what version of his life would come out. On the other hand, he might continue where we had last broken off, in which case Sally might pop straight out of her socks if she wasn't warned what to expect.

So I planted my puzzled wife in a chair in the living room of Lo Blanc. I went over the subject of how Lucy and I had first got Harry to recount his history and then, in stages, I told her as neutrally as I could the whole absurd business. She got the lot: Harry the vampire, Harry and the Dreyfus Affair, Harry the friend of Churchill, Harry as Rudolf Hess. She took it well: amused by it; laughing at it. I think she imagined us whiling away the fleeting hour listening to Harry as if he were a conventional author reading his latest work of fiction to a gathering of a few friends. What I could not convey was Harry's insistence that his stories were true or my own uneasy sense that they were told with some deep purpose and full of hidden meaning; though she did consider the idea and asked, 'Is he crazy, then?'

'I don't know. Certainly he's sick – probably dying. Cancer, I think.' I explained that Harry injected drugs: heroin, he said, but more likely morphine to suppress pain. Although I had tried to protect him by concealing his habit from the enquiries of the police, in truth I discounted the notion that he was buying smack from a dealer in Mirepoix. 'And there's something else,' I said. 'The stories are building up to a sort of climax: something that happened in America, in a town called Hotzeplotz, and involved a man called Clarence Quimby. Harry has hinted that at some time in the fifties he was locked away in a lunatic asylum. I don't know why, but I think that part of his history may be true. In fact, the whole affair of the stories may have its origin in that episode. It may be that in some weird way he's trying to work out and explain what happened to him then. At all events it's a theory.'

'You mean that the stories have to make sense?'

'Don't they?'

Sally shrugged. 'I don't know,' she said; and we passed on to talk of other things.

I described the etiquette of dinner with Harry: the clothes, the food, the booze, the dope. She was surprisingly relaxed about both the drink and the marijuana, more mellow than I remembered; and, though she cautioned me against excessive indulgence, there was no censoriousness in her voice – indeed I began to wonder if it had ever been there or if it was a meaning I had read into her tones from my own fragile and often compromised morality.

'Harry will have to take me pretty much as I am,' said Sally. 'I didn't bring a lot in the way of clothes with me, a change of underwear and a clean cotton frock.'

'I'm sure you'll do,' I said and felt inexplicably proud of her as though I'd set her a test and she'd passed it .

So we went to Harry's place. But first, because we had the time, Sally suggested we drop in at Mike's and have an aperitif. She hadn't seen Mike or Marie-Paule for a couple of years and wanted to chat with them for old times' sake; earlier they had spoken only briefly. Marie-Paule took her into the back room to gossip.

Mike gave me a leery look. 'You two seem to be very pally,' he said.

'It isn't what you think. Things were never bad between us – I mean we didn't argue and there was no bitterness. You know for yourself that she's staying the night here with you and not with me up at the cottage.'

'Whatever you say. Oh, while I remember, there's more news about the Moineau kid.'

'Yes?'

'It seems he hadn't been swimming when he died.'

''Was it suggested that he had been?'

'He was naked when he was found.'

'I didn't know that.'

'So the first theory was that he'd been swimming and hit his head on some driftwood. Or maybe he'd dived into the water and struck a tree root.'

'That sounds possible.'

'Except that the blow on the head didn't kill him outright. If he'd been in the water he'd have drowned, but there was no water in his lungs. Also his body was found on the bank, under those trees a good twenty feet from the lake where the kids go for an *al fresco* shag. It was naked and had been arranged.'

'Arranged?'

'You know – *arranged*. And the clothes, too. They were spread out in the bushes' – he hesitated – 'Like Lucy's.'

So there it was, the connection between the two cases for anyone like me who was hoping it didn't exist.

I asked, 'Was he sexually molested, the Moineau boy?'

'I don't know,' said Mike. 'I spoke to Alain Huppert, who found the body when he was walking his dog. He saw nothing to indicate ... then again, he was hardly going to *look* – and what would he look for? I understand ... with that sort of thing you don't know what really happened until you do tests.'

I said, 'I thought you told me one of the Germans found the body?'

'I did? I must have made a mistake. You know how stories get mixed up.'

I didn't want to hear more, and Mike apologised. 'I didn't know what to do for the best. Whether to tell you or not. In some ways it's best to know the worst, and you needed to be prepared in case the police paid you another visit. You can't trust those bastards.'

'Gérard seems all right.'

'Sure, Gérard's okay.'

I told Sally none of this. She'd hadn't asked about Pierre Moineau and assumed his case to be an accident. I saw no reason to distress her with insoluble conundrums. Let's be frank: I didn't want her thinking of the increasingly sinister circumstances surrounding Lucy's disappearance. I was only just recovering a modicum of self-respect in my dealings with her and I didn't need her to suspect me of murder.

Harry had prepared dinner. I had told him that Sally was vegetarian and we ate a simple soup flavoured with fresh coriander and a dish of wild mushrooms. The old man was more subtle than I expected. He'd detected in Sally a mature calmness, a balance and innate moderation; and he didn't set out to affront her. He offered only a single bottle of muscadet, and the dope and the gear for his opiate addiction were kept out of sight. His conversation was attentive, directed at setting Sally at ease, with enquiries about her work, her taste in music, Jack and his career. I was relieved at this display of normality, but, as always with Harry, I suspected a subtext beneath anything that he said. Not that it was hard to find. Sally hadn't changed: it was only that my detachment gave me a new clarity. She was, put at its simplest, decent, caring, intelligent, attractive, good-humoured and – it was so obvious – intensely desirable. She wasn't like Lucy, who, for me, burned with a fierce animal attractiveness made even more alluring by a spirit of playful magic. Rather she possessed a simple feminine sensuality, only hinted at in her outward appearance but unfeignedly passionate when enjoyed; a sensuality which was achieved, in one sense, artlessly in that she made no effort to disguise her age and had no shame or regret at the effects, but which did not tend to the natural consequences of neglect because the unadorned materials of her body were instinct with her own sense of beauty, quickened by it and transformed. The question that Harry was posing to me was: how could you ever lose this woman? And to Sally: why did you marry this jerk?

Harry told us his story. He began diffidently by saying to Sally, 'I guess Johnny has told you all about me.'

'A little.'

'Then it's kind of you to pay me a visit, honey. And I guess, too, that you're waiting for old Harry to lay out the next chapter of his life?'

'Only if you want to, Harry.'

He looked at me. 'Oh, I think this business has gone beyond what we want or don't want. Some things you can't stop once you've started. Ain't that the truth?'

'I think perhaps it is,' said Sally.

So Harry got on with it and we learned how Harry Hess or Rudolf Hess or whatever you want to call him fled Germany and was helped by Churchill to a new life in America. As I have said, the story came in the form of a play produced from the carpet bag; and Sally and I had to sit dumbfounded in the dim light while Harry strutted the room, declaiming the lines with mock solemnity. I didn't know what to make of it. Indeed I had difficulty following the narrative line beneath the words. And it came to me that Harry didn't care. He was defiant. Through excess of artifice he had gone beyond artifice: treating with contempt the proposition that we should suspend our disbelief. His arrogance was as gross as it was splendid. If I was right, we were invited to believe him not because of any device designed to persuade us, but out of our own naked need and longing to believe. In no other way can I explain the agony I felt lest I was missing something, or my desire to cry out, 'Help me, Harry! I want to understand!'

But I didn't cry out. I clutched Sally's hand and sat silently through the show. Was it well done? Probably not, if one was not there to see and hear. Was I moved by the outrageous farago? It would be more truthful to say that I was benumbed. But, when Harry writhed at the pain and terrors afflicting Hess in his cell, I had to restrain Sally, who feared that Harry's grief was genuine.

That night Harry was arrogant, tragic, funny and cruel. And, when the play was finished, he allowed me to keep my copy of it as if to say, 'See. There's nothing in it. Look what one can make out of nonsense if one tries. Don't trouble yourself to find a meaning in the text. Only think on the experience.'

Like a fool, all I could say was, 'You had the photograph? The one taken in 1900, which hangs in your bedroom?'

'*Précisement*. I called in the favour which Winston owed me.'

Well, that made a sort of sense – within the context of Harry's stories. There was a question, but it took Sally, who was uncertain of the rules, to put it. She said: 'I thought Rudolf Hess died in Spandau?'

'Conspiracy,' answered Harry. 'Read the books about it. Next you'll be saying that Oswald shot Kennedy and

Elvis is dead. There are wills within wheels. Always was and always will be.'

I glanced at Sally. *Answer that one*. But she backed off and I thought that was the end of the night's entertainment, with no further clues to enlighten me as to Harry's motives. Then after a few seconds he added a brief remark, a sort of coda or, perhaps more accurately, a sad grace note such as might fall after a tremulous pause from the hands of a pianist who has been too much moved by the piece he has just played.

'And without all that,' murmured Harry wistfully, 'I'd never have met Dolly and Charlie.'

There was silence when he had finished. I had a question, but Sally signalled me to hold it. I looked at her and her face seemed very still. She wasn't a creature of facile sympathies, ready to blurt them out; in fact she was sceptical of sentimentality, which she considered an attribute of men. Her compassion was either active and useful or else silent in anticipation of that exact moment when its expression would be valued and remembered. So, as I say, she was silent and she gave Harry time to shake himself and propose that he fix a cup of coffee, 'And for you, Johnny, maybe a small cognac?'

Outside, the long summer evening closed in a light shower of rain.

He returned from the kitchen with the coffee and brandy. We lit cigars. Harry put some questions about Sally's stay in France. She told him about the Mortimers' villa near Montaillou and the problems with the swimming pool.

'Do you propose to stick around here, Sal?' he asked.

'I don't know,' she said. 'There's nothing in particular to take me back, but I don't have many clothes with me. And I don't know how John feels.'

'I've no objection,' I said.

'Then I may do.'

We drank the coffee and I let Harry snap out of the slight melancholy he'd seemed to feel at the end of his story. Then I raised the point that aroused my interest.

I said, 'You've never mentioned Charlie before. Who is he?'

A tremor passed through Harry's body. He looked pained and an expression passed across his face, a sort of furtiveness which I had seen before only in habitual liars. It was there only for a second and then vanished as if discarded rather than suppressed.

Harry said, 'Charlie was a "she" not a "he". Dolly had a little girl.'

'Your daughter?' asked Sally.

He shook his head and answered slowly, 'No, I never had any kids. Dolly and I always took precautions. It was too risky.' He smiled frankly. 'The vampire stuff. You got to be careful.'

I felt a flash of excitement. I had Harry on the run! I knew that in his connection with Dolly and Charlie I would drive him out of the fortress of his fantasies and pin him in a corner where, God willing, there was a glimmer of truth. I pressed him.

I asked, 'Is Charlie dead, Harry?'

He seemed not to hear.

'Is Charlie dead?'

John!' exclaimed Sally.

'What? Don't you want to know? Come on, Harry you've told us everything else and had it your own way. Can't you for once give a straight, honest answer? Is Charlie dead?'

'He's crying,' said Sally. She turned on me. 'That was cruel, John – brutal!'

She was right. Harry was crumpled in an agony such as I'd never seen, and I could justify myself only by thinking that this was the sort of shock he needed to drag the truth out of the darkness of metaphor and lay the undead to rest.

What, after all, was my role as the listener to Harry's stories if not as a kind of therapist? So let's get on with it since, at last, we all know why we're here and it's not because I've got anything to learn from Harry and I can stop beating my brains out searching for any message directed at me.

And if you believe that self-serving crap, you'll believe anything.

Overnight someone stole Sally's clothes.

She'd brought only a small bag with a change of underwear and a fresh cotton dress. On the evening of that first day, before we left to take an aperitif with Mike and then dinner with Harry, she rinsed through the clothes she'd worn and hung them to dry in the garden. It was something I could scarcely forget, because at the scent of the soap, the sight of her washing the clothes with fluent movements, and at the idle chat with which we passed the moment, a silly smile played on my lips and I drifted off into one of my reveries in which a hundred other similar occasions (now consolidated into one archetypal memory) passed before me; and, in particular, I thought of some drawings in chalk by Degas, in which, in muted colours, a woman was depicted washing herself over a bowl, unconscious of being observed. It was this image, so unsentimental in itself, that evoked sentimentality in me. In fact it contained something essential, a key to the criteria by which I judged feminine beauty, an appreciation of female physicality in itself, quite unconcerned to answer the demands of men but occupied in its own tasks and burdened with its own flaws (the woman in the picture seeming frozen, studying perhaps the blue traces of a vein in her leg) so that I saw it without any ornament but only in its plain otherness.

'It's annoying, but I shouldn't be too bothered,' I said, remembering what Mike had told me. 'Apparently there's someone in the village who steals clothes.'

'How odd.'

'It's not a recent thing. Mike said it's been going on for quite a while. He suspected the Moineau boy and tried to catch him. But, obviously, it isn't him.'

'No, but it's a damned nuisance. For now' I can wear the things that I had on last night, but I'll have to ger some more clothes from somewhere.'

For a moment I thought she might suggest running through Lucy's wardrobe. But, of course, the idea would never occur to Sally and, in any case, Lucy was a different size and had different tastes. Either in the clothes themselves or in the way Lucy matched them, there was a note of feyness that would have seemed absurd in Sally. Instead she would wear something simple and inexpensive: something which on her would look graceful and elegant, but which on Lucy would look clumsy and cheap.

With a sinking feeling, I asked, 'What do you propose? Do you intend to go back to Montaillou?'

Sally looked at me quizzically, then said, 'I could do. Alternatively we could go to Mirepoix for the day.'

'We could do. But today's Friday. As I remember, the market is on Monday.'

'I wouldn't buy clothes in the market, and in any case I don't recall it as that sort of market. Well?'

'I'd like that.'

'So should I.'

It was as an afterthought that she suggested we invite Harry to come along.

Harry was touched that we should ask him. 'You kids are too nice to me.' He'd recovered from last night's distress, about which I could think only shamefacedly. As a concession, he dressed in a halfway civilised fashion in a plain blue short-sleeved shirt, slacks and a pair of canvas deck shoes. Only a natty little hat with a painted silk band acted as a reminder of the old sinner.

We travelled in Sally's hired Renault, and, in such close proximity to Harry, I felt a little uncomfortable with my recollection of dinner. He anticipated me by saying, 'Don't feel bad about last night, Johnny. I have some memories which are kind of hard to deal with.'

'You don't have to talk about them, Harry. I was in the wrong.'

'I guess I'll get around to them sooner or later, but you have to let me get there in my own time and my own way.'

'Whatever you say.'

I was familiar with the road to Mirepoix and was no longer a tourist in the ordinary sense. I spent my time reflecting on what had happened. In the back of my mind I thought I could detect an emerging pattern in which the dominant motifs were vampires, Dolly and the spectre of Clarence Quimby. One way or another we always returned to these. Admittedly Harry had said little about Dolly: she hadn't figured as a character in any of the stories, just as a passing but recurrent reference, and I had no picture of her in my mind. Nonetheless I found this reticence significant, as if Harry could neither talk about Dolly nor leave her alone. The point is that I was convinced that Dolly was real. The others were fictional even if, strictly speaking, historical. Only prosaic Dolly appeared without the trappings of fantasy. And Quimby?

Clarence Quimby seemed genuine, more so than could be expected of a character who had a purely fictive existence. Also – and this might be important – Harry had reported his enemy as having been present in America. He had figured at the trial of Hateful Harry the Hotzeplotz Horror. I was certain that Harry had spent a considerable amount of time in the States – everything about his voice and demeanour seemed to confirm it. Accordingly (so my lawyer's logic told me), it seemed to me that the closer the stories drew to America, the closer we came to the point where fiction could no longer hide the substratum of fact. I was conscious that I was supporting this analysis by some dubious psychology and I wasn't certain to what conclusion it tended – perhaps a sort of Hitchcockian dénouement full of phony Freudianism (refer to Larry, Curly and Mo) – but this was where my thinking had got me to as we drove to Mirepoix. And, let's face it, I was more comfortable with this line than with plumbing my own psyche for explanations.

I also had to account for Charlie.

'Regarding Charlie,' said Harry after we'd been driving for a while in silence, 'I want to apologise for getting upset last night.'

'You don't have to talk about her,' said Sally gently.

'I don't intend to. I mean: I haven't got myself to a state where I feel I can do. All I wanted to say was sorry.'

'That's all right.'

'You're a sweet guy, Johnny – and you're a hell of a gal, Sal.' Harry looked out of the window and made a comment about something we passed. When he next spoke his mood had changed. He sounded relaxed. He said, 'Okay, I've decided. I'm going to tell you about everything – not today but some time soon – my time in America, Quimby, Dolly, Charlie, J. Edgar Hoover, the whole *megillah*!'

I looked round from my position in the front passenger seat and scanned Harry's face for any indication of what he might mean.

J. Edgar Hoover?

Harry was smiling and I thought it was a smile I knew. I'd experienced that same sense of contentment when, writing the Great Indian Novel, I'd manoeuvred round some angle of the plot in a fashion which worked. If I was right, Harry had, for his own obscure purposes, done the same, and he had, to his own satisfaction, completed the history of his life.

What had he said? That he told the truth simply as he remembered it? It would have been more accurate to say that he told those truths he could bear to remember.

Charlie. I'd glimpsed her so briefly: a fleeing figure without an age, a face or a character. Charlie, to whom, I was convinced, something terrible had happened. From the haze of Harry's stories she'd emerged like a creature struggling towards the light. And, as quickly, she'd vanished.

We reached Mirepoix and parked the car. Fatigued by the drive, Harry came hobbling after us. We'd got a few yards ahead before realising the old fellow was in trouble, but to Sally's show of concern he answered, 'No, no, it's okay, *mes enfants*. You go on and do whatever it is you got to do. I have an errand of my own to see to. *Dépechez-vous!*' That was fine by me and, calculating that we would not be above an hour about our business in such a small place, I proposed a time to meet and named a restaurant where we would take a leisurely lunch.

Mirepoix is a small town with some resemblance to the *bastide* villages of the south-west. The shops are mostly limited to rows of half-timbered buildings round a central square, at one end of which stands a pleasantly seedy cathedral, in its atmosphere reminding me of a shabby old man of intolerant opinions, who, in his dotage, has grown too tired to argue.

First we took a coffee and sat for half an hour reading a two-day-old newspaper. The last time we had been here was three years before. By then Jack was already living most of the time away and we'd gone to Puybrun for a week on our own. Lately this had been possible and that visit had been – so we told ourselves – the model for the future, and the prospect pleased us. I am, as I've indicated, an unadventurous man and content to take my pleasures quietly. Even my elopement with Lucy wasn't out of character, but in the nature of an accident, as a man sitting peaceably in the comfort of his home may have his house burn down. Which isn't to say that I disclaim responsibility. At all events, to sip coffee with Sally in the shade of an arcade was a reprise of life as it used to be – as I wanted it to be. And if, in the conflict of my loves and desires, I betrayed both Sally and Lucy and showed my inconsistency, selfishness and folly, then so be it: it's how I was. I could contemplate the problem calmly and think my ruthless thoughts. There's nothing so black-hearted as an English gentleman.

After coffee we took a turn about the square and Sally bought some salad stuff and flowers, freesias. Fresh flowers were for her a necessity and the house at Virginia Water was never without them; in particular, I remember the scent of forced hyacinths which filled the bedrooms at New Year.

We pushed on. I went inside and grunted at the right moments when Sally paraded herself before me in a variety of frocks, and she laughed wistfully, since she knew of old that I was faking interest. My mind was elsewhere, sailing on a scent of freesia across oceans of recollection which now were beginning to appear limitless.

'Fine,' I said. 'Buy it. I'll pay. Let's eat.' I blamed Harry for the rush. We'd fixed a time to meet him.

When we reached the restaurant, we looked inside, where some families were noisily lunching, and outside under the arcade. No sign of Harry. We took a table outside, where, in the shade, we could look on the square as it shimmered in the midday sun, and ordered mineral water and a Dubonnet with soda while we waited for him to turn up. He didn't.

Sally was concerned. I was callous, telling myself that Harry, having nothing else to do, was quite capable of finding a bar where he would buttonhole a stranger and explain that he was Count Dracula. I said this to Sally, who laughed. But there were reservations in her smile.

We ordered lunch. France is not a country for vegetarians but we persuaded the *patron* to rustle up a mixed salad with goat's cheese, and I took a steak with the pulse still beating. I called up a bottle of claret with a disapproving glance from Sally, telling myself that, when Harry joined us, he would drink most of it. Most likely, however, I was feeling the strain of his absence and also, perhaps, a perverse desire to destroy the new rapport I'd established with my wife: to shake it and test it.

Still no Harry.

I finished the food and the wine. I ordered coffee and a cognac. I suggested we pay the bill in the next ten minutes and then go looking for the old guy, though I had no idea where to look.

The *patron* returned. 'You are English, Monsieur?' he enquired.

'You're darn tootin',' I replied wittily.

'Pardon, Monsieur?'

'Yes. I am.'

'Very good. I wonder, then, if you can give me some assistance.'

I told Sally that the *patron* needed my help: probably to translate something. I swaggered after the man and he led me through the restaurant and a set of doors at the rear.

'Where are we going?' I asked.

'Everything will explain itself,' he answered and I noted under the influence of alcohol that he seemed a kindly person. We reached the toilet. The *patron* rapped on the door and we went in.

259

Harry was lying on the floor of the cubicle. There were flecks of blood spattered on the wall. A needle and all the other crap he used for injecting heroin lay beside him.

CHAPTER TWENTY-TWO

Puybrun
15 April

Dear Willie

I am writing to you as agreed, poste restante, Athens, not knowing if you will get this letter – though why I should say this, I don't know, since if you don't get it these words will remain unread.

Weather fine, place beautiful, house comfortable, wish you were here – all the usual stuff.

Honestly I do wish you were here.

I'm lonely. In fact, if it weren't for a funny old man I've met, called Harry Haze, this would be a boring place. I know I have John and – when he thinks about me – he is the kindest man imaginable and, especially compared to you-know-who (how is Theo, by the way?), he doesn't have a jealous bone in his body.

Also he's rich, cultured (by my standards, at least), and amusing company when he puts himself out. I know what you're thinking: Why am I bleating on? (Unless you're wearing your all-men-are-bastards head, which you sometimes do – you know you do – in which case you'll say: Serves you right!) All in all, I should be happy.

The fact is, Willie, that I'm a little frightened.

There, I've said it.

I'm not sure when it started, or whether I can explain it in a way that will make sense to you. Like most things, it has to be experienced.

John was always a little fussy. I knew that when I was his secretary, very determined, very single-minded. I suppose you have to be that way to be a successful lawyer. The job requires very intense concentration on the task in hand. Of course there are some flamboyant characters who do it (naming no names, but the one who used to grope me). But the majority are like John, more or less obsessive.

When we came to Puybrun, John was clear that he was taking one or two years away from his career to sort himself out and, you know, make things work between him and me. Of course, being here for such a long time means that it isn't like a regular holiday. You've got to find things to do.

John started with painting. The tubes of paint and all the other bits and pieces mean there's plenty to fuss with, and the painting itself means that you have to be alone in your head and concentrate. It fitted well with the way John is, and, honestly, I didn't mind.

After the painting we get the writing. We still have it, and it's even more time-consuming – more to the point <u>attention</u>-consuming. John prides himself on the clarity of his legal drafting and can't accept that he may not be able to write 'literature', though the two things aren't the same at all. The book is, as you might expect with a first novel (remember, I did study a teensy bit of American literature), cumbersome, self-consciously 'arty', and obsessed with the writer's own problems. In John's case he's trying to work out what went wrong between him and Sally and how he feels about life, the universe and everything. He's hiding himself behind fictions, and we're supposed to work out the subtext – though I don't know who would bother since, apart from those of us who love him, I can't imagine anyone would find him <u>interesting</u>. I try not to think about what he's doing, because when I do think about it, it reduces me to a symptom rather than a person.

At the beginning of the year – I mean the depths of winter – John decided, without any sort of explanation that made sense, that be wanted to go biking in the 'garrigue' (which is French for 'garrigue' – don't ask me, I've never been there). It was scary. People don't do that – not on their own – not men like John who aren't outdoor types. He could have been killed! I could see he was determined and, after the business of the painting and the writing, knew that he couldn't be talked out of it. I laughed it off, hoping he'd see sense on his own and the whole idea would go away. It didn't, but – thank God! – he came back safe and sound. Meanwhile I was left with Harry, who's a dear old chap and has led an interesting life which he tells me about.

So that's how things stand. Looking back, it seems to me that these different things – the painting, the writing, the hike in the garrigue – are all parts of the same picture: John's obsessions – especially about the past. I haven't mentioned that, though in some ways it's the most painful subject of all.

You know that he's much older than me. So does he. So do I. We've never disguised the fact from ourselves, indeed we've made a joke of it.

What I hadn't realised was that the age difference was not the same problem for both of us. Of course I was aware that our experiences have necessarily been different, but for me the problem always appeared to concern the <u>future</u>. I'm speaking of considerations such as children, who'll still be at school when John has retired. And – to be frank and a bloody-minded bitch – John is going to <u>die</u> before me.

For him, on the other hand, the problem concerns the
<u>*past*</u> *and I don't mean a sentimental journey down memory*
lane, which would be boring but bearable. Actually that's
how it started off: John talking about his childhood, which
sounds positively Victorian, event though he was born in
the late fifties. Then he started having flashbacks – sort of
Proustian moments, as the saying goes, though he says
not. When he talks about these memories he says he isn't
interested in the 'metaphysic' of memory but the 'ethic'
(which, in Proust's case, was the other way round – I
think). The 'ethic' of memory – according to John – is its
function in building and maintaining relationships and as
a guide to action. As you would say: 'Oh yeah? Well,
maybe.' If you want the truth – philosophy aside – I sniff
his wife Sally behind all this, though I don't blame her.
Did I tell you I met her a few times? She's quite a decent
woman.

Don't mistake me. John is in his heart genuinely a very
good man. It's that fact, I suspect, that is causing his
difficulties. He wants to be a good, moral, upright, faithful
<u>*adulterer*</u>*, and he can't be. And I'm frightened that the*
contradiction is driving him towards a breakdown. Then
what? Sometimes I wonder if, though he could never admit
it to himself, he wouldn't prefer it if I simply disappeared
by some sort of miracle or act of God that would relieve
him of all responsibility.

What a dismal soul I am! I haven't asked about your
news. Is Theo keeping on the straight and narrow? What
an ever-hopeful soul you are to put up with him. Which
reminds me: I was taught that there are only seven plots to
describe all the fiction ever written (seven, eight,
whatever). Well here's another one:

Girl meets Vampire.
Girl loses Vampire.
Girl discovers all men are Vampires.

I'll explain when I next see you. In fact, why don't you drop in on us here at Puybrun on your way back from Greece?

Enough! The sun is shining and I feel better after getting everything off my chest. On reflection, don't treat this letter too seriously.

I love and miss my 'other half'.

Ta ta for now!

    Lu

CHAPTER TWENTY-THREE

I should have noticed Harry's deteriorating physical and mental condition; and would have done so if I hadn't been so absorbed in my own affairs. In my defence I can say that I was too close: that the declining trend was hidden by the daily ups and downs. But that isn't the excuse of a true friend.

Writing now and in retrospect, I see a change of pattern in the way the old man was telling his stories. What had begun as simple tales – admittedly bizarre as to subject and touched by notes of whimsy and black humour – had become more extravagant. What had been a fairly straightforward narrative had become burdened with tedious word plays, leaden alliteration, obscure allusions and a sloppy heap of slapdash parodies: a complexity of form in which Harry could hide any meaning he chose. I don't think I'm mistaken in this. It's possible – even likely – that in my initial surprise, when, if you like, I wasn't attuned to Harry's wavelength or as attentive as I later became, I missed some of the nuances, and in recollection have oversimplified what Harry said in the earlier tales. Even so, I think that as he approached closer to whatever 'truth' he was trying to reveal, Harry was throwing more tricks into his pot of conundrums to mask his pain and uncertainty as to whether he should continue.

In other words, what happened in the restaurant at Mirepoix wasn't an accident.

The *patron* asked me, 'Do you know this gentleman?' And, when I said yes, he was too relieved to reproach me with the character of my friends.

I asked, 'What do you suggest we do?'

'I don't care, as long as you remove your friend from my restaurant.' The *patron* was a civilised man, but his eyes held the alternative of calling the police.

'He shouldn't be moved,' said Sally. 'He needs a hospital, or at the very least a doctor.'

I didn't find this a helpful suggestion. I foresaw all kinds of problems if Harry fell into the hands of the authorities – not just in relation to his drug habit, but also over his identity papers. And if, in the course of questioning, the Nazi vampire came out of his lair, the old fellow might find himself on the way to the booby hatch. More clearly than Sally, I saw that, in his own interest, we had to get Harry home.

The problem was that I had no idea how to handle a heroin overdose. Or even how to recognise one, except that I thought that the victim fell into a coma. If I was right, then there were some grounds for optimism since Harry, who must have taken his fix an hour or more ago, was beginning to revive. He was still slumped on the floor of the cubicle and as floppy as an old teddy bear, but I saw his eyes open and his lips move silently to play with a few words. I said to Sally, 'Let's get him out of here first. Then we can decide what to do with him.'

With the help of the *patron* I got Harry into a fireman's lift and staggered under the weight of him through the restaurant under the indifferent eyes of the dining families. I sent Sally to bring the car into the square, and, when she arrived, dumped Harry in the rear seat and made him as comfortable as I could. His hair was disordered and spattered with filth and blood; there were piss dribbles down the front of his trousers and a brown skid mark on the seat; and, looking at him, I realised that the more crazy and pathetic he seemed, and despite my profound suspicions, the more I was coming to love the poor devil.

'What do you intend to do?' asked Sally.

'I want to get him home. We can't take him to the hospital.'

'He's sick.'

'I think he's going to come round. If he takes a turn for the worse, I'll call a doctor.' I went on to explain the problems, as I saw them, if we involved the authorities.

Fortunately, just as Sally was raising her objections, Harry himself came to my rescue by mumbling his first coherent words. He said: 'It looks like I've let the regiment down, old boy.'

I laughed and answered, 'You certainly have. But are you okay?'

'I shan't be shooting elephants for a while.'

'That's all right. They're out of season.'

He said nothing else, but what he had said was enough to satisfy Sally, and we drove back in silence to Puybrun. Once at Harry's house, we took him inside and, at Sally's suggestion, stripped and bathed him and put him to bed. Tidying his clothes, Sally came across several small bags of heroin that he must have bought that morning. As she was about to dump them, I stopped her and pointed out that this wasn't the right time to throw Harry into cold turkey; that the stress might kill him and it was the sort of thing best done under supervision. Reluctantly she agreed and we put the stuff in a drawer with the rest of Harry's gear. And then we settled to keep vigil over him; and to talk about the past.

Harry passed the night quietly. I don't know if this is normal under the circumstances. In any case, he didn't seem to have much truck with normality. I dozed in an armchair while Sally took a spare bed, and in the morning, leaving her sleeping, I fixed coffee and ambled down to the baker's to buy bread and croissants. There I learned that the police had returned in force and were messing down by the lake.

Harry was awake for breakfast but kept to his bed. In my absence Sally had woken and looked in on him, so that when I saw him he was sitting up, fairly spruce, with his white hair clean and brushed. I asked him how he felt.

'Fine,' he said.

'You had a close call yesterday.'

'I've had closer.'

'You should give that stuff up.'

'At my age? With all I've been through? Get real, John. What does it matter if it's heroin or pneumonia that kills me? I've told you why I take it.'

'The vampire thing.'

'Give the kid a prize. Cold turkey is nothing compared with the frozen dodo you get when the fresh haemoglobin stops coming. They said I was crazy at the Nuremberg trials – and that was five years after I came off the Count Dracula High-Calorie Diet Plan. Believe me, it don't get any worse.'

'Whatever you say, Harry.'

He grinned. 'So what's new? By the way, I want to thank you and Sal for hanging in there with me.'

'It was nothing.'

'I still appreciate it.'

'The police are back.'

'Uh huh.'

'They're down by the lake.'

'I see. Can you give me a hand with this pillow? The lake? Maybe you should go down there, take a look-see.'

'I think I may,' I said.

When I got there I found that the water was out of bounds, and those tourists who hadn't decided that this was a day to go sightseeing were hanging around Mike's hut. Antoine was there too. But this morning the big fellow looked puzzled rather than guilty and, putting aside my earlier suspicions, I felt no inclination to talk to him. As for the police, the baker was right: they were out in force, perhaps twenty of them, six doing the work and the rest cheering the team.

Mike said, 'They're dragging the lake.' I could see two men plying grapples and draglines and a group of divers making ready on the sand. 'What do you think they're looking for? They've got young Moineau's body and his clothes. What do they expect to find – a weapon? I think they're barking up the wrong tree. I knew that kid. He was just the sort to get himself killed in an accident.'

'They expect to find Lucy,' I said.

Mike stared at me. 'Christ, you're a cool one!'

'I haven't killed her,' I reminded him. 'In fact, I'm not convinced she's dead.'

'Still…'

'Still nothing.' I relented (I was putting on an act) and added, 'I have to keep my hopes up, don't I, Mike?'

'Yes … sure. And Sally? How's she taking this?'

'Fine. She hasn't talked much about Lucy – not about her disappearance.' But about other things. While Harry slept and we kept watch, we'd had a long conversation which, after we'd covered all the polite stuff, came round to the headlines of the day: or how John Harper, respectable middle-aged lawyer, had got himself into this mess; with a failed marriage, a disappearing mistress, and a drug-addicted Nazi vampire in the next room.

I'd always known that Sally was her own woman. It was one of the things I loved about her. More than that, it was this very quality that brought me to like and admire women generally. Sally knew how I felt and said that, for that reason, she'd never worried I would engage in a casual sexual fling: treating some woman to the dubious joys of a one-night stand with the great John Harper. If I fell (and she was realistic enough to know I might) I would at least escape the worst degree of shabbiness – but only at the cost of our marriage. For me there couldn't be any compromise: no secret weekends away on spurious business trips; no occasional visits to a flat in St John's Wood. Whatever I'd done to Sally, at least I hadn't deceived and short-changed Lucy. For what I was worth, she had the whole of me. Put like that, I almost sound a good guy.

That night at Harry's we went over this old ground: laughed a little and, I admit it, cried a little. But there was no going back; leastwise not as long as Lucy was alive and I loved her. Nor, I think, was Sally looking to recreate the past; only purge the last residues of bitterness at what I'd done to her. We could be friends again, she implied, but nothing more. She didn't regret our years together; but, as the saying goes, that was then and this was now. The fact was that she didn't *need* me any longer.

When I returned to La Maison des Moines, I found Gérard's car parked outside; and he and Barrès were just leaving.

'We have spoken to Monsieur Haze,' said Barrès.

'He's sick,' I objected.

'He was well enough to talk.'

'I see.'

I remembered the question I was supposed to ask. 'Do you have any news of Lucy – Mademoiselle Western?'

'No,' answered Barrès blankly.

'You'll let me know?' I asked fatuously.

'Of course.'

'Thanks.'

Sally told me she'd objected to the interview, but the police had been insistent and Harry had been agreeable.

'How is he?'

'He's fine. He has an incredible constitution for his age.'

'Has he taken any more…?'

'No. He says his habit is only a small one; he doesn't need it all the time.'

'Good. I'll just have a word with him, and then I want to go to the cottage for a shower and a shave.'

'I'll come with you. My clean clothes are there.'

When I went in to Harry he was dozing but he woke and gave me an affectionate smile.

'Hi, Johnny.'

'Hi, Harry.'

'Any news from the lake? What are they searching for?'

'Lucy's body.'

Harry considered this. 'Will they find it? I guess I shouldn't ask, since you wouldn't know the answer – would you, Johnny?'

'What did Barrès want to know?'

He brightened. 'Oh, just the whole story about what happened between Sunday and Wednesday.'

'I see. And what did you tell them?'

'The truth as I remembered it. Except that – like you asked – I said that on Tuesday night I took you straight home from Mike's bar at ten thirty. Nothing about you coming here and our little chat. Why did you ask me to do that? I could have given you an alibi for eleven thirty.'

'It doesn't matter. Did they ask about you?'

'Me? Why should they want to know about old Harry?' He chuckled. 'Aw, you're a sweet guy, *mon brave*. You were trying to keep me out of trouble.'

'The heroin ... the stories. Would you have told them what we talked about?'

Harry looked at me carefully. 'I guess we'll never know,' he said slowly. 'But the truth of my stories is kind of a point of honour with me. As George Washington said, I cannot tell a lie, except about girlfriends and taxes.'

'And you knew George Washington?'

'Who's to say? I forget a lot. Maybe I did.'

We walked up the lane to Lo Blanc. A tractor had gone by; as its dust settled, the air sparkled white. We were at the hot, still, tired, midday hour when nothing moved except some swallows spinning round the castle. We held hands. I think it was out of unconscious habit. At all events I don't recall reaching out for Sally's hand, though when I found hers in mine the sensation was pleasant.

A vehicle was parked outside the cottage, a patched-up VW van of the kind I associate with the sixties. The driver was in his seat, eating a sandwich. A woman was at the rear, squatting to take a pee in the road. He was black-haired, black-eyed, unshaven and wearing a denim shirt. She was dark-haired, pale-skinned and wearing a biker's leather jacket and a long muslin skirt the colour of crushed raspberries, streaked with bleach marks. They were both aged about thirty.

I ignored them and they me until I got to the garden gate, when the woman looked up and said, 'You must be John Harper.'

'Yes?'

'My name's Willie. I'm Lucy's sister. That's my boyfriend, Theo, in the cab. Theo,' she called, 'there's somebody come back.'

The man got out of the cab. I saw cut-away denim shorts, sandals and a pair of legs as black and hairy as a monkey's. He extended an equally hairy hand and, with his mouth full, grinned and said, 'Theo. Pleased to meecha.' I heard a north London accent and suspected he was Cypriot rather than strictly Greek.

'Well?' said Willie in an Essex drawl that I knew to be phony since she came from Nottingham. 'Ain't you going to invite us in?' She glanced indifferently at Sally.

'Yes, of course … Have you come far?'

'From Paris. Drove overnight. Crazy, really. It would have made more sense to come here first and then go to Paris. But Theo wouldn't listen.'

'There was this concert,' said Theo.

Willie shrugged.

We went inside and I asked whether I could offer tea or a snack. Willie flopped on the settee. Theo started fiddling with the knick-knacks that came with the house. Willie said, 'I'll have some wine if you've got it. Theo drinks beer, doncha, love? Lu said this was a nice place, and she was right.'

I threw a can of beer to Theo and opened a bottle of wine. I asked Sally what she wanted and she said a spritzer. She added, 'I'll go, if you want me to.'

'That's not necessary.'

Theo opened the can, blasted froth over his face and laughed. Willie spared him an indulgent glance and turned to me. 'Is Lu around?' she enquired innocently.

I took a sip of wine. I asked, 'When did you arrive in France?'

'I dunno. Theo?'

'Last Friday.'

'Last Friday,' repeated Willie. When she wasn't confronting me with her direct stare, I was trying to assess her resemblance to Lucy. Same dark hair and pale skin. Same fine features and, so far as I could judge beneath the clothes, same small breasts and slender figure. In fact, when I concentrated on these purely static bodily features, I persuaded myself that the two sisters could pass for one another. Yet at another level of appearances, that would be quite impossible. There were small details of difference: I noticed that Willie wore a diamond stud in her nose and a fine gold ring in her right eyebrow. But more than that, there was an overwhelming difference of style – of which these points were just indicators – which immediately and so radically distinguished the two women that no one would believe them to be sisters, and which, unless one supposed that they were consummate actresses, would be quite impossible to imitate convincingly. My Lucy was full of fun and, in an unaffected way, had a certain chic combined with simplicity. Willie, on the other hand, with her sullen directness, fake accent and general slovenliness, seemed all affectation, reminding me of a form of coarseness which had once been in fashion but, I suspected, no longer was. At all events, she didn't appeal to my fastidious tastes, and I disliked her.

And she had been in France since Friday.

'Theo, will you stop pissing about with those ornaments,' snapped Willie. 'You're making me nervous.' To me she said, 'Well? When do you expect Lu back?'

'I'm not sure.'

'Not sure?'

'I haven't seen her since Sunday.'

So far as I could tell, her surprise was genuine. She asked, 'What do you mean by that? Are you saying she's left you?'

'Possibly. I thought you might know.'

'How the hell would I know?'

'She might have told you.'

'Come again? Me? She might have told you! Or are you saying she went to the door to put the cat out and just never came back?'

'Something like that. I don't know how to explain this, but the fact is we went to bed on Sunday night and, when I woke on Monday, she was gone.'

'Just like that? No note? No fight?'

I shook my head.

'I don't believe you.'

'I can't help that. I've told you the truth.'

I watched as she took this information in. I debated whether to give her the rest: Lucy's failure to pack a bag, the absence of transport out of Puybrun, the discovery of her clothes and watch, the suspicions of the police – all the indices of murder – and decided against it. She would find out these things in good time. But for now I couldn't stand her and wanted rid of her. I suspected her of an irrational and vengeful personality. She reminded me of those people who, in the teeth of compelling new evidence, insist that an innocent person should remain in prison, rather than allow a crime to go unpunished.

I cast an eye at Theo, who had only a walk-on part in this little drama. His lips were fluttering between a sheepish grin and invisibility, and I could see that, like many inadequate men, he had no idea of the appropriate reaction. I had an ear for the sense of Willie's abusive manner and knew that she was in love with him. And I knew, also, with certainty, that she was doomed to grief. As soon as they returned to London, he would leave her and in a week or so, to save his self-respect, would be telling his friends about the woman he took to Greece – what a slag; what a complete cow. I've become a connoisseur of that kind of relationship.

Meanwhile Willie was saying, 'I'm going to stay on until this business is sorted out. Can you recommend somewhere?'

'What do you want? I imagine there are hotels in Lavelanet, and there's a campsite here in the village.' I wasn't going to offer them Lo Blanc, though there was a spare room. However, I softened a little. I said, 'You can use this place as a base, if you like. For washing and the other facilities. The telephone, if you need it to make enquiries.'

She nodded. She didn't say thank you. And only now did she pay any attention to Sally, which made me think that she didn't get on with other women, and how lonely and vulnerable that must make her. Except that she had good old Theo, of course.

She looked Sally up and down with her unsympathetic eye. But when she spoke, it was to me. She said, 'Who's this?'

Did I hesitate? Probably.

I said, 'Let me introduce Sally. She's my wife.'

I heard the catch of breath. Saw the unfakeable wide-eyed stare and look of hostility.

Willie said, 'Well, ain't that just fucking marvellous!'

CHAPTER TWENTY-FOUR

My portrait of Willie is bleak and no doubt wrong or, at best, oversimplified. That is the risk you run when you place yourself in the hands of a narrator. To others I imagine she is more complex and sympathetic. I hope so. As I've said, I like women; though I should add that Sally, who has good judgment, didn't take to Willie, albeit her dislike was less visceral than mine.

I was not a detective. I was a murder suspect, an uncomfortably passive role for which nothing prepares you and all patterns of behaviour seem oddly inappropriate. When Willie and Theo had gone, I had nothing to do, no steps to take which might contribute to solving the mystery. Though ordinary life had ceased to exist, the demands of the day called for business as usual. After a light lunch I took up a book to read, exactly as I might have done a week before; and this mundane activity seemed the strangest thing in the world, stranger even than if I'd been a murderer, when it would have had an obvious and relevant purpose: the masking of my guilt.

We stayed in the garden until three, I with a mystery story and Sally with the manuscript of the Great Indian Novel. A thunderstorm, heralded by a stirring of the trees, blew in from the west, and for an hour we sat inside in purple darkness, lit fitfully by yellow flashes, talking quietly about this and that.

Sally finished my manuscript and placed it carefully on the table. For a few seconds she stared at it, as if uncertain what it was. I said. 'Well?'

'Yes,' she said musingly. 'What can I tell you? It's difficult for me to judge. I can't say I'm enjoying it, though it's interesting enough. The problem is I can't be objective. When I'm reading, it sticks out of the text every time I hear your voice: a turn of phrase or an idea you've expressed. And' – she smiled – 'I get a very peculiar feeling, finding myself in the book.'

'You recognised the character of Allison?'

'Obviously. Of course, she isn't me as I see myself – or not entirely. But the likeness is there, and someone else might say you've captured me to the life.'

'Have I embarrassed you?'

'No. "Embarrassed" is the wrong word. I just find it odd, the shift of viewpoint. I'm not used to seeing myself from the outside, without my behaviour being explained by my own thoughts. And it's uncomfortable, the notion of being on the page for everyone to see, as if you've borrowed a piece of me. I can't say I like it, though I certainly don't object.'

'I see.'

She examined me, as if cautious about going on. 'I find the tone a bit odd,' she said.

'In what way?'

'You've clearly put a lot of effort into characterising the two women, but it comes over as misogynistic – which isn't like you at all.'

'Misogynistic?' I was genuinely surprised.

'Yes. Perhaps it's because the story is told through the hero's eyes and he's trying to justify himself. I don't know. I'm not meaning to be critical. It seems to be an aspect of the way men write – even good authors. Females are too thinly drawn or somehow implausible, or, as I say, there's an undertone of hostility. Women writers don't seem to have the same difficulty. Their men are usually completely believable. What do you think?'

Disappointed, I had to say, 'I suspect you're right. I don't know what the explanation is. Maybe women are more observant. Especially about relationships.'

'I think that's because relationships interest us. Men tend to subordinate them to the action of the plot. For us they are the plot. That's probably why we enjoy soap operas so much.'

'I'll go over what I've written again,' I said, hoping to end the subject. But, apparently, there was a more important point Sally wanted to make.

She said, 'Haven't you noticed? I'm in your book and, obviously, you are. But Lucy isn't.'

'Susheela,' I reminded her. 'She stands in for Lucy.'

'That's precisely my point. She stands in for Lucy, but she isn't Lucy. She's just a device to make the plot work. She doesn't resemble Lucy in the slightest. The subject of your novel is the hero and his wife and the problems between them. Susheela is only a convenience so that you can explore them.'

And my poor, sad, vanished Lucy was just a convenience to the same end. Sally was not cruel enough to say so, but I was cruel enough to think it. And perhaps it was true. What, then, of my love for Lucy? It is often said that the congenitally blind can have no conception of colour, but I suspect that isn't so. From the conversation of others, a blind man will learn that leaves are green, wood is brown and tomatoes are red and he will, in his own mind, build lists of green, brown and red things, and deploy those words appropriately in his own conversation and they will not be meaningless; for if someone were to say to him that a tomato was blue, he would be surprised and immediately recognise the incongruity, a reaction that would be impossible if 'red' and 'blue' were mere sounds that evoked nothing in the mental world of the blind. Which brings me to my love for Lucy and a point of comparison. Obviously I have a conception of love and I

deploy the word in contexts that seem appropriate –
leastwise I've never been accused of talking gibberish, of
using 'love' instead of 'banana' on the right occasions. But
if Sally were right? On this analysis, I am no longer John
Harper, the lover, but Mister Magoo.

The rain had ceased a half-hour ago and the sun was
shining through the last wracks of cloud. I heard some
vehicles stop outside and, looking through the window,
saw Gérard's car and a van full of ordinary coppers.
Gérard and Barrès came up the path.

'Gentlemen,' I said, 'what can I do for you? I take it
you've found nothing in the lake.'

'You don't seem surprised,' said Barrès.

My conversation with Sally had left me depressed, and
I restored my self-esteem by sounding flippant. 'You
forget that I know something that you don't know.'

'Really? And what is that?'

'That I haven't murdered Mademoiselle Western. In
fact I don't believe she's dead.'

'I see. And what makes you so confident that she is
alive?'

'The fact that she must have left voluntarily on Sunday
night or I'd have been woken by the noise. And the fact
that you obviously haven't found a body.'

Even as I was speaking, I knew I was creating the
wrong impression. My comments sounded tricky rather
than sincere – the comments that might be made by a
deceitful man who considered himself smarter than the
police. Yet, knowing this, I continued in the same vein of
smug superiority.

Barrès said, 'The problem with your explanation,
Monsieur Harper, is that you confine yourself to what you
say happened on Sunday. But what do you say to the
breaking of Mademoiselle's watch on Tuesday and the
discovery of her clothes only on Wednesday?'

'No explanation is ever complete. Not all facts are relevant or can be accounted for.'

'You have something in mind?'

'There is someone in the village who steals clothes. Speak to Monsieur Miller; he'll confirm it to you.'

It was obvious that neither Barrès nor Gérard knew of this.

'You think it is relevant?' asked Barrès.

'I have absolutely no idea.'

Something else came to mind, an odd detail I'd noticed when the two policemen arrived. The garden gate was hanging from one of its hinges. It hadn't been so only a little while ago when I opened it to show Willie and Theo out. The only time it could have happened was when Sally and I took shelter from the storm. I considered mentioning the matter to Barrès but decided not to, since there was no reason to suppose this trivial event was in any way connected to Lucy. However, it did aptly illustrate my thesis.

Gérard was looking at Sally.

'Do forgive me,' I said. 'I'd forgotten that you haven't met. This is my wife. She was on holiday with friends at Montaillou when she heard of my problem and decided to pay me a visit' – and, by the way, in case it has slipped your attention, she had the motive and was conveniently placed on Sunday, Tuesday, Wednesday, or any day you like, to pop on over to Puybrun and bump off my mistress. Except that, unlike you, I know her and the whole notion is inconceivable – well, not actually *inconceivable*, since I just thought of it, but you know what I mean.

Sally introduced herself and exchanged some remarks about weather and journeys with Gérard. With her unerring eye she'd seen that my behaviour was unhelpful, and that, of the two, Gérard was the person on whom one could make the more sympathetic impression. And, indeed, when he next turned to me to put a request, he made it sound the most natural and insignificant thing and not a demand from the police.

'Monsieur Harper,' he said, 'we've come to ask your permission to dig up your garden.'

I was fleetingly minded to stand on my lawyerly dignity and demand a warrant. But what was the point? I knew they wouldn't find Lucy's body there. The soil had remained undisturbed since she left, except that Sally had lifted a few weeds.

'Of course,' I answered, and immediately Barrès was on his feet and calling on his lads, like a handler whistling up dogs.

'I need to make a phone call,' said Sally.

'You know where it is. I suppose I ought to keep an eye on these clowns.' I moved to the doorstep, from where I could overlook the operation. Barrès had brought half a dozen men with mattocks, spades and coarse sieves to sort through the soil. Already they were attacking the garden, levering up bushes beneath which there couldn't possibly be any body. Then, thinking of Barrès mind-set, I wondered if by chance he would dig up something – a piece of lost jewellery or the bones of an old pet – and this rubbish would become evidence in the case: something to be explained, and thus obscuring explanation. Ah well, let him do it, I thought.

Sally joined me at the door. 'I've just spoken to Pauline,' she said.

'Yes?'

'The problem with the pool has been sorted.'

'Good.'

'So there seems no reason not to return to Montaillou.'

'You're going to leave me here?'

'I don't think my presence is likely to help, do you? The police are probably curious as to why I'm here at all. If I stay any longer, they'll become downright suspicious.'

'It makes no difference. They can suspect what they like but they'll prove nothing.' I looked Sally in the eye. 'Trust me, I'm a lawyer.'

She grinned, then said, 'No, really, I have to go. I can't carry on with just a couple of dresses and knickers I have to rinse every night. And, unless Lucy suddenly turns up, who knows how long this investigation is likely to go on? I've been planning to return to England in a week in any case.'

'I'd rather you stayed.'

'No,' she said firmly, though without hostility. 'Let's go inside. Tea? I don't want anyone else overhearing our affairs.'

Sally went to make the tea. I fixed myself a brandy, which gave me a momentary lordly feeling as I watched the police slaving in the heat. The next instant I felt like a little boy about to be rebuked by teacher, since I knew Sally was going to remind me that these days, by my choice, we were living separate lives and it wasn't appropriate for me to look to her for support. (Reconsider that last sentence for a moment, and substitute 'lecture' for 'remind'. To a fastidious ear the original may clang with misogynistic tones. With the change, the noise is deafening. Sally was right about the way that men perceive such scenes, both in fiction and – in the present case – in fact.)

'You're determined to go?' I asked as she came from the kitchen with tea and a shortbread biscuit.

'Yes,' she said, and added slowly, 'I've enjoyed seeing you again, but I can't see the way forward very clearly. There are too many unresolved issues on my agenda as well as yours. And nothing can be clear until we're certain what has happened to Lucy.'

I didn't doubt that she was right. What I resented was the very fact that she was right. However, I had the wit to recognise the feeling for what it was. So I nodded and agreed, and after our civilised cup of tea I walked with her to the broken gate and watched as her hired car rolled down the lane to the *route nationale*.

The squad of police coolies finished their labours when there was still light left in the cool of the evening. Barrès said unenthusiastically that they would return and finish the job in the morning, and he posted one of his men in the garden so that I shouldn't run off with any stray stiff or other treasures that might be lurking under the soil. I wished him well and strolled down to La Maison des Moines, feeling restless and hoping to find Harry *compos mentis* so that I could propose a walk.

'Sure,' he said. 'Why not? I'll grab a stick and we'll go. Where do you fancy? The lake?'

'Not the lake. How about the castle?'

'Whatever, as long as you don't mind my being slow on my pins up the hill.'

We took the circular walk past the chapel. At the top of the saddle I looked back at the village. This time I wasn't dazzled by light and heat, and I experienced no visions. Puybrun lay in a mosaic of soft blues and russets except for the spire of St Hilaire, which still captured the last bands of sunlight.

From the saddle we walked up the gentle slope to the ruins. I sat on a stone from the crevices of which grew spirals of toadflax, and studied the ivy-covered wreck of the donjon, from which the early bats were emerging. Harry asked about the castle and I gave him a story of how Simon de Montfort had stormed it during the Albigensian crusade, and how, somewhere nearby, the wife of Albert, Count of Puybrun, had been burned for adhering to the Cathar heresy.

'And what happened to Albert himself?' enquired Harry.

'He found another wife.'

Harry had been down to the lake after the storm cleared. The police frogmen had packed their gear and left, with nothing to show for their efforts except a small mound of waterlogged branches and junk. My prediction that Lucy would not be found in the lake had been borne out. I told him that the police had begun digging up the garden of Lo Blanc and also that Sally had left to return to Montaillou.

'She was probably wise,' said Harry, and added, 'Nice lady.'

I said, 'I've introduced you to both Sally and Lucy, but you've never compared them. Why is that?'

'What's to compare? They're different. Or are you asking me which one is better? Don't be a bigger idiot than you are, Johnny. I don't judge these things. People who live in coffins shouldn't complain if the neighbours stink.'

I accepted the rebuke. In any case I hadn't expected a clear answer. I was moving still further away from the idea that anything Harry said was wise or meaningful. It was as if he had at last convinced me that he was merely reciting his memoirs like an old gaffer and that the correct response was to listen with half an ear and agree where agreement was called for. At all events, the question of belief or disbelief no longer seemed an issue between us, and I no more judged him than he did me. So it seemed perfectly natural to ask, 'What was it like, being a Nazi?'

'Fun.'

'Fun?'

'Sure. If it wasn't, why would anyone bother?'

'And being a war criminal?'

'Pretty much the same. Have you ever seen pictures of Goering at the Nuremberg trials? Believe me, he loved every minute. He was able to take a trip down memory lane while all the world watched.' Harry sighed. ''What wouldn't you give for such a dose of fame and nostalgia together in one glorious hit? And afterwards exit with a touch of bitter cyanide rolling over the tongue. Put like that, it's kind of Proustian, ain't it?'

'I doubt it's what Proust had in mind.'

'No? 'Well, maybe not. But wisdom comes from misunderstanding the work of great writers. Leastwise, it does for us poor dumb bastards who aren't capable of anything better.'

I turned to study the horizon again. The line of cliffs had descended into shadow. Above it stretched a strip of cloud that had caught the reflecting sun in a blaze of peach and gold.

Harry rambled on. 'You can't expect to understand what it was like, unless you were there. We'd get up of a morning, have breakfast, go to the office, put in a couple of hours at the monstering stuff, have lunch and, like as not, watch a film in the afternoon.'

'The banality of evil,' I said, quoting Rebecca West, I think.

'Hogwash. Happiness is banal. Evil is exciting, a bundle of laughs as long as you're on top. Whoever said "Goodness is its own reward" didn't know diddly. Evil is its own reward. Goodness is rewarded some other place – maybe in Heaven.'

I wasn't interested. If this was wisdom, it too was ordinary. I said, 'So you left Europe and went to America?'

'Uh huh.'

'And met Dolly and Charlie?'

'My ass is getting numb with sitting.' Harry stood up and slashed at some bindweed with his stick. He asked, 'Why do you want the story of my life? What are you doing with it?'

'I've started making notes.'

'And? What? You'll put them into a book?'

'Perhaps. I haven't decided.'

'Then I should tell you, old boy, that you won't be the first.'

I was surprised. 'You've told your stories to someone else?'

'Volodya Botkin.'

'The writer you met in Berlin?'

'And later. He emigrated from Germany to the US of A, where he made a pile setting down the sufferings of poor old Harry Haze so that the world could laugh.'

'Do I know the book? Is it a vampire story?'

Harry stooped to pick a pale trumpet of bindweed. He spun the flower in his fingers. He said, 'Volodya was too clever to use the V-word, but what he wrote was a vampire story right enough.' He looked at me. 'But don't let that fact put you off writing whatever it is you want to write. Your version and Volodya's won't be the same. Like as not you won't even recognise them as dealing with the same subject.'

'I see.'

'No, you don't see, Johnny. Even I don't see.' Harry dropped the flower and ground it underfoot. 'Write what the fuck you like.'

'I will,' I said and added, slightly prissily, as though taking dictation from a recalcitrant boss, 'Okay. So we've dealt with your career as a Nazi war criminal. What happened next?'

'I went to America, became a Jewish stand-up comedian and met J. Edgar Hoover,' said Harry.

CHAPTER TWENTY-FIVE

Harry's Tale

Members of the jury if I am to ask for your understanding – your forgiveness – I have to put my character on the line. I am prepared to swear on my father's coffin (wherever the old guy happens to keep it these days). *Enfin, coupons à la chasse!* Put on the spot, I must, like Hamlet, 'sling fortunes at outrageous Arabs'.

As a fugitive Nazi, I was the most loyal citizen ever to grace the fair shores of America in the Year of Our Lord 1946. Indeed, who but I could swear in better conscience that I was not and never had been a member of the Communist Party? As for advocating or taking steps towards the overthrow of the constitution of the United States of America by force, that was the last thing I had in mind. For was not this land of Goshen my shield and buckler against mine enemies? No, folks, though you may beat me about with rubber hoses, you won't make the disloyalty rap stick as long as I've got a lawyer.

As my first witness, I call my fellow founder members of the Legion of Funny Jewish Guys Against Everything Un-American. (I apologise for the indifferent initials, but this is 1946 and we haven't yet figured out the witty potential of the acronym.) Just to prove that we kikes can be counted on in this Age of the Soviet Threat, we have persecuted other Jews through the forty-eight states on the grounds that they are not funny, Jewish or American enough for our tastes.

Those who forget the past are condemned to relive it.
Those who remember it are condemned to tell jokes or go
crazy. Experience equipped me for life as a kosher comic.
Adolf and the boys were a mine of Jewish jokes, and it
was simply a case of cleaning up the language. Scholars
may also care to refer to my monograph *The Dreyfus Case
as a Source of Jewish-American Humour* (Las Vegas,
1948).

During '46 and '47, I put in a couple of seasons
working the resort hotels of the Catskills, ladling laughter
and latkes, two shows a day, and all the while I was as
happy as Larry, as merry as Moses. Or would have been if
I had not sensed that Fate in the form of Clarence Quimby
was coming tippy-toe after me like a bail bondsman.

You are entitled to instances to prove that the
Eumenides were weaving the skein of events to their
purposes. I give you my agent, Mr Hyman Kaplan, whose
letter of 1 April 1947 (exhibit 365 in the People's bundle)
directs me to go to the Beaver Creak Country Club, where
I am booked for two weeks in July. Except that the
dyslexic Mrs Hymen has typed on her Remington not
Beaver Creak but *Beaver Crack*. I place no blame. Mrs
Highball has a weakness for cocktails, but in other respects
is a respectable lady and I will take my oath that she has
no sense of humour. You may rest assured that if that good
matron has, instead of naming an hotel of unblemished
reputation, put her finger on one of Quimby's aliases, it is
because she has been nudged by Greater Forces.

I can give other examples of how Quimby set symbolic
traps along the path of that summer's itinerary. What make
you of the Happy Clam Restaurant (22-27 May)? Or my
seven-night stint at the Menorah *Cuntry* Hotel (courtesy
again of *la belle dame sans Macy's*)? It was with relief at
her delicacy that, in August, I deposited my worldly goods
at the Grand View, Maiden Falls.

That establishment was a gothic pile built on the edge of the virgin waters, where the waxwing flies and the shagbark grows. Imagine a series of cavernous rooms with coffered ceilings and renaissance fireplaces large enough to burn a sizeable coven of witches, and you have an idea of 'the olde worlde charme of the King Tudor period'. Imagine, too, a high tower from which Rapunzel or some other nice Jewish girl might have let down her hair, plus a room furnished with the newe worlde charme of the Woolworth period, and you have a notion of where Humorous Harry was required to park his hide on an old army cot in view of a sign admonishing: 'Cabaret artistes are requested to refrain themselves from washing their hands in the hand basin as the practice is unhygienic and the smell causes offense'.

Already, on my arrival, I was shaking. Or, if you prefer it for the sake of stylistic verisimilitude, I was shaking already. I opened my fibre suitcase and prepared a heroic dose of heroin, and when I awoke from the arms of Morpheus the only shaking I experienced was from the tremor of King Tudor's plumbing, and night was falling. Still I was gripped by a feeling of dread.

To what did I owe this experience? It ran counter to my past life, in which Harry the Transylvanian Terror and Notorious Nazi had often instilled fear in others but had not been on the receiving end. I tasted the air and it made me shudder with a dim frisson of recollection. Again I sniffed, and this time I detected a musty odour; but whether of sod or sodomy I could not tell, since the acuity of my senses had declined with the waning of my vampire powers, and the clarity of my memories been muddied by too frequent and excessive use of opiates.

My nearest neighbour was one Irving Greenbaum, who was Jewish *d'appellation controlée* and not a *juif d'occasion* such as I. He acted the part of host to falling maidens among the guests, assisted by a *shone-twos* named Shadelle and a black-face band whose name I decline to give out of a desire to avoid offence, since I understand this form of nigger minstrelsy has become deeply unfashionable. While I sat on my bed in a state of nameless terror, I heard Irving's heeltaps clatter down the staircase, followed by the rustle of tissues being stuffed by Shadelle into her Berleigh bra. A moment later the Deeply Unfashionable Band struck up a chorus of their 'Ole Kentucky Shtetl' or something equally appropriate.

I trust I am making myself clear. If not, the jury will shortly hear the testimony of three learned psychoanalysts who will elucidate how an acute anxiety state and sense of temporal displacement are symptomatic of severe psychotic disorder. They will explain to you that the symbology of hotel names, though meaningful to the patient, is meaningless with regard to a description or interpretation of external reality beyond the accidental congruity of similar sounds or ideas. Mrs Hyman Kaplan's distressing dyslexia is, at most, the manifestation of a Freudian slip (or Freudian avalanche, in the opinion of Mr Haze) and is relevant to *her* psychopathology not *his*. Furthermore and fifthly, such a playful awareness of words as the patient, Mr Haze, exhibits is the hallmark of the schizophrenic as well as the writer, as is the ability to assume fictitious characters and memories. While lastly and tenthly, they will adumbrate that a heightened olfactory awareness is often delusional; so that, if the patient claims that the savour of a *petite madeleine* is the foundation of an important revelation, it is nevertheless improbable that he is a great writer and more likely that he is *aussi fou qu'un rat de WC* and will end his days in a cork-lined room.

However, temporally displaced Harry Haze is unconcerned by this mumbo jumbo. He can see a year or two hence when Herr Doktor Haze, that suavely secretive gentleman, shall descend on the leafy shades of

Hotzeplotz, and Dolly and Charlie be fascinated by his quips, quibbles and quimbies.

I am speaking of tragedy. Of death and dolour. For the smell in Harry's nostrils, as he sits on his bed in a Catskills hotel and debates whether he can descend the stairs to the room where the Deeply Unfashionable Band is playing shvartzeh music to the sheenies, is the stink of the crypt.

To steady my nerves and in tribute to my Ole Frenchie Home, I drank a shot of bourbon and crept downstairs and into the wings of the small stage area. The Greenbaumettes were playing away and *les invités* still chomping the chow. That was the deal. Once the guests reached coffee (without milk, natch), Irving would make with the intros and Hilarious Harry would spring on to the stage and knock 'em dead – to speak metaphorically.

(By way of digression, you may like to know that, in my experience, there are few Jewish vampires. I think it's because of the blood thing. Deuteronomy has something to say about it.)

The smell, of course, was Quimby and I put away another slug of Jim Beam as I scanned the hubbub of Hebrews for some clue to his presence. I laboured under the disadvantage that I had not seen him since 1938, when as a minister of the Reich I had got NBC to post him to Zembla, and I had supposed and hoped that the Russians had swept him up and dropped him in a remote oubliette after their conquest of the Baltic states. It was my ill luck that he should, so to speak, have come back from the grave at this juncture.

Though I could not see him, the certainty of his presence confirmed that the code I had detected in the hotel names was not a mere caprice of fortune. Indeed, I had a sudden insight into the brilliant mind of the man. For not only were the individual hotel names the enunciators of his presence, but the whole project of my sojourn in the

Catskills had been not a manifestation of my free will but a part of his fiendish manipulation. How so? Consider, then. Where 'Cat' appears substitute 'Pussy'. The result yields 'Pussy-kills', a Quimbyish formulation if ever one existed, and proof positive before any disinterested tribunal that he was here and now at Maiden Falls.

The shock of this new discovery near bowled me over and I took another nip from my flask without its suppressing the graveyard reek that afflicted my nostrils. I was astonished that no one else could smell it and I put this down to the fact that my situation as a recovering vampire had made me sensitive in the way that a reformed smoker or alcoholic may gag on his former stimulants. However that may be, what had begun as the faintest of odours had now become a miasma both oppressive and soporific. So, when Irving had made his introduction and the Deeply Unfashionable Band delivered a drumroll followed by a clash of cymbals, I could only croak, 'Nyah, the smell!' and faint upon the spot.

In praise of Irving, I have to say that, apart from an initial and understandable lapse when he murmured, 'God damn it, the sonofabitch is drunk!' he acted like a Christian. He directed the black-face drummer to sling me over his shoulder and the *shone-twos* to guide the way. Then, shining his smile on the audience, he said sportingly, 'Well, ladies and gentlemen, we have a problem tonight, we surely do.' Gaining in inspiration, he continued, 'But seriously folks, Harry has just heard that his Momma is ill and may not pull through.' He raised a hand. 'I know how you feel. Another person than Harry would have taken the night off. But Harry isn't another person, he's – Harry, I guess. And so *he* had to try because *he* knew how disappointed you folks would be. Well, we can understand that, can't we? I mean, can't we? It's the American Way, to try – am I right? Darn right I'm right! So now let's hear it – I want to hear it – a Maiden Falls

294

welcome for a trooper who did his best. I repeat: let's hear it! For Harry! And – *for Momma!*'

Which, indeedy, we did. The best round of applause I ever got. Yes, so convincing was Irving that Shadelle was in tears and all the way back to my room blubbered, 'Poor Harry! Poor Momma!' so that I do believe some amorous exercise might have been in order. Except that on opening the door to my room I saw a figure rise from the shadows with a Martini glass in his hand and a voice proposed: 'May I offer you a drink, old sport? Gin Sling? Singapore Sling? John Collins? Michael Collins? Mai Tai? My Lai? My my! What was that? Forgive me, old sport, but it seems that we run only to bourbon.'

I stepped into the room, leaving Shadelle blinking myopically into a darkness which only my eyes, after years, yea centuries, of practice could penetrate.

'Is there someone there, Harry?' asked *ma share shone-twos*.

'Who's the frail?' asked Quimby. 'Hey, sister, take a powder!'

'I suggest you go,' I said, closing the door on her but not without wistfully treasuring a pair of nacreous tears she let fall on her cheek. I took a seat on the army cot. 'Well, Clarence,' I sighed, 'it seems you haven't changed.'

'You cut me to the quick, heart of my heart. *Où sont les neiges d'antan?* Should auld acquaintances … I forget. Come to me, oh buddy mine!'

'How has life – or for that matter death – been treating you?'

'*Comme ci comme ça.*' He wagged his finger. 'You know. It wasn't very kind of Herr Rudolf Hess to have my press credentials revoked. I did not like Zembla at all – Zembla, where I walked in the shade of hazels – no, not at all. It was rather like Mordor – whoops! I shouldn't have said that; the book hasn't been published yet – this temporal displacement is the very devil, *n'est-ce pas*? It was rather like Atlantic City during a *very* rainy winter.'

'It was necessary,' I said. 'You took advantage of our relationship too much to indulge in your ... um ... proclivities. And you were excessively untidy in leaving bodies around.'

'Pish!' retorted Quimby scornfully. 'Fie, and double pish! There were far too many bodies lying about the Reich for my small contribution to be noticed. And I was perfectly willing to reach an accommodation. Why, I should have been entirely happy to feast off Jews and gypsies. I could have performed a service.' He shook his head. 'No. Reluctantly I have to conclude that you never loved me.'

'Vampires don't love.'

'Tell that to Anne Rice. Whoops! Another anachronism. I must reset my watch. I'm late for the Queen.'

I helped myself to one more bourbon. Bearing in mind the injunction against washing my hands in the wash basin, I took a piss in it. I used the opportunity to examine my guest. Though evidently annoyed with me, he was looking prosperous and I could only conclude that the Home of the Brave offered opportunities for a working vampire. My complaint against Clarence had been that, in addition to foisting an unwelcome friendship on me, he was a sloppy eater who gave the trade a bad name.

'Do you still practise?' I asked.

'I dabble. And you?'

'I gave it up.'

'*Quelle horreur!* How did you manage?'

'The war. My imprisonment. I had no choice.'

Quimby shuddered, but brightening he said, 'Well, it's an ill wind ... your new reformed and respectable condition means that you are even better placed to assist me.'

'How did you find me?'

'It wasn't easy. I spoke to Eddie Mars, and he fingered Moose Malloy. Then, once I figured why the Brasher doubloon –'

'You had help?'

'Some. The difficult part, sweetheart, was your habit of changing name and appearance. Have you been following the Alger Hiss story in front of the House Committee on Un-American Activities?'

'A little.'

'You had me fooled. I thought he might have been you. Esterhazy – Hess – Hiss.'

'Understandable.'

'Then I set my nets – the eminently bribable Mrs Hyman Kaplan and her kind – which drew you to me by the power of words as like attracts like, synonymantically. I refer to my little game with the names of hotels.'

'It worked.'

'It surely did.' Quimby grinned, and I noticed for the first time that he had acquired a moustache and beard, which grew in wiry curls around his fleshy, fruity mouth. 'And now it's party time!'

The hotel was quiet. Nothing was stirring, not even a moose. Quimby and I descended to the courtyard, where he had parked his gossamer-grey Packard coupé in the dappled shadow of some hazel bushes.

'Where are we going?' I asked.

'Fear not, Cinderella, you *shall* go to the ball. Washington, if that's all right with you, kiddo.'

I took a seat on the passenger side. Quimby took his place and started the engine. 'Hang on to your hat, pardner. The sooner they invent safety belts, the better.'

So we were off, and, *quelle surprise*, we arrived in Washington three hours before we left Maiden Falls. Which, I admit, is an impressive feat for mere mortals, but *un morceau de gâteau* for magical realist novelists or a brace of temporarily temporally displaced vampires. At all events, when we arrived before a tall white house (in Georgetown, I believe), it appeared to be hopping with life, especially after the hotel which we had left in its maidenly slumbers by the plangent falls.

A black footman in full fig, frogged and wigged, admitted Quimby and me to the house. Quimby threw his hat, careless of whether it would be caught by another flunkey, and cried, 'Arthur, is the Boss here?'

'He sho' is, Massa Clarence,' replied Arthur, winking at me waggishly. 'Lordy, but it do ma ol' heart good to see you agin.'

'That's enough of that,' said Quimby.

'Where's the bar?'

'In the Jefferson room.'

'Very good. Come with me,' said my guide briskly, and I followed.

We entered a large reception room painted yellow and white and lit by a cascade of brilliants from a central chandelier. Another band – Cuban to all appearances – was playing, and a stout woman, vividly dressed in colours reminding me of the flag of a banana republic, was singing; caressing a microphone with one hand while, with the other, seemingly steadying a mountainous perruque topped with hot-house fruits. Quimby procured a bourbon for me and ordered himself a bloody Mary which, after he had dunked his snout in it several times, encrusted the rim of beard and moustache and accentuated the red gash that sat in the fold of his face-fur.

'*La toute* Washington is here,' said Quimby complacently. He seized the arm of a passing grandee. 'May I introduce you? Mr Haze, this is Colonel Latoot Washington, the senior senator for the Pelican state. *Ong-shone-tay de vous rev-wire, mon colonel.*'

'Hell, don't snow me with that Frenchie shit, Clarence,' said the senator cheerfully. 'Say, that reminds me, are you going to take me up on that invitation to see my whores? And you, too, Mr Hess. You do like to ride good whores, don't you?'

'Well…'

'The Colonel has the best stables in Louisiana,' explained Quimby as he led me away.

My next interlocutor was a fellow with steel-grey hair who wore a white tuxedo. Quimby sought him out and again made the introductions. 'Mr Harry Haze, this is Mr Ted Gottlos. Ted is a major Party contributor but more famous for his religious and charitable works.'

'The Ted Gottlos Baptist College in Hotzeplotz, Ohio,' said Gottlos genially. 'Where'd you say the other Hotzeplotz was, Clarence?'

'Zembla.'

'Jeez, where 'n hell is that? Never mind. I also broadcast on the radio for the comfort of the righteous and the salvation of the ungodly. You heard of the Hellfire and Happiness Hour, Mr Hiss?'

'An occasional mention, perhaps.'

'Well, good for you! I didn't know nobody could listen in outside of the great state of Nevada. I like you, son. Do you care for Latoot?'

'Excuse me?'

'I said: would you care for a toot? *Comprende?* A toot of cocaine?'

'I don't do cocaine.'

Gottlos looked at me solemnly and placed a hand on my shoulder. He said, 'Seriously, son, you should consider it. There are tribes in South America or South Africa or someplace who use it in the worship of Almighty God. You got to move with the times. And I got to move too – do you know where the horses are?'

'Louisiana.'

'Louisiana? You're joshin' me. I'm looking to get laid tonight, not next week.' He patted my arm and said, 'Clarence, you take care of this boy of yours.'

When Gottlos had disappeared, I asked Quimby, 'Why have you brought me here?'

'Because, old sport, this is America, the land of minorities, and we have got to stick together.'

'I told you, I'm not a vampire any more.'

Quimby buttonholed me. 'Listen, Jim Crow. Jus' cos you can pass fer white, don' mean you ain't a nigger like the rest of us folks.'

'I can try,' I said.

Before the conversation could continue further, the music stopped and the singer got down from the dais, sashayed in my direction, and, with a nod to Clarence, asked me in deep, honeyed tones, 'Well, hi there, sailor. Care to dance?'

To avoid any further dispute with my companion, I agreed. The band had struck up a rumba and I took the floor with my partner, who said her name was Velda. She was, for my taste, somewhat coarse-featured and stricken in years, but she could move in a reptilian fashion, fat and sleek like a boa constrictor. I felt the pressure of her fingers on the muscles of my arm.

She said admiringly, 'What brings you to see Washington?'

'The Colonel?'

'That *shlemiel*? No, child, the city.'

'Clarence Quimby invited me to meet people.'

'Clarence! Well, you're in good company, sailor, even though that face-fungus makes his face look like a cunt – if you'll pardon my French. Speaking of which, do you do French?'

'I'm sorry?'

'French? I asked if you speak French. You bein' you-row-peen an' all.'

'Yes, as a matter of fact I do. Why? Do you want to learn French?'

Velda laughed. 'Heck, no. I was just makin' conversation. My only interest in French is gobblin' dicks. But y'all knew that, didn' you, darlin'?'

The music stopped. Quimby came over and eased me out of Velda's embrace. To her, he said, 'You'll have to excuse us, Edgar. Harry and I have got to talk.'

I was taken aside to a billiard room where several drunks were laid out on the table and being serviced by whores or horses, I forget which. I whispered to Clarence, 'Velda was Edgar – as in J. Edgar Hoover?'

'The very same, *il capo di tutti capi*. I wanted you to see him.'

'Why?'

'To see what we're up against.'

'We?'

'Nosferatu.'

'I've told you … in any case, what interest does Hoover have in … *us*? '

'I'll explain.' Clarence glanced over his shoulder and said urgently, 'But not here. Come on, would you like to see the horse?'

'The whores?'

'Are you deaf or something? I said "horse". These old places have stables at the rear. Most of them are converted for servants or garages, but Latoot keeps a carriage.' He tugged my sleeve and we left to find Arthur, who showed us through the menial offices to the mews behind the house where, sure enough, a horse was kept. I patted its muzzle, felt its breath on my hand, and listened to the whiffle of that same breath. The air was warm and smelled of hay and grave earth.

'So?' I asked.

'Okay,' said Quimby. 'What do you make of this Red Menace? The loyalty oaths? The blacklists? McCarthy and Nixon?'

'It seems rather overdone.'

'Exactly!'

'Yes? And?'

'Do you know how many Communists there are in America?'

'I've no idea. Thousands, apparently.'

'In America? Come on, old sport, try harder.'

'A few hundred?'

'There are *five*,' said Quimby. 'And four of those have doubts. If we were talking about Jews, they couldn't say prayers. Now do you follow?'

'I'm afraid I don't.'

Exasperated, Quimby stalked up and down the yard. The horse whinnied and I patted him. Fixing me with his bloody eye, Clarence said, 'This Red Scare is just a front. Hoover doesn't care about Reds. he doesn't believe in them.'

'I see. A front for what?'

'For Edgar's campaign against vampires.'

'*Vampires?*'

'Sure. He can't *stand* vampires. He thinks we dress better and have more interesting sex lives than he does.'

'And you?'

Quimby eyed me shiftily. 'I'm helping him while secretly protecting our own. He doesn't suspect me.'

And, members of the jury, why should he? Which of us suspects the vampires in our midst?

CHAPTER TWENTY-SIX

That night, Saturday, was the sixth after Lucy's disappearance, and I had a dream. Or possibly not. Sometimes, when dreaming, I am conscious and able to comfort myself, saying, 'This is a dream,' which is usually enough to bring it to an end. More commonly, however, and no matter how absurd the content, at the time it carries complete conviction and my ability to define the experience as 'a dream' comes from comparisons and reflections made in my waking state which override all prior conviction and destroy it by the tests of logic and plausibility. If this were not so, 'dreaming' and 'waking' would have no certain meanings and, no doubt, I should go mad.

Yet intermediate cases do exist: experiences that persuade us at the time but in retrospect seem implausible, yet cannot definitely be rejected as impossible. I am speaking about Lucy. If there were no proof that she was dead, it's possible that I saw her, isn't it?

For supper I must have eaten something containing raw onion, a food that repeats on me. Combined with jetlag, it was one of the banes of my travels in India, where onion often slipped unnoticed into relishes and pickles and I knew about it only when I found myself tossing and turning, neither awaken or asleep but in an exhausted twilight state. In such a condition I would turn on the television and watch a house movie, or read a few pages of my book – or I would think that I might have done these things, but could never be certain since I had no recollection of the film or the text, and could only infer the explanation from circumstantial evidence such as the movement of a bookmark to an unfamiliar place in the text; evidence that was inconclusive since the bookmark might have been placed by the boy who cleaned the room, or I might have read the pages prior to retiring and yet forgotten because I was tired. My memories of travel are full of these nights haunted by vague sense impressions, no more substantial than the after-images left by a bright light. And, if we consider time past as 'dead' and time present as 'live', these nights (which, because of their unresolved details, lack individuality) form a species of 'undead' time, not transfixed and laid to rest by the firm recollection of real events, but continuing as vampire memories. Fortunately, such memories are, for the most part, of no importance.

I woke in darkness, too disorientated and distracted to read. My abdomen felt gassy and bloated. My breath tasted foul. I went to the kitchen and helped myself to a glass of mineral water; then, feeling too restless to return to bed, put on some clothes so I shouldn't get cold.

I don't know how long I sat in a chair staring at the window, but at some point I decided that a walk would help to settle the gas and keep me warm. Also my mind, which had been sunk in animal inactivity, was now firing off random thoughts about Sally and Lucy and Harry's stories. From experience I knew that fresh air would help me think more coherently and that this would be better than being, as it were, an uneasy audience to a clamour of random voices.

I went to the door and opened it. These last few nights, the moon had crept closer to full and the garden was bathed in a pale light. So, too, in the distance, was the steeple of St Hilaire which rose above the blackness of the village like an iceberg floating in a calm, dark sea. Still further away, the vertical line of cliffs and crags captured its share of moonlight in crevices and planes of reflection, and I thought of the edge of pack-ice, behind which would stretch an infinity of snow, menacing, quiet, and majestic.

A police car was parked in the lane. I remembered that Barrès had posted a man to keep watch over his excavations. My eye turned to these and I saw that what had once been Lucy's garden was now an expanse of spoil heaps and pits like empty graves. As for the man himself, I found him in the seat of his car, still sitting upright as if he had been on the point of driving away when struck by a sudden enchantment so that he seemed not truly asleep but spell-bound by the moon.

I walked down the path. La Maison des Moines was shuttered and in darkness and I felt under no urge to disturb Harry, or, rather, as though that natural urge had been placed under a ban it would be dangerous to violate. I reached the *route nationale*, where I paused out of habit, looking in both directions for the non-existent traffic along the grey tarmac ribbon; pausing longer than circumstances would warrant; conscious that I must let the ghost cars pass.

So on into the village and past the silent baker's shop and the Bar des Sports and across the bridge where the two medieval toilets, normally the cause of amusement, kept sentinel. I heard the first sound other than my own footfalls. The stream was still rolling in a gentle lilt over the rocks, though it was invisible in the dark chasm between the flanking houses.

Beyond the bridge, a short stretch of narrow street ended in the square. I saw a length of shadow, like the figure of a tall man, though this unknown person was only the object of mild curiosity and I almost looked forward to meeting him, in the way that, when lonely, we seek the company of strangers to lighten our thoughts with the sound of a human voice. But there was no one, only the war memorial, which was made to seem more spare and static by the scurrying of a cat.

I had a notion to go into the church. It occurred to me that I had not seen the windows and their images of Albert the Good and the Châtelaine d'Échalotte by moonlight. I doubted anyone ever had: not even the priest saying mass on a winter's evening, when the altar candles and the lights in the nave would ward off the moon as if she were the devil. It was not the fact that the church was certainly locked which restrained me, but the sense that I was following an ordained path which was my only source of safety. I could in any case enter the place in imagination and I knew that, as the earth rotated, so the chancel was filled with two figures of fleeting moonlight, telling off the hours of the night with a dance.

It was clear to me now that my goal was the lake. I was reminded of Sir Bedevere who was commanded to return the sword of the dying Arthur; and of those perilous places that are not perilous to those of a pure heart. Pure – not perfect. Sir Bedevere was tested by the doubts and desires of his own nature, and only at the last attempt brought to obedience. Even when the path seems clear to those who do not have to follow it, those who undertake the enterprise find it obscured by clouds of revenants: spirits and vampires of inclination and memory; conjurors of false glamours. It is for this reason that the future is so often a revisiting of the past and so rarely seen as such. And the path that seems to lead directly and unimpeded to the lake, will in fact turn and take us into the shadow of the osiers where we have often walked before.

If nothing else, it is clear that, waking or dreaming, I was overwrought. I was seeing not objects in a landscape but a series of figures, none of which was complete in itself but each referring by simile or speculation to something ineffable. No doubt the details of my vision were those of a commonplace mind, but the criticism hardly matters: certainly not enough to diminish the fact of the vision or its intensity. And yet at the surface of my mind and in my actions I felt calm as if, for example, I had met Harry, also sleepless and taking the night air; in which case we would have expressed surprise and pleasure and explained why we were up and about so late; and in a few words the enchantment of the night would have been dispelled, we would have walked home together; and in the morning I would recall as a fact not a dream that I had gone for a pleasant stroll and afterwards drunk a cup of chocolate to settle my nerves.

But I did not meet Harry. I saw the still lake with the moon floating on it, moonlight on the silver sand, moonshadow under the trees. And Lucy walking at her ease, flickering in and out of the osiers along the avenue, dragging her feet slowly like a little girl, who, bored with following her parents, dawdles with only half an eye on them and talks in her head to friends who are not there.

Of course I did not know it was Lucy. I was too far away. What I saw was a dark-haired, bare-legged, barefooted woman in a white dress, who, in the rhythm of walking, vanished and reappeared with the regular rhythm of the trees. A figure whom I might have dismissed as an illusion, a construct of moonlight and shadow. But what illusion carries a pair of sandals in her right hand, swings them playfully, and twirls one on her finger?

I quickened my pace, frightened of disturbing her. I reached the beginning of the osier avenue, which stretched out in bars of alternate light and shadow between the glimmer of the lake on one side and the black descent to the fields on the other. As if in a succession of tableaux, Lucy stepped from darkness into light into darkness, but, though her face was hidden, I saw her clearly enough to know that she was no mere apparition. I do not think that, even in my imagination, I would have created a figure who, except in her pale colouring, was so at odds with the mood of the night, being, so it seemed, blithe and unaware of her surroundings. I fancy she was humming a tune. I fancy she halted for a second, quite unconcerned, shook out her hair and ran her fingers though it.

I called, 'Lucy' – not loudly, since the night was so still it seemed the slightest sound would carry to the world's end. The woman stopped and her face turned, not abruptly but with a curiously mechanical circular motion. In the fugitive light I tried to fix an image of Lucy, but the truth is I could not say if it were she or not, and already the opportunity was gone. She had turned and was running away from me. I followed but, Lucy or not, she was younger, fitter and less earthbound than I was, so that, although I could prevent the distance between us from increasing, I could not close it.

We emerged from the avenue at the point where the bank curved to turn back by the far side of the lake; the place where the regular line of osiers ended in dense scrub and isolated trees, where the clothes of the Moineau boy had been found. I floundered for a minute until, regaining my bearings, I saw her a distance away walking along the sand, still swinging her sandals unconcernedly.

I set to running again. As soon as she saw me, she too began to run. But this time, even though I could not catch her, I could at least hear her panting breath, which reassured me that, if I were not dreaming, she was a creature of flesh and blood and no mere phantom.

So on, and the lake was behind us and we were running in the dark lanes of the village. Again I found myself in the square, where the shadow of the memorial had rotated with the transit of the moon and now pointed at me accusingly; a sinister detail but one that suggested I was experiencing the passage of real time.

I paused, out of breath, not knowing which exit my quarry had taken. I listened, and heard the slow, flat flop of sandals in the street directly ahead. I followed at a rapid walk and glimpsed her by the small arcade where the market was held. She was swinging by an outstretched arm as if one of the columns was the pivot of a carousel, and her pale face and dress fluttered in and out of the light of a single faint lamp. Seeing me, she gave a little gasp and vanished, but I knew that she was running towards the *route nationale*, since I could hear the noise of her sandals, and again I glimpsed her as she emerged from the street on to the open highway and as quickly disappeared. Within seconds I was at the same spot, and automatically I paused to allow the ghostly traffic to pass.

To left and right the road ran to Quillan and Lavelanet. Directly on the other side it forked between the path leading uphill past La Maison des Moines to Lo Blanc and the cemetery and the road to Chalabre, which inclined more gently in a narrow defile overlooked by the gardens of Harry's house and his neighbours'. I was convinced that the figure in white had taken this latter way, in which case I should find her quickly, because this was the extremity of the village and the road was fenced in by steep banks with no way of escape.

But I did not find her. Nor could I hear her. I walked along the road for the better part of a kilometre until I reached the junction where another, narrow route wound its way to Quillan. There I stopped, and was able to survey the fields around me and look back towards Puybrun. It was possible, of course, that she had hidden in a hedge or ditch and that a still patch of moonlight spattered with leaf shadow was the trace of her dress; and perhaps by beating about the deserted fields I might have started her, as one flushes out a hare, but by now I was convinced that I was dreaming, and I told myself that, come morning, I should be able to reflect on what had happened and test it for its correspondence to comfortable, credible reality, or, even better, I should have forgotten – which would be the perfect touchstone of a dream.

I was woken at ten by the sound of the police working at their fool's errand in the garden. I looked out of the window and saw two of them in their shirtsleeves digging a grave, under the eyes of Gérard, who was sitting on the wall, silent and smoking like a melancholy Hamlet. Taking pity on them, I stuck my head out of the door and offered some coffee. When it was brewed, I decided to drink my cup outside and so perched myself next to the *brigadier*.

He said, 'You seem very confident that we shall find nothing.'

I answered, 'I am. I haven't killed Lucy, and I doubt that anyone else could have popped a body into the garden without my knowing.'

My language was too flippant, but unlike Gérard I was more and more certain that Lucy was alive. Although I couldn't be sure about the events of the previous night, I felt that, even if not 'real' in the conventional sense, they nevertheless reflected an aspect of the truth. To take a naively Freudian viewpoint, my 'dream' – if that's what it was – was an essay at unravelling the clues to the mystery using data that were as yet only partly assimilated in my conscious mind. It was an imperfect solution, but it gave me confidence to believe that, at some level of awareness, I knew the truth.

'What will you do next?' I asked Gérard.

'It is not permitted to say.'

'Have you sent the papers to the *juge d'instruction*?'

'What if we have? Does that bother you?'

'No. You forget that I'm a lawyer. These things have to be decided according to evidence, and there is no evidence.'

Gérard looked at me coolly and thoughtfully. He said, 'You seem to want to make some sort of impression upon me, as if we are playing games. I don't know many Englishmen – in fact, Monsieur Harper, you are the only one – but I've heard of the famous sense of humour. You should be cautious of behaving in inappropriate ways simply because they amuse you''

I accepted the rebuke. 'I'm sorry' I said, and asked him sincerely, 'But what does "appropriate" mean? Surely, what is appropriate when someone is dead is not the same as when she is living?'

'That's very true and, if that's all it is, there are grounds for being uncertain how to behave. But have you in fact told me everything, Monsieur Harper?'

'I've told you everything I know.'

'Everything you *know* you know.'

'If you like.'

I went inside and read for an hour or so until I heard the sound of Gérard and his men leaving and then the arrival of another vehicle in the lane. It was the old VW van containing Willie and her Greek. This morning she was dressed in an unattractive blouse and a skirt worn to mid-calf; her legs were bare and needed shaving; her feet were encased in all-terrain sandals; and she gave me the impression of a disappointed schoolmistress who wished to give a pupil a dressing-down for wearing earrings during a games lesson. That impression was, however, only brief and was succeeded by the feeling that she was a sad woman who was obscurely angry with life.

'Good morning, Willie, Theo,' I said. 'What brings you here? Can I offer you something?'

'Beer,' said Theo.

'Nothing for me,' said Willie. We were still outside. She flopped into a rattan chair, cast her eyes over the excavations and continued with calm acidity, 'What's all this about? The police been looking for my sister's body, have they, you bastard?' She enunciated 'bastard' as if it were my title, like 'doctor'.

'The police don't know what's happened to Lucy. No one does. They have to look into all possibilities.'

'But you do know what's happened, don't you?'

'I know no such thing.'

'Yes, you do. You've bloody well murdered her.'

'No, I haven't.'

I got the beer for Theo. Seeing it, Willie said, 'I've changed my mind. I'll have some wine.'

'White or red?'

'As it comes. Bring the bottle. Are you drinking?'

'I think I'll have a brandy.'

I fixed the drinks and brought out the tray. I took a seat in one of the free chairs. I said, without being ironic, 'You're taking things very well – drinking with a murderer.'

Willie didn't look at me. Squint-eyed in the sunlight, she was taking in the view. 'Yeah,' she said. 'I know. I'm still getting my head around the idea.'

'Did you find a hotel?'

'Naw. We camped in the village.'

Noticing her cream-coloured skirt and blouse, an idea occurred to me and I asked. 'Did you go for a walk round the lake or through the village last night?'

'Do me a favour.'

'I take it you didn't?'

'I was knackered after all the travelling. Now it's my turn for a question. Why did you kill Lucy?'

'I didn't.'

'Why didn't you tell me yesterday that her clothes had been found and the police called in?'

'I didn't want to distress you.'

Willie snorted. 'What a gentleman!' She helped herself to another glass of wine. A tear crept down her cheek. I glanced at Theo. He had the puzzled expression of a family dog which senses but does not understand the mood of a quarrel between its owners. Dog-like, he snuffled in his beer. 'Well, aren't we the civilised ones!' continued Willie. 'You've fucked my sister and then fucking killed her, and here we are chatting about it like characters in a fucking Mary Wesley novel.'

'I don't think they swear so much,' I said.

'Then fuck 'em if they don't,' murmured Willie.

We fell silent for what must have been a few minutes, during which there were only a few exchanges between Willie and Theo in Greek; and, once, Theo, after a second beer, asked convivially, 'What do you think of the football, eh? Wicked or what?'

I remembered my earlier conversation with Gérard. Willie's demeanour seemed to me as bizarre as mine had earlier seemed to him, and I wondered from where we get our notions of what is appropriate to situations of which we have no experience outside fiction. The difference between us – between myself and Gérard – was that, however suspicious I might be of Willie, I could recognise in her oddity genuine bewilderment and grief; but in my case Gérard was unable or unwilling to make that leap of imagination. And this in turn made me wonder if it were because I was a lawyer: so practised in detachment and the fabrication of emotions and stories to defend unworthy causes that, in the last analysis, nothing I did or said could ever be entirely believed.

At length Willie said, 'Did you love Lucy?' Past tense.

'I do love her.'

'Uh huh. And where's whatsherface?'

'Sally? She's gone back to Montaillou. She's staying there with friends.'

'Then why did she come here – assuming you guys haven't got together again?'

'She heard through my son, Jack, that there was some sort of problem, and she was concerned.'

'Concerned for a shit like you? Christ, what a saint.' Willie sounded sceptical yet admiring; willing to consider that Sally was a good woman, even if fit for a zoo. As for 'a shit like you', she used the expression in the same neutral tone in which she had called me 'bastard', and I glanced at Theo, who, I suspected, was a fellow-member of the Shits and Bastards Club. She might, of course, be right about both of us, but I pitied her for this black view of men. It seems to me that there are some propositions which, even if true, should not be accepted by a well-balanced mind. At all events, I thought that Sally, with her willingness to accept the risks of love, was a more sensible person than Willie.

'I suppose you thought Lucy adored you, didn't you?' said Willie.

'I wouldn't say "adored". I think she loved me – *loves* me.'

'She thought you were going nuts.' Willie gave me this information as easily as two old women might complain of their husbands' reluctance to change socks.

'I don't believe you,' I said.

'No?' retorted Willie, her voice rising in pitch. 'Then believe this!'

She had a bag with her, very old, once very expensive; the kind picked up for five pounds at antiques fairs. In some ways it paralleled Harry's carpet bag in that it was the kind purchased only as a token of something else that is dreamed of. She fumbled at the tarnished clasp and then at the torn black moiré lining. And finally she produced an envelope bearing a French stamp, from which she extracted several pages of a letter. She handed this to me, saying, 'All right, you asked for it. Prepare yourself for a revelation.' I read it.

The letter was from Lucy to her sister, addressed *poste restante* Athens and dated April. It set out in some detail the history of our time together in France. As a bald statement of fact, it was accurate in reciting my successive attempts at painting and writing, and my expedition into the *garrigue* during the winter. In its interpretation, however, and in particular its characterisation of me and of

314

Lucy's response, it was, as Willie had promised, a revelation. I'd known – I've never denied – that my behaviour during that period was eccentric. It was – is – rationally explicable in the light of the stress of the experience I was going through; which was the more acute because of the regularity of my previous life, my unadventurous nature, and my acknowledged feelings of guilt. But the letter did not describe eccentricity. It described obsession and, moreover, not an obsession that was fading as I worked towards the solution of my problems, but, rather, increasing – one need only consider how what had begun on a few sketches made around the village had become an insane journey into the mountains. Most of all – and this is what was most pitiful – no reader except Lucy herself, who was blinded by love, could fail to detect the sinister note in my behaviour or be unaware that Lucy was stumbling headlong into danger. If one believed the letter.

'Did you reply?' I asked evenly.

'I sent a card.'

'I've read your card. The tone is quite cheerful – not what I'd expect from someone who'd received this.' I tapped the letter slowly. 'In fact, your card makes no reference to it.'

Willie opened her mouth as if astonished, closed it, smiled slyly and asked,' Are you cross-examining me? Jesus H fucking Christ! Theo, are you listening to this? This rotten, cold-hearted bastard is cross-examining *me!*'

'Answer the question. Why doesn't your card refer to Lucy's letter? Why is it so cheerful? Didn't you care what was happening? Even if the letter didn't frighten you, why didn't it evoke a single word of commiseration? It wouldn't have been difficult. In fact I could write the card for you – the card you *would* have written if you'd really received this letter. Doesn't it go like this: "Dear Lu, Thanks for your letter. I always warned you that the Bozo was a dangerous bastard, just like all men." Do you want me to go on, Willie? Why didn't you write *that* card?'

'Because I knew you'd read it,' said Willie softly.

We stared at each other in silence for some moments. Theo fidgeted uncomfortably and then proposed, 'Shall I get some more drinks? That bottle looks empty. Another whisky, or was it brandy, for you, John? I think I can find my way around inside. Beer in the fridge?'

'Make mind brandy, too,' said Willie. To me she said, 'Well? Satisfied?'

I asked, 'Are you and Lucy twins?'

Willie laughed. 'What? Us? Twins? Where'd you get that idea from?'

'Why does Lucy call you her "other half"?'

This time she was genuinely amused. 'It's a joke from when we were kids. Lu was always the good, perfect little girl – and I was always the bad one. Together we were two halves of a normal child.'

'It sounds as if you didn't like Lucy.'

'That shows how little you understand. I loved her. And I don't give a shit whether you believe me.'

'You're not twins?'

'No! I'm a year younger than Lu. Second children are always the most difficult – if that's how you like your psychology. Christ, what's all this about? What does it matter?'

In that unguarded moment of enquiry Willie looked almost like Lucy. Indeed I saw then that there was in fact a very close physical resemblance, but one that was disguised by differences of style and, more especially, by differences of experience and character that had etched the younger sister's face with lines of resentment and a dozen other abuses, as if she were Lucy's portrait in the attic.

I picked up the letter again and studied it more closely. The handwriting was to all appearances Lucy's; but – something which hadn't struck me before – it was also that of Willie's postcard from Greece. The sisters shared that, too, and it gave me a clue – if not the total explanation of what had happened.

I tore the letter up under Willie s incredulous eyes.

She cried. 'You can't do that! It's evidence!'

'It's evidence of nothing,' I answered coldly. 'You wrote that letter, not Lucy. That's why I couldn't recognise Lucy in it. I don't know what's happened to her, but I think that you and Theo do. And, if you don't want me to take my suspicions to the police' – I looked down at the shreds of paper lying on the ground – 'you'll say nothing about a letter that doesn't exist.'

I was calm. I'm trained to be calm, and my calmness means nothing. But Willie couldn't be expected to understand, and she had her own position to defend.

She said, bitterly, 'I don't know what you're talking about, but I'll tell you something for nothing, John.'

'What's that, Willie?'

'You're a dangerous fucking madman.'

CHAPTER TWENTY-SEVEN

Harry's Tale

Hotzeplotz, my Hotzeplotz!
'Tis mad I am for Thee!
Where flows the Ole Meshuggeneh
Through cornfields to the sea;
Where burbles, too, the Mishegoss
Through haze that mars the dawn.
Lay me down beneath their hazels;
Let me rest there when I'm gone.

Let me rest there when I'm gone,
Let me rest there when I'm gone.
When I and Ole Meshuggeneh
Are finally at one.

How high, Ohio! Oh, I owe
A debt that can't be paid
Until by Ole Meshuggeneh
My corpse at last is laid.
My sanity depends on Thee,
And this is what I crave:
That in the shade of hazels.
I rest quiet in my grave.

I rest quiet in my grave,
I rest quiet in my grave.
For I shall be Meshuggeneh
When there is nought to save.

Ding dong! Vampire calling!

Or so the bells of hell ring in the ears of Homeless Harry as he stands with his carpet bag of nightmares on the porch of the Humperl household and talks to *gnädige* Frau Humperl through the fly screen.

Let me set the record straight on this point. Dolores, alias Dolly, Humperl was above the age for statutory rape in the State of Ohio, or indeed anywhere else, being by her own admission twenty-nine years old and by everyone else's thirty-five. She was also a registered Republican voter, a condition not permitted to persons under thirty without a certificate signed by two doctors. I emphasise this because the fantasies of my kleptobiographer, Volodya Botkin, have it that Dolly was a nymphet still a couple of years shy of bobby sox. Whereas, *im Gegenstand*, I aver that she was a woman mature in both mind and body, a pert, plump (not to say porky) little number capable of engaging what remained of affection in my bloodless heart. Let me be further plain about this. When Volodya was knocking out his book, my patron and dancing partner J. Edgar Hoover was still waging his campaign against Undead American Activities. It was, put at its simplest, unsafe for Volodya to treat my existence in a manner which the prurient might claim would lead to emulation. How much wiser to write of nympholepsy, a perversion far less plausible, less attractive and less widespread than vampirism.

Meanwhile on the porch of Casa Humperl.

'Ye-es? You are?' says the welcoming winsome creature.

'Permit me, dear lady. I am Doktor Heinrich Haze, visiting professor of Comparative Literature at the Ted Gottlos Baptist College. You have heard of me? Been advised to expect me? The registrar – Mrs Merkin, I believe – informed me that she had arranged accommodation.'

'You are German?'

'I speak German. My nationality, until the Soviet Union invaded my country, was Zemblan.'

Dolly beams. 'You speak German! Wonderful! I mean *wunderbar*! I am delighted. *Ich bin empört*.'

She opens the fly screen and Hopeful Harry feels the faintest stirrings in his withered loins. To be clinical, Dolly is five three and about a hundred and thirty pounds, a goodly number of which are stacked about her chest. Harry suspects – rightly, as it turns out – that her munchable mammaries will sag a little on intimate inspection but, taken as a whole, she is in fair shape; her body has had one careful lady owner and the coachwork is in good order. For the sake of the film script I go on to add that her hair is à la Veronica Lake and her nose and mouth pleasantly asymmetric, lending interest and a note of good humour to her face. She tenders a hand, which Harry, whose blood flows cold and sluggish, takes in his own chill paw

'My!' she coos. 'We're not very warm today, are we, Herr Doktor? Still, it is a little early in the season and you've walked from the station. Did you walk or use a cab? If you walked, you must have taken in the views of our lovely Meshuggeneh river.'

'I took a cab.'

'*Wie Schade!* Still, you have a pleasure in store. Our river is *sehr schön* and famous hereabouts. It has a moderating effect on our climate, which can be cold in winter. There's a spot, only a little ways out of town, where a small lake is formed. We call it Joy Hole. In summer it's very shady on account of all the hazel trees. We must go there in the summer. I mean if you decide to stay, of course!' She laughs as if she has made an indecent suggestion.

Why am I here, talking to this delightful lady instead of still pursuing pussy in the Catskills? To understand that, you must refer to my vampire chum, Clarence. Since our trip to Washington, he has continued to harass Harry through his quimomantic games with the map of New England. I have been invited to stage my act at the Love Nest Tavern, the Amorous Valley Restaurant and the Warm Nook Hotel. The Fur Trappers of America were kindly pleased to ask me to their ball. Some realtors tempted me to invest in the Dark Gulch Fun Resort (New Mexico – a little out of my territory). The life of a stand-up comedian requires fine timing and steady nerves quite incompatible with Clarence's distractions. I sought a quieter life.

'I'd invite you in straight away,' says Dolly, 'but the house is being cleaned.' She detects herself making a faux pas and puts a hand prettily to her mouth. 'Oops! I don't want you getting the wrong idea that we have *servants*. It wouldn't do at all to give that impression to the neighbours, who know for a fact that it's only Mrs Kowalczyk who comes in twice a week.' She adds secretively, 'She's *Polish*, you know. Isn't Zembla near Poland?'

'Very close. May I put my bag down?'

'*Natürlich!* Oh, how rude I am not to notice, and so heavy I don't doubt, with books and things you need as a professor. And what a pretty carpet bag! So old and so quaint, where did you get it?'

'In Greenwich Village.'

'I *love* quaint – or do I mean quaintity? In Hotzeplotz we have so little that is quaint except some very religious Jewish people, on account that the town isn't very old. On the other hand, along the banks of the Mishegoss (which is a stream flowing into the Meshuggeneh at Joy Hole) you can pick up arrowheads which, if not exactly quaint, are at least *old*, and that's almost the same but not as *nice*.'

Out of the blue, courtesy of US Mail, had come a letter from Ted Gottlos inviting me to leave my lair in the Catskills and visit him in Las Vegas. I travelled by Greyhound in the company of GIs returning home in that brief interlude between wars. I fed myself on furburgers in bus-station diners liberally sauced with neon light and unfiltered Camel cigarettes. I watched lonely people reading copies of *True Crime* over cups of cold coffee and reflected sentimentally on the days when they had been meat on the hoof for my cannibal appetite: the days when derelicts and winos were the original version of fast food, eaten on the run and the rubbish discarded in an alleyway by the trash cans.

In 1948 Las Vegas had not yet been civilised by the Mob. My empty billfold and a Quimbyish whim directed me to a cheap cabin at the Red Snapper Motor Court, where an emblem of said fish flickered intermittently in the purple evening. The following morning I attended on Ted at his office in the Strip. He was in a religious mood and coked to the eyes.

To digress within a digression, I was never one with an eye to dress and merely asked my tailor to equip me *à la mode*. Also 1948 is a ways away and my memory, unlike Marcel's, is a little hazy. But for the benefit of the MGM costume department, I recall Ted wearing a wide-lapelled charcoal suit, soft-collar shirt and a felt hat (I believe hat brims were tending to become narrower). Stanislavsky was not yet in vogue, so in the scene that following I was spared any mumbling on my host's part.

'Brother Harry!' announced Ted. 'The Lord has sent you unto me like Paul was sent unto the Corinthians and Ephemerals and all those other guys, to be a Light unto the Gentry. Did Brother Clarence speak to you?'

'I haven't seen Clarence since we met you in Washington.'

'Uh-huh? You don't say. Cigar?' He offered me a cigar like a gift-wrapped turd. He parked himself in a leatherette executive chair and invited me to another. 'Hal – can I call you Hal? – what do you know about books?'

'I've read a few.'

'I guessed it . Being a European, I figured you'd read somewhat.' He grinned. 'But, what the hell, Hal, does it take talent to teach literature to a bunch of kids who only want to play football? Wasn't Paul a tent-maker? And didn't Mark or Matthew – I forget which – work for the IRS? And those guys wrote Holy Scripture already!'

'Indeed they did,' ventured Harry, who had a sniff of employment more congenial than amusing his fellow Hebrews with Polack jokes.

'I own a college back in Ohio,' said my prospective employer. 'The Ted Gottlos Baptist College in Hotzeplotz. You may have heard of it? Our motto is "Pray hard and shoot straight". And that's what I am, a straight shooter, whether in bed or boardroom.'

'You intrigue me.'

'I surely hope so.'

We exchanged what is commonly called a 'knowing' smile, though as often as not it signals no more than conspiratorial ignorance.

'You'll have tea?' says Dolly. Although she is unsophisticated, she has that commendable sense of equality which I admire in American women. She opens the fly screen and does not wait on a reply, granting me a tantalising glimpse of the interior of Schloss Humperl, and calls, 'Mrs Kowalczyk, could you break off of what you're doing and make tea for myself and the gentleman.' To me she says, 'Being a European, you'll take it with lemon, I know. I have lemon substitute, which I bought this morning, expecting you. I can put in a regular order, if you like.'

I loathe lemon, but for this fetching lady I will consume it by the grove. But I wish she would allow me to leave the porch. Since I gave up flying on batlike wings, I've taken to walking and my dogs are killing me. Notwithstanding the journey by cab, I want a bath (not a shower, since I am a filthy foreigner) and then to ensconce myself in Mrs H's spare room, which I imagine to be roomy and spare.

'Oh my!' she says, looking to the heavens. 'I think we're in for a storm.'

I follow her gaze to the sky and see anvil-heads flickering with lightning on a horizon so distant it could be in another state.

'It'll be here in an hour,' says Dolly. 'I hope my storm shutters will stand the strain.' She smiles.

Indeed the storm will come. The vampires are at your door, Dolly my darling. I have not spotted how Nature is playing along with the pathetic fallacy, but she is, yes indeedy. The vampire and the maiden will go inside the house and the storm, with its due accompaniment of thunder, will rattle about us as gothic as you like. Dolly, naturally, will not understand this. She will take comfort from the presence of her undead soon-to-be-lover, having no notion that he has brought the thunderbolts down on her as surely as a lightning rod.

'What is your opinion about paying taxes,' asked Ted Gottlos, putting his hands together as if to ask, 'Are you saved?'

'I no more like paying them than the next man.'

'It's Ungodly,' pronounced Reverend Ted, which was enough for me. 'The Good Book is quite clear on this point. When Satan offered the Kingdoms of this World to Our Lord, he could not offer what was not his. *Therefore*, those kingdoms – which for this purpose I believe to include republics – belong to Satan and should not be supported by the taxes of Christians. Do you follow me?'

'I do.'

'Praise the Lord!'

'Okeydokey!' Did I really say that?

'Then let's come down to cases. The college is a nice tax racket and the Lord don't care shit if you teach those kids diddly, if and so long as their souls go to Heaven. Catch my drift? There's a job for you, Hal, provided I have your word that you won't rock the Ark of the Lord.'

I gave my word.

Meantime here comes Mrs K bringing T for D & H.

'With lemon substitute,' says Dolly daintily.

I don't know what lemon substitute is, but it appears to be powder from a small sachet. I smile my suave smile and wet my lips on the rim of the cup. For good measure I stick out my pinkie, which is a European kind of thing.

'The storm shutters,' says Dolly. 'I confess' – *confess* because it is a sophisticated word in the circumstances – 'that I have come down in the world – does one say *unterirdisch*? – and getting little jobs done, like the shutters fixed, has become *exceedingly* difficult.'

At various times Harry has been decidedly *unterirdisch* and I sympathise.

Looking around, I see what she means. A fresh coat of paint is a year or two overdue; a shutter is tied in place with string; and one of the boards on the porch creaks like an old man who wants to join in the conversation.

'Is there a Mr Humperl?' I ask.

Dolly sniffs. She is so full of words and gestures that are used because she considers them appropriate – so *comme il faut*, so *wie es sein muss* – that I love her for it.

'Mr Humped was killed in the war,' she answers sadly.

I do not ask how. The Humperls of Ohio die because they are caught on the latrine when a bomb falls. We shall leave the deceased's heroism acknowledged but undiscussed. I have been given his rocking chair, which has a pretty gingham cover. Old Norman, as I shall learn to call him, was a smoker and also left-handed – there are burns on the rocker arm, insignificant details, but Marcel would have loved them. Also, I shall discover, such matters appeal to Volodya Botkin who, to his credit, makes a sincere effort to get inside my head and improve on my style. Then he buries me in his book. He writes a vampire story but never admits it. I have a file of complaints I wrote from the sanatorium.

The avenues of Hotzeplotz run north to south and are named after poets. The cross-streets are numbered. The Ted Gottlos Baptist College stands at the corner of 9th and Sirin. Sirin was a Zemblan poet who wrote in the style of Alexander Pope. By way of history when Zembla was a province of the Russian Empire, the Tsar (Nicholas I, I believe) expelled a sect of polyandrous Lutherans, who trekked to the banks of the Meshuggeneh and planted Hotzeplotz in the middle of Ohio. Their traces are the Mishegoss Church, which is at 10th and Poe, and a recipe for a local delicacy, 'clam in dark meat' (it sounds better in Zemblan), a reputed aphrodisiac.

When I arrived at the college I was met by the registrar, Mrs Merkin. She collared a passing giant and got him to carry my bag. Then she showed me around the 'educational facility', as she called it.

We stood outside the gymnasium looking over at the football field where two gangs of trolls were slugging it out. A few attractive co-eds had parked their butts on the bleachers and when a point was scored (an event, I confess, which was incomprehensible to me) they set up a chorus of the college anthem: *Hotzeplotz, My Hotzeplotz!* et cetera.

'You appear to have no lecture halls,' I remarked to my companion.

'An appropriation is included in the budget for the next fiscal year,' said the Merkin, stroking her wiry hair.

'But where am I to teach?'

'I thought that Reverend Gottlos had explained. We follow a very liberal policy within the limits of strictly conservative principles. We grant the students credits for their life experiences. Teaching, as such, is rather new with us. I suggest you arrange informal tuition at the soda fountain and the drive-in. You'll find the Joy Hole Drive-In on the highway near the lake of the same name.'

As the storm moves in across the cornfields, the light changes. The sky is as purple as an African, the earth as yellow as an octoroon. Until the storm breaks over us, that is to say, until vampire and victim are shivering in terror at the wind and lash of rain, the effect is quite romantic.

Dolly is naturally a soft person. The love she demands is no more than a moderate kindness which even Hapless Harry can manage. She reads magazine articles of the How-to-Take-Care-of-Your-Man variety and is prone to springing surprise dinners with candles and Hawaiian-style meatloaf. She believes that culture is something knitted, crocheted or covered, and the raw forms of everyday household items are masked in small white starched pieces of daintiness. There are a lot of framed photographs. Dolly thinks they are important in order to establish a tradition in the family.

Do I sound as if I am mocking her? For shame! I *adored* her – though this fact of adoration did not become clear to me until I could see her only through the shade of hazels. I, who had been buried in the past, had never met someone so rooted in the present. I, who had been self-absorbed, had never met someone whose sense of self and will to selfishness were suppressed by a benign desire to follow convention and the good opinion of her neighbours. Dolly was as divinely banal as a Deity who thinks that keeping an eye on the least little sparrow is a good way to run a universe. And she was as worthy of worship.

'You know,' says Dolly as we sip our tea and I keep an ear open for Mrs Kowalczyk to finish and bid farewell, 'I feel as if we've known each other for ever. I'm sure we're going to get on famously. I assume you like old-fashioned home cooking. Or, if you like something exotic, I mean like veal or something – Oh! Forgive me. You're not one of *those people*, are you?'

'Those people?'

'Of the Jewish persuasion?'

I convert on the spot. 'No, you need have no fear – if that's the right word – on that score.'

'Please,' says Dolly, concerned at giving offence (a sin somewhat more heinous than murder, which, I fervently trust, is occasionally forgivable), 'I hope you don't think I'm full of small-town prejudices. It's quite enough for me that Our Lord Jesus Christ was Jewish – though, strictly speaking, only on his mother's side.'

'I have no prejudices either way. Do you think we should go inside before that storm breaks?'

'It's still a ways off. Tell me,' she adds kittenishly, 'is there, or has there been a Frau Doktor Haze?'

In a flash I acquire a wife and bump her off – a performance even Reno cannot better.

'Alas,' I say, 'I had a wife.' I shake my head and debate inwardly whether to elaborate on the tragic circumstances. Did she fall to consumption, clutching a posy of camellias to her pale bosom? Or have the villagers driven a stake through her heart and chopped off her head? If Harry were prone to inventing stories, instead of scrupulous in his regard for truth, he could tell a tale that would get him ejected here and now without passing 'Go' and thereby spare Dolly the horror to come. But Dolly is cursed by kindness; which is why she married that schmuck Norman Humped, who did her no favours. Now, for a change in her sad, respectable life, she is on the receiving end of another's kindness. But the kindness of vampires is a cruel thing.

Of all the colleges in all the world, Volodya Botkin walked into mine. And I didn't even know he was coming. I was too busy teaching literature or, at least, literacy to chronic morons; or staring at the cleavage of my student *la bellissima* Largizione; or tousling Dolly's nether hair. In my absence, the Merkin booked him through the lecture circuit to speak to a few sophomores and a large contingent of IRS agents wanting to know what kind of operation Ted Gottlos was running. And, of course, Prof Haze attended, accompanied by the lovely Mrs Humperl, his landlady if you believe it, hum hum.

That evening was, I guess, the peak of our bliss. We had just returned from vacation and for months there had been nary a sight of the Transylvanian Terror's former habits. Rather Harry the European gent had hand-kissed his way into Dolly's circle of intimates and – quite unlike Botkin's fantastic creature, forever weighed down by his vanity, his guilt and his perversion – I was blithely unconcerned.

To explain this, let me enlighten you with a story. I was once asked, 'Weren't you guilty about being a Nazi war criminal?'

To which I answered. 'Sure.'

'And?'

And nothing. I got over it. Sane people do.

Granted that I was, for a time, *clinically* insane, I maintain that I was at all times *morally* sane. Don't mistake me. I am not against feeling guilty. But one shouldn't wear guilt like last year's fashions.

What I want to know is: am I ever going to get off this damned porch? My hair is tingling as the anvil-heads get closer. Already they are playing the devil with the power supply and Dolly has asked Mrs Kowalczyk to bring out the candles and kerosene lamps. In the street a dog, sensitive to the charged atmosphere, slinks like a serial killer, and the birds have been advised by their attorneys to stay *shtumm*. Dolly does not see that I am fretful. That I am frightened. That I want a taste of Humperlish delights so that I can live in the present and not for ever in my memories.

Goddamn it, I want to be *bored*!

Vampire legend has it that the undead cannot cross a threshold unless invited. However, in my case it is mere politeness that restrains me. Dolly, like an inexperienced salesman, does not know when the punter has bought the goods.

She says, 'Did you and Frau Haze have any children?'

'We weren't blessed,' I answer sanctimoniously.

'Not...? '

'There were religious objections on her part,' I say, waggishly hinting that she might have belonged to a flagellant cult of the Virgin. 'And you?' I ask.

'I have Charlie.'

Charlie did not come to the Botkin lecture. I paid the generous Miss Largizione to sit for the night – a good-hearted Grace Poole who would keep our secret safely locked in the attic.

The gymnasium hall with its smell of sweat and floor wax was converted for the occasion. An abundant supply of crêpe paper and the industry of those students in our remedial class who aspired to no more than inheriting a fortune gave it the air of a railway car from which some sleazebag politician would canvass our votes. For my sins I had to inform myself of what Volodya had written over the near thirty years since I had met him in Berlin. Since I had neither read nor even heard of his books, I proceeded on the assumption that they had been critically well received. There are conventional ways to open such events. I scorn to parody them.

The porch has become like the setting of a classical tragedy. We are confined to a single locus. The events are confined to a single day. All significant action occurs off-stage. And the storm rumbles as an admonitory chorus.

'Charlie?' I repeat.

'Her name is Charlotte,' says Dolly.

'I look forward to meeting her,' I volunteer without enthusiasm.

'I hope you'll like her,' says Dolly, and I detect but cannot fathom a look of tenderness and hopefulness.

Is Charlie a beautiful shining nymphet? I swear that no such thought crossed my mind. Volodya's imputations on this account have no basis in reality, only in art and his own dark imaginings. I was the common enemy of humanity, not a specific predator on little girls: and, in any case, was making a pathetic attempt to suppress my vampire nature. And there we have the tragedy. Waiting on the porch for admission into the sanctum of Humperldom, Harry is conscious only of the utter innocence of his intentions. Even those sluggish movements of his member do not betoken lust. Though Dolly is attractive in her physical parts, her mind, coloured by convention and conversations with her neighbours, is anaphrodisiac. Sex is not of the essence of Humperlity. The Humperls only occasionally hump.

Enough! I am fluttering like a butterfly round the subject of Botkin, whose bodkin is going to pin me to the specimen card. If, God forbid, I were to use vampirism as a metaphor rather than a description of my too too sullied flesh, Volodya would be *numero uno* for the honour of Nosferatu and Harry no more than an unsuspecting maiden. However, on that night at the gymnasium I had no notion of my plight, no notion that the trade of author is of its nature foul and unprincipled. On the contrary I thought I was in the company of an old friend I hadn't seen for the better part of thirty years.

After the speech was over and we had retired from the dais to the Dean's office, where the more dextrous of our educationally challenged Neanderthals served us with orange juice and canapés, we had a conversation, Volodya and I. It went somewhat as follows.

'Long time no see.'

'Sure, long time no see.'

'How goes it?'

'So-so. And you?'

'So-so.'

'Uh-huh.'

'Say…'

'Yeah?'

'No, you first. You were about to…'

'Isn't that – over there?'

'Where? Who?'

'Sorry my mistake. You were saying?'

And so on for about half an hour like the dialogue in an off-Broadway play. What I did not hear was Volodya slurping the blood out of me to infuse into the golem he was about to make. I should be flattered. My fictional self is more erudite, more eloquent, more debonair, more witty, than his shambling original. And if I had never been a vampire, I would nevertheless remain for ever undead in the pages of Volodya's book.

It is too sad.

The outriders of the storm are with us now. Winds are rocking the bushes in the front yard and bowling trash down the road. Mrs Kowalczyk, mounted on her thick, sturdy, storm-proof ankles, emerges on to the porch and says, 'I'd better get home before I get soaked through. I've left Charlie's room until next time. You need soapflakes, bleach and ammonia.'

'Did you find your money by the telephone?' asks Dolly.

For some curious reason whores and cleaning women are always paid this way.

'Yes, I did, Mrs Humperl,' says Mrs Kowalczyk.

'And Charlie?'

'She was having a nap, which is why I left her room. I heard her getting up. She'll be here in a moment.'

Dolly smiles at me. Girls will be girls. Mrs Kowalczyk says something I do not catch and then exits, holding her hat against the wind.

Shall I ever get off this porch? Apparently not. Dolly, who is quite an outdoor gal, has a smile on her face and an ear to the wind. But she does not hear the warnings in its aspirated gusts: *Hateful, Hazardous, Harry Haze, the Hotzeplotz Horror is here!* She does not hear it sigh, *Have care! Hush! Hide! Have care!* The creak of tree and fence and the frantic clatter of a child's toy windmill nailed to a post in the yard cover the whispers of truth like the patter of a preacher.

'Charlie!' she exclaims as her sleepy-eyed darling opens the flyscreen. 'Charlie,' she says as her heavy-footed dearest slouches joyfully towards her, 'this is Herr Professor Haze, who will stay with us if he likes us and our home. You must make the curtsey Momma showed you. And say as Momma said: *Es freut mich…*'

'*Sfroymee.*'

'*Sie kennenzulernen.*'

'*Zicklern.*'

'What do you think of that?' Dolly asks me rapturously. 'Hasn't Charlie done well?' she whispers. 'Please encourage her.'

Behold, then, my nympholept's joy, my paedophile's paragon. My Charlie, who at thirteen years old has five words of German *and* can write her name. Squat and lumpish, thick-tongued and thick-waisted, she beams through her thick lenses at Horrible Harry and steals his heart so that henceforth he will live or die for her. But, lest we get sentimental about the brat, let us bear in mind that God, in His infinite compassion, has given her kind a dicky ticker and will bump her off before the age of thirty if the Vicious Vampire doesn't do for her first.

CHAPTER TWENTY-EIGHT

Harry or I: which of us was insane? According to Willie, I was the madman who had killed her sister; and even though I knew the allegation to be untrue I found myself searching my memory as if it were one of the minor incidents of life, no sooner done than forgotten: an incident to whose recollection the memory must be prompted; as if someone were to ask, 'Didn't I see you on Sunday night?' to which the answer would be 'Sunday? I watched TV and went to bed early,' followed by a pause and a note of uncertainty. 'No – I tell a lie – *that* was the night I murdered Lucy.'

'Do you mind if I take a bath and wash out a few things?' asked Willie as I swept up the remains of the letter and put them in the bin.

'No. Make yourself at home. Help yourself to food and drink, if you like.'

'Thanks, mate, you're a gent,' said the genial Theo, who had no prejudices against murderers.

'What are you going to do?' enquired Willie.

'I don't know. Go for a walk. Read a little.' I picked up a Sarah Paretsky novel. 'Take your time. There's no need to lock up when you go.'

'You're taking all of this very coolly,' said Willie.

'Yes, I am.' I gave her a wintry smile. 'Peculiar, isn't it?'

She laughed. 'Fucking barmy, that's what you are.'

'Possibly.'

I walked down the lane and called at La Maison des Moines. It took me a minute to rouse Harry. When he appeared, he looked ragged and dirty. Concerned, I asked if he was all right.

'Sure, sure. What do you want?'

'I'm going to the lake. Coming?'

'Give me ten minutes to clean myself up. I'll meet you there. Get me a beer.'

At the *buvette* I saw Mike. We exchanged a few words, and I discovered that, after the initial excitement, murder generates only the same small talk as any other subject. I learned that the police team had cleared out of Puybrun except for Gérard, who was haunting the lakeside, as lonely as a sex offender. Antoine was also there. It was his day off and he sat on his own, pale and flabby, but reminding me of Seurat's bather in the shimmer of midday.

When Harry arrived, I still thought he looked unwell.

'I'm sleeping badly,' he said. 'It happens.'

'Why?'

'Memories. Can't seem to get rid of them.'

'Is that because of all the questions I've been asking?'

'I don't blame you. I've kept that stuff to myself too long. It festers.'

'Maybe you should try telling the truth instead of fictions.'

Harry looked at me and his eyes flickered with sorrow. 'I don't know what you mean,' he said.

I drank my beer and ate a *merguez* or two. I thought of Willie, who was no doubt ransacking my place for evidence. The beer relaxed me and I opened my shirt to catch a little sun. In this mellow mood I turned to Harry and asked, 'What happened next? After you met Quimby? You gave up work as a comedian?'

'Ted Gottlos and the FBI found me a job teaching at Hotzeplotz. It was forty-eight. Hoover was spying on everybody. I was one of his stooges.'

'Hotzeplotz: that's where you met Dolly and Charlie?'

336

'For my sins – and for theirs, too, I guess. Though I'll never know what they did to deserve me.' Again Harry looked at me, and he said, starkly and quietly, 'What happened was too terrible, Johnny.'

We strolled along the osier avenue – that same avenue where, by night, I had seen Lucy flitting in shadow and moonlight. Now it was dappled with sharp patches of sunshine between the leaves and I was reminded of another picture, this time by Monet, of a woman carrying a parasol. She wears a white dress and in the flecks of light and shadow seems to be merely an effect of the sun. I thought of Proust, too, and imagined him in pursuit of Albertine during his stay at Balbec. I had no specific passage of his book in mind but merely an impression, which could easily be false, of a promenade by trees and water to the accompaniment of the cries of young girls. But, as I admitted with an inward smile, neither Harry nor I was Proust; we were merely two madmen troubled by memories.

Harry told me his story. Stripped of his elaboration, it was of his arrival in Ohio, the taking up of a college teaching post and his meeting Dolly and her daughter. It was the first of his tales I believed to be true, at least so far as concerns those basic facts. And it came to me that I was hearing a love story.

As I have indicated before, I am trapped by words: those that Harry chose to use. And always – *always* – they were profoundly changed by the way Harry spoke: by accent, stress and interval; by glance and gesture; by sighs and silence. I can set down the conceits of his inflated language. I can confess that I found his grotesque waggishness irritating. I can admit my confusion as to whether I had grasped even the literal sense of what he was saying. But where I fail is in capturing the mood. Harry's coarseness masked his delicacy; his brutality hid his sympathies; his savagery was an expression of tenderness. If I have understood anything, it is that his stories were poignant and utterly tragic. And that he was sincere in claiming the truth of his memories, inasmuch as they were the twisted wreckage of a past he had lost.

There was more to come and I was afraid of it. It is unbearable to be sad in the sunshine, and as we returned across the little beach where children played raucously under the somnolent eyes of their comfortable parents, I found my eyes pricking with tears and I was glad to see Theo sitting at one of Mike's tables with a circle of beer cans in front of him. I called, 'Theo!' and he gave a friendly wave and gestured to buy a drink.

'You don't mind drinking with a murderer?' I asked.

'Naw. Live and let live is my motto.'

'Willie doesn't seem to agree.'

'Yeah. Well, that bird is a cow when she gets a bee in her bonnet.'

'By the way, this is Harry.'

'Hi, Harry.'

'He's a vampire. Do you have anything against vampires?'

'Naw. I've slept with a few.'

We made up a threesome and ordered a round of beers. I asked, 'Where's Willie?'

'Still up at your cottage, last time I seen her.'

'What was she doing?'

Theo shrugged.

'Searching the place?'

'Could be. I told her she was wasting her time – that you was too fucking clever to leave evidence lying around, even if you did kill Lucy. Which I don't believe, by the way.'

'Thanks for saying so.'

'My pleasure.'

338

'I'm going back to Lo Blanc,' I said to Harry. 'I'll leave you with Theo.'

I don't know why I hurried back to the house. It wasn't that I had any fears of what Willie might find. Perhaps I suspected her capacity for malice. I didn't know what she might destroy or whether, rather than discovering evidence, she might plant some. But when I arrived everything looked peaceful, and in the garden clothes were hung to dry in the late-afternoon sun.

The lounge was empty when I entered. I called, 'Willie?' There was no reply. I went into the bedroom, intending to change my shirt. Lucy was lying naked and asleep on the bed.

Except that it wasn't Lucy. It was Willie, seeming to occupy a body I knew so well; borrowing even Lucy's face in repose; distinguishable only by the stud in her nose and ring in her eyebrow. She stirred lazily, opened an eye and murmured sleepily in a Nottinghamshire accent, 'Oh, hullo, John. Sorry. I was dozing.'

'Take your time,' I said and, closing the door behind me, I retired to the lounge, took up my book and stared without comprehension at the pages.

The bedroom door opened and Willie padded naked into the lounge and squatted on the chair opposite mine. She looked down at her bush and combed through it distractedly with her fingers.

'Are you going to put on some clothes?' I asked.

'Why? There's nothing you haven't seen before.'

I went to the bedroom, picked up a blouse and skirt, returned and threw them to Willie. She let them lie where they fell. She was feeling her breasts, testing them for lumps as I'd seen Lucy do.

She said, 'My mum died of cancer.'

'I didn't know.'

'My mum was fifty.'

'That's young.'

'Isn't it? It gives you a different outlook on life.' Finished with testing, she cupped her breasts, lifted them, pushed them together to accentuate her cleavage. 'Like this? Or like this? Lu and me always wanted bigger tits. Perhaps you're not a tit person? You just like them young.'

'It wasn't as simple as that. I wasn't looking to have an affair. It just happened.'

'Our dad used to abuse us – if you know what I mean. I was nine and Lu was ten. It went on until Lu was seventeen and we both left home.'

'I didn't know.'

'You don't know much, then, do you? Did you never wonder what Lu saw in you? It's bloody obvious what *you* wanted, but did you never ask what *she* was looking for? I suppose not.'

I didn't answer. It crossed my mind that she was testing me with lies.

She got out of the chair and stretched herself so that both breasts and belly became taut, and as she turned and touched her toes I caught a brief glimpse of labia.

'Do you fancy a fuck?' she asked.

'What is this about?'

'Sex? Curiosity? I've never shagged a murderer.' She took a step towards me, raised one foot and placed the toes in my groin. 'You've got a hard-on. It seems a shame to waste it.'

'You're even crazier than I am.'

'Maybe. Lu and I used to exchange boyfriends. She was a randy little thing. Did you ever suspect?'

'I don't believe you.'

'Sharing lovers is a bit like incest, when you come to think of it.' She removed her foot and did more touch-toes and stretching exercises, pausing to let me see the fall of her breasts and the gape of her vagina. She continued conversationally, 'Do you know that most people are killed by parents, spouses and lovers?'

'Yes.'

'I see you like murder mysteries. But they get it wrong, don't they?'

'Do they?'

'Oh, yes. Because the real mystery isn't whodunit.'

'No?'

'No. The real mystery is to identify who was killed. Once you know who the victim is, then the murderer is pretty bloody obvious.'

'I suppose so.'

'Definitely. In fiction the murderer disguises himself. But in real life he disguises the body. He chops it up. He hides it. And why is that? Because the only thing that stands between the murderer and conviction is being certain about who was killed. It's a question of evidence.'

'You may be right.' I said. 'Is that what you've been doing? Looking for evidence?'

'That's what the police are doing. If they can prove that Lu is dead, there isn't any real doubt that you killed her, is there?'

'I haven't killed Lucy.'

'Then where is she?'

I shook my head.

'You know something?' said Willie, smiling at me and touching in turn each of her nipples so that they stood proud. 'Most men wouldn't be able to resist sex if it was offered to them on a plate. Not even if they thought it was wrong. In fact, that would add to the excitement. But you can resist, can't you?'

I asked, 'What are you getting at?'

'I just wanted to find out how cold and calculating you are.' The lasciviousness in her expression vanished. She said, 'And what I've found is that you're the most chilling, frightening person I've ever met.'

I was angry but I kept the same measured voice in which I had answered all her points. I said, 'Your notions of pop psychology don't interest me. Nor your attempt to project your own problems on to me.'

She was not put down. She went on, 'You're very anxious to appear to be a 'good' man, aren't you? That's more or less what Lu wrote in her letter. Good little Johnny has betrayed his wife and doesn't know how to live with himself as long as the wicked temptress is alive. So he has to get rid of her. Oh!' – she put a finger to her mouth in a stagey expression of surprise – 'but we have a problem! How can Johnny kill his mistress and still remain a good boy? Do you want to hear my theory?'

'If I must.'

'Right!' she said. 'Willie's theory!' She grinned. And if my even temper and rationality may be considered frightening, Willie's fevered imaginings were even more terrible. She continued, 'I think that Johnny got blind drunk and stoned out of his mind at Harry's party on Sunday night. I think that afterwards he murdered Lucy.'

'I see.'

'No. No!' Willie cried. 'You haven't heard the funny part!'

'There's a funny part?'

'Oh, yes!'

'Go on.'

She paused. She began again. 'I think that Johnny murdered Lucy. And…'

'Yes?'

'Good boy Johnny can't bring himself to remember what he did!'

I hadn't killed Lucy and forgotten for the sake of my delicate conscience. Willie's theory was no more than cheap psychology covering the bitterness of a troubled woman. It's true that I want to regard myself as a decent man in my own eyes. But it's equally true that I'm aware of my shortcomings and try to face up to them. If this isn't so, I am indeed mad.

Willie dressed and we exchanged a few mundane remarks. She asked if I had any objections to her underwear being left out to dry. I said I had none. She told me that Theo was pressing her to leave Puybrun, because he had things to do in London. Reluctantly she was returning with him. In the end her own neediness was more important than the fate of Lucy. If I were entirely cruel, I could have pointed this out. I could have pointed out, too, that she was making a useless gesture to save a relationship that was bringing her neither meaning nor happiness. But, though I disliked Willie, I was sorry for her. For Lucy too, I suspect, and for much the same reason: namely that she had chosen – and would always choose – the wrong man.

I worked into the evening, writing up my notes of Harry's stories. For dinner I made myself a green salad with some goat's cheese. Outside the light faded and the bats came out and I heard the voices of German holidaymakers who had taken the walk up to the castle and descended by way of the cemetery. Writing my notes, I wasn't looking for the symbolism within Harry's tales – assuming it to exist. In the end I could approach them only from the limitations of my own understanding; and, as a lawyer, I looked for the core of factual truth, attaching no special meaning to the word 'truth', seeking no wisdom or insight. What Willie had falsely believed of me was, I suspected, true of Harry. Something had happened in America which was too terrible for him to bear, and I was certain that it involved murder. And about one thing, Willie was right: the mystery of murder is to know in the fullest sense who has been killed; for it is the victim who defines the murderer.

Someone had been murdered. Perhaps Dolly, or Charlie, or (which seemed to me most likely) Clarence

Quimby. Harry's stories, full of complexity and misdirection, were in effect pointers to the grave where the body was buried; and I, so I now realised, was playing the role of the innocent man who walks his dog through the thickets of the past, allowing the beast to root among the leaf-fall and the turned earth; ignoring the first discovery of scattered bones; telling himself they are those of a wild animal, and the rags of discarded clothing are just the leavings of a tramp. How often does the man pass by, whistling up his dog and returning to the comfort of home? The world is full of missing people, and the woods of unmarked graves.

If I were right, Harry's stories were a confession.

I finished writing and took a walk into the village to drink a nightcap at Mike's place. I didn't call on Harry. Mike quizzed me on the latest news about the police and Lucy. He told me that Theo had stayed drinking at the hut all afternoon and then suddenly turned ugly and picked a fight with one of the Germans. Willie had arrived in a bad mood, started quarrelling; and Theo had given her a black eye. I listened with only half an ear. It was too dreary, too predictable. Instead of being pleased that my prejudices had been vindicated, I felt ashamed, as if by understanding the situation I'd become complicit in it.

I returned to Lo Blanc, put aside the novel I'd been reading and picked up another by Agatha Christie. I sat for an hour taking comfort from a world in which murder is not the dismal and inevitable working out of human failure, and murderers are not known by their victims.

I heard a noise from the garden.

At first I thought it must be the wind, but the day had been calm, and this wasn't the season for winds. I'd closed the shutters and so had to go to the door to investigate. I saw a figure removing Willie's underwear from the line.

'Antoine?'

I called his name because I suspected that, in his loneliness and inadequacy, stealing women's clothes was a plausible sin. I wasn't especially perturbed at discovering him.

The figure didn't reply. Indeed, I couldn't be certain it was Antoine, though it was undoubtedly a man. He seemed fixed to the spot. I took another step towards him, repeating in a friendly enough fashion, 'Antoine?' Almost too late, I noticed he was carrying a stick or club. He raised it and took a swing that would have smashed my skull if I hadn't faltered backwards and then fallen.

He was off. And, like a fool, I was after him, running blindly in the darkness down the lane. Thank God, he wasn't someone used to violence. It no more occurred to him than it did to me that he could have stood his ground and killed me unnoticed by anyone in the silent village. His only interest was flight.

We crossed the *route nationale* and continued the descent down the street towards the village. Then he cut into one of the narrow side lanes. I followed, but he had the advantage of me in that I had never had reason to walk these dark streets of houses and small gardens and had only a vague idea where they led. He would have lost me if he had not been wearing clogs, which I heard alternately dragging or clattering on the stones.

'Antoine?' I murmured, adding somewhat pointlessly in English, 'Come on, mate. Give yourself up. I'm sure we can sort things out.'

There was no reply, but the footsteps ceased and I heard only breathing, somewhere ahead in the shadows.

Belatedly I realised that I was acting stupidly. I felt a first twinge of fear. More from bravado than anything else, I called, 'Well, fuck you then! Do you hear me, Antoine, you sad bastard?' When no answer came, I decided that honour was satisfied and turned to go home. Antoine was standing behind me, blotting out the moon.

He had come up silently in a pair of outsize sneakers. He wasn't wearing clogs. He was looking at me strangely and then I understood that in fact he was looking beyond me to wherever the other man was hidden. I said unheroically, 'Christ, you almost scared me to death.'

'I was watching you,' he mumbled in his thick patois.

'Who is it?' I asked, indicating the darkness.

'The thief.'

'Do you know his name?'

'He steals clothes.'

I saw no point in arguing with the poor fellow's slow wits, and he wasn't interested in me. He brushed past and disappeared in the far darkness. A moment later I heard voices and the sound of a struggle. Knowing that the thief was armed, I was cautious of joining in, but a sense of obligation to Antoine and my own curiosity got the better of my prudence. As it happened, my help wasn't needed. I'd gone only a few steps when the noise of fighting stopped. I called out the big man's name again and got a modest 'Oui, Monsieur?' in answer. Then Antoine emerged quite suddenly and close beside me, and he was holding the underwear thief in a bear-hug. It was Édouard Moineau.

A light was burning at the Bar des Sports. Mike had closed up and was washing glasses. I hammered on the door until he opened.

He asked, 'What the bloody hell is going on, John? 'Who've you got with you?'

'Édouard Moineau and Antoine.' I urged him, 'Come on, Mike, let us in. And get on the 'phone to Gérard. He needs to come here as quickly as he can.'

'Oh? And why should he do that?'

'Because I think that Moineau is about to confess to killing his boy.'

'Jesus Christ!'

Mike stood back to allow us in. I bundled the dispirited Moineau into a corner chair. Antoine, who was curiously indifferent, took his usual place by the football machine. Mike volunteered drinks and then said, 'Before I call Gérard, I'd like to know what's going on. Are you sure of what you're saying?'

I nodded. I explained that the older Moineau was the thief who had been stealing women's clothes from around the village. 'He was at my place tonight. I disturbed him and chased him. But the credit should probably go to Antoine for catching him.'

'Okay,' said Mike. 'I follow that. But how do you get from there to killing his boy?'

'The way the clothes were said to have been folded and laid out. Pierre wouldn't have done that himself. But his father has a fetish about clothes. I imagine that somewhere in the village he has a shed of some kind, for tools or gardening or whatever. When the police find it, they should also find the rest of what he's stolen, and I'm willing to bet the clothes will be laid out in the same way.'

'Is that right?' Mike called to Moineau. Then he asked, 'Why did he kill Pierre?'

'I don't know. And I doubt that he does.' I didn't have a better answer. Parents kill their children, and the immediate cause is almost invariably trivial. Perhaps the father lost his temper at his son's pranks. Perhaps the boy taunted him about his fetish. Édouard Moineau had probably been in a state of undiagnosed clinical depression since the death of his wife and, if Mike were right, he was an alcoholic. If it was his habit to carry a stick with him, there was always a risk that a small source of anger might lead to disproportionate consequences. I doubted he had intended to kill Pierre.

'Well?' said Mike, again to Moineau. 'Is he right?'

Moineau nodded slowly.

'Fair enough,' said Mike. 'I'll call Gérard.'

I asked, 'Where's Marie-Paule?'

'In bed. Do you want me to get her?'

'No.'

'Are you happy being left with him?'

'I've got Antoine to help me, haven't I?'

Antoine grinned. I wondered exactly how much he knew and how much he was capable of explaining.

Mike went into the back room to make the call. I helped myself to a brandy and poured beers for the other two. I took Moineau's to his table set it down and sat opposite him. I said something facile like 'Cheer up. It'll soon be over.' And then I asked the question to which above all I wanted an answer.

'Have you killed the Englishwoman, Mademoiselle Western?'

Moineau addressed himself to the beer. 'Thank you, Monsieur.'

'Have you murdered Lucy?' I pressed him.

He looked from his glass to me, to his glass again. He grunted, 'No.'

In the following silence between us I heard Mike in spirited conversation with Gérard's wife. I turned to Moineau once more. I was not sure that the beer was a good idea. He had a low tolerance and his eyes were becoming unfocused.

I said, 'Have you seen her body?'

'No,' he answered. Then, more emphatically, 'No, Monsieur!'

'But it was you who arranged her clothes in the bushes along the path, wasn't it?'

'Yes, when I learned she had disappeared. I did not want to be found with them.'

'I understand. That was on Wednesday.'

Moineau shrugged.

'And you stole the clothes on Tuesday night, yes? That's when you dropped the watch and broke it?'

Again a shrug. Evidently the days meant little to him, but only my chronology made sense of the facts.

I asked, 'Where were you on Tuesday night? Where did you find the clothes?'

Moineau looked at me with the innocence of ignorance. I doubted he had any notion of the agonies and uncertainties he had caused. In his quiet distress he seemed otherworldly and for a moment I wondered if he were capable of answering my question. If time meant little to him, the same might also be true of place.

I put my hand on the beer glass to take it from him. That small threat of animal deprivation stirred the other man's sluggish thoughts. In a voice faintly glimmering with intelligence, he asked me to repeat my question.

When I did so, he nodded with understanding and answered, 'I found them at the American's house.'

CHAPTER TWENTY-NINE

Moineau had stolen Lucy's clothes from La Maison des Moines. I pressed for more details and got out of him that he had found the stuff hung to dry in the garden behind the house. He agreed he had broken the watch, which confirmed these events as occurring on Tuesday night. He'd known the identity of the owner from the contents of Lucy's bag, and disposed of everything on the following evening when he learned that she was missing. The repetition added little except to convince me that Moineau was speaking the truth.

I asked Mike, 'Is Gérard coming?'

'Yes. He's trying to contact Barrès.'

'Good. I have to go.'

'Go?' Mike was surprised. 'Where to? What am I supposed to do with him?' pointing at Moineau, who was sitting in the corner staring at his beer.

'He won't give you any trouble, and you have Antoine to help you.' I wanted to leave in any case. The ordinariness of Moineau's tragedy depressed me. He understood nothing and could teach nothing; though my pity may have owed much to a feeling that my situation was no better.

I left the bar and walked the short distance to Harry's house. The moon was still fooling the senses with its pale impression of day. The air was tepid and scented faintly with lavender. The night whimpered and rustled like a child asleep in another room.

Once at La Maison des Moines I didn't go directly to the door. A path of moon-washed paving led to the garden at the rear of the house, though the term 'garden' describes a high terrace looking down on the Chalabre road. It was small and neat and gravel-surfaced, possessing a very ordinary charm of potted plants and plastic garden furniture. A line was strung from a hook on the wall to a further pole and here, I assumed, Édouard Moineau had found Lucy's clothes; though why her purse and watch should have been placed outside escaped me for now.

I returned to the front of the house, where no light showed through the shutters. I banged the door. I felt myself ranking my emotions like suits in an unfamiliar card game: anger, self-pity, disappointment, curiosity, detachment. At times I wonder if I experience authentic feelings or merely lifeless imitations to which I give familiar names from convention, being ignorant as to their true nature. Tonight I tasted them and found them insipid, as if watered with grief.

I banged on the door again and rattled the shutters and, from somewhere, borrowed a voice and shouted Harry's name; and after a minute or two of this heard the old man muttering and drawing the bolts. His tired face appeared in the gap of the half-opened door and I pushed my way inside.

'This isn't friendly, Johnny,' he said wearily. He was wearing faded cotton pyjamas. The room stank of dope. 'What time is it? Holy cow, shouldn't we all be in bed?'

'Where is Lucy?' I asked. 'Is she here? Did you kill her? What the hell happened?'

'I see,' he answered without elaboration. He gestured at a wine bottle and a dirty glass on the table. 'Can I fix you a drink?'

'I've been talking to Édouard Moineau,' I told him.

'Oh?'

'He stole Lucy's things from your garden.'

Harry smiled. 'Wow.'

'So I know that Lucy came here when she left me.'

He put his hands up. 'You got me.' When I didn't react, he let them fall, went to the table and poured himself a drink. He took a seat. Evidently I hadn't disturbed him, and this perfect indifference made me lose my composure.

I asked him, 'Why? What's the point, Harry? Were you trying to teach me something?'

'No,' he said slowly. 'At least, I don't think so. Sit down, Johnny.' He patted the chair next to him. He sighed. 'I'm so old I've become part of history. And d'you know what history is? It's just stuff that happens. It doesn't claim to teach – but that doesn't mean there's nothing to be learned. And that's me, Johnny. I just do stuff that seems right. I don't understand why. It's kind of an existential thing, I guess.'

'And Lucy? Is she alive?'

'She's changed.'

'What does that mean?'

Harry shrugged.

I noticed a door. It was ordinarily bolted and I understood it to lead to the cellars underneath La Maison des Moines; I'd never had occasion to visit them. But tonight the bolt had been slipped.

'You've been hiding Lucy in the cellar?'

'Her choice. I never forced her to do anything,' said Harry.

'Is she there now?'

'She may not want to see you.'

'Why not?'

'I don't know. I never was good at explanations.'

'I have to see her.'

'That's your prerogative.'

I went to the cellar door and opened it. A short flight of steps descended and took a turn to the right where I couldn't see. I asked Harry, 'Is there a light?'

'At the bottom. To the left of the door.'

He was referring to a second door at the turn in the steps. I found the switch and turned on a pale striplight. It illuminated a clean room with a floor of terracotta tiles. Shelves ran along two walls. They held a few wine racks, power tools, garden implements and the usual range of gadgets that mystify someone as impractical as I am. A third wall, by my calculation, faced the lane and was plainly plastered and studded with hooks and more gardening stuff. The fourth, which must have supported the terrace overlooking the Chalabre road, showed signs of ancient stonework: a row of shallow Romanesque arches, infilled with fieldstone, rubble and mortar; proof of Harry's supposition that the house had been built on old monastic foundations.

I called Lucy's name, though it was obvious she wasn't there. Then I noticed, behind a stack of old deck chairs, an opening which seemed to descend to a lower level. It was the head of one more flight of worn steps ending in a door let into another rounded arch. The door was unlocked, but there was no light in the chamber beyond it.

I returned to the upper cellar. Searching the shelves, I found a small oil lamp and some matches. I lit the lamp and went down again to the lower chamber.

At first I could see very little. I seemed to be closed in by a wall, but as I felt along it I discovered a broad pillar supporting some barrel vaulting. The lamp revealed another pillar and I understood that this ancient cellar or crypt – whatever it was – was the base on which the entire structure rested: not merely Harry's house but the row of which it formed a part.

Next I noticed speckles of light that were not from my lamp. Pale flecks of moonlight were breaking through the ruin of a small wicket gate. Scarcely the height of my waist, it formed a narrow exit in the exterior wall on to the bank above the Chalabre road, and I imagined from the outside it was largely masked by tangles of broom. Its existence could explain the disappearance of the ghost figure I had chased the previous night.

But where was Lucy? The monks' chamber was very dark, very silent. The floor was of beaten earth marked here and there by tumbled stones that might have been roof-falls from the vaulting, half-cut ashlars abandoned by the ancient masons, or the remains of something innocent and domestic such as barrel stands, ovens or butchers' slabs. I had no reason to suppose otherwise. None at all.

I called, 'Lucy!' and heard the echo of my voice and soft footfalls on the earth. I held out the lamp and glimpsed a fluttering of cobweb grey. I stumbled towards it, finding that the floor rose sharply and formed a loose spoil where the ground had slipped. By now I had a sense of the extent of the chamber, though possibly exaggerated by imagination, the series of tight perspectives framed by the columns; and the darkness, too, which caused me to impute a distance of which I had no knowledge. Whatever the reality, it seemed vast, silent and empty and there, where the floor had risen to within an arm's length of the ceiling, the stone vault closed down upon me like a lid and I could not see the way by which I had entered.

There, too, where earth and ceiling met, the echoes ceased. I listened to my own breathing as a diver must hear only his in the mute world of the sea. I repeated Lucy's name, not knowing if it were loudly or softly. The faint grey sheen flitted between a pair of columns. And suddenly I felt an agonising fear that the lamp would go out and I should be left buried in earth and stone. Of course, I was not alone. Lucy was there – so Harry had assured me. But not my Lucy: rather one transformed by whatever conjuration the old man had worked on her. I did not fear vampires – I did *not*. They were mere fiction and metaphor. What I feared was far more real, namely: ignorance; loss of predictability and control; the disordered emotions and impulses of other people; the collapse of my moderate, unadventurous and reasonable world, whose workings could be picked over by my rational intellect and whose gaps were made comprehensible by the comfortable prejudices of an unchallenged mind.

I cried out, 'Lucy! For God's sake help me!' and scuttered down the loose earth mound, clutching the lamp that was the last barrier against terror. I hit the bottom in a half-roll, heard the oil sloosh in the reservoir, saw the wick flare and, in that brief second of brightness, stared at Lucy as she stood black-haired, pale-skinned and dark-lipped, and offered me a hand.

I took it and she lifted me.

'Hullo, John,' she said.

She offered her mouth. which was warm, human and alive.

We left the ancient cellars of the monks hand in hand. And they fell into black stillness behind us. Lucy shut the door and bolted it. She smiled at me and said in her natural voice. 'I hope I didn't scare you. I was frightened of seeing you, after what has happened. I thought you might be angry. Are you?'

I felt around in my emotions as a householder, in the ruins of his burned-out house, might rummage through the wreck of his possessions, finding something that bore the shape of a familiar object, only to discover that it was useless. Anger? Yes, I remembered it. I sensed its vague appropriateness to my situation. My mind ran blind fingers over it.

'No, I'm not angry.'

'You've had a shock,' said Lucy gently.

'Yes, I've had a shock.'

'Harry and I did discuss how we might break matters to you.'

'That was kind of you,' I said without deliberate irony.

'You *are* angry...'

'No. I feel … absolutely nothing.'

Harry had tidied himself up and put on a dressing gown of burgundy velvet, frogged in a deeper purple. Beer, wine, brandy, and three clean glasses stood on the table. He had rolled three spliffs, which lay unsmoked on an ashtray by a plate of biscuits.

'Well, *mes enfants*,' he said cheerfully, 'you kids don't look too miffed with each other.' More barbed, he added, 'I always knew you could trust Johnny to be a gentleman. What can I offer you? Wine? Cognac? Smoke? All three or none of the above? How about a kick in the teeth for old Harry? Say the word and I'll take them out to make it easy for you.'

'You bastard,' I muttered.

'That so? Well, maybe. But you'll remember I told you I was a vampire and a war criminal. When did I ever say I was a nice person? C'mon, have that drink!' He put an affectionate arm round me and steadied me to a seat. As he did so I saw him wince, and he slipped his free hand into his pocket and popped a couple of pills.

'Are you in pain?' I asked. Lucy had shot an anxious look at the old fellow.

'Just the usual crap that flesh is heir to. Some inheritance, huh? Don't worry it'll pass. And you, Johnny, how do you feel? Relieved? Angry? Curious? I'll bet on curious.'

Shakily I poured a brandy. My lips trembled on the rim of the glass.

Harry lit the three spliffs and passed me one, murmuring like a mother to a child, 'Take it easy with that.'

The alcohol hit my stomach. The dope settled on my brain. I felt a different kind of nothing, one that was warmer and more settled.

Lucy had taken a chair and was sitting leaning forward, regarding me intently. She was wearing a white dress printed with small sprigs of flowers. I'd bought it for her and forgotten. I'd not missed it when I'd gone through her possessions for anything she might have taken. I realised then that my impression that she had vanished naked into the night was a product of ignorance or, more accurately, indifference to that aspect of her life.

I spoke to Harry. 'Did you plan all this?'

He laughed modestly and shook his head. 'Nope. I don't plan things. I never understood enough for my plans to work.'

'Was it some sort of revenge?'

'*No!*' cried Lucy, alarmed.

'Hell, no,' said Harry. 'Don't think so bad of yourself. You never did anything so terrible it demanded revenge.'

'Then you were teaching me a lesson?'

'I don't teach. Maybe some things teach themselves. I can't say. Lucy?'

She shook her head.

I looked from one to the other and believed them. I thought: they have done this to me and it is without malice or meaning. And I sighed.

I asked, 'Can you tell me what happened? Just the facts?'

'Where do you want me to start?' said Lucy.

'I don't know. It's your story not mine.' I hesitated before my next question. 'Did you ever love me?'

Lucy groaned, 'Oh, God! Of course I did.'

'Thank you,' I said.

She looked from me to Harry and back again, and I had a curious notion that, contrary to appearances, I was not interrogating them. Rather, we were on the same side, each in a state of ignorance, putting questions to an absent person who alone knew what had happened. I thought of my favourite reading: the drawing-room murder. The suspects had assembled in order to have the solution to the mystery revealed, but the detective had failed to appear.

What then? Was an unrevealed solution in truth a solution at all? Did it in any meaningful sense exist outside the mind of the detective? I considered then a philosophical point raised by Berkeley. If a body is buried in a forest and there is no one to see and no one to hear, has there been a murder?

'After Harry's party,' said Lucy, 'we went to bed.'

'For a long time I used to go to bed early.'

'Pardon?'

'I'm sorry – something Proust wrote. Go on.'

'I went to sleep – in fact I passed out for two or three hours. You know how drunk we both were. And then, suddenly, I woke. Or rather I came to, as though I'd never been to sleep at all, as if I'd just gone to bed and was saying to myself, "It's time to go to sleep."

'I didn't know where I was. I heard a bird – an owl, I suppose – and a car. Someone was driving up the lane very slowly. But the only place in that direction is the cemetery. A few minutes later he came back, stopped outside the house, and then drove off again. It wasn't sinister. Poignant. Even at that late hour there was someone about – perhaps a doctor on an emergency call – and the driver was obviously lost. He didn't want the cemetery but somewhere else he couldn't find. So he stopped and took a map from the glove compartment and sat in the car trying to make sense of it. He didn't know – he couldn't have guessed – that there was someone awake in the house, who might have helped him.

'The car disappeared and I tried to sleep. I tossed and turned and then saw that I was in bed with a stranger.'

'You mean me,' I said.

'You were very still, not moving at all. Your skin was very pale and covered in a film of sweat as if it were made of wax. I'd never seen you like that before. You looked old.'

'Thanks.'

'No – no, that didn't bother me. What frightened me was that you seemed like an object, not a person. And when I said to myself, "I'm in love with John," I couldn't relate that feeling to the object lying in bed with me.' Lucy sobbed. 'It was terrifying. We'd lived together for more than a year and, yet, when I looked at you, I saw this strange *thing* that seemed half dead.'

I put my hand on hers. Harry looking on sympathetically, poured another glass of wine and passed it to her. I thought of the half-dead thing lying in the bed next to Lucy and shuddered.

She continued. 'I decided I had to leave. I didn't think about the decision. I didn't give myself reasons. The bed belonged to the stranger I was sleeping with and I had no place there. I got up, dressed and packed a bag with a change of clothes and I left the house.'

'Where were you going?'

'Nowhere. I walked down into the village and out to the lake. It was dark – a week ago there wasn't much of a moon. I wandered round the lake without any idea of why I was there, and then I decided to take the Cathar trail and walk up to the castle. I think I wanted to sit there and simply look at the view.'

'Look at the view?'

'Yes.' Lucy giggled and squeezed my hand. 'It doesn't make a lot of sense, does it?'

'Is that what you did?'

'No. Where the trail follows the stream I got lost in the dark and fell into the water. I was soaked – my clothes, my purse, everything except the bag, which I dropped.'

Harry intervened. 'She came here, to my place.'

'That must have been a shock.'

'Stranger things have happened. I cleaned her up and put her to bed, and in the morning she told me she'd left you and didn't want to see you again.'

'And that made sense to you?'

Harry shrugged. 'I'm stupid. I don't expect things to make sense.'

'What did you intend to do?' I asked Lucy.

'I had a vague idea of going back to England.'

'You could have told me. On Monday, when Harry knew I was looking for you, you could have spoken or sent a message.'

'On Monday it didn't seem so important. It was obvious I'd left you. There wasn't any question of murder.'

'She spent most of Monday sleeping,' Harry explained. 'Most of Tuesday, too.'

'I put my clothes, my purse and my watch outside in Harry's garden to dry,' said Lucy. 'Someone stole them.'

'That was Édouard Moineau,' I said.

'Oh? I thought it might have been Antoine.'

I told her the sad business of the death of the Moineau boy and that his father had killed him. She nodded through it and then began to cry very quietly. I was reminded that people who are in distress at their own affairs will sometimes find a sudden sympathy for others, as if their own concerns are too small to hold the volume of their emotions. Or perhaps they find new and unsuspected connections with others; connections which are not apparent in the world of self-contained contentment.

Lucy said, 'By Wednesday night, when my clothes were found, things had got out of hand.'

'They could have been retrieved. You could have gone to the police. All it would have cost you was some embarrassment. Wasn't I worth that? To spare me the misery?'

'I stopped her,' said Harry sharply. 'And don't get self-righteous. You were never in serious danger, and a bit of misery wasn't going to harm you.'

'But why?' I cried, in frustration as much as anger.

'What are you going to tell me?' said Harry. 'That what we did wasn't kind? Wasn't the thing that decent respectable people do? No, it wasn't either of those things. But it was *right*. I gave you a reason to poke around in the rubbish heap of your character and find stuff you never knew you had.'

'So there *is* a lesson to this?' I pointed out acidly. 'I thought you said you didn't teach?'

Harry threw up his hands, but he was mocking me. 'So I'm inconsistent. I'm not a philosopher. I just tell stories. They fall out the way they fall out. I don't know what in Hell's name they mean.'

I jumped out of the chair, headed for the door, stopped and then paced the room, flinging my arms about. I was too angry to stay, too fascinated to leave. I felt like a child humiliated by a lesson that was beyond his intelligence. I felt that the tools of logic and analysis on which I prided myself had been dashed from my hands. It seemed, too, that their supposed sympathy was entirely false: a disguise for a mad complacency at their success over me. I hated them both.

Lucy began to speak again, hesitantly unravelling clues within her own thoughts. She said, 'Your problem, John, is that you look for explanations in the wrong place. Do you remember when we heard the first of Harry's stories? We wondered why Harry was telling them, what they meant – as if there were an explanation outside them. There isn't. Harry told his stories in the only way he knew. If he had understood more or differently, the stories would have been different. Do you follow me? The stories can't be explained – at least not by Harry. They *are* the explanation.'

'I see,' I answered, unconvinced. 'And you? Your behaviour?'

I was grateful that she didn't look to Harry for help: that she accepted her own responsibility.

'I can't debate with you,' she said. 'Life isn't a thesis. It can't be explained as a series of deductions from an incontrovertible premise. If I try to argue my position as if it were morally coherent, you would smash my case to pieces. You would bully me with words and logic.' She looked at me defiantly but not challenging me: rather willing me to understand. 'I don't have to let you do that. And I won't. I've made my argument. It's in the way I've behaved. Your answers are all there, and you must find them for yourself. As far as I'm concerned, what I've done isn't something that calls for explanation. It is the explanation as best I can give it.'

'Are you telling me that I just have to accept it?'

'No,' said Lucy. 'You have a choice. You can listen for the meaning. Or you can treat what I've done simply as material for your mind to grind down with its own preconceptions. You're still free to despise me and be angry. I haven't taken that away from you.'

'And are you intending to come back to me?' I asked, without considering how bizarre this might sound.

She shook her head.

'Will you stay with Harry?'

'For the moment. I haven't any longer-term plans.'

'Do you love him?'

Lucy smiled. 'What a sad, conventional question.'

'I'm sorry.'

'I don't love him in that way. In fact, if you want the truth, he frightens me.'

'That's my girl!' said Harry jovially.

'You have to remember,' Lucy continued, 'that, at heart, Harry is still a vampire.'

At the outset I said that this was a murder mystery. I wasn't referring to the death of the Moineau boy, which may or may not have been murder, depending upon how one feels about that poor devil his father. And in any case it wasn't a mystery. All that happened was that a few questions were raised on the way to an inevitable solution.

But there was another murder. It happened in Hotzeplotz – wherever that may be. And Harry was involved. All his stories, viewed in this aspect, were merely steps down the path to a small college town where terrible deeds were done. And I – if we pursue the vampire metaphor – was Dr van Helsing, who had chased Harry from the coffins he had prepared for the ashes of his past and finally driven him to his last lair.

We fell to smoking and drinking, but not in relaxation: rather, watchfully as if arming ourselves for a perilous venture. The centre of our attention was Harry. Lucy and I studied him and exchanged glances of mutual support. The old fellow meantime took drags on his cigarette, nibbled a biscuit and chugged at a can of beer. And when I glimpsed into his misty eyes, I saw him falling away into a pit of memories, beckoning us to follow.

Suddenly Harry grinned mournfully. He put down his biscuit, spun the can between his fingers and said, 'Funny how I'd forgotten about the beer. But now it all comes back to me.'

'The beer?' I repeated.

'Yes, the beer,' said Harry. He shook himself and looked at us. 'Quimby and I had a beer together that night – the night when it all happened.' He put the can to his lips, tasted it, savoured it. He went on. 'We drank Schlitz – or was it Bud?' He tasted again. 'Clarence wouldn't drink Miller – said it gave him gas.' He laughed and tears poured down his cheeks. He sobbed. 'The house was full of blood, but Clarence wouldn't drink Miller because it gave him gas!'

Then he told us a murder story, the last story I ever heard from him.

CHAPTER THIRTY

When, at last, Harry decided to speak, it was in a way I'd never heard before. To say that it was natural is probably inaccurate, because it implies the old man had another mode of speech than his odd confections. The most I can say is that he spoke without deploying the full range of his accents and without the note of archness that characterised his normal narrative style. He was, if you like, more human. Yet – and here is my difficulty, since I can reproduce only words – his vocabulary, his phrasing, and all the verbal trickery of his language were there as before. So he spoke in the most unaffected of manners; and in the most affected of terms. I can only guess at his reasons, but I believe that by the frankness of his voice he was trying to convince me of the essential truth of his story even as, by other means, he was trying to hide it. I see no purpose in trying to resolve the inconsistency by rational analysis.

Harry's Tale

For a season or a century I was a vampire full of verve and vitality, a victor over circumstances, a happy bunny. In our comfortable, humperlish cottage, Dolly, Charlie and I were as blissful as the Winstons – a simile which won't mean much now, but will if you are still watching television in the year 2020 – and that is to say that we experienced a mindless and uncomplicated joy. Poppa Bear, Momma Bear and Little Baby Bear discovered, as each wanderer in this Vale of Tears must for himself, that lasting happiness is the quiet, sensual enjoyment of habit; and bliss is a bowel movement every day.

Which is not the best way to introduce a tragedy. But what is tragedy, except comedy without the jokes?

I loved Dolly and therefore I lied to her. There is a theory that love is about telling the truth, but I don't accept it. Americans believe in the truth and, in consequence, kill each other and get divorced. This at least proves they are sincere. Civilised people, on the other hand, tell lies. Bad people tell hurtful lies; good people don't: that's the only difference. As the Apostle said, when I became a man I put aside vampirish things and (I blush for shame, Johnny) told Dolly a wholly fictitious story of my life back home in Zembla.

My lumpishly loveable Charlie was what is unpopularly known as a retard. That summer, as we took a vacation touring in the east, we were consigned to dreary cabins on the remotest part of motor courts, and dark tables in secluded corners of restaurants, so that my darling child should not frighten the human beings. But Happy Harry was unconcerned, because for the first time in his life he had a family. As for my trusting Dolly, I don't believe she ever asked herself what manner of creature would take on a woman at the brink of middle age and an ugly child who would only be a burden in her declining years. For a space I was Harry the Hero.

For the benefit of geographers, this was our itinerary starting from Newell. First Maine, where we saw Lake Aghmoogenemook, Whittequrgaugaum, Nomjamskilli-cook, Sekledobskus, Genasagarnagum and Absequoit. Then Vermont, home to the towns of Dog Hollow, Skunk's Misery, Devil's Den, Nine Holes and Goose Green. Virginia gave us Buzzard Roost, Pole Cat, Bull Ring, Dog Town and Negationburg. North Carolina revealed the joys of Lazy Level, Bull's Tail, Lick Lizzard, Burnt Coat, Tear Shirt, Snatch It, and Purgatory. Students will note that, among the lot of them, not one Quimbyish place-name figures. It seemed that I was free of him.

The highest form of postmodernist literature is the blackmail letter. Who can fail to admire its minimalist beauty? In it the author demands money *tout court* without claim to style, fine language, plot, subtext or philosophy. He dispenses with publishers. He proclaims the death of the novel. He does not even seek popularity – surely the mark of an artist?

The letter awaiting me on our return to Hotzeplotz ran as follows:

> *Five thousand dollars,*
> *Or else I tell the police.*
> *Details will follow.*

I put it down as fortuitous that my blackmailer had adopted the form of a haiku, but his next communication made me revise that opinion. It read:

> *You are a vampire.*
> *I have the goods on you, bud.*
> *I want cash. Okay?*

Disappointingly, the writer lacked the courage to grasp the essential shapelessness of his chosen genre. In succession I received a sonnet, sestet, ballade, rondeau, virelay, triolet, terza rima, quatrain, Spenserian stanza and twenty lines of alexandrines in passable French. My correspondent was in every way as inventive as I in expending effort without ever coming to the point. When Dolly enquired about this considerable increase in my mail. I attributed it to *Reader's Digest*.

Only once did my tormentor give his name. It came with the following verse:

RECHERCHE

A vampire name of Haze
At teaching spends his days.
Of his life story let it be said
That he is better dead than read.

The signature was 'Hugh Clary', but I fancied that that 'Clary' was 'Clarence' and that Quimby had found me again.

I telephoned Ted Gottlos to see if I could discover what turn in Quimby's affairs had set him on my trail once more. I was, after all, a stool pigeon in good standing. In my regular reports to the FBI I had dutifully betrayed my friends and colleagues if by word or deed they displayed any Communist leanings. Staunchly I had advocated that the members of the college should take loyalty oaths on every possible occasion, as faithful as Muslims at prayer. And, in private correspondence marked for Hoover's eyes only, I informed him of my suspicions whenever I caught a whiff of grave dirt or cerements disturbing the balmy air of Hotzeplotz. What more could my country demand of me? I would have laid down my life for America, had I not laid it down on many previous occasions only to have it returned like a suit from the garment-cleaner.

'The Lord has judged him,' said the Reverend Ted, 'as He judged the inhabitants of Sodom and Gomorrah.'

(By way of aside, while I am tolerably clear about Sodom, what exactly did the inhabitants of Gomorrah *do*? Park against a hydrant? Fail to put out their trash?)

'In what way?' asked Harry.

'He quarrelled with Edgar and was subpoenaed by the House Committee.'

'And?'

'He wouldn't answer questions. He took the Fifth,' said Ted ominously.

Well, that was that. If Clarence had lost the support of Hoover, his goose was *bien cuit*. But I was puzzled that Quimby should turn his resentment and attention upon yours truly.

As the proverb has it, forewarned is firearmed. I went down to my friendly neighbourhood specialist in slaughter and enquired as to suitable artillery with which to meet Quimby if he should ever turn up in my neck of the cemetery. I explained that I had a single homicide in mind, and he informed me that an instrument known as the Saturday-Night Special was the weapon of choice for the domestic or amateur murderer. I demurred. The name suggested a less than whole-hearted commitment to blood-letting, a purely token weekend killing like the sexual effort of a middle-aged commodity broker who, on the following morning, needs the sight of a flaccid condom to remind him that he has done anything at all. I wanted a Weeklong Sooper Dooper, man enough to wow all the girls at a party and nail them good.

Thus armed with my purchase, a weighty chunk of metal whose grey and brutal aesthetic appealed to my determined frame of mind, I returned home to Dolly and apple pie, and waited on the arrival of my Nemesis.

Prescience or simple fear made that fall in Hotzeplotz an especially poignant time. Most days I would persuade Dolly and Charlie to walk with me by the river and even bathe in the pool where the last of the summer's heat warmed the chill ichor in my congealed veins. I told Dolly and Charlie that I loved them. I used not the words of great literature but the cheap sentiments of dime store fiction – the language that articulated Dolly's heart – and thus convinced her of my sincerity. \We went to movies, and listened to schmalz on the phonograph. We held hands in public. We ate meatloaf by candlelight.

Did Dolly suspect? Did she detect the immortal sadness in the eyes of her melancholy monster as he painted the porch and fixed the storm shutters? I think not. I hope not. She was experiencing the wholly innocent selfishness that comes with a shower of happiness after a long drought.

And Charlie? Who knows? Did I see in her dull orbs a fey flicker of awareness? Was that a question hanging from her thick, drooping tongue as she trundled after Pop? I know she was frightened. But she was often frightened.

So passed the fall. I gathered leaf litter from the front yard and burned it in large, odiferous piles. I looked forward to Hallowe'en, when, for one night in the year, we undead were just plain folks. My spell at Hotzeplotz was between blossom time and fruit, between the annunciation of pink petals and the epiphany of ripe apples; and as one summer is the archetype of all summers and those of childhood are all the same, so my season in Ohio seemed but one in an infinity of seasons now forgotten; and even now I relive them in memory and wait in tense expectancy as if they are not truly lost to me but merely delayed as summer is delayed by a long, frosty spring.

Meanwhile Destiny is bowling down the highway in a stolen Oldsmobile, knocking over liquor stores and killing state troopers as need and whim take him. I have to tell you that at this stage of his career Clarence is entirely lacking in class. Harry, *au contraire*, is pushing for a Good Citizenship citation, pedalling his bicycle around the leafy lanes of our little burg, leafleting for leftovers – clothes for refugees in Europe, I believe. I don't want to advertise my own virtue, but for that one brief period in 1948 I took a stab at sainthood.

Fifty miles north of Hotzeplotz the highway first meets the Meshuggeneh. Here Clarence camps for one last night before hitting town on the morrow. To celebrate, he pots a hitch-hiker and, after a good dinner, buries the remains by the riverside. Harry dines on a seasonal pumpkin pie and has a sleepless night through indigestion. Charlie is fretful. The moon is three-quarters full.

Cometh the dawn. Harry stills his stomach with a seltzer. Charlie does not want to go to school: she is frightened. Dolly is grey and has monthly cramps. Clarence, in a fit of sentiment, digs up the hitch-hiker and contemplates taking a trophy – a penis? a set of testicles? But trophies are for rubes, not *cognoscenti*. He confines himself to pummelling the corpse until it is pulpy and then, bored, abandons it unburied.

That day my students are exceptionally stupid. Looking at the afternoon sky, I say to one of my fellows that the days are short and winter is drawing nigh.

Why is this night different from any other night? Well, that ain't no mystery. Mayhem and madness are in the air, and the Boogie Man is abroad. But not yet. Not for a little while, since a bunch of the boys are whooping it up in the Hotzeplotz Saloon, and the juke-box in the corner is playing a Gershwin tune. Ted Gottlos's Finest have won their victory game in the Major Moron League and Prof Haze, the good sport, has agreed to fill them with beer after dutifully calling Dolly to say he will be home late. Afterwards he cycles unsteadily through the poetic streets of the town as though browsing an anthology of American verse, and the stars shine down on Ohio and probably Alabama, too.

He reaches the house. It is in darkness but he doesn't notice. Opening the gate in the picket fence a domestic thought strikes him: next year, God willing, he will paint it and also erect a swing in the front yard to entertain Charlie. Happiness bubbles in his heart like a pan of Dolly's chicken soup and he curses cheerfully as he wrestles with bicycle and gate and finally abandons the former on the grass.

He reaches for his keys. He fumbles over the Fearsome Firearm that he carries with him at all times. He pulls it from his pocket, fondles its grim greyness by moonlight, and puts it back, giving it a comforting pat. He stumbles up the porch steps and hears the loose board creak like a frog by the river. He opens the door.

'Oh ho-oney, I'm ho-ome!' he calls.

He feels for the light switch. Click-click. *Zip*. Gosh, golly, gee! That gale reported upstate on the radio must have brought down the lines and the gosh darn power company hasn't fixed them. Still, in the basement there are torches, candles and hurricane lanterns. And hopefully the bugs are keeping quiet since the roach man zapped them in the summer.

Speaking of bugs, the house smells damp, kind of like the fetid haze that blows over the Mishegoss when the fallen leaves stew and rot in its quiet pools. Harry shivers with unquiet memories, slides the bolt on the basement door and descends the steps. His feet plop softly on the earth floor.

In the pitch darkness the possessions of the late Norman Humperl are set like spring guns to catch the unwary. Although they are notionally inert, Harry suspects the paint cans and old motor parts of scurrying between his feet like rats. He picks his way blindly tippy-toe between the beasts. The candles et cetera are on a shelf and Harry can hear them shuffling places with the reluctancy of volunteers. He wants a torch but must make do with a kerosene lamp. *Scrape. Flash.* By matchlight the junk runs for cover. The moment the lamp is lit and Harry can hold it up to survey the basement, the objects have settled in their places as demurely as children on teacher's return. He grins at his own fears. Is this the same Harry for whom, at one time, there was no crypt like home?

With a blithe and inebriated skip, he returns upstairs. The lamp grabs sections of the rooms out of darkness and throws shadows around as if dealing cards. The rumbling of his belly says chow time, and he wonders if Dolly has left anything in the icebox. For that matter, where is Dolly? 'Search me,' says Quimby.

'Pardon?'

'I said, "Search me," ' Quimby repeats. 'Are you going deaf or what?'

Harry turns. He holds the lamp up, down, in, out. The room is empty. The furniture huddles together for security and whispers every time Harry takes a step.

'Where are you?'

'That's for me to know and you to guess, old sport.'

'Are you in the room?' A face glimmers in a mirror but when Harry turns, it is gone.

'Peekaboo!'

'Where *are* you?'

Disappointed and annoyed, Quimby asks, 'Look, old bean, are we going to play hide-and-seek all night, or talk this thing over, ghoul to ghoul? What say you pull up a chair and park your corpse?'

'What do we have to talk about?'

Peevishly: '*I* don't know. If I did, I probably wouldn't need to talk. I could just kill you and leave. I'm a busy fellow. The night is frosty and I have miles to go before I sleep.'

'Then why are you here?'

'*Qui sait?* Most likely it's got something to do with the plot.'

'Whose plot?'

'God's plot! Deuce take me, Harry but you are becoming dense. Don't you know your elementary theology? We creatures of the infernal regions exist only by the Grace of God and serve His purpose so that by our foul deeds we shall instruct mankind and bring it to salvation. We're kind of like teachers in a remedial class. It's a tough job, but somebody's got to do it.'

'You mean our story has a purpose?'

'I'm just guessing.'

I turn up the wick on the kerosene lamp, hoping to surprise Clarence out of the shadows.

'I've given up the vampire stuff,' I say.

In a jolly rumble deeper than his normal voice, Clarence answers, 'You are a card, Mr Haze, really you are!'

'It's true, nevertheless.'

'Nonsense! Have you been truthful with Dolly and little Charlie? Have you told them the peccadilloes of your past, the bodies buried by life's highway? I think not, *mon ami*, I think not. Your history is a fiction, one evasion after another. Truth and story-telling are not the same thing. Neither are fine language and a fine soul. Do you know why vampires fear mirrors?'

'No.'

'Because we see nothing in them. We are unable to see ourselves. Why do we change shape?'

'Tell me.'

'Because we have no real form of our own. We steal from others to give substance to our own insubstantiality.'

'Trite psychology!' quoth Harry scornfully. That hurts Clarence's vanity. I hear him sulking, even though I cannot see him. During the pause I help myself to one of Dolly's cigarettes, lighting it at the funnel of the kerosene lamp. In that first puff of smoke a face forms briefly.

'Let me tell you something, Mack,' the face says in a reasonable tone. 'There ain't nothing clever or original about wisdom. You can write it on one of those slips of paper in a fortune cookie. What did Jesus say? "Love God and your neighbour"? Wow! *That's* profound, or what? You need a whole *book* to say *that*? Are you with me, pal? So don't come hoity-toity with me for teaching you something you already know. Instead, think about why you have to be told the same simple things again and again.'

'Enlighten me.'

The answer comes down the chimney, rattling the lid on the wood stove. Harry jumps.

The voice says: 'Because wisdom isn't a bright idea. It's a *trick* by which we take a dumb, stupid, obvious notion and actually figure out how to incorporate it into our lives.'

I ask, 'And what was the point of the blackmail letters?'

'To get your attention. To make you think while I told you a few home truths. The letters were flimflam, nothing but a story.'

I am thirsty. I propose, 'I'm going to get a beer from the icebox. Can I get you one? Or can't you materialise?'

'I'm working on it. Bring a beer. You have Bud?'

'I think so.'

'Bud or Schlitz – not Miller, it gives me gas.'

I go into the kitchen, pop the corks on two beers and take out the Fearsome Firearm. I slip the safety catch and put the gun back as before. When I return, I see Clarence sitting dull and foggy in a club chair. He smiles innocently and says, 'Put the bottle on the table. I'll pick it up when I'm able. You got snacks?'

'Crackers?'

'On second thoughts, I already ate – two courses.'

'It's no trouble.'

'I said forget it!'

'All right already.'

I take the opposite chair, sip my beer, and wipe the foam from my lips. Alternately smiling and grimacing in pain, Clarence forms up some more, his features clarifying and the first washes of colour filling out his shape. Like everything, materialisation takes practice.

He says, 'You haven't asked about Dolly and Charlie.'

'They're out,' I say. I try to remember what Dolly must have told me.

'Wro-ong!' croons Clarence.

'Where are they, then?' I ask.

'In the shade of the hazels, where *you'll* never find them.'

I snap, 'If you've-!'

'If I've what, dearest?'

'Charlie...'

'What's your problem, Mack? Don't go sentimental on me. The kid was just lunch on legs. Less brains than a rabbit. If I'd only known you cared, I wouldn't have gone to the trouble of raping her first – whoops! I used the "R" word.' He simpers. 'Honestly, honey, she meant nothing to me. I hope you're not going to let her come between us and spoil what we have.' He leans forward and leers. And in that instant he materialises in all his bloody horror.

'Golly!' he apologises, coyly flicking a gobbet of flesh from his leather pilot's jacket. 'Ain't I a messy feeder!'

The lamp flares, and when it settles the shadows vanish and the room, which I thought was in regular order, is revealed as a wreck of smashed furniture and blood spatters. Clarence is sitting at ease in the club chair. He is dressed for the outdoors in leather jacket, tartan shirt and jeans. The shirt is soaked in blood. Blood leaks from ears, nose, mouth and eyes. It seeps from beneath his fingernails. It drains through anus and penis to stain his pants. His face is dirtied, and fragments of leaf and twig litter his hair.

'Lord, I must look a fright,' he says. 'I've been sleeping under the great blue sky and sorely need a bathroom. *Entre nous*,' he adds, 'I'm frankly feeling frazzled. When our Master, the great Lord God Almighty, finally gets off His ass and decides to drive the plot of His story forward, He shows no consideration for us mere soldiers of sin. But isn't the war between Good and Evil like any other? The poor goddam infantry must fight the battle without understanding the campaign. By the by, how are you feeling? Not too shocked, I hope?'

He smiles complacently and with the tender generosity of victory continues, 'I think I should be on my way. I've sent another brace of souls to Jesus and delivered the moral of my tale. I do hope you understood it? Personally, I thought it rather confusing. Speaking confidentially' – Clarence points a finger heavenward – '*He* tends to narrate history with vulgar *coups de théâtre*, which, while entertaining enough, obscure the clarity of the message. Not my business, I suppose, but I do hate cheap fiction. Or cheap fact, for that matter. Of course, *He* claims the prerogatives of truth-telling. But sincerity is the excuse of every third-rate poet. *He* accuses the Demiurge of shoddiness, but I say it takes one to know one. By the Lord Harry, you're not paying attention! Wake up and look shipshape, laddie! Cat got your tongue?'

'May I see Dolly?' I ask humbly.

Quimby stares at me. He says sternly, 'I wouldn't advise that. Too gruesome, dear boy. I can tell you all you need to know. The killing itself went off in the usual manner – perhaps a little more violent, a little more bloody because of the struggle. And her *language*, old chap, was absolutely *shocking*. I'm afraid she didn't die a lady.' He taps a thoughtful lip and murmurs, 'What can I say of the rape? Brutal? Yes, of course. Repellent? *Mais oui*. Cruel and painful? Excessively so, I'm afraid. I experienced – ahem – technical difficulties in pumping up the old pecker before poking the pork prong into the poor darling, if you'll allow the awful alliteration. No, no, Henry – may I call you Henry? – you wouldn't like to see her. Not at all.'

Your Honour, gentlemen of the jury – Johnny: I deny that I murdered Dolores and Charlotte Humperl with *malice prepense* or at all. If I killed them, it was not with fang and claw but by inflicting a vain, cruel and self-regarding nature that could not give them the love and protection they deserved. As Clarence more or less admitted, he did

376

not come *to* me: he was drawn *by* me, as if to fill a vacuum. There was nothing in his shifting shape that was not calculated to fit itself to the emptiness within me. Vampires are created out of emptiness. That is what being undead means. Blood calls to blood and the needy cling to the needy. Dolly was calling out from the grave before she was ever sent there.

However, Heroic Harry has time for a final flourish. While Clarence shakes the creases out of his pants, and makes noises like a guest who has outstayed his welcome, and promises to write and keep in touch, I remember that the Fearsome Firearm is still packed away in my pocket. I cannot save Dolly or Charlie, but I can cause Clarence some modest discomfort – say, with a slug in the chest, a stake through the heart, and his head cut off and burned in the stove.

I pull out the gun.

Quimby freezes. He glances at me contemptuously and drawls, 'Howdy, pardner. That's a fine shootin'-iron you got there.'

'It sure is,' I say by way of unimaginative riposte. (You can't always rely on a murderer for a fancy prose style.)

'I hope you know how to use it.'

'Try me.'

'I may do that.'

I raise the gun.

I take a bead on Quimby's forehead.

I squeeze the trigger.

Unfortunately, Clarence also has a gun and is quicker than I. He fires and puts a forty-five slug through my cold heart and kills Harry Haze stone dead..

CHAPTER THIRTY-ONE

When Harry and Lucy were finished, I do not know if I was angry, amazed or horrified. I do know that I wanted sleep, the refuge of a troubled mind. And, however improbable it may sound, on that most improbable of nights that is what I did. I curled up then and there on Harry's couch and drifted off. I believe Lucy kissed me. When I woke in the morning, they were both gone.

I was left not in a theatre of wonders but in a rented house in a nondescript village in the south of France. The picture of Chronos, the photograph of Churchill, the battered carpet bag – every scent and sign of the pair had disappeared. By the wan daylight I saw the faded decoration and the used furniture and I was in possession of only a palimpsest from which all physical trace of meaning had been scraped. So I am left, as Le Grand Meaulnes must have been after his own vision of miracles, to scour the earth for evidence of what has passed; to glimpse it in its attenuations, as a manor house in ruins, seen through a screen of trees on a dull day, and feel for a moment a magical excitation of the spirit, only to find that it is not the true lost domain, merely a house abandoned by a bankrupt speculator; and the voices of ghosts are the cooings of pigeons fluttering in the deserted lofts.

I made some enquiries as to whether anyone had seen Harry leave. No one had. I said nothing of Lucy. If she had been seen, she would have been such an object of surprise that of necessity I would have been told. Nothing was said, and I stayed silent. I returned to La Maison des Moines, searched it for a note or any indication where the fugitives had fled. Finding nothing, I closed the door behind me, and left it as a quiet, empty, ordinary cottage that stood in a country lane.

For some days I remained at Lo Blanc. But it was unbearable to stay longer, purposeless and gnawed by a feeling of utter emptiness. Barrès and Gérard called only once, when both suspicious and apologetic, they returned my passport and said that for the present I was not involved in their further investigations. Édouard Moineau had admitted killing his boy. He had admitted stealing Lucy's things from Harry's garden. And, although he had denied murdering Lucy or having any involvement in her disappearance, he was the prime suspect until she or her body was found – in which case, who knew how the facts would present themselves? I did not say that Lucy was alive and that I had seen her again. I could not produce her; and two unexplained disappearances were beyond the credulity of any normal mind. I was unconcerned. Indeed, I had never been particularly worried. I was a lawyer and I knew that in the confusion of circumstances and the absence of a corpse, there had never been any evidence against me. I am a believer in evidence.

I returned to England. After some recriminations and an adjustment of finances, I was allowed to resume my partnership in the law firm and the mundane pursuit of millions. I rented a flat in Pimlico and lived alone, following quiet occupations and dining each night in the corner of a restaurant, ignored by everyone.

For my sins I took up writing the Great Indian Novel again and, after twelve months, completed it and sent it to Messrs Lawrence, Lockig and Mowlem in the hope that it might be publishable. The reply I received was evidently written on a Friday by an editor who had just lost her job and therefore felt entitled to tell the truth. The material part read:

Your book is at heart a whodunit of a kind that went out of fashion twenty years ago and is marred by the middle-class anxiety and smallness of ambition which have brought the modern English novel into disrepute. The style is pedestrian, as one would expect from a lawyer. The supposed subtext – which you were kind enough to explain for the benefit of the illiterate – comprises banalities that obviously trouble your commonplace mind but fail to engage the interest of someone who is less sad.
Get real! Get a life!

I laughed. Truly I did. I saw, clearly and at last, that I did not have Harry's courage to face the dangers of story-telling. I had believed, falsely, that it was a progress towards the light. I had not realised that it was a headlong rush into darkness in which understanding was not a guide to the way ahead but a beast in the shadows behind, who pursued like a monster. Nor did my vapid and kindly soul possess the necessary spirit of amorality to recognise in story-telling a form of criminal enterprise demanding the suavity of a confidence trickster and the brutality of a rapist. At bottom, I was too fainthearted for the task.

For relaxation I returned to Proust. After a lapse of thirty years, I hoped that with time and maturity I'd be able to tackle his book's monstrous bulk and find understanding.

But, though I still pick it up and struggle over a few pages, I have to conclude that I'm no wiser now than I was as a student. Sometimes I think this is a sad reflection on my life. At other times I feel oddly cheerful, as if it is the very failure to find wisdom today that gives me the hope to continue tomorrow.

One passage in particular did grab my attention. Proust wrote: 'The artist knows that he has created his masterpiece out of the effects of attenuated light, out of the

380

action of remorse upon consciousness of guilt, out of women posed beneath trees or half-immersed in water like statues.'

This seems to me to describe what happened at Puybrun, but when I press the text to yield a meaning that is more exact and usable, it resists. On reflection I doubt that Proust had my situation in mind. I don't know what he did have in mind. Perhaps they are only time-washed words found like driftwood that has lost all mark of its original purpose and, according to the mood of the finder, is an ornament or kindling for the fire.

I went to see Vernon Machin. He has an office in one of the Edwardian blocks along Holborn, and his firm of enquiry agents does occasional professional work for me. This was in one of the periods when I felt the need to take positive steps about my life; when I told myself that what had happened was not a metaphysical fantasy and that Harry Haze was a creature of flesh and blood who had trailed his spoor across the real pages of history.

I told Vernon the bones of Harry's story, conceding that the bulk of it – his lives as Dracula, Esterhazy and Hess – was plainly absurd.

'The whole of it sounds bloody daft,' said Vernon, who teases his clients with the pretence of being a rough Yorkshireman.

'I don't agree,' I said. 'I think Harry's account of what happened in America has some sort of basis in fact.'

'Oh aye? Specifically?'

'I believe that Harry was teaching at a college in Ohio in 1948. I also believe somebody murdered Dolores Humperl and her daughter – and quite possibly Clarence Quimby, too. And I think that Harry was brought to trial for the murders.'

'Do you honestly suppose those names are genuine?' asked Vernon sceptically.

'Possibly not – in fact probably not. But Harry played games with words. If the ones I've given you aren't correct, they'll still contain clues to the true names.'

'Maybe – if you're clever enough to spot' em.'

'We can only try. I'm convinced that Harry's stories are intended to be understood.'

'They may still mean nothing, even if they are understood.'

'I'll take that risk.' I said.

I went to see Sally at Virginia Water in the spring, some eighteen months after coming back to England. I'm not sure why I left the visit so long, but these things are sensitive to timing, and I had to go with my feelings. My love for Lucy was dead, but not from running its natural course. It lay like a corpse found in a wood under a fall of leaves: sinister – but not necessarily so – mysterious; and, in the last analysis, inexpressibly poignant. I couldn't see Sally when I was still dressed in mourning.

The day was chill and clear, but Sally had already put out the garden furniture. I can't say which flowers were in bloom, except that there were drifts of bluebells beneath the trees. Sally wore woollens and I wore tweeds and we sat outside, looking a middle-aged, middle-class couple.

Our conversation was a long recital of domestic events as two old friends might have, who have not met for some time. Though I would not say we spent our time in laughter, it sparkled whenever, through the surface of the present, we glimpsed bright moments of the past. I believe we made our peace. However, you must ask Sally about that. I've made too many mistakes to be certain.

Will we get together again?

Sally said, quite frankly that, while we may be friends, married life – in particular, marriage to me – offers her nothing she needs and many things she doesn't need. Marriage is a state appropriate to its own time but not necessarily all time. We are in our fifties, our child-rearing is behind us and we each have our own security for the future. The case for re-marriage is a poor one, but I think Sally will have me back on her own terms; and I shall accept them, since I know she will be a generous victor.

We have become occasional lovers.

Vernon invited me to his office. He had received the report from his American correspondent, who had done the actual investigation. After the usual preliminaries, he came down to the facts.

'As you might expect, Harry or Henry Haze is a fairly common name, especially under the spelling H-A-Y-E-S, but none of the genuine Harry Hazes remotely matches your profile for the place and time. There are no real Dolores and Charlotte Humperls. Ditto for Clarence Quimby.'

'I see.'

'As to other details,' continued Vernon, 'there is no Ted Gottlos Baptist College and no Hotzeplotz in Ohio or any other place in the United States.'

'I didn't expect there would be.'

'No, nor did I.'

'And?'

'We've searched newspapers and federal and state court records for Ohio in the late forties and early fifties to find a murder case under another name that comes close to Harry's. There are quite a few mother-and-daughter cases that could be the one we're talking about, but in those days the killers were executed and so couldn't be Harry.'

'Unless he were acquitted.'

'That's a possibility. Do you want me to check?'

'No. Harry spoke about being locked up in – I think it was a sanatorium.'

Vernon grunted. 'I can look again, but where we know who the killer was, he doesn't resemble your man. Harry was a European and an academic. He stands out from the farm boys and mechanics who were slaughtering their families in Ohio.'

'And that's it?'

'That's it.'

'Thanks, Vernon.'

'*De nada*,' said Vernon in a Hazey way. He took his holidays in Spain.

Finished for ever with the Great Indian Novel, I set to and wrote down Harry's stories, working up the notes I had made in Puybrun. I struggled with the difficulties of detail and accent and made what I could of the welter of allusion and parody, always conscious that I might lose the essential Harry. I was also conscious too that, as with Proust, I might simply fail to get the point.

I dreamed about the stories. I don't mean that I relived them, walking through the scenes in which Harry had taken part. Rather, I saw them as things without content, imagining them cosmologically as if there had been, in an impossibly remote past, an *Urgeschichte*, a singularity exploding into a universe of stories in clusters, galaxies, stars, planets, moons, down to grains of dust and an infinitude of atoms; no story true and complete in itself but always partial and capable of being understood only imperfectly in relation to all the others. At times they came to me as an all-embracing light, but one which did not reveal the truth, since it was too bright – too, too bright for human eyes to see. At other times, for all the vastness of their number they seemed mere specks orbiting round something still vaster but for ever dark. In this last image the stories were not true – they were never true, being always too small and too fragmentary. But against the face of utter darkness, it was only these particles of light that allowed me to know that the darkness existed.

To dream like this I had to be drunk.

Vernon called me in again. I asked him, 'Have you found the truth about Harry Haze?'

'Not exactly,' he said. But for the first time he looked interested. Hitherto he'd acted as if the Haze case were the fantasy of a client it was well to humour.

'Well, what have you found?'

'A case to the point. Don't get too excited. It's not your man – it can't be. But it *may* be the source from which he made up what he told you.'

'Very well,' I said. 'Tell me.'

'Have you heard,' said Vernon, slowly and with relish, 'of Heinrich Dunst, the Vermont Vampire? By the way, shall I ask Sandra to get you a coffee while you listen to this?'

I doubt that Vernon noticed, but I was shuddering with shock not unmixed with fear. For I *had* heard of Heinrich Dunst. I couldn't remember the details, or where I'd read about him, but the bluntness of the name was unforgettable. Quickly I scrabbled for a hold in the loose shale of memory and surmised that I must have come across the case in one of those anthologies of real-life murders which marked an occasional interval in my diet of mystery novels.

'Shall I go on?' asked Vernon.

'Yes, do.'

'Dunst was a Jew from Hungary or Silesia or some place in Eastern Europe – the sources aren't clear. He may have been married – again the record isn't certain. At all events, during the war he was sent to the extermination camp at Treblinka, and, as you might expect, was lucky to survive. He was badly traumatised. He suffered from Holocaust survivors' guilt. He thought that he was dead, or that he should have died, or that he was responsible for those who died and was as bad as the Nazis. There are psychiatrists' reports on him, and they all agree that his personality was very fragile, very damaged.'

Sandra came with the coffee. We talked about milk, sugar and biscuits. I said, 'Go on.'

'After the war, Dunst was allowed to emigrate to America – this would be in forty-six. For a couple of years he seems to have held down odd jobs, nobody's sure. Then, in the spring of 1948, he fetched up in a small town in Vermont and got a job at the local college.'

'As professor of comparative literature.'

'Are you telling this or am I?' Vernon put me down firmly. 'No, as it happens you're wrong. That was the other fellow.'

'What other fellow?'

'I'll come to him. Now, where was I? Yes. Dunst taught *history*.'

'Was he married – I mean in 1948?'

'Single. He found rooms with a widow, a Mrs Dorothy Hammick. She was a perfectly ordinary woman, but she had a daughter Charlene, who had some mental disability – Down's syndrome, I think.'

'*Charlie*,' I whispered.

'If you like,' said Vernon. 'Dunst was by all accounts very fond of both of them. Nothing improper. He was able to produce character witnesses.'

'Right.'

'I'll come to the murder, for which we have only Dunst's version. which wasn't believed. First, however – I'm not telling this right – I should mention George Duke Cunniliffe.'

'Who?'

'Dunst's best friend. A fellow in his forties. He was the professor of comparative literature. They used to chat and play chess together, sometimes at Cunniliffe's place and sometimes at the Hammick house.'

'I follow. And?'

'It was the beginning of November 1948. According to Dunst, a chess match was planned at the Hammick home. But the college team had won some competition or other and he stayed late, drinking with the older students, and forgot about his appointment with Cunniliffe.

'When he got to the house it was in darkness. Cunniliffe was already there, sitting in the dark, covered in blood. It was obvious what had happened, but in any case – according to Dunst – his friend confessed that he'd raped and butchered Mrs Hammick and the child. So far so good.'

So far so good. Vernon, however, had not heard the other version of the horrors of that night. I didn't want to hear any more – still less, hear it in Vernon's indifferent tone. But I had asked for this and must listen.

'Now we come to the strange part. If Dunst had called the police then and there, it would have been all done with. But he didn't. According to Dunst, he and Cunniliffe stayed talking literature and philosophy for two hours and then Cunniliffe was allowed to leave and Dunst waited another six hours before the police came. His psychiatrists claimed that this was the effect of shock and his trauma in the camp.

'When the police finally arrived, too long had passed for the time of death to be clearly established. Within the margins allowed by the pathologist, Dunst *could* have been in the house even according to his own account. His only hope was to nail Cunniliffe. And that's where his story fell down. Cunniliffe said he had been at home all evening. He had no witness to the alibi, but there was no one to say they'd seen him going either to or from the Hammick house, and the bloodstained clothes, if they ever existed, had been destroyed. In the absence of that evidence. no one would believe Dunst's story.'

I nodded. That was so even if Dunst had told the truth, as to which there was no knowing.

'What happened?' I asked.

'The defence denied that Dunst was the killer, but their main plank was psychiatric testimony and character witnesses. The whole business of the camps came out. Dunst himself put on a plausible performance of being crazy in court. The jury found him guilty but insane.'

We paused. I asked Vernon for a cigarette, though I hadn't smoked for years. I wondered, 'What's your opinion? Was Dunst guilty?'

'That's the interesting part,' said Vernon enthusiastically. 'On the evidence at the time, I'd have said yes. But since then some commentators have challenged the verdict. They point to two other vampire-style murders in Vermont: one in 1951 and another in 1953; which by definition Dunst couldn't have committed. The forensic details – injuries and so forth – are very similar to the Hammick murders. Cunniliffe died of a heart attack in 1954 and the vampire killings stopped.'

'You think he did them?'

'There's a doubt, that's all one can say,' he answered. 'Because people were convinced that Dunst killed the Hammick women, nobody connected that case with the later murders. And in the absence of that connection, no one thought to investigate Cunniliffe. He might have had a solid alibi. Or maybe not. Who can say?'

'Indeed. Who can say?' I shuffled in my chair, wanting to go but wanting to know more. I said, 'I can see the similarities between Heinrich Dunst and Harry Haze. But you said they can't be the same person. Why not?'

'It's a purely practical question,' said Vernon. 'You told me that Harry is eighty – there or thereabouts. But according to the record Dunst was sixty-three in 1948. In the extremely unlikely event that he were still living, he'd be well over a hundred. And that isn't the end of it.'

'No?'

'No. Dunst was released in 1956 because he had cancer of the pancreas. He couldn't have lasted six months.'

'Unless he were a vampire,' I said. And who knows if I was being facetious?

Are Heinrich Dunst and Harry Haze the same person? I believe it is possible though unlikely. A slip of a clerk's pen could have recorded Dunst's age as sixty-three instead of thirty-six. Cancer may be misdiagnosed or go into remission. But does this supposed identity have any real meaning? Dunst and his shabby tragedy exist only as the object of lurid articles in true-crime magazines bought at grocery checkouts. How can he be compared with fabulous Harry Haze in all his terrible glory? The connection between them diminishes both and adds nothing. It sacrifices truth to mere facts.

Harry and Lucy vanished and I do not know where they are. Willie has received no news. She still phones me and calls me a murdering bastard and a madman and I listen to this abuse, out of sympathy I suppose. Only after that final evening at Puybrun did it occur to me that I never asked Lucy if she had in fact written the letter to Willie – the one that branded me a dangerous obsessive. If Lucy were never to reappear, that letter would be the only real evidence that I was a murderer. I destroyed it, but it lingers like the memory of a person I wish to forget, or perhaps one whom I never truly knew. Yet I am sure I am not a murderer.

I can only imagine the pair, and I see them in an hotel in Deauville or one of the other resorts where old men go to die. They live in a cheap room for which they pay the out-of-season rate. They walk along the promenade, hand in hand, exchanging secret and affectionate glances. When they look outwards, then, like Proust at Balbec, they see an infinity of ocean in an infinity of moods. And behind them a little band of girls plays games while waiting for a boy to arrive.

Already I imagined him at night
enveloping his daughter in a coat
and leaving with her for new adventures.

I read these closing words of *Le Grand Meaulnes* more than thirty years ago, and, though they evoked passion and mystery, those qualities were in a purely abstract form without meaning in the concrete life of an eighteen-year-old and after a while the sensation provoked by them (which I had felt intensely, having no equivalent in experience which by its reality would suppress a mere fiction) faded. Then recently, when setting out my books on the shelves of my new flat, and putting my nose to each one to sniff out its place in my life as if I were running my fingers over filing cards, I came across my school copy of the book, in a tattered Émil-Paul edition. An emotion which had floated freely began to fix itself and I turned to the last page, intending to regain a sense of the whole by reading a short passage, in the way that a little phrase of music will recall an entire sonata and the time and place when it was first heard. It was then that I read the words quoted and they sprang fresh off the page, as if they had never truly gone away but simply lain in wait to provide a key that would interpret something that was beyond my own powers.

Living alone, I have often had opportunity of an evening to reflect on Harry's stories and what happened at Puybrun. Lucy suggested that the stories and the events are in themselves the explanation, but that statement, though it may be true, goes against the natural inclination of my mind, which seeks to reduce matters to an account that is logical and coherent. I have done this and, if I assume that everything was designed to teach me a lesson, the lesson was banal, uninteresting, disappointing: a few truisms that could be written on a small piece of paper. And I cannot swear that there is anything more. Both our stories – Harry's and mine – may be trivial.

Perhaps some day I shall act wisely. If it happens at all, wisdom will probably come in some small way and I shall not recognise it for what it is. Still less will I know the source or even that it comes from outside me. Memory will fail.

It is this prospect of learning wisdom in forgetfulness that makes me smile.

READERS' NOTES

Recherché is my second novel in an exercise of revisiting the central subject of the classic murder mystery, namely the murder itself, to see if there's anything new that can be done with it. In this case, on reflection, you should see that there's a question over whether a murder has in fact occurred at all, and, if so, which, because two possible murders present themselves: the disappearance of Lucy in the main narrative, and the terrible night of slaughter at Hotzenplotz in the fantastic story told by Harry Haze. Yet it's not clear that Lucy is dead, or that the events of Harry's tale ever actually happened. They are both creations of storytelling.

This is the main theme of the book. The Narrator, dizzy from listening to Harry, wonders why the old fellow is telling him his literally unbelievable life history. Is there a lesson in it? Harry never says and the Narrator and by extension the reader are left to speculate. In a similar vein, there is something "off" in the Narrator's version of his last encounter with Lucy. Did he really see her again as he claims? As with Harry, we should ask ourselves; why is the Narrator telling us this tale? Is he hiding the terrible truth that he did in fact murder Lucy? Indeed is Harry Haze himself nothing more than an invention of the Narrator to distract us from his confession?

In fact these questions can't be answered because, we must remember, the novel is purely fiction: there are no "real" events behind the narrative; there's no story before, after or outside what's written on the page. The murder exists like Schrödinger's cat, in an indeterminate state until fixed by the reader's decision that the Narrator did or didn't murder Lucy, and that Harry did or didn't exist.

The second theme of the book – given away by its title and various allusions to Marcel Proust – is memory. It's related to the main theme because memory is a particular instance of storytelling, a point worth bearing in mind in reading Proust because his book is itself only an illusion of a life remembered: the reality of his own life being somewhat different. Harry's stories by their extravagance remind us that our memory is not an accurate record of our "real" past but a reconstruction distorted partly by flawed material and by our need to impose coherence and meaning on things that may originally have been chaotic and meaningless. Harry's life story may not be true, but it's the life story he wishes to have at the point when he tells it. This aspect is revealed in a small "tell" by the Narrator, who informs us that he is sure he didn't kill Lucy, rather than simply saying as a *matter of fact* that he didn't kill her. His superficial certainty is in truth a measure of his uncertainty about his own memory.

Finally, in deciding what this present book is "about", it's worth remembering a point made by Lucy to the Narrator when trying to explain the meaning of Harry's stories. She tells him that Harry's stories are themselves the explanation rather than a thing to be explained. If he could have explained himself better, he would have done so.

So, if you like, this book is the explanation, and you shouldn't look to some other book that I didn't write.

June 2013

Connect with Jim Williams and Marble City Publishing

http://www.jimwilliamsbooks.com/

http://www.marblecitypublishing.com

Join Marble City's list for updates on new releases by Jim
Williams:

http://eepurl.com/vek5L

Follow on Twitter:

http://twitter.com/MarbleCityPub

Other Marble City releases by Jim Williams:

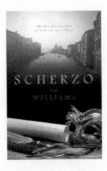

Scherzo by Jim Williams, in e-book and paperback

MEET two unusual detectives. Ludovico – a young man who has had his testicles cut off for the sake of opera. And Monsieur Arouet – a fraudster, or just possibly the philosopher Voltaire.

VISIT the setting. Carnival time in mid-18th century Venice, a city of winter mists, and the season of masquerade and decadence.

ENCOUNTER a Venetian underworld of pimps, harlots, gamblers, forgers and charlatans.

BEWARE of a mysterious coterie of aristocrats, Jesuits, Freemasons and magicians.

DISCOVER a murder: that of the nobleman, Sgr Alessandro Molin, found swinging from a bridge with his innards hanging out and a message in code from his killer.

Scherzo is a murder mystery of sparkling vivacity and an historical novel of stunning originality told with a wit and style highly praised by critics and nominated for the Booker Prize.

Tango in Madeira by Jim Williams, in e-book and paperback

A disillusioned soldier looks for love. An exiled Emperor fears assassination. Agatha Christie takes a holiday. And George Bernard Shaw learns to tango.

In the aftermath of World War I, Michael Pinfold a disillusioned ex-soldier tries to rescue his failing family wine business on the island of Madeira. In a villa in the hills the exiled Austrian Emperor lives in fear of assassination by Hungarian killers, while in Reid's Hotel, a well-known lady crime novelist is stranded on her way to South Africa and George Bernard Shaw whiles away his days corresponding with his friends, writing a one act play and learning to tango with the hotel manager's spouse.

A stranger, Robinson, is found murdered and Michael finds himself manipulated into investigating the crime by his sinister best friend, Johnny Cardozo, the local police chief, with whose wife he is pursuing an arid love affair; manipulated, too, by Father Flaherty, a priest with dubious political interests, and by his own eccentric parent, who claims to have been part of a comedy duo that once entertained the Kaiser with Jewish jokes. Will Michael find love? Will the Emperor escape his would-be killers? Will any of the characters learn the true meaning of the tango?

The Argentinian Virgin by Jim Williams, in e-book format

A sensuous novel of erotic fantasy, obsession, jealousy and betrayal set in the dreamlike atmosphere of a Riviera summer in wartime.

Summer 1941. France is occupied by the Germans but the United States is not at war. Four glamorous young Americans find themselves whiling away the hot days in the boredom of a small Riviera town, while in a half-abandoned mansion nearby, Teresa and Katerina Malipiero, a mother and daughter, wait for Señor Malipiero to complete his business in the Reich and take them home to Argentina.

The plight of the women attracts the sympathy of 'Lucky' Tom Rensselaer and he is seduced by the beauty of Katerina. Tom has perfect faith in their innocence, yet they cannot explain why a sinister Spaniard has been murdered in their home and why Tom must help them dispose of the body without informing the police.

Watching over events is Pat Byrne, a young Irish writer. Twenty years later, when Tom has been reduced from the most handsome, admired and talented man of his generation to a derelict alcoholic, Pat sets out to discover the facts of that fateful summer: the secrets that were hidden and the lies that were told. It is a shocking truth: a tale of murder unpunished and a good man destroyed by those who loved him most.

The Hitler Diaries by Jim Williams, in e-book and paperback

A stunning literary prophecy! The international bestseller that caused a sensation when it was published 9 months before the famous Hitler Diaries forgery scandal.

A French aristocrat and his mistress are murdered. A mysterious businessman offers the Fuehrer's diaries to a new York publishing house. Are they a hoax or a record of terrifying truth? A controversial historian and his beautiful assistant are commissioned to find out the answer following a trail that draws them into a terrifying web of conspiracy and slaughter as competing forces fight to publish or suppress Hitler's account of the War and of secret negotiations with his enemies.

But are the Diaries genuine or just a plot to destabilise contemporary politics? A shattering revision of history whose revelation must be prevented at all costs: or a fake, just a sinister manoeuvre in the Cold War?

If the Hitler Diaries are authentic, then who left the bunker alive?

Made in the USA
Charleston, SC
06 March 2014